The Tycoon and I

JENNIFER FAYE

KANDY SHEPHERD

BARBARA WALLACE

HarperCollins
P U B L I S H E R S
Since 1817

First Published in Great Britain 2017
By Mills & Boon, an imprint of HarperCollins*Publishers*
1 London Bridge Street, London, SE1 9GF

THE TYCOON AND I © 2017 Harlequin Books S. A.

Safe In The Tycoon's Arms, *The Tycoon And The Wedding Planner* and *Swept Away By The Tycoon* were first published in Great Britain by Harlequin (UK) Limited.

Safe In The Tycoon's Arms © 2014 Jennifer F. Stroka
The Tycoon And The Wedding Planner © 2014 Kandy Shepherd
Swept Away By The Tycoon © 2014 Barbara Wallace

ISBN: 978-0-263-92950-8

05-0217

Our policy is to use papers that are natural, renewable and recyclable products and made from wood grown in sustainable forests.The logging and manufacturing processes conform to the legal environmental regulations of the country of origin.

Printed and bound in Spain
by CPI, Barcelona

SAFE IN THE TYCOON'S ARMS

BY
JENNIFER FAYE

In another life, **Jennifer Faye** was a statistician. She still has a love for numbers, formulas and spread-sheets, but when she was presented with the opportunity to follow her lifelong passion and spend her days writing and pursuing her dream of becoming a Mills & Boon author, she couldn't pass it up. These days, when she's not writing, Jennifer enjoys reading, fine needlework, quilting, tweeting and cheering on the Pittsburgh Penguins. She lives in Pennsylvania with her amazingly patient husband, two remarkably talented daughters and their two very spoiled fur babies otherwise known as cats—but *shh*. . . don't tell them they're not human!

Jennifer loves to hear from readers—you can contact her via her website: www.JenniferFaye.com.

For Viv.

Thank you for being such a good friend over the years. Your helpful advice and unending support are deeply appreciated. Here's to the future of possibilities.

CHAPTER ONE

A DEAFENING CRACK of thunder rumbled through the darkened house. Kate Whitley pressed a hand to her pounding chest. She'd hated storms since she was a little kid. A brilliant flash of lightning sent shards of light slashing across the hallway while rain pelted the window.

Mother Nature certainly had a wicked sense of humor. Actually, it seemed as though life as a whole was mocking Kate. Absolutely nothing was going according to plan, no matter how hard she fought to put things right.

Her fingers pushed against the cold metallic plate on the swinging hall door. Inside the kitchen, the glare from the overhead light caused her to squint. What in the world was going on? She could have sworn she'd turned everything off before going upstairs. Hadn't she?

She sighed and shook her head. Her mind must be playing tricks on her. The long nights of tossing and turning instead of sleeping were finally catching up to her. And it couldn't have happened at a worse time. In a few more hours, she had to be fully alert. There were decisions only she could make—lifesaving decisions.

If only she could get a little shut-eye, she'd be able to think clearly. But first, Mother Nature had to quiet down. No one could rest with all this ruckus.

It didn't ease her nerves being away from home, even if she was staying in a New York City mansion. This place was nothing like her two-bedroom, ranch-style house in Pennsylvania. Though this oversize house contained some of the most breathtaking architecture, there was something missing—the warmth that made a building more than just a place to hang your coat, the coziness that made it home.

In a big city where she barely knew anyone, she and this house had a couple of things in common—being lonely and forgotten. Somehow it seemed like fate that she'd ended up in this deserted mansion. A warm, loving home had somehow always eluded her, and just when she thought she'd made one of her own, it too was about to be snatched out from under her.

Sadness weighed heavily on her as her bare feet moved silently across the kitchen tiles. The coldness raced up through her pink painted toes to her bare legs and sent goose bumps cascading down her arms. Spring may have brought warmer days, but the nights were still chilly. She rubbed her palms up and down her arms, willing away her discomfort. Perhaps her long T-shirt wasn't the warmest choice for this soggy night, but with her living out of a suitcase, her choices were quite limited.

She yawned and opened the door of the stainless-steel refrigerator. She hadn't had any appetite until now. With so much riding on this upcoming meeting, she'd ended up with a stress headache for most of the day. But back here ensconced between these quiet, peaceful walls, the pain had loosened its vicelike grip.

Now she needed something to ease her hunger pangs. Other than a few meager groceries she'd placed in there earlier, the glass shelves were bare. The friend who'd let her stay here free of charge said the owner was out of town and wouldn't be back anytime soon. From the empty cabinets to the dust-covered bedrooms, Kate deduced no one had lived here in quite a while.

With an apple in hand, she filled a glass of water. She'd

just turned off the faucet when she heard faint but distinct footsteps. The hairs on the back of her neck rose. Either this place had some mighty big rats…or she wasn't alone.

"Stop right there!" boomed a male voice.

So much for the rat theory.

Her heart lodged in her throat, blocking a terrified scream. Who was this man? And what did he want with her? Her lungs started to burn. Was he a thief, a desperate junkie…or worse?

She struggled to suck air past the enormous lump in her throat. A nervous tremor in her hand caused droplets of water to spill over the rim of the glass. Why had she put herself in such peril by making the rash decision to stay in this deserted house alone? After all, what did she know about her newfound friend? Not much. They'd only met a week ago. The older woman had seemed so nice—so understanding in Kate's time of need.

She wondered if a scream would carry to any of the neighboring houses on the block. Probably not. This house came from an era when structures were built with thick, sturdy walls. She was on her own.

"You shouldn't be here." She fought to keep her voice steady. "This place has a burglar alarm. It won't be long until the police show up. I haven't seen your face. You can escape out the back and I won't tell anyone."

"I don't think so. Turn around."

Not about to let this stranger know how much he frightened her, she placed the glass on the counter, leveled her shoulders and took an unsteady breath. When she went to turn, her feet wouldn't move. They were stuck to the floor as though weighted down in concrete.

A crescendo of thunder reverberated through her body. The house plunged into darkness. Kate bit down on her bottom lip to keep a frightened gasp bottled up.

Don't panic. Stay calm.

Could this really be happening? What had she done to piss off Fate and have it turn on her? Hysterical laughter swelled in her throat. With effort, she choked it down. It wouldn't help anything for this man to think she was losing it.

Drawing on every bit of courage she could muster, she forced her feet to move. Once fully turned around, she squinted into the dark shadows but could only make out the man's vague outline. Who was he? What did he want with her?

Then, as though in answer to her prayer, the power blinked back on. When her vision adjusted, she found herself staring at a bare male chest. *What in the world?* Her wide-eyed gaze dropped farther past his trim waist but screeched to a halt upon the discovery of this stranger's only article of clothing—navy boxer shorts.

This night was definitely getting stranger by the second.

She couldn't resist a second glance at her sexy intruder. He definitely wasn't a kid, having filled out in all the right places. She'd only ever seen defined muscles like his in the glossy pages of magazines, and this guy would qualify with his washboard abs. He must be around her age, maybe a little older.

When her gaze rose up over his six feet plus of sexiness, she met a hard glint in his blue-gray eyes. He obviously wasn't any happier about discovering her than she was of stumbling across him.

"What are you doing here?" The stranger's deep voice held a note of authority as though he were used to commanding people's attention.

"Wondering why you're standing in my kitchen."

The frown lines on his face etched even deeper. "This is your place?"

Technically no, but she wasn't about to explain her unusual circumstances to Mr. Oh-So-Sexy. She merely nodded, affirming her right to be there.

His brow arched in disbelief.

Who was he to pass judgment? When she pressed her hands to her hips, she realized he wasn't the only one scantily dressed. With the hem of her worn but comfy shirt pinched between her fingers, she pulled it down as far as the material would allow. Instinct told her to run and put on something more modest. But in order to do that, she'd have to cross his path. Not a great idea.

Her gaze strayed back to the doorway. Sooner or later she'd have to make her move. She wanted to believe he wasn't there to hurt her—wanted to accept the notion that there was some crazy explanation for the nearly naked man standing in front of her, but her mind drew a blank. She glanced back at him, taking in his blondish-brown wavy hair tousled as though he'd just woken up. And his lack of apparel left no room for doubt that he was unarmed.

"Don't look so panicked. I have no intention of hurting you." His deep voice was as smooth and rich as hot fudge. "I just want some answers."

She stuck out her chin. "That makes two of us."

"I guess you should start explaining." He looked at her expectantly.

Kate crossed her arms. He wasn't going to boss her around. She had every right to be here. Then an ominous thought came to her: Who was to say Connie hadn't made a similar offer to this man? But wouldn't it have crossed her friend's mind that this would create an awkward situation to have two strangers—a man and a woman—alone in the house?

As she kept a wary eye on him, she noticed something familiar about him. The thought niggled at her. She couldn't put her finger on where she'd seen him before, probably because the only thing keeping her on her feet right now was adrenaline. She needed sleep. Desperately. But how would she get this man to put on some clothes and go away?

"No more stalling." Lucas Carrington's patience was worn razor thin. Tired of talking in circles, he cut to the chase. "Who are you? And what are you doing here?"

Her lush lips pursed as her eyes narrowed. "My name is Kate Whitley and I have every right to be here—"

"Impossible. More likely you're homeless and broke in here seeking shelter from the storm."

Kate's chin tilted up and her unwavering brown gaze met his. "I'm not homeless. In fact, I'm an interior designer and a darned good one, too."

She did have an innocent girl-next-door look about her, but he knew all too well that things were never quite what they seemed. "Are you trying to tell me you broke in here because you had this overwhelming desire to redecorate the place?"

Her thin shoulders drew back into a firm line. Her threadbare cartoon T-shirt pulled snugly across her pert breasts. He swallowed hard. Okay, so maybe his first assessment of her hadn't been quite right. Gorgeous. Sexy. Curvaceous. Those were much more fitting descriptions.

She continued to glare at him, seemingly oblivious to the fact her demeanor was more alluring than intimidating. And like some hormone-fueled teenager, he found himself unable to turn away from her tempting curves.

"There's no need to sound so condescending." Her voice filled with exasperation.

With effort, his gaze lifted to meet hers. "I'm calling the police. They can deal with you." But there was a wrinkle in his plan—his cell phone was in the other room and the landline in the kitchen had been disconnected ages ago.

"Go right ahead."

Her confident tone surprised him. Did she expect her

beauty to get her out of this mess? Or was she attempting to pull a con job on him? Not that any of it mattered. He didn't have a problem calling her bluff.

"You seem fairly certain you won't get in trouble—"

"I won't."

Lucas was having a hard time focusing on the conversation given that his unexpected visitor was standing in his kitchen with nothing on but a T-shirt, which clung to her shapely curves and exposed her long, long legs. He was definitely beginning to understand why she might rely on her looks. And if he kept staring, this could get embarrassing for both of them.

He forced his gaze to her face, not that it was any less distracting. Was she wearing makeup? Or was her skin naturally that smooth and creamy?

Even more troubling than how beautiful he found her was the way she reminded him too much of the past—a past that had nearly destroyed him. Not so long ago another beautiful woman had stood in that spot. She'd made him promises but ended up breaking each and every one of them. His jaw tightened. The last thing he needed was this stranger's presence to dredge up memories he'd fought so hard to seal inside. He refused to let it happen.

Refocused and clear about his priorities, his gaze returned to her warm brown eyes. She stared directly at him. Pink stained her cheeks, but she didn't glance away. She stepped forward, using the kitchen island as a shield. It was far too late for modesty. Her sexy form was already emblazoned upon his memory.

Stay focused. Soon she'll be gone. One way...or the other.

He cleared his throat. "Okay, you've got my attention. Why won't you get in trouble?"

"I have permission to be here. Temporarily, that is. You know, while the owner is out of town." Kate's eyes narrowed, challenging him. She certainly was confident. He'd give her that. "And now it's your turn to do some explaining. Who are you?"

"My name's Lucas."

"Well, Lucas, I assume you must know Connie, too."

His gaze sought out hers and held it. "Connie? Is that who let you in here?"

Kate nodded as hope sparked in her eyes. "Connie Carrington."

He had liked it better when he thought Kate was a squatter looking for a warm place to sleep. "To be sure, describe Connie."

"Short. Brunette. Sixtyish. Very sweet and generous. She has a friendly smile and volunteers at East Riverview Hospital."

"That's her." It still didn't prove Kate was telling the whole truth, but it was sure looking that way.

"Here's the thing, Connie obviously offered me this place first. And I don't think us sharing the house is going to work."

How dare this woman—this stranger—kick him out of his own house? He opened his mouth to give her a piece of his mind but then closed it. Obviously she didn't recognize him, a small wonder after that ridiculous magazine article earlier in the month had named him Bachelor of the Year. His quiet life hadn't been the same since then.

Kate was a refreshing change from the headline seekers and the husband hunters. Maybe if this were a different time under different circumstances, he'd welcome this beautiful intrusion. But right now all he wanted was to be left alone.

A clap of thunder rattled the windows. Kate jumped. She obviously wasn't as calm as she'd like him to believe. Perhaps they both needed a moment to gather their thoughts. He certainly could use a minute or two to tamp down his unwanted attraction.

"This conversation would be a little less awkward with some more clothes on. I'll be right back." He started out of the room, then as an afterthought he called over his shoulder, "Don't go anywhere."

Lucas strode from the room. His teeth ground together. He didn't want this woman here. He never had company and he preferred it that way. In fact, the less time he spent here, the better he liked it. When he'd asked his aunt to look after the place, he'd never expected her to turn it into a B and B. What in the world had she been thinking?

Maybe his aunt had planned for him to never find out about Kate. After all, he wasn't even supposed to be home for another week. But one untimely setback after another at the future site of Carrington Gems' expansion in San Francisco had ground construction to a halt.

Still, it was more than losing money hand over fist due to bureaucratic red tape that had him cutting his trip short. He put a stop to his thoughts. He wasn't ready to contemplate the devastating situation he'd faced before catching his cross-country flight home.

And the last thing he needed was to return home to find a half-dressed woman making herself comfortable in his house. The image of her bare legs teased his mind, clouding his thoughts.

He cursed under his breath and pulled on the first pair of jeans he laid his hands on. But if he was going to stay focused, his beautiful interloper needed to cover up. He grabbed a heavy robe that should modestly cover her and give him some peace of mind. With a T-shirt in hand for himself, he rushed back to the kitchen clutching both articles of clothing.

"Here." He held out the robe to her. "Put this on."

Her wary gaze moved to his outstretched hand and back. It was then that he got a close-up view of her heart-shaped face and button nose. His thoughts screeched to a halt when he spied the dark shadows beneath her eyes. Sympathy welled up inside his chest. Not so long ago, he'd worn a similar look. It hadn't happened by missing a night or two of sleep. In fact, it'd been the worst time of his life. His gut told him that Kate had a devastating story of her own.

He'd always been good at reading people. It was what helped him run Carrington Gems and hire a reliable staff. So why had he immediately jumped to the wrong conclusion about Kate?

Had his experience with his ex-wife jaded him so badly that he wasn't even willing to give this woman the benefit of the doubt? Or was it the fact she was standing in this house—a place so filled with pain and loss?

Kate's cold fingertips brushed over the back of his hand as she accepted the robe. His instinct was to take her hands in his and rub them until they were warm. But he resisted the temptation. She wasn't his guest…his responsibility.

While she slipped on the robe, he stepped back, giving her some space. He pulled the shirt over his head. Now they could have a reasonable conversation.

Fully clothed, he glanced up, finding Kate's brows furrowed as she stared at him. He followed her line of vision to a large hole in his jeans above his knee as well as the army of white smudges marking up both legs. He really should consider tossing them, but they were just so comfortable. Wait. Why should he care what this woman thought of him or his clothes? After tonight he'd never see her again.

Kate shoved up the sleeves on the robe and crossed her arms. "What do you propose we do?"

In any other situation, he'd show her to the door and wish her well. After all, she wasn't his problem. And being drawn in by her very kissable lips and the memory of how that threadbare shirt hugged her curves was a complication in his life that he just didn't need.

But her pale face with those dark smudges beneath her eyes dug at his resolve.

And he couldn't dismiss the fact his aunt had sent Kate to stay here. Not that his aunt didn't help people on a daily basis, but she knew this house was off-limits to everyone. That meant Kate was someone special. Now he really needed to speak to his aunt, but first he had to make things clear to Kate.

"There's something you should know. This is my house."

CHAPTER TWO

KATE EYED UP Mr. Oh-So-Sexy's faded T-shirt and thread-bare denim. Even her ratty old jeans were in better condition. Did she look gullible enough to swallow his story that he was the owner of this mansion? That would make him wealthy. Very wealthy. And he sure didn't look the part.

"Why should I believe you own this house?"

He frowned. "Because I'm Lucas Carrington. Connie's nephew."

His unwavering tone gave her pause. She studied his aristocratic nose, piercing blue eyes and sensual lips. The wheels in her mind began to spin. No wonder he seemed so familiar. During her many hours at the hospital, she'd ended up thumbing through one magazine after the other. It was within one of those stylish periodicals that she'd skimmed over an article listing this year's most eligible bachelors.

Lucas Carrington had been named Bachelor of the Year. And he had been by far the steamiest candidate on the list. And that had been before she'd garnered a glimpse of his ripped abs. Her mouth grew dry at the memory. She instantly squashed the thought.

The reality of the situation at last sunk in. That man—the hunk from the popular magazine—was standing in front of her in his bare feet. And she was accusing him of being an intruder. This had to be some sort of crazy, mixed-up dream.

"I see my name has rung a bell." Smugness reflected in his captivating eyes. "Perhaps my aunt mentioned me."

The fact he'd been holding that ace up his sleeve the whole time instead of introducing himself up front annoyed her. She wasn't about to fold her hand so quickly—even if she had been beaten already.

She conjured up her best poker face. "Actually, Connie went to great pains not to mention you. She merely said the owner was out of town for an extended period. In fact, when I saw the condition of this place, I didn't think anyone had lived here in years."

A muscle twitched in his cheek as his gaze moved away. "I only need a couple of the rooms. Even when I'm in town, I'm not here much."

"I see." What else could she say? That it was a bit strange to live in a mansion filled with cobwebs and covered in a blanket of dust? But who was she to judge? She was living out of a suitcase, and by the end of the month, she would be technically homeless. The thought of being adrift with no place to call home sent her stomach plummeting. But she could only deal with one problem at a time.

Lucas shifted uncomfortably. "Why do you keep looking at me strangely?"

"I'm trying to decide whether I should believe you. I mean, I wouldn't expect such a wealthy man to wear… umm, that." She pointed at his tattered jeans.

Even though she knew that he was in fact Lucas Carrington, she didn't want to let on just yet. After all, he hadn't readily taken her word that she wasn't a squatter. Why not let him see what it was like not to be believed?

He shrugged. "So they're old jeans. It doesn't mean anything."

"I don't know. This could all be an act. How am I to know that you aren't pretending to be the owner? Maybe I should call the police and let them sort this out."

Instead of the angry response she'd been anticipating, the corners of his mouth lifted. Was that a smile? Her stomach somersaulted.

"I guess I deserve that. Wait here." He set off in the same direction he'd gone to grab his clothes and the robe he'd loaned her.

The scorching hot image of him in those boxer shorts flashed in her mind. Her pulse kicked up a notch or two. If Lucas wasn't already wealthy, he could make a fortune as an underwear model. She'd be first in line to buy the magazine.

Still a bit chilled, she snuggled up in the robe, noticing the fresh scent of aftershave. She lifted the plush material to her nose, unable to resist inhaling even deeper. *Mmm...*

"Is the robe okay?" His smooth, deep voice filled the room.

"Umm...yes." She smoothed the lapel. "I was just admiring its...its softness."

He nodded, but she wondered if he'd caught her getting high off his very masculine scent. No man had a right to smell that good or look that hot with his clothes on...or off.

He skirted around the kitchen island and headed for her. Kate held her ground, all the while wondering what he was up to.

"Here." He flipped open a black wallet. "This should clear things up."

Her fingers slid across the worn smooth leather. She really didn't need to see his driver's license, but she had started this, so she might as well follow through.

She glanced at the photo of a neatly groomed man in a suit and tie. Definitely Lucas, but the spiffed-up version. The funny thing was she liked him in his worn-out jeans and sloppy T-shirt as much if not more than his business persona.

"So now do you believe me?" he asked with a tone of smug satisfaction, as if he'd just one-upped her.

She didn't like him thinking that he'd gotten the best of her.

"I don't know." She held the ID up beside his face, hmming and hah-ing, as though trying to make up her mind. "There's definitely a resemblance, but I'm not sure."

He yanked the card from her hand and stared at it. "Of course it's me! And that's my address…this address."

At last he'd fallen off his cool, confident edge. A smile pulled at her lips. The action felt so foreign to her after the past few stressful months, but the lightness grew, erupting into laughter. The more she laughed, the deeper Lucas frowned. It had been so long since she'd had an occasion to laugh that she didn't want it to end. It felt so good. So liberating. So freeing.

His brow arched. "Have I amused you enough?"

Her cheeks started to ache and she forced herself to calm down. After dabbing both eyes, she gazed up at him. "Sorry about that. But you don't know how much I needed that laugh."

His brows rose higher, but he didn't ask why and it was just as well. She wasn't about to spill her sorrowful tale to this stranger. In fact, she suddenly felt guilty for her outburst. Not because it was at Lucas's expense. He was a big boy who could take a little ribbing. It was the thought of her little girl in the hospital that sobered her mood. Under the circumstances, Kate had no right to smile, much less laugh.

If the hospital staff hadn't invoked their stupid policy, she'd still be there—sitting by Molly's bed or haunting the halls. But the nurses had insisted she needed some rest so she didn't wear herself out.

"Hey, what's the matter?" Lucas stepped closer. His hand reached out as though to touch Kate's shoulder, but then he hesitated.

She blinked back the rush of emotions. "I'm fine. I'll just get my things and get out of your way."

His hand lowered to his side as he glanced around the room. "Where exactly are your things?"

"Upstairs."

"But those rooms aren't fit for anyone. I dismissed the maid service as soon as… It doesn't matter. The only important thing is keeping you out of that mess."

"It isn't so dirty now." At the shocked look on Lucas's face, she continued. "Or at least the room that I'm staying in is mostly clean."

"What room?" His face creased with worry lines.

A crack of thunder sounded, followed by the lights flickering. Kate wrapped her arms around herself. "The one at the end of the hall."

His shoulders drew back in a rigid line as his brows gathered in a dark, intimidating line. "Which end?"

Kate pointed straight overhead.

His shoulders drooped as he let out a sigh. "What in the world was my aunt thinking to send you here?"

Kate had wondered the exact same thing, but she'd come to the conclusion that Connie had only the best intentions… even if they were a little misguided. Now it was time to move on.

Lucas watched as Kate snuggled deeper in his robe. A resigned look etched across her weary features as the dark circles made her eyes appear much too large for her face. She reminded him of a puppy who'd been kicked to the curb and forgotten.

His thoughts rolled back in time to the day when he'd found a stray pup and brought it home. Everyone but his aunt had told him to get rid of the filthy beast. Aunt Connie had been different. She could see what the others couldn't be bothered to look at—the puppy's need to be loved and cared for. More than that she recognized Lucas's need for something calming in the upheaval that was his life.

Lucas brought his thoughts up short. Kate wasn't a stray puppy. She was a grown woman who could care for herself. He had enough problems. He didn't need to be embroiled in someone else's. He should wish her well and be done with it.

A loud boom of thunder shook the very floor they stood on. Kate wrapped her arms around herself as her wide eyes turned toward the window. This storm was showing no signs of letting up. Definitely not a night to be out and about.

If only he knew why his aunt had sent her here....

Kate turned and started down the hall.

"Wait." Unease mounted within him as he realized what he was about to do.

"For what?" Kate asked, stepping back into the kitchen.

He noticed how the rest of her short dark brown hair was tucked behind each ear as though she'd been too busy to worry about what she looked like. The concept of a woman going out in public without taking great pains with her appearance was new to him. This mystery woman intrigued him and that was not good—not good at all.

But more than that, he'd witnessed how every time it thundered, she jumped and the fear reflected in her eyes. He couldn't turn her out into the stormy night—especially when he suspected she had nowhere else to go.

Going against his better judgment, he said, "You don't have to leave tonight."

"Yes, I do."

"Would you quit being so difficult?"

She glowered at him. "But you just got done telling me that you wanted me out of here right away. You're the one being difficult."

He inwardly groaned with frustration. "That was before. Give me a moment to speak with my aunt."

"I don't see how that will change anything. Unless you're still worried that I'm a liar and a thief."

"That isn't what I meant." He jerked his fingers through his hair. "Just wait here for a minute, okay? In fact, sit down. You look dead on your feet."

Her eyes narrowed. Her pale lips drooped into a frown. He'd obviously said the wrong thing…again, but darned if he knew what had upset her. Maybe it was mentioning how tired she looked. In his limited experience with women, they never wanted to look anything less than amazing, no matter the circumstances.

When Kate didn't move, he walked over and pulled out a chair at the table. "Please sit down. I won't be long."

He stepped inside the small bedroom just off the kitchen, which at one point in the house's history had been the domestic help's quarters. Lucas now claimed it as his bedroom—not that he spent much time there. His cell phone was sitting on the nightstand next to the twin bed.

He selected his aunt's name from his frequently called list. His fingers tightened around the phone as he held it to his ear. After only one ring, it switched to voice mail.

"Call me as soon as you get this." His voice was short and clipped.

He couldn't help but wonder where she might be and why she wasn't taking his call. Would she still be at the hospital doing her volunteer work? He glanced at the alarm clock. At this late hour, he highly doubted it.

With his aunt unaccounted for, he'd have to follow his gut. He'd already determined Kate wasn't a criminal. But what would he do with her? Sit and hash out what was bothering her to see if he could help? Certainly not.

He rubbed his hand over his stubbled jaw. He didn't want to get pulled any further into her problems. No matter what her circumstances were, it had nothing to do with him. Come tomorrow, she'd have to find other accommodations.

Still uncomfortable with his decision, he stepped back into the kitchen. Kate was seated at the table. Her arms were crossed on the glass tabletop, cradling her head. He must have made a sound, because she jerked upright in her seat.

Kate blinked before stretching. "Did Connie confirm what I told you?"

"Actually she didn't—"

"What? But I'm not lying."

"No one said you were. But my aunt isn't available. So how about we make a deal?"

A yawn escaped her lips. "What do you have in mind?"

"I'll give you the benefit of the doubt, if you'll do the same for me."

Kate was quiet for a moment as though weighing his words. "I suppose. But what does it matter now?"

"Because you and I are going to be housemates for the night."

"What? But I couldn't—"

"Yes, you can. Have you looked outside lately? It's pouring. And it's late at night."

Her lips pressed into a firm line as she got to her feet and pushed in the chair. "I don't need your charity."

"Who says it's charity? You'd be saving me from a load of trouble with my aunt if she found out I kicked you to the curb on a night like this."

Kate's hand pressed to her hip, which was hidden beneath the folds of the oversize robe. "Are you being on the level?"

She didn't have any idea what it was costing him to ask her to stay, even for one night. This place was a tomb of memories. He didn't want anyone inside here, witnessing his utter failure to keep his family together.

But there was something special about her—more than the way that he was thoroughly drawn to her. There was a vulnerability in her gaze. Something he'd guess she'd gone to great pains to hide from everyone, but he'd noticed. Maybe because he'd been vulnerable before, too.

"You don't look too sure about this."

He was usually much better at hiding his thoughts, but the dismal events of the day combined with the lateness of the hour were his undoing.

"I'm not. Let's just go to bed." Her drooping eyelids lifted and he immediately realized how his words could be misconstrued. "Alone."

CHAPTER THREE

THE SUN HAD yet to flirt with the horizon when Kate awoke to the alarm on her cell phone. Though she'd only snuck in a few hours of sleep, she felt refreshed. Her heart was full of hope that today her most fervent prayer would be answered.

It will all work out. It has to.

As she rushed through the shower, the what-ifs and maybes started to crowd into her mind. Finding a cure to her daughter's brain tumor had been rife with negative diagnoses. That was why they were here in New York City—to see a surgeon who was willing to do the seemingly impossible. But what if—

Don't go there. Not today.

With her resolve to think only positive thoughts, she pulled on a red skirt and a white top from her suitcase. The light tap of the continued rain on the window reminded her of the night before and meeting Lucas Carrington. He definitely presented a distraction from her attack of nerves. She wondered if he'd be just as devastatingly handsome in the daylight. She tried to convince herself that it'd been the exhaustion talking, that no man could look that good. But she'd seen the magazine spread with him shaved and spruced up in a tux. He really was that good-looking. Which raised the question: What was he doing living here in this unkempt, mausoleumlike house?

Kate proceeded down the grand staircase, with her suitcase in one hand and her purse in the other. She hated the fact that she would never learn the history or secrets of this mansion. This would be her last trip down the cinematic steps. She paused to take one last look around.

She was in awe of the house's old-world grandeur. Her gaze skimmed over the cream paint and paused to inspect the various paintings adorning the walls. Her nose curled up. She knew a bit about art from her work as an interior designer and these modern pieces, though not to her liking, would still fetch a hefty chunk of change at auction.

Even though the current decor didn't match the home's old-world elegance, she still saw the beauty lurking in the background. In her experience, she'd never found such charm and detailed work in any of the newer structures. Sure, they were all beautiful in their own unique ways, but this mansion was brimming with personality that only time could provide. She'd be willing to bet that if the walls could talk they'd spin quite a tale. She was certain that given the opportunity to rejuvenate this place, she could learn a considerable amount about its history. But she'd never have that chance.

With a resigned sigh, she set her suitcase by the front door before heading back the hall to the kitchen. She couldn't shake the dismal thought of Lucas turning a blind eye to the house's disintegrating state and letting the place fall into utter disrepair. Who could do such a thing? Was it possible he didn't realize the real damage being done by his neglect?

If the man took the time to walk upstairs once in a while, he'd notice the work that needed to be done. Some of the repairs were blatantly obvious. It was a little hard to miss the *drip-drip-drip* last night as the rain leaked through the ceiling of her bedroom. She'd used a waste basket to collect the water. Maybe she should say something…

No. Don't go there. This house and Lucas are absolutely none of your business.

She paused outside the kitchen door and listened. No sounds came from within. She wasn't so sure she was up to facing him in the light of day after getting caught last night in her nightshirt. Still she refused to just slip away without thanking him for his generosity.

She pushed the door open and tiptoed into the room, hoping not to disturb him since his bedroom was just off the kitchen. Now if only she knew where to find a pen and some paper to write a note.

"You're up early."

Kate jumped. It took a second for her heart to sink back into her chest. She turned to find Mr. Oh-So-Sexy sitting off to the side in the breakfast nook with the morning paper and a cup of coffee. Yep, he looked just as delicious in the morning. Now she'd never get him off her mind.

She moved to a bar stool and draped his robe across it. "I didn't expect you to be up so early."

"I'm a morning person."

His intense stare followed her. What was up with him? She nervously fidgeted with the Lucky Ducky keychain she kept around as a good luck charm.

When she couldn't stand to be the focal point of Lucas's attention any longer, she faced him. "Why do you keep staring?"

"It's just you don't look like the same woman I met last night."

"Is that your attempt at a compliment?"

"Actually it is. You see, my brain doesn't work very well this early in the morning until I finish my first cup of coffee." He held up a large blue mug. "But if you'd like me to spell it out, you look radiant."

Had she heard him correctly? Had a man, a drop-dead gorgeous hunk, just said she was radiant? *Radiant.* The word sounded as sweet as honey and she was eating it all up. Heat swirled in her chest and rushed up to her cheeks, but for that one blissful moment she didn't care.

"Umm, thanks." Her hand tightened around the keychain. "I'm all packed up."

"What's that in your hand?"

She glanced down, realizing she was squeezing the rubber duck to the point of smashing it. "It's just a keychain. No big deal."

He nodded in understanding.

"Do you have any more coffee?"

"I'll get you a cup."

He moved at the same time she did and they nearly collided. Kate froze, but not before she caught a whiff of his intoxicating male scent. He had on a light blue button-up with the sleeves rolled up and the collar unbuttoned. His hair was combed but still slightly damp. And his face was clean-shaven. He looked like a man ready to conquer the world.

Her heart tripped in her chest as she pictured them chatting over a morning cup of coffee and bagel. He'd tell her what he had on tap for the day and she'd tell him about her plans.

Lucas cleared his throat and pointed. "The cups are in the cabinet behind you."

She had to get a grip and quit acting like a high school student with a crush on the star quarterback. The best way to do that was to make a fast exit before she made a complete fool of herself. "On second thought, I don't have time for coffee."

"It's awfully early to be in such a rush. Is something the matter?"

"Nothing's wrong." She crossed her fingers behind her back like she used to do when she was a kid and her father asked her if she'd cleaned her room before allowing her go outside to play with her friends.

Lucas nodded, but his eyes said that he didn't believe her. She never had been good at telling fibs. That's why her father had caught her every time.

A sense of loss settled over her. What had made her think about that man after all this time? She grew angry at herself. As far as she was concerned her father was dead to her. She certainly didn't miss him.

Maybe being alone in a new city had gotten to her more than she thought. It didn't help that she'd witnessed the supportive clusters of families at the hospital while having no one by her side. That must be it.

Stifling the rush of unwanted emotions, she made a point of checking her wristwatch. "If I don't leave now, I'll be late."

"But you haven't even eaten. Don't let me scare you off."

"You haven't. I just have things I must do." She walked over to the doorway and paused. "By the way, did you ever speak to your aunt?"

"No. I think it was too late last night and she had her phone switched off. I'm sure she'll call soon."

"I understand." But Kate still wanted that little bit of vindication. The chance to flash him an I-told-you-so look. "Thank you for letting me spend the night. By the way, there's some food in the fridge. Help yourself to it."

And with that she started down the hallway headed for the front door. She had no idea where she'd find a cheap place to stay tonight. All but one of her credit cards was maxed out since she'd been forced to give up her job to travel with Molly to the long list of specialists. She dismissed the troubling thought. There were other matters that required her attention first.

"Hey, wait!"

Kate sighed and turned. She didn't know what else they

had to say to each other. And she didn't have time to waste. "Surely you aren't going to insist on searching my luggage, are you?"

"Are you always so feisty in the morning? Or are you just grumpy because you skipped your caffeine fix? I know that first cup does wonders for me. See, I'm smiling." His lips bowed into a ridiculous grin.

She rolled her eyes and shook her head. She honestly didn't know what to make of the man. His personal hygiene was impressive, but other than the kitchen his house was a disgrace. And last night he was crankier than an old bear, yet this morning he was smiling. He was one walking contradiction.

Lucas held out his hand. "Let me have your keys and I'll pull your car up to the door so you don't get soaked."

"I don't have one." She'd left her car in Pennsylvania, figuring city driving was not something she wanted to attempt.

"Did you call a taxi?"

"I don't need one." She pulled a red umbrella from her tote. "I'm armed and ready."

"Have you looked outside? It's still pouring. That umbrella isn't going to help much."

"Thanks for caring. But I've been taking care of myself for a long time now. I'll be fine."

When she started to move toward the front door, he reached out and grabbed her upper arm. His touch was firm but gentle. Goose bumps raced down to her wrists, lifting the fine hair on her arms. She glanced down at where his fingers were wrapped around her and immediately his hand pulled away.

"Sorry. I just wanted a chance to offer you a lift. I'll go grab my wallet and keys." He dashed down the hallway without waiting for her to say a word.

This was ridiculous. She couldn't let herself start going

soft. There was only her and Molly and right now, her daughter needed her to be strong for both of them. She would walk to the hospital as planned. It wasn't that many blocks and she'd already done it a number of times.

She quietly let herself out the front door, feeling bad about skipping out on Lucas. For some reason, he was really trying to be a good sport about finding a stranger living in his house. She wondered if she would have been so understanding if the roles had been reversed.

"Kate, I've got them." Lucas called out from the kitchen. "We can go now."

Lucas had never met a woman quite like her. Her tenacity combined with a hint of vulnerability got to him on some level. He sensed she wasn't the type to ask for help and would only take it if it was pressed upon her. Maybe that was why he was going out of his way to be kind to her—because she appeared to be in need of a friend and would never ask for one.

He strode to the foyer with his jacket on and keys in hand. But Kate was gone. He called out to her, but there was no sound. Surely she hadn't skipped out on him.

He stepped outside to look for her. The rain was picking up and so was the wind. But there was no sign of Kate in either direction. This was not a day where an umbrella would do a person much good.

Without taking time to question his next move, he was in his car and driving around the block. She couldn't have gotten far. And then he spotted a perky red umbrella. In the windy weather, Kate struggled to keep a grip on the umbrella with one hand while clutching her suitcase with the other.

He slowed next to her and lowered the window. "Get in."

She ignored him and kept walking. A gust of wind blew hard and practically pulled the umbrella free from her hold.

In the end, she'd held on to it, but the wire skeleton now bowed in the wrong direction, rendering the contraption totally useless.

"Get in the car before you're soaked to the skin."

She stood there for a second as though ready to burst into tears. Then pressing her lips into a firm line, she straightened her shoulders and stepped up to the car. He jumped out to take her things from her.

Once they were stowed away, he climbed back in the driver's seat. "Where are we off to?"

"East Riverview Hospital."

Her face was devoid of any expression, leaving him to wonder about the reason for her visit. She'd mentioned meeting his aunt there, but she hadn't added any details. Was she visiting a sick relative? Or was there something wrong with her? Was that the reason for her drawn cheeks and dark circles under her eyes?

He wanted to know what was going on, but he kept quiet and eased back into traffic. If she wanted him to know, she'd tell him. Otherwise it was none of his business. He assured himself it was best to keep a cordial distance.

Kate settled back against the leather seat. She hated to admit it, but she was thankful for the ride. She hadn't any idea that there would be so much ponding on the sidewalks. Her feet were wet and cold.

As though reading her thoughts, Lucas adjusted the temperature controls and soon warm air was swirling around her. It'd been a long time since someone had worried about her. For just a second, she mused about what it'd be like to date the Bachelor of the Year—he certainly was easy on the eyes and very kind. More than likely, he had his pick of women. The thought left her feeling a bit unsettled.

She couldn't let herself get swept away by Lucas's charms. She had a notorious record with unreliable men.

Why would Lucas be any different? After all, she knew next to nothing about him—other than he was a lousy house-keeper. He'd dismissed his desperately needed maid service. And he went out of his way for strangers he found squatting in his house. Wait. She was supposed to be list-ing his negative qualities.

She needed to make an important point not only to him but also to herself. "You know, I would have been fine on my own. You didn't have to ride to my rescue."

"I had to go out anyway."

"And you just happened to be going in the same direc-tion."

"Something like that."

The car rolled to a stop at an intersection. Lucas glanced at her. His probing eyes were full of questions. Like what was a small-town girl doing in the Big Apple? And how had she befriended his aunt? And the number one ques-tion that was dancing around in his mind: Why was she going to the hospital?

He didn't push or prod. Instead he exuded a quiet strength. And that only made it all the more tempting to open up to him—to dump the details of the most tragic event in her life into his lap. No, she couldn't do that. No matter how nice he was to her, letting him in was just ask-ing for trouble.

Afraid he'd voice his inevitable questions, she decided to ask him a few of her own. "What's the story with the house? Why does it look frozen in time?"

Lucas's facial features visibly hardened. "I haven't had time to deal with it."

"Have you owned the place long?"

"My family has lived there for generations."

Wow. She couldn't even imagine what it would be like to have family roots that went that deep. Her relatives were the here-today-gone-tomorrow type. And they never bothered to leave a forwarding address. Once in a while a postcard would show up from her mother. Her father... Well, he'd been out of the picture since she was young.

She tried not to think about her lack of family or her not-so-happy childhood. It didn't do any good to dwell on things that couldn't be changed. The only thing that mattered now was the future. But there was one thing she could do to help Lucas hold on to a piece of his past.

"You know the house is in desperate need of repairs, especially the upstairs," she said, longing to one day have an opportunity to work on an impressive job such as his historic mansion. "I'm an interior designer and I have some contacts that could help—"

"I'm not interested."

The thought of that stunning architecture disintegrating for no apparent reason spurred her on. "But houses need to be cared for or they start to look and act their age. And it'd be such a travesty to let the place fall down—"

"It's fine as is. End of discussion."

She wanted to warn him about the leaking roof, but he'd cut her off. She doubted anything she said now would even register in his mind.

With a huff, she turned away. Frustration warmed her veins. Here was a problem that could so easily be resolved and yet this man was too stubborn to lift up the phone and ask for help. If only her problems could be fixed as readily.

Her thoughts filled with the possible scenarios for today's meeting with Molly's specialist. This surgeon was their last hope. Kate prayed he wouldn't dismiss the case as quickly as Lucas had dismissed the problem with his house.

She tilted her head against the cool glass. It soothed her heated skin. She stared blindly ahead, noticing how even at this early hour, the city was coming to life. An army of people with umbrellas moved up and down the walks while traffic buzzed by at a steady pace. Her world might be teetering on the edge, but for everyone else, it was business as usual.

Now was not the time for self-pity. As the towering hospital came into view, she straightened her shoulders and inhaled a deep breath, willing away all of her doubts and insecurities.

"Which entrance should I drop you at? Emergency?"

"No. I told you I'm fine. Fit as a fiddle." She forced a smile to her lips before gathering her things.

"You're sure?"

"Absolutely. The main entrance will do."

"You know hospitals aren't a great place to be alone. Is there someone I can call for you?"

He surprised her with his thoughtful offer. How could a man be so frustrating in one breath and sweet in the next?

"No, thanks. I have some people waiting for me."

He pulled the car over to the curb. "Are you sure?"

She nodded. What she failed to tell him was that the people waiting for her consisted of the medical staff. No family. Except for Molly. She was all the family Kate needed.

"Thank you for everything." She jumped out into the rain. "I just have to grab my suitcase."

Lucas swiveled around. "Leave it."

"But I—"

"Obviously you have enough to deal with already. Besides, I'm planning to work from home today. Call me when things are wrapped up here and I'll give you a lift to your hotel."

She had to think fast. Without an umbrella, the rain was soaking her. She really should end this here and now, but she'd feel more confident for the meeting if she wasn't lugging around an old suitcase. Lucas was only offering to keep her possessions for a few hours, not asking her to run off and have a steamy affair or anything. The errant thought warmed her cheeks.

"Thanks for the offer, but I'm not sure how long I'm going to be."

"No problem. Let me give you my number."

In seconds, she had his number saved on her cell phone and was jogging up the steps to the glass doors. Thoughts of Lucas slid to the back of her mind. She was about to have the most important meeting of her life.

She refused to leave until she heard: "Yes. We will help your daughter."

CHAPTER FOUR

"I THINK WE can help your daughter but—"

Kate's heart soared. She'd been waiting so long to hear those words. It took all her self-restraint not to jump for joy. She wasn't sure what the surgeon said after that as the excitement clouded her mind.

For months now, they'd traveled to one hospital after the other. Every time she located a place that offered a possibility of hope, they were there. Now at long last they had come to the right place. The weight of anxiety slipped from her shoulders and left her lighter than she'd been in recent memory.

When a stack of papers was shoved in front of her, she glanced down, spotting her name and a very large dollar figure. Her excitement stuttered.

"What is this?" She couldn't move her gaze from the staggering dollar figure.

"That is the amount you'll need to pay up front if we are to perform the operation."

This couldn't be right. She had health coverage and it wasn't cheap. "But my insurance—"

"Won't cover this procedure." Dr. Hawthorne steepled his fingers and leaned back in his chair. "It doesn't cover experimental procedures. I'm willing to donate my time, but in order for the hospital to book the O.R. and the necessary staff, you'll need to settle this bill with Accounts Receivable." He paused and eyed her up as though checking to see if she fully understood. "You also need to be aware that this is an estimate. A conservative one at that. If there are complications, the bill will escalate quickly."

Kate nodded, but inside her stomach was churning and her head was pounding. Her gaze skimmed over the long list of charges from the anesthesiologist to medications. How in the world was she going to raise this staggering amount of money?

Her daughter's smiling face came to mind. She couldn't... no, she wouldn't let her down. There had to be an answer, because this operation was going to happen no matter what she had to do to make it a reality.

"You should also know that we normally like to treat children on an outpatient basis until surgery but with this tumor's aggressive growth rate and with it already affecting her mobility, I feel it's best to keep her admitted under close observation."

Kate nodded in understanding even though her head was spinning with information. "I understand."

Dr. Hawthorne cleared his throat. "Will you be able to come up with the funding?"

Without hesitation, Kate spoke in a determined voice. "Yes, I will."

The surgeon with graying temples gave her a long, serious stare. She didn't glance away, blink or so much as breathe. She sat there ready to do battle to get her daughter the necessary surgery.

"I believe you will," Dr. Hawthorne said. "I need you to sign these forms and then my team will start working to reduce the tumor's size before surgery."

Kate's lungs burned as she blew out a pent-up breath. She accepted the papers and started to read. Her stomach quivered as she realized the overwhelming challenge set before her.

A half an hour later, with her life signed away to East Riverview Hospital, Kate took comfort in knowing she'd done the right thing. This surgeon had performed miracles before. He could do it again. Kate was spurred on by the thought of Molly healthy once again. She could do this—somehow. She just needed time to think.

The elevator pinged and the doors opened. Kate stepped inside. A man stood in front of the control panel.

"Five, please." She moved to the other side of the elevator and stared down at the paperwork in her hand, wondering how she'd pull off this miracle.

"Kate?" a male voice spoke.

The door slid shut as Kate lifted her head. When her gaze latched on to the man, her breath caught. This couldn't be happening. Not here. Not now.

"Chad, what are you doing here?"

His dark brows scrunched together beneath the brim of a blue baseball cap. "Now, is that the way to greet your husband?"

"Ex-husband." She pressed her hands to her hips. "I tried to reach you months ago. You didn't have time for us then. Why have you suddenly shown up now?"

"My daughter's sick. My family needs me—"

"That's where you're wrong." There was no way she was letting him walk in here and act as if he was their saving grace. "We don't need you. We've been fine all of this time without you."

His gaze hardened. "I've been busy."

After he'd refused to settle down in one place and create a nurturing environment for their daughter, he'd left Kate on her own to have their baby. He'd succeeded in confirming her mistrust of men.

The elevator dinged and the door slipped open. Kate stepped out first and left Chad to follow. They stopped outside Molly's door. Kate didn't want anything to upset her little girl, not after everything she'd been through in the past several months. And certainly not now that she was scheduled for a very delicate procedure.

"How is she?"

"The tumor is causing her some mobility problems."

"Is she in pain?"

Kate shook her head. "Thankfully she feels fine…for now. If they don't do the surgery soon that will change. But…"

"But what?"

"Money has to be raised to cover the surgery. Lots of money." Kate stood between Chad and the doorway to Molly's room. "You should go before she sees you."

He crossed his arms. "I'm not going anywhere." His voice rose. "My Molly girl will be excited to see her daddy."

Before she could utter a word, Molly called out. "Daddy, is that you?"

"Yes, sweetie. I'm here." He leaned over and whispered, "I always was her favorite."

Kate bit back a few unkind words as she followed her ex into the room. She hated how he dropped into their lives whenever it suited him and disappeared just as quickly.

Maybe that was why she'd been initially drawn to him— he was so much like her family, always chasing happiness in the next town. Having a child had been too much for her father, who'd split when she was ten. But her mother had stuck it out until Kate's eighteenth birthday, before skipping town with the current flavor of the month.

But when Kate became pregnant, her priorities changed. She wanted her child to have a real home. She promised herself that her little one would have something she never had—stability.

The same town.

The same house.

The same bed.

She wondered what it'd be like to live in a home like Lucas's, rich with family history. The man didn't know how good he had it. The errant thought brought her up short. Why should she think of him now? And why did just the mere thought of him have her heart going pitty-pat? Maybe because she hadn't anticipated his kindness after finding her, a total stranger, in his house.

"Yay! Daddy's here." Molly's smile filled the room with an undeniable glow.

Chad gave their daughter a kiss and a hug. Kate watched the happy reunion and wondered whether she should be furious at her unreliable ex or grateful he'd made Molly's face light up like Christmas morning. A child's ability to forgive was truly impressive. And right now Molly's happiness was all that mattered.

"How long are you sticking around?" Kate asked, wondering if she had time to grab some much needed coffee and gather her thoughts.

"For a while. Molly and I have some catching up to do."

"Daddy, wanna watch this with me?" Molly pointed to a cartoon on the television anchored to the wall.

All three of them in the same room for an extended period would only lead to problems. Chad had a way of finding her tender spots and poking them. And having Molly witness her parents arguing was certainly not something her little girl needed right now. Kate struggled to come to terms with the fact Chad was suddenly back in their lives.

"I'm just going to step out and get some coffee. I'll be right back." Kate couldn't help thinking that she was a third wheel here, an unfamiliar feeling. "You should know she sleeps a lot."

"No need to rush." Chad used his take-charge tone, which caused every muscle in Kate's body to tense. "How about I stay until this afternoon and then you can spend the evening with our girl. No need for both of us to be here. After all, you have money to raise."

Just the way he said the last part let her know that coming up with the money for the surgery would be solely her responsibility. Her blood pressure rose. What else was new?

She was about to inform him of his responsibilities toward their daughter when common sense dowsed her angry words. An argument between her and Chad was the last thing Molly needed. Still, with all three of them crowded in this small room all day, an argument was inevitable.

"You can leave," Chad said dismissively.

"Yeah, Mommy. Daddy and me are gonna watch TV."

Maybe it was the best way to keep Molly happy. She caught Chad's gaze. "Are you sure you want to stay that long?"

"Absolutely. Molly and I have lots of catching up to do. Is that a stack of board games over there?" He pointed to the corner of the room.

Before Kate could speak, Molly piped up. "Yeah. Wanna play?"

While Chad wasn't reliable for the long haul, when he was with Molly, he was a good father. Kate smiled at her daughter's exuberance. "What time should I be back?"

"Three. I have some things to do then."

"Okay. I'll see you both at three." And to be certain of Chad's intentions, she added, "You will still be here, won't you? Because I can come back earlier."

"I'll be here."

Kate kissed her daughter goodbye and hesitantly walked away. She assured herself Molly would be fine with Chad. In the meantime, she had planning to do. Four weeks wasn't much time to come up with enough cash to cover the bill.

The thought made her chest tighten. She didn't have access to that kind of money. As it was, her house in Pennsylvania was being sold to pay some prior medical bills. What in the world was she going to do?

"Elaina, you have to be reasonable." Lucas struggled to maintain a calm tone with his ex-wife. "All I'm asking is for you to let me see Carrie when I fly back out to San Francisco."

"And I told you it's too confusing for her. She has a dad now—one who doesn't spend his life at the office. Don't come around again. All you'll do is upset her."

"That's not true." His grip on the phone tightened. "You know you could make this easier for her by not yelling at me in front of her."

Elaina sighed. "When you show up without invitation, what do you expect? And I'm only doing what's best for my daughter—"

"Our daughter. And if I waited for an invitation, I'd be an old man. Don't you think her knowing her father is important?"

"No. Don't keep pushing this. Carrie is happy without you."

A loud click resonated through the phone. His teeth ground together at the nerve of his ex-wife hanging up the phone while he was trying to reason with her.

The kitchen chair scraped over the smooth black-and-white tiles as Lucas swore under his breath and jumped to his feet. He paced the length of the kitchen. The sad thing was Elaina meant her threat. She would make his life hell if he didn't play by her rules. She'd done it once by skipping town with their daughter and leaving no forwarding address. This time he didn't even want to think of the lies she'd tell Carrie about him.

This was the reason he'd decided to let his daughter live in peace without the constant shuffle between two warring parents. He wanted a better childhood for Carrie than he'd had.

His thoughts drifted back to his childhood. He'd hated being a pawn between his parents and being forced to play the part of an unwilling spy. Those two were so wrapped up in knowing each other's business and with outdoing the other that, in some twisted way, he figured they never really got over each other.

But if that was love, then he wanted no part of it. That's why he'd decided to marry Elaina. They had a relationship based on friendship and mutual goals, not love. A nice, simple relationship. Boy, had he made a huge miscalculation. Even without love things got complicated quickly. Now he couldn't let his daughter pay the price for his poor decisions.

Lucas stopped next to the table and stared down at the unfinished email. The cursor blinked, prompting him for the next words, but he couldn't even recall what he'd written.

Nothing was going right at the moment. First, his ex-wife declared war if he pursued his right to spend time with his little girl. Then there was the San Francisco expansion, which was hemorrhaging money. His only hope was the launch of his newest line: Fiery Hearts—brilliant rubies set in the most stunning handcrafted settings.

The launch of this line had to be bigger and better than any other he'd done. Fiery Hearts had to start a buzz that would send women flocking to Carrington's, infusing it with income to offset the cost of getting the West Coast showroom up and running. He raked his fingers through his hair, struggling for some innovative, headline-making launch for the line. But he drew a blank.

He closed the laptop and strode over to the counter. He went to refill his coffee cup only to find the pot empty. The thought of brewing more crossed his mind, but he had a better idea—getting away from the house by going to a coffee shop. Between the hum of conversation and his laptop, it'd keep him occupied. And if Kate needed her suitcase, she had his number.

Satisfied with his plan of action, he grabbed his keys and wallet when his cell phone buzzed. A quick glance at the illuminated screen revealed it was his aunt.

"Aunt Connie, I've been trying since last night to get you. Are you okay?"

"Of course. Why wouldn't I be?"

"I'm not used to you being out so late and not taking my calls."

"Sorry. I was at the hospital, sitting with a woman whose husband underwent emergency surgery."

"Did everything go well?" he asked, already having a pretty good guess at the answer. His aunt was too upbeat for things to have gone poorly.

"Yes, the man has a good prognosis. So, dear, how are things going in San Francisco?"

This was his opening to find out what exactly was going on here. "I got back late last night."

There was a quick intake of breath followed by silence. He wasn't going to help his aunt out of this mess. She owed him an explanation of why a stranger was living here in his home without his permission. He might love his aunt dearly, but this time she'd overstepped.

"Oh, dear. Umm…I meant to call you—"

"So you're admitting you invited Kate to stay here without consulting me?"

"Well, yes. But I knew you'd understand." Uncertainty threaded through her voice.

If Connie were an employee, he'd let her have an earful and then some. But this was his aunt, the only family member who'd ever worried more about his happiness than the company's bottom line…or having the Carrington name appear on the society page with some splashy headline. He couldn't stay angry with her, even if he tried.

"It might be best if you ask in the future, instead of assuming." He made sure to use his I'm-not-messing-around voice.

"I'm sorry. She doesn't have any family for support or anywhere to go. And I would have sent her to my place, but you know after the last person I took in, my roommate insisted I never bring home anyone else. How was I to know that woman liked to borrow things?"

"Without permission and without any intention of returning them."

He was so grateful that his aunt had Pauline to look after her. If it weren't for Pauline, he'd never feel comfortable enough to leave town on business. His aunt was too nice, too unassuming. As a result, people tried repeatedly to take advantage of her to get to the Carrington fortune.

"Kate isn't like the others," Connie insisted. "She has a good heart."

"Still, you shouldn't have sent her here. This house… it's off-limits."

"I thought after all of this time you'd have let go of the past."

He'd never let go. How could he? It'd mean letting go of his little girl. A spot inside his chest ached like an open, festering wound every time he thought of how much he missed seeing Carrie's sweet smile or hearing her contagious laughter. But he didn't want to discuss Carrie with his aunt…with anyone.

Hoping to redirect the conversation, he asked, "What do you know about Kate?"

"Didn't she tell you?"

A knock at the back door caught him off guard. He wasn't expecting anyone as he never had visitors. And if it was some sort of salesperson, they'd go to the front door.

"I've got to go. Someone's at the door. I'll call you back later."

"Lucas, be nice to Kate. She has more than enough on her plate. She can use all of the friends she can get."

And with that the line went dead. What in the world had that cryptic message meant? He didn't have time to contemplate it as the knock sounded again.

He let out a frustrated sigh as he set his phone on the center island. So much for getting any answers about Kate. Now all he had were more questions.

The knocking became one long string of beats.

"Okay! I'm coming."

Lucas strode over and yanked open the door. A cold breeze rushed past him. His mouth moved, but words failed him.

There standing in the rain, completely soaked, was Kate. Her teeth chattered and her eyes were red and puffy. This certainly wasn't the same determined woman he'd dropped off at the hospital. Where her hair had once been styled, the wet strands clung to her face. What in the world was going on?

Without thinking he reached out, grabbed her arms and pulled her inside. His mind continued to flood with questions, so many that he didn't know where to start. But finally he drew his thoughts into some semblance of order and decided to start at the beginning.

"Why didn't you call?" He slipped her purse off her shoulder and set it on a kitchen stool. "I'd have picked you up."

Were those tears flowing down her cheeks? Or raindrops? He couldn't be sure. Obviously he'd have to hold off getting to the bottom of this. His first priority was getting Kate warmed up.

"We need to get you in a hot shower." She started to shake her head when he added, "No arguments. You'll be lucky if you don't catch pneumonia. If you hadn't noticed, it's awfully cold to be walking around in the rain."

He helped her out of her jacket, which definitely wasn't waterproof. Next, he removed her waterlogged red heels. When he reached for her hand to lead her to his bathroom, he noticed how small and delicate she was next to him.

She looked so fragile and his instinct was to protect her—to pull her close and let her absorb his body heat. He resisted the urge. It wasn't his place to soothe away her worries. When it came to relationships, he should wear a sign that read Toxic. And that was why he intended to grow old alone.

In his bedroom, he had her wait while he grabbed a towel and heated up the shower. When he returned, she was still standing there with her arms hugging herself, staring at the floor. What in the world had happened? Did she have bad news at the hospital? Had someone died?

Not that it was any of his business. He wasn't a man to lean on. He had no words of wisdom to share to make whatever problem she had go away. If he had, he'd have used it to fix his own messed up life. He'd have gotten his family back. The house would be filled with the sounds of his daughter's laughter. Instead the silence was deafening. He shoved the troubling thoughts away.

"Let's get you in a hot shower." He showed her to his bathroom. "Will you be all right in there alone? Or should I call my aunt?"

In a faint whisper, she said, "I'm fine."

Sure she was. And he had some oceanfront property in New Mexico to sell.

"Just yell, if you need me. I won't be far away."

While she warmed up in the shower, he rushed to the front door and returned with her suitcase. His thumbs hovered over the locks. He stopped. Opening her suitcase would be prying—something he hated when people did it to him, no matter what their intentions. Instead, he retrieved his robe and laid it on the bed, just in case she was still chilled.

Trying not to think of how good she'd looked in his robe, he returned to the kitchen. He grabbed the coffeepot and filled it with water. His idea to step out for a bit was permanently on the back burner. Once he got Kate situated in a hotel, the afternoon would be shot. And so would his patience.

He flung himself down on a kitchen chair, determined to concentrate on something besides his unwanted guest. He opened up his laptop and skimmed over his unfinished email. He had absolutely no desire to work. This realization for a renowned workaholic was unsettling, to say the least. What was wrong with him? Was it the way things had ended in San Francisco with his little girl looking at him with fear in her eyes when he went to pick her up?

He inhaled an unsteady breath. He'd made his choice, not to make his daughter a pawn between him and his ex. It was the right decision…for Carrie. Now he had to get a grip. After all, Carrington Gems was all he had left.

With one ear toward the bathroom and his eyes on the monitor, he started to type. He'd gotten through a handful of emails by the time Kate emerged from the bedroom wearing his robe. Her dark brown hair was wet and brushed back from her face and her cheeks were tinged pink from the shower.

The robe gaped open, revealing a glimpse of her cleavage. His overzealous imagination filled in the obscured details. He should have looked away but he couldn't. He was drawn to her like a starving bear to a picnic basket.

He shifted uncomfortably, fighting back this wave of desire. Sex was not the answer. It only complicated things, even in the simplest of relationships.

The fact he'd never met anyone who was so fiercely independent but at the same time looked worn to the bone only made him more curious about Kate. What was her story? Where had she come from? And what was she doing at the hospital?

He swallowed hard. "Do you feel better?"

She nodded. "I'm sorry to be such a bother."

Was this where he was supposed to step up and comfort her? He hesitated. He never was one of those soft, mushy people. He was a Carrington—strong, proud and unfeeling. Or at least those were the words his ex had thrown at him numerous times and he'd never had a reason to disbelieve her assessment. Until now....

There was something about Kate that bore through his defenses and made him want to fix whatever was broken. But he didn't know anything about comforting people. With each passing moment he grew more uncomfortable, not knowing how he should act around her.

Taking the safe approach, he got up and pulled a chair out for her. "Have a seat while I get you some coffee. Do you take milk or sugar?"

"A little of both, please."

That he could do. It was this talking stuff that had him knotted up inside. He wasn't sure what to say or do. Silence was best. Silence was golden.

Once she finished her coffee, he would see about getting her moved to a hotel. His life would then return to normal. Or whatever qualified as normal these days. And he wasn't going to ask any questions. Her life was none of his affair.

CHAPTER FIVE

KATE SANK DOWN on the black-cushioned chair, mortified that she'd shown up on this man's—this stranger's—doorstep and fallen to pieces. The staggering hospital bill already had her worried beyond belief, but combined with the unexpected appearance of her ex-husband it was just too much. It wasn't often that she let down her guard. And she really wished it hadn't been in front of Lucas.

The steaming shower had helped clear her mind. She'd given in to a moment of fear that she would fail her daughter, but the time for uncertainty had passed. She must be strong now. Besides, she refused to fall to pieces again in front of Lucas. He must already think that she was... what? Pathetic? Weak? Looking for a handout? Or all of the above? She wasn't about to confirm any of his suspicions—not if she could help it.

He pushed a cup of steaming coffee in front of her. "Drink this. It'll warm you up while I run to the deli and get us some lunch."

"Thank you. I'm sorry for imposing again. I...I just started walking and thinking. Eventually I ended up here."

Her hands were clammy and her muscles tense as she clutched the warm ceramic cup. Her gaze strayed to Lucas as he strode over to the center island where his jacket was draped over a stool as though he might have been headed somewhere before she showed up. His strides were long and his dark jeans accentuated his toned legs and cute back-side. His collared shirt was unbuttoned just enough for her to catch a glimpse of his firm chest. He'd certainly make some woman a fine catch—except for his lack of house-keeping skills.

He slipped on his jacket. "You can play solitaire on my computer."

"I hate making you go out in the rain—"

"I was going out anyway. I guess one of these days I need to do more than just drive past the grocery store." He flashed her a lighthearted smile. "Do you want anything in particular to eat?"

She shook her head. "I'm not picky."

"I won't be long." He rushed out the door.

Kate was exhausted, but there was no time for sleep. She needed to plan out how to raise the funds for the sur-gery. Her lengthy walk had given her time to think and she knew there was no way a bank would lend her that kind of money. And she didn't have any rich aunts or uncles lurking in the family tree. That only left a fund-raiser. A big one!

Lucas had said she could use his computer. She pulled up a search engine and began typing. Eventually she stum-bled across the fact that the Carringtons used to organize fund-raisers, some even taking place in this very mansion.

Somehow Lucas must have missed the social gene. This house wasn't fit for him to live in much less provide a venue for entertaining. If only the mansion had been better main-tained, it'd be ideal for a premium ticket event.

Before she could search for alternate locations that might attract wealthy donors, Lucas returned with a large bag. "Hope you're hungry."

"Looks like enough to feed a football team."

"I wasn't sure what to order. So I got a little of this and a little of that."

They quietly set the table and spread out the food. Kate's

belly rumbled its anticipation. She eagerly munched down her sandwich before Lucas was even halfway done with his. He pushed another foil-wrapped sandwich in front of her.

"That must have been some walk," Lucas said as she unwrapped the food.

"I had a lot of thinking to do."

After she'd left the hospital, she'd tramped around the bustling streets of Manhattan. She'd been surrounded by people from all walks of life and yet she had never felt more alone—more scared that she'd fail as a mother. But thanks to Lucas's kindness the panic had passed and her determination had kicked in. She would see that her little girl got what she needed—one way or the other.

"And did you get everything straight in your head?"

She glanced away, unsure how to answer. She didn't want him to think any less of her for losing complete control of her life, but she hated to lie, too. She took the middle road. "I still have a lot to figure out."

"You know, I find when I have problems at the office that talking them through usually helps. We conduct brainstorming sessions where my key people sit around tossing out ideas, no matter how crazy they might sound. One thing leads to another until we have some potential solutions. Would you like to give it a try?"

She didn't know why he was being so nice to her. A warm shower. His übercomfy robe. A cup of hot coffee. More food than she could ever eat. And now a sympathetic ear. His kindness choked her up and had her blinking repeatedly.

"Hey, it can't be that bad." Lucas squeezed her forearm.

The heat of his touch seeped through the robe, igniting a pulse of awareness. The sensation zinged up her arm and short-circuited her already frazzled mind. Then just as quickly as he'd reached out to her, he pulled back. It was as though he realized he'd crossed some sort of invisible line.

She sniffled. "Actually my life is a nightmare right now."

"The visit to the hospital—was it because you're sick?"

"I wish that was the case."

His brows lifted and his eyes grew round. "You want to be sick?"

The horrified expression on his face made her laugh. She couldn't help it. Maybe this was the beginning of some sort of nervous breakdown, but the look Lucas shot her across the table tickled her funny bone. He probably thought she'd lost control of her senses. But she was perfectly sane and this was deadly serious.

Her laughter was immediately doused by the thought of her daughter. "I don't want to be sick. But if someone must be ill, it should be me. Not my four-year-old daughter."

Lucas sat back in his chair as though her words had knocked him over. "What's the matter with her?"

"Molly needs an operation. That's why we came to New York. No one else was willing to take the risk. But before anything can be done, I have to come up with the money to pay for the surgery."

Lucas's brows scrunched together as though he were processing all of this information. "Excuse me for asking, but don't you have insurance?"

"It doesn't cover experimental procedures. And every cent I have won't make a dent in what I owe."

His blue eyes warmed with sympathy. He nodded as though he understood. That or he ran out of kind words to say. Either way, she'd already said too much.

"I'm sorry. This isn't your problem. I only stopped back to get my things."

"Where will you go?"

"I…I don't know. I hadn't gotten that far yet. But I'll figure out something. I always do."

She got to her feet a little too quickly. The room started

to spin. She grabbed the back of the chair and squeezed her eyes shut, willing the sickening sensation to pass.

The sound of rapid footsteps had her opening her eyes. A worried frown greeted her. "I'm fine."

"You don't look it."

"It's nothing. I just stood up too fast." That combined with three hours of shut-eye the night before and plodding around in the rain on top of the news that she owed the hospital a small fortune had left her drained and off-balance. But she refused to play the sympathy card. She didn't want him thinking any less of her. Then again, was it possible to sink lower in his estimation? She stifled a groan.

"I think this news has taken its toll on you." Lucas stared at her, holding her gaze captive. "Do you have family around to help?"

Did Chad count? Not in her book. "No. My mother is out of town and my father… He's not in the picture. It's just me and Molly."

"I'm sorry to hear that."

An awkward silence ensued. Hoping to fill in the gap so he didn't feel that he had to say anything sympathetic, she added, "We do okay on our own. In fact, I should get back to the hospital soon."

"I'm sure your little girl misses you."

The mention of her daughter had her remembering Lucky Ducky. She pulled the keychain from the pocket of the robe and fidgeted with it.

"I see you have your duck handy. Is it special? Or do you just like to have something to fidget with?"

Kate stared at the trinket. "My daughter gave it to me after winning it at Pizza Pete's Arcade. She said it was to keep me company. I tossed it into my purse and eventually it became sort of a good luck charm."

"He looks like a reliable, no-nonsense duck. No quacking around."

She found herself smiling at his attempt at levity. "He's definitely seen me through some tough times. Now, I should get cleaned up. Molly's dad will be leaving soon and I need to be there when he does so she isn't alone."

His gaze moved to her bare ring finger. "You're married?"

"No. Chad's my ex-husband. And…" She shook her head, fighting to hold back another yawn and…losing the battle. "Never mind. I keep rambling on when I need to get out of your way. I'm sure you have better things to do."

"What time are you expected back at the hospital?"

"Not until three. It's best if my ex and I keep our time together at a minimum. Molly has enough to deal with. She doesn't need to see her parents arguing."

"You still have a couple of hours until you have to be back. Why don't you take a nap and later I'll give you a ride to the hospital?"

His offer filled her with a warmth that she hadn't felt in a long time. "I couldn't ask you to do that. You don't even know me."

"You aren't asking. I'm offering. And after I kept you up late last night, I owe you this."

"But it isn't necessary—

"It's still drizzling outside. You don't need to get wet again. So do we have a deal?"

"How is it a deal? What do you get out of helping me?"

"Let's just say it feels good being able to help someone."

She had a feeling there was more to his statement than he let on. Was he wishing that someone would help him? What could a wealthy, sexy bachelor need help with?

She looked into his blue-gray eyes. "Are you sure?"

"I am. Now do you promise you won't go sneaking off again?"

She was exhausted. And he seemed determined to be a Good Samaritan. What would it hurt to accept his offer?

"I promise."

A ball of sympathy and uneasiness churned in Lucas's gut. He knew all too well the hell a parent went through when they felt as if they'd lost control of their children's safety. When his ex-wife had up and left him, she'd written only a brief note saying she'd take good care of their little girl. Until his private investigator had tracked her down in California, he hadn't been able to function.

This thing with Kate hit too close to home. But how could he turn his back on her when her daughter was in such shaky circumstances?

He needed time to think. In fact, that's all he'd been doing since Kate went upstairs to lie down. But it was almost three and he hadn't seen any sign of her. The memory of her pale face and the dark smudges under her eyes had him thinking she was still asleep. Perhaps she'd forgotten to set the alarm on her phone. Or maybe she was so tired that she'd slept right through it. He couldn't blame her.

He should wake her, but the thought of going upstairs left a sour taste in his mouth. He hadn't been upstairs in a long time. There was nothing up there but gut-wrenching memories of everything he'd lost—his family...his little girl.

Still he had to do something. He'd given his word that he'd get her there on time. The thought of a little girl—the image of his own daughter crystallized in his mind—sick and alone spurred him into action.

He moved to the bottom of the steps. "Kate!" Nothing. "Kate, are you awake? It's time to head to the hospital."

He waited, hoping to hear a response or the echo of footsteps. There were no sounds. Surely she hadn't left again without saying anything. Unease churned in his gut. No.

She'd promised and he sensed that she prided herself on keeping her word.

"Kate, we need to go!"

The seconds ticked by and still nothing. There was only one thing left to do. His gaze skimmed up the staircase. He'd been up and down those stairs countless times throughout his life and he'd never thought anything of it. Then came the day when he'd climbed to the second floor only to find his wife was gone along with his baby girl. The memory slugged him squarely in the chest, knocking the breath from his lungs.

That never-to-be-forgotten night he'd cleared out his personal belongings and moved to the first floor. He'd wanted to avoid the memories…the pain. Now because of Kate and her little girl, he had to climb those steps again.

Putting one foot in front of the other, he started up the stairs. He faltered as he reached the landing with the large stained-glass window, but he didn't turn back. He couldn't. This was too important.

He turned, taking the next set of steps two at a clip. His chest tightened and his hands tensed.

Don't look around. Don't remember. Just keep moving.

His strides were long and fast. He kept his face forward, resisting the instinct to survey his surroundings, to let the memories crowd into his mind—not that they were ever far away.

Lucas stopped in front of her door and blew out a pent-up breath. He rapped his knuckles on the heavy wood door. "Kate, are you awake?"

Nothing.

He knocked again. Still no response.

Was it possible she was sick? Walking around in the cold air while soaking wet certainly couldn't have done her any good. And he wasn't going downstairs until he knew she was all right.

He grasped the handle and pushed the door open. The drapes were drawn, allowing shadows to dance across the spacious room. When his eyes adjusted, he spotted Kate sprawled over the king-sized bed. Her breathing was deep. The stress lines were erased from her beautiful face. And her pink lips were slightly parted and very desirable.

He squashed his line of thought. Now wasn't the time to check her out, no matter how appealing he found her. Relationships weren't in the cards for him. In the end, people just ended up hurting each other. And he wanted no part of that.

"Kate." His voice was soft so as to not scare her. When she didn't stir, he stepped closer. "Kate, wake up."

She rolled over and stretched. The robe fell open, revealing a lace-trimmed pink top that hugged her curves and rode up, exposing her creamy white stomach. The breath caught in his throat. She was so gorgeous. He shouldn't look—he should turn away. But what fun would that be? He was, after all, a man. A little glimpse of her fine figure wouldn't hurt anyone. Right?

Her gaze latched on to him and the moment ended. She bolted upright.

"Lucas. What are you doing here?" She glanced down, cinching the robe closed. "I mean I know it's your house and all…but what are you doing in my room…umm, your guest room." She pressed a hand to her mouth, halting the babbling.

"I tried calling up the steps and even knocked on the door, but you were out to the world."

"What do you want?"

The question was a loaded one and set off one inappropriate response after the other. The first of which was for her to move over in bed. The next thought was for her to kiss him.

He cleared his throat, hoping his voice would sound normal. "It's time to go back to the hospital." He turned for the door. "I'll meet you downstairs."

Drip... Drip... He paused and listened. *Drip...*

Lucas turned on his heels. "Is the faucet in the bathroom leaking?"

"Umm…no."

"But that sound. Something's dripping." He squinted into the shadows. Frustrated, he moved to the light switch. "Can't you hear it?"

"Of course I hear it. I'm not deaf."

He flipped on the overhead light and spotted a wastebasket in the corner. A quick inspection of the ceiling showed water gathering around the bloated section of plaster. Droplets formed and dropped. Bits of fallen plaster littered the floor.

"What the—" He remembered his manners just before cursing. His mother had been the epitome of proper form. Carringtons should never lower themselves with vulgar language, she'd say. Especially not in front of guests.

"It's been like that since the rain started. You need a new roof."

His jaw tightened. "Thanks for pointing out the obvious."

"I told you when we met that I'm an interior designer. I know more about houses than just how to properly hang a painting."

"So you do roofing, too?"

She smiled. "No, I'm not a roofer, but that doesn't mean I can't find someone qualified to do a rush job. Because if you'd look around, you'd realize that isn't your only leak."

This time he didn't care about his manners. "Damn."

He'd turned a blind eye to the house to the point where he had no idea this place was in such bad condition. This went far beyond the mopping and cleaning he'd envisioned.

There was considerable damage to the ceiling that was now bowing, and the crown molding was warped and crumbling.

Kate listed everything she'd noticed that needed repair. Unable to bear the guilt over the devastation he'd let happen to his childhood home…to his daughter's legacy, he turned his gaze away from the ruined plaster. Kate continued talking as though she was in her element. Who knew that fixing up old houses could excite someone so much?

She got to her feet and straightened the bed. "If you want I can make a few phone calls to get people in here to start fixing things up. Maybe they can change things up a little and give this place a makeover—"

"No. I don't want people in here, making changes." He ground out the words.

A frown creased her forehead. "Of course there will have to be changes. Nothing ever stays the same. Life is one long string of changes."

The only changes he'd experienced lately were bad ones that left him struggling to keep putting one foot in front of the other. Like his last visit with his daughter in California—when she'd turned away from him because he was now a stranger to her.

"Listen to me," Kate said, moving to stand right in front of him. "You're going to have to make some decisions about this place. You can already see the neglect is taking its toll. Once it's fixed up, you can move out of that tiny room in the downstairs—"

"I'm happy there."

She frowned at him as though she didn't believe a word he said. "Perhaps then you might consider moving to someplace smaller and selling this house to some lucky family who will appreciate its charms."

He glanced around at the room. This had been his aunt's room, back when he was a kid. In this room, he'd always felt safe and accepted just as he was. This house was a scrapbook of memories, some good, some not so good. He couldn't turn his back on it all.

Ghosts of the past filled his mind. The walls started to close in on him. Each breath grew more difficult. He needed space—air. He headed for the door, ignoring Kate's plea for him to wait. With his gaze straight ahead, he marched down the hall, his breathing becoming more labored. It felt as though the oxygen had been sucked out of the house.

No matter how much he hated to admit it, Kate had a point. This mansion was in worse shape than he'd ever imagined. His shoulders drooped beneath the weight of guilt. His parents and grandparents would be horrified if they were still around to see the neglect he'd let take place. They'd entrusted him with the care of the Carrington mansion and he'd failed. His chest burned as he rushed down the stairs.

Even if he someday won over his little girl—if she no longer looked at him like a scary stranger—he couldn't bring her here. He couldn't show her the numerous portraits of her ancestors that his ex-wife had stashed in the attic. The dust. The peeling and cracking plaster. And most likely mold. It just wasn't fit for a child—or for that matter, an adult.

In the foyer, he yanked open the front door. The cool breeze rushed up and swirled around him. He stood in the doorway as the rain pitter-pattered on the pavement. He breathed in the fresh air—the coolness eased his lungs.

As his heart rate slowed, his jumbled thoughts settled. Kate was right. The house did need more repairs than he'd ever thought possible. And he was way past putting it off until another day. Then a crazy idea struck him. But could it work?

CHAPTER SIX

UPON HEARING KATE'S approaching footsteps, Lucas turned. "You're right."

"I am?" Her pencil-thin brows rose. "Is this your way of apologizing? And perhaps asking me to make those calls for you?"

"Yes, that was an apology." Why did she make him spell everything out? He thought he'd made it clear from the start.

As for having her involved with the repairs, he wasn't sure. Guilt niggled at him. Here she was with so much on her plate and she was worried about him…er, rather his house. This was all so backward. He should be offering Kate a helping hand.

Wouldn't things have gone more smoothly for him when his daughter went missing if he'd let someone in? Instead he'd closed himself off from the world. Lost in his own pain, Carrington Gems had teetered on the brink of disaster. Even today, he was still paying for the poor choices he'd made back then.

Was that the way Kate was feeling now? He glanced into her eyes, seeing pain and something else…could it be determination? Of course it was. She might have had a case of nerves earlier, but he could see by the slight tilt of her chin and her squared shoulders that the moment had passed.

Still, he wasn't quite ready to throw in with a woman

he barely knew…even if his aunt trusted Kate enough to open up his home to her. Still she seemed so excited when she talked about the house. He couldn't make any decisions now. It'd take him some more thought.

He glanced at his watch. "We should go. You don't want to be late."

"But what about the roof?"

"It'll keep for a few more hours. We can talk it over when you're done at the hospital."

He ushered her out the door into the gray, drizzling day. Deep inside he knew that Kate's appearance in his life was about to alter things…for both of them. He didn't know how, but he sensed change in the wind. And after years of trying to keep the status quo, this knowledge left him feeling extremely off-balance.

But no one could understand how hard it would be for him to help this woman with a sick child—a child the same age as his own daughter…who no longer even recognized him. Regret pummeled him. He should have been home more and tried harder to work things out with Elaina, if only for the sake of his little girl. Then it would be him she was calling Daddy—not someone else.

Silence filled the car, giving Lucas too much time to think about what he'd lost and how inadequate he felt as a human. He glanced over at Kate. "What has you so quiet?"

"I was thinking about how to raise money for the surgery."

The streetlight turned green and Lucas eased down on the accelerator. "Do you have any family you can reach out to?"

"No. My family is small and not close-knit. My mother was around when Molly first got sick, but she doesn't have a lot of patience. The longer the tests and hospital visits went on… Well, now she's off in Los Angeles, or was it Las

Vegas, with the new flavor of the month. She calls when she gets a chance."

That was tough. Even though his mother had remarried after his father's death and moved to Europe, he knew if he ever picked up the phone and asked for help that she'd come. She was never a warm and affectionate mother, but she did protect what was hers.

"So without a rich uncle in the family and knowing I won't qualify for a loan, I'll have to organize a fund-raiser. Something that can be arranged quickly and without too much overhead."

He paused, searching for a solution. "I'll help you as much as I can. You just hit me at a bad time as I'm fully invested in expanding Carrington Gems to the West Coast." He didn't bother to add that they'd hit one expensive stumbling block after the other with this project. In comparison to what Kate was facing, his problems paled considerably. "If I think of something that might work, I'll let you know."

"Thanks. And my offer is still open to make those phone calls. I have some contacts in New York who can hook me up with a reliable crew."

The depth of her kindness struck a chord with him. "You'd really do that with everything you have going on?"

"Of course I would. You let me stay at your house for almost a week, rent-free…even if you didn't know it. I owe you so much."

He grew uncomfortable when people started thanking him. He wasn't someone special—definitely not a selfless person like Kate appeared to be. He was a workaholic, who'd lost focus on his priorities and wound up with a house of memories and a business in jeopardy because he'd pushed too hard, too fast to gain the expansion into San Francisco.

"You don't owe me a thing. All I did was let you stay in a leaky bedroom. Not very gallant of me."

She sniffled. "You could have had me thrown in jail. Most other people who find a stranger in their house would call the police first and ask questions later."

Lucas slowed the car as they neared the hospital. Once he maneuvered into a spot in front of the main sliding glass doors, he shifted into Park and turned to her. "Listen, you shouldn't put me up on a pedestal. You barely know a thing about me. Trust me, I have an ex-wife who would vouch for the fact that I'm no saint."

"You're far too modest—"

"Don't let a little kindness fool you. I'm a Carrington. We don't have hearts—instead, there's a rough diamond in its place." His fist beat lightly on his chest. "Harder and colder than any rock you'll ever find."

"I don't believe you."

"It's true. My grandfather told me. I was too young to truly understand what he meant, but now I do—"

"You definitely have a heart or you wouldn't have been so kind to me."

"And you're too sweet for your own good."

The way she stared at him with such assuredness made him want to be that man for her. The kind that was giving and thoughtful instead of focused and driven. For a moment, he was drawn into her dream—drawn to her.

When she lowered her face, he placed a finger beneath her chin. He wasn't willing to lose the connection just yet. Her eyes glinted with... Was it longing? His body tensed at the thought. How could this slip of a woman— a near-stranger—have such an effect on him? And why did he have this overwhelming urge to pull her close and kiss her?

Without thinking of the consequences, he leaned forward. His lips sought hers out. They were soft and smooth. A whispered voice in the back of his mind said he should not be doing this. Not with Kate. Not with anyone.

But when her mouth moved beneath his, logic escaped him. It'd been so long since he felt this alive—this invigorated.

He went to pull her closer, but the seat restraint kept them separated except for his lips moving hungrily over hers. His hand reached out, cupping her face. His thumb stroked her cheek, enjoying her silky, smooth skin. All he could think was that he wanted more—more of her kiss… more of this connection.

A bright flash broke the spell. Lucas pulled back, struggling to catch his breath. His gaze moved to the window. Immediately he spotted a photographer smirking at him. Lucas surmised from past experience that the guy would take the picture and fabricate an eyebrow-raising headline to fit it.

"Wait here. I'll be back." Lucas jumped out of the car and started after the photographer. "Hey, you! Stop!"

The reporter had too much of a head start and slipped into a waiting vehicle. Lucas kicked at a pebble on the side of the road and swore.

What had he gotten himself into this time? Of all the foolish things to do. He'd been so touched by her insistence in believing in him that he'd momentarily let down his guard. He hadn't thought about where they were or what he was about to do. He'd just reached out to her, needing to feel her warmth and kindness.

How was he supposed to know there was a photographer at the hospital? And how could he anticipate that they'd be noticed? Normally it wouldn't have been a big deal, but with Kate involved it was different. She already had so much on her plate. She didn't deserve to have to put up with the press. Those news stories, as they loosely called them, were nine times out of ten malicious pieces of gossip—such as the story his ex-wife had read about him being involved with one of the Carrington models. But it had been only one crack in an already crumbling marriage.

Kate hadn't signed on for any of this media mayhem. She didn't deserve to have her name associated with some trumped-up story. He just wished he could shield her from the public eye. With a frustrated sigh, he climbed back in the car.

"What's going on?" Kate's eyes filled with concern. "Why were you chasing that man?"

"The man was a reporter and he took a picture of us—"

"What?" Her face lost most of its color. "But why? None of this makes any sense. Why would he be interested in me? In us?"

Lucas raked his fingers through his hair. "Normally it wouldn't matter. And any other time the paparazzi wouldn't have given us a second look, but last month there was this magazine article—"

"The one announcing you as Bachelor of the Year."

"You saw it?" His muscles tensed, hating the thought of being played by her. "You knew who I was from the moment we met, didn't you?"

"That's not true." She held up both palms, feigning an innocent expression. "At first, I didn't recognize you in your boxers. I guess I was a bit distracted." Color rushed back into her cheeks. "The more important question is what will this reporter do with the photo?"

He shrugged. "My guess is he'll sell it to the highest bidder—"

"But he can't. If it gets out people will think that you and I are…uh—"

"Involved." He wasn't used to women being repulsed by the idea of being romantically linked with him. "Is the idea of people thinking we're a couple so bad?"

"Yes."

Her snap answer stung. He didn't know what to say, so

he leaned back in the driver's seat. Maybe he should be relieved by her lack of interest, but he wasn't. And that knowledge only aggravated him more.

"I'm sorry." She fidgeted with her purse strap. "I didn't mean for that to sound so harsh. I'm just not used to the paparazzi. And I really don't want my picture in the news."

Now that he could understand. His family had been making headlines longer than he'd been alive and he still wasn't comfortable with it.

"Most likely something more newsworthy will come along and they'll forget about us."

"Oh, good." The stress lines eased on her pretty face.

He didn't really believe it, but there was always a sliver of hope. And right now, Kate looked as if she could use some positive thoughts.

Later that evening, Kate made sure to double-check the dead bolt on the door. She glanced out the window, relieved to find that no one had followed her.

"Anything wrong?"

She jumped at the unexpected sound of Lucas's voice. "Umm…no."

Had she imagined someone had been watching her at the hospital? Definitely not. She might be a lot of things but paranoid wasn't one of them.

"Listen, if you're stressed about what happened between us earlier, don't be." He shuffled his feet and wouldn't look her in the eyes. "It was all my fault and it won't happen again."

Kate didn't know whether to be insulted or relieved. She hadn't been able to forget that kiss either—that mind-numbing, toe-curling kiss. And he was right—there shouldn't be a repeat.

"If you don't make a big deal of it, neither will I."

He looked as if he wanted to say more, but then he turned away and headed for the kitchen. "I ordered pizza, if you're hungry."

She followed him. The aroma of tomato sauce and sausage wafted across the kitchen. "Smells good. Did you by chance order a salad to go with it?"

"Yes, I did." He looked very proud of himself as he pulled a bowl from the fridge.

"Thank you."

She sat down at the counter, still unsettled. She kept going over the memory of that man lurking in the hallway at the hospital. She hadn't thought anything of him at first. But as the evening wore on, she'd noticed him again.

Lucas waved a hand in front of her face. "Kate?"

What had he said? She hadn't been paying attention. "Umm…sure. Whatever."

He placed a slice of the thin-crust pizza on a plate and pushed it in front of her. She didn't make a move as she kept replaying the events from the day.

"I wasn't going to ask," Lucas said, "but you obviously aren't going to eat until you resolve whatever has you so distracted."

"There was a man lurking in the pediatrics unit this evening. At first, I thought he was there to visit someone, but he stayed in the shadows and sort of watched everyone. I wasn't sure about leaving, but when I mentioned him to a nurse, he just sort of vanished."

"I hired him," Lucas said in a low, even tone.

That news had her sitting up straighter. "You hired someone to spy on me?"

"He was there to protect you."

"Protect me?" Her voice rose. "From what?"

"Remember the photographer outside the hospital?" Her hands pressed the countertop as she nodded and he continued. "I didn't want him or any other reporters to bother you with questions, so I sent an off-duty security guard from Carrington to make sure that didn't happen."

"I thought you said the press wouldn't make a big deal of it."

"I just wanted to be sure they left you alone."

"So you do think they'll go ahead with the photo?"

He wanted to assure her that she had nothing to worry about, but he couldn't lie to her. "Probably."

Her eyes lit up. "You can stop them."

"Me? How am I supposed to do that?"

"Pay the guy off. Bid on the photo. I don't know. There has to be a way."

"Even if I wanted to stop him, I don't have the man's name."

"How am I supposed to throw myself on people's mercy and ask for money after my name and face have been tangled up in some tabloid scandal?"

"So you've come up with a plan to raise the money?"

She sat back with a huff. "We're thinking of making it a costume party. Something unique. Your aunt offered to help."

"You've been talking to my aunt?"

"Since I don't know anyone else in this city except you, I approached her to help me organize the fund-raiser. Your aunt seems to know everyone, and if she doesn't know them personally, she knows someone who does. Your aunt loves to talk. We even talked about this house."

His eyes widened. "What exactly did you tell my aunt about the house?"

"Not much. Just that I found this place fascinating. The house is rich in architecture and history. I find it almost as intriguing as its owner."

"You do?" He searched her eyes as she smiled at him.

Was she flirting with him? He gave himself a mental jerk.
He didn't need to hook up with her. He just needed her professional expertise. "I have a proposition for you."

CHAPTER SEVEN

LUCAS HAD BEEN considering his plan all day. Kate obviously needed some immediate monetary assistance plus a roof over her head. And he needed someone to oversee the mansion's repairs—someone who appreciated its old-world charms. Kate fit that bill perfectly—if only he could forget how tempting her lush lips were.

She eyed him up tentatively. "What sort of proposition do you have in mind?"

"Since you like this place so much, what would you say if I offered you a job working here?"

Confusion reflected in her brown eyes. "You want me to work for you? Even after the run-in with the photographer?"

"Don't worry. I'll bet the article will be a small, obscure piece. Hardly anyone will notice it." He crossed his arms and rocked back on his heels. "As for the arrangement I'm proposing, it can benefit both of us."

She paused, glancing around the house. He could practically see the wheels in her mind spinning. He'd hired enough people to know when they were eager for a position.

"I...I can't. My daughter is in the hospital and I need to get this fund-raiser off the ground."

She did have a very valid point. But there had to be a compromise. He could see how tempted she was to work on the house, and he knew from his experience with stressful situations that a diversion would do her some good.

He cleared his throat. "The thing is, I have a couple of projects with Carrington Gems that are going to take all of my time." He stopped, realizing his responsibilities paled in comparison to hers. "The real truth is I can run a business, but I don't know how to turn this mess into a home again."

A smile touched her lips and her shoulders straightened. "What makes you think I can turn this place around?"

He didn't want her taking this the wrong way, especially after she thought he'd hired someone to spy on her. He'd have to phrase this carefully. "You got me to really think about this mansion and what my neglect is doing to it. And you mentioned that you have interior design experience. So I checked out some of your prior work. It's good."

Surprise lit up her eyes. "Thank you."

"And I really like your website."

She smiled broadly. "I built it myself."

"You're a woman of many talents. Maybe I should have you consult on Carrington's upcoming web campaign."

Interest sparked in her eyes. "Are you launching a new line of jewelry?"

He nodded, not surprised that she was familiar with his company. His father's lifelong dream had been to make Carrington Gems into a household name. In fact, they still used his father's slogan—*Carrington Gems for the queen of your heart*.

"I'd love to see the new jewelry." Kate's face lit up with excitement. "Your magazine ads already have a distinctive look. I like that they are never overdone and always tasteful."

He stood a little taller. Though he had a team that put together the ad campaigns, he was an active member, adding his input here and there. He was after all a Carrington and he had a vested interest in any images that represented his company.

"I'm also in the middle of an expansion project, which

needs more attention than I'd anticipated. So you can understand that I won't be available to oversee things here. However, I'm more than willing to compensate you for your time."

"My daughter has to be my priority—"

"Of course. We can work around that. Your ex-husband, is he still planning to be at the hospital part of the day?"

Kate nodded. "Actually, I do have a few ideas for the house."

"What would they be?"

Kate began listing off everything she'd like to do to the house, most of which hadn't crossed his mind when he'd offered her the job. Yet she had so much passion in her voice that he didn't want to stop her. The things he'd read about her and her work online didn't live up to the impressive woman standing before him.

As she continued explaining her vision, he couldn't believe someone could be so passionate about working on a house. His ex-wife, Elaina, had only ever been this excited about new clothes or jewels. Kate was definitely a different breed.

She paused and looked at him expectantly. "What do you think?"

"If I do what you suggest, will you take the job?"

"A good contractor can take care of everything."

Lucas shook his head. "I'm not going to let a bunch of people I've never met come in here and take over. You've already displayed your ability to take charge by getting me to see the condition of the house. You'll keep those workers in line and make sure that no changes are done without my authorization."

"I appreciate your faith in my abilities, but I can't be here every minute of the day while my daughter's in the hospital."

He knew he was asking a lot, but he needed to know that

his most treasured memories were handled with the utmost care and respect. "You said so yourself—you can't be there when your ex is with your daughter during the day. I'm offering you a chance to do what you obviously love while earning some money—"

"But what if my ex suddenly decides to skip town, as he's been known to do in the past?"

"We'll deal with that if or when we have to. But this will give you something to do besides sitting around, worrying. There's nothing worse than a day filled with worrisome thoughts and nothing but time on your hands."

"Sounds like you're speaking from experience." When he shrugged but failed to add any details, Kate continued. "And what do I do about the fund-raiser?"

He'd thought about this, too. "I think between my administrative assistant, who is practically a party-planning pro by now, and my aunt, who knows everyone who is anyone, you'll have time to spare. But if you decide to pass on the job, I totally understand. I'm sure I'll find someone to oversee things…eventually."

"This isn't a wait-and-see problem. One more big rain and you'll have untold damage. You need a new roof, and who knows what else, today."

"Does that mean you accept the position?"

Kate was impressed by the speed and ease with which Lucas solved problems. A snap of his fingers and all was right in the world—except for this time.

As tempting as it was to take on this exclusive job and add it as a crowning jewel in her portfolio, she still had a much bigger problem. She needed money for the operation. And though she didn't doubt that Lucas's assistant and aunt could throw together a lavish party, it was still her responsibility. And its success was paramount.

"As much as I'd like to, I can't accept your offer. I have to concentrate on the fund-raiser."

Frown lines creased his forehead. "How is that going?"

She shrugged. "The location is going to be a problem as there are a lot of spring weddings taking up the prime locations, not that I have enough for a deposit on the plush venues anyway. I have some phone messages in to other places—I'm just waiting for them to get back to me."

"I'm sure it'll all work out."

She couldn't help but wonder if he really thought that or if he was just telling her what she wanted to hear. "Connie helped me come up with a theme. It's going to be a vintage costume party. Hopefully people will have a lot of fun dressing up."

"My aunt is a great lady to have around to help plan a party. She's had a lifetime of experience. Between my great-gran, my grandmother and my mother, there was always some sort of social function going on here."

"Really? I've never been to a formal party other than a friend's wedding."

"Not even a work function?"

"By the point where I was in a position to be invited to client parties, I had Molly to consider. I didn't get to spend enough time with her as it was, so I stayed home. We put on an animated movie and ate popcorn."

"You're a very dedicated mother."

Heat flared in her cheeks. "I…uh… Thank you."

"Don't worry, you didn't miss much at those parties."

Her mouth gaped. "Of course I did. It's a girl's dream to get all gussied up and go to the ball. You can say that because you've gone to countless parties. Just once I'd like to check it out for myself."

He chuckled. "Beneath the jeans and T-shirts, I guess you really are a girl."

She frowned. "You actually had doubts about me being a girl?"

"Not at all. You just struck me as being different from the other women I've known."

"I'm not sure if that's good or bad."

"It's neither." He cleared his throat, looking exceedingly uncomfortable. "What if I throw in free room and board if you work for me?"

The man certainly didn't give up easily. "From what I've seen in the kitchen, I'd probably starve to death."

"You've got me there. But I have all of the local take-outs on speed dial. And…maybe I'll entertain some of your design ideas."

She had to admit she was impressed, but she couldn't spread herself too thin. She opened her mouth to turn him down…again.

"No." He held up his hand to silence her. "Don't answer so quickly, because this will be my last offer and I can see the glint of temptation in your eyes."

On second thought, her serious consideration of his offer would give her license to browse around. She'd love to check out the closed-up rooms she hadn't dared explore before. "Do you mind if I look around? To see what I'm getting myself into?"

He waved his hand, granting her free passage. "Help yourself."

She jumped to her feet and hurried down the hallway. She noticed how he trailed her—so close that the scent of his spicy cologne wrapped around her. She paused in front of the double doors just off the foyer and glanced over her shoulder as though making sure he hadn't changed his mind about her nosing around the place.

"Go ahead." His tone was reserved and a bit hesitant.

She turned and pushed the doors open. This was her first glimpse of the living room and she was impressed by its sheer size. Her entire ranch house could fit in this one room with space to spare. And the ceilings were at least twelve feet high, giving the room a wide-open feel.

But there was something not quite right. She scanned the area again, taking in the furniture. Though of high quality, it was too contemporary for the house. And the impressionistic artwork on the walls didn't quite fit. A stately home such as this deserved to be decorated with items that exuded grace and elegance, not flash and fad.

With no throw covers, everything was coated in heavy dust that tickled her nose and made her eyes water. Beneath the filth, the house looked as though the occupants had gotten up one morning, gone about their day but never returned.

Throw pillows were haphazardly strewn about as though people had tossed them aside and forgotten to pick them up. Even a newspaper was spread across the glass coffee table, open to the sports page. Was that why Lucas lived like he did? Was he waiting for someone to return? A lost love?

Kate recalled him mentioning an ex-wife. Was that it? Was he still grieving the loss of his marriage?

A white-and-pink figurine caught her attention. Drawn to it, like a curious feline to a buzzing fly, she couldn't stop herself from picking it up. It was of a mother holding her baby girl. Her fingers stroked over the smooth surface. The mother and child were smiling at each other as if they'd just spent a marvelous day together. It touched something deep inside Kate and had her frowning at the thought of never spending another carefree day with her daughter.

"Put it down."

Kate jumped at the boom of Lucas's voice. Her fingers tightened around the porcelain figurine to keep from dropping it. With the knick-knack safely returned to the dust-covered end table, she faced Lucas. "You know you're going to have to learn to trust me or this will never work."

His expression transformed into one of contrition. "Sorry. I… Oh, never mind."

She noticed a deep sadness in his eyes and wondered what had put it there. But she knew it was none of her business. He probably didn't want to talk about his past any more than she did.

"The good news is from what I've seen of the downstairs, there's no damage. The rooms need a thorough cleaning and a fresh coat of paint. How attached are you to the furniture?" She tried to sound impartial just in case he actually liked the pieces.

"It can go as far as I'm concerned. Does this mean you've accepted the job?"

Oh, she was certainly tempted. "This place is so big. You know you could clear away the furniture and dance in here."

"It's been done before."

"Really?"

He nodded. "My great-grandmother started the tradition of throwing grand parties here at the house. She considered it her duty to entertain clients of Carrington Gems. She'd think up some of the grandest parties. It didn't matter the occasion as long as she could get together the city's movers and shakers to flaunt Carrington's latest creations."

Already Kate could imagine the big-band music, the beautiful dresses and glitzy jewelry. "Oh, how I'd have loved to attend. It must have been something."

"Great-gran was a crafty one. She knew these women were quite wealthy and hated to be outdone by anyone. So my great-grandfather ended up employing the finest craftsmen to design something unique for each of them."

"Those must have been some grand parties."

"They were. In fact, there should be pictures of them around somewhere." He paused as though trying to remember what had happened to them. "Then again, I think they might have been packed away in the attic. Elaina, my ex, didn't like to have antiques and memorabilia around. She called it clutter."

Without thinking, Kate blurted out, "Did Elaina by chance redecorate the house?"

Pain showed in his eyes. "I thought it'd make her happy. She made a mess of the house and…" He pressed his lips together as though realizing he'd said too much. In a blink, the glimpse into this man and his closely guarded feelings was once again hidden behind a wall. "About my offer—are you willing to take me up on it?"

Looking around the place, she was filled with ideas. "How would you feel about making a deal?"

"I thought that's what I'm trying to do. Name your price."

"It isn't your money that interests me." She worried her bottom lip. Should she do this? She had to be crazy, but what did she have to lose?

"What sort of deal do you have in mind?"

"When the work is all said and done, I'd like to borrow your house for an evening." The words poured out of her mouth like a breached dam, but at least they were now out there. "We could hold the fund-raiser here. In honor of your great-grandmother, we could have a 1920s flapper party—"

"What?" He reared back as though slapped.

"Think about it. You could show off your new line of jewelry."

"Impossible. I don't want people parading through my house like it's some sort of museum. You'll have to find another way to advertise your interior design work."

Her hands pressed to her hips. "That's what you think? That I'm planning to line potential clients down the block to have a look-see at your house? Well, you don't have to worry—the thought never crossed my mind."

She had more to say about him misjudging her, but she

bit back her tongue. She couldn't forget how much was riding on her making a successful deal.

He eyed her up as though trying to make up his mind. "Maybe I jumped to the wrong conclusion. But the days of parties being thrown here are over. We'll find you another venue."

"Not one with so much allure or history. We could double or triple the ticket price for people to come to the Carrington mansion." Lucas shook his head, but she couldn't stop. The ideas were coming hard and fast. Her hands waved around as she talked. "Think about it. This could provide publicity for Carrington Gems, too."

She didn't see why they couldn't both benefit from this production, but she could tell he wasn't quite sold. Now how would she nudge him into agreement? She didn't have a clue, but there had to be a way.

"Do you really think people are going to line up to come here?" He glanced around at the dirty surroundings.

"I know it needs a little TLC, but this place will draw in lots of curious folks."

"I don't think so."

Her insides quivered as she stepped up to him. "Please. I'll beg if I have to."

CHAPTER EIGHT

A BALL OF SYMPATHY churned in Lucas's gut. He knew all too well the private hell a parent went through when they felt as if they'd lost control of their child's well-being. But Kate was asking him to open up his home—a piece of himself—to public scrutiny. His life was already disrupted enough by that magazine article. He didn't need people he didn't even know coming in here and whispering behind his back.

He needed time to think. But not here. Not now. He turned on his heels.

"Wait!"

His steps faltered, but he didn't turn back. He couldn't. It would be utter torture to witness the desperation written all over her delicate features. Or the disappointment when he denied her what she so badly wanted.

"I'm not finished." Her voice cracked with emotion. "At least hear me out."

He didn't know what else she had on her mind, but he at least owed her the decency of hearing her out. He stopped in the foyer and turned. The desperation on her face ate at his resolve.

"I'm sorry." She caught up to him. "I don't mean to pester you. I just… I need to do everything to help my daughter."

Lucas shifted his weight from one foot to the other. This

wasn't his problem, no matter how bad he felt for her and the awful situation she was facing. He couldn't let himself get sucked back into the miserable murkiness of helplessness. Yet turning his back on Kate clearly wasn't an option either.

When the silence dragged on, Kate spoke up. "Do you like my idea about planning a party like your grandmother might have done? You know, displaying the new line of jewelry?"

He actually liked her suggestion a lot. "I'd need to find someone to wear the jewelry."

"I'm sure you must have some beautiful models on hand. Any woman would die to wear Carrington Gems."

"But this will have to be done right. The clothes and hair will all have to be choreographed to give the gems the best display possible."

"You make it sound very planned out."

"It will be. Trust me. Only the best for Carrington."

The smile dipped from her face and she suddenly looked quite serious. "Does this mean we have a deal?"

"Not quite." Though a voice inside him said he was crazy to open his home to the public, business sense told him this personalized campaign might make a big difference to the Fiery Hearts jewelry launch. "I want daily progress reports, including any surprises or unexpected delays. If I find at any point you aren't completely forthcoming, the deal is off."

He wasn't the first client to micromanage a project. Having Lucas looking over her shoulder wasn't her preferred way to work, but she'd make do. "Not a problem. I can write up a daily summary of our progress."

"I'd prefer to have these updates in person. Say over dinner each evening."

"You want us to dine every night?" She hadn't counted on that and after the kiss in the car, she wasn't so sure spending time together was a good idea. She wasn't ready for a relationship—she wasn't sure she ever would be again. They hurt way too much when they ended.

"Considering we'll be living here together, I don't see where that will be such a hardship."

"But I'll be at the hospital."

"No problem. I'm used to eating late. I'll have something waiting when you get home." He sent her a don't-argue-with-me look. "I'll let you think it over."

"I don't need to." His eyes lit up with surprise, but the truth was she didn't have any time to waste. This place needed lots of TLC. "It's a deal. Now would you mind if we went upstairs? I'd like to get your input on some things."

His head lowered and he spoke in a strangled voice. "I can't go back up there."

Not *I won't* or some other excuse, but rather *I can't*. What was up with that? She was tempted to ask—tempted to ease his pain. But she reminded herself that this was a business relationship. Nothing more.

"Lucas, thank you...for all of this." When his gaze rose to meet hers, she noticed a poignant sadness in his eyes. "Tell me, what do you plan to do with this house? You know, once it's fixed up?"

He ran a hand over the back of his neck. "Does it matter?"

"Actually it does. If you're planning to sell, then the interior should be more neutral to invite people to envision their family and possessions within these walls. But if you have plans of keeping it and living here then we can tailor everything to your taste."

"It doesn't matter. Use your best judgment."

Frustration bubbled up in Kate. She'd never encountered this problem before. Usually her clients had too many ideas—ideas outside of their budget and she'd have to rein them in. And though she was tempted to run with the utter freedom he suggested, something told her that Lucas wasn't as apathetic to the house's remodel as he wanted her to believe.

She lifted her chin and looked him straight on. "If you would walk through the rooms with me and give me a basic idea of what you have in mind, I could come up with some sketches for you to look over."

"I only have one requirement. There's a room upstairs at the other end of the hallway from yours. I don't want anyone in there. It's locked and it's to remain that way."

"But this place is filthy. You might not want to paint the room, but we'll need to clean it."

"No. I don't want you going in there. Period."

What in the world was his hang-up about that room? Had it been the room he shared with the ex-wife? Was he secretly pining for her? Somehow his reaction still seemed over the top.

Perhaps someone had died in the room. If so, that would explain why he was acting so strange. And it'd be a more reasonable explanation for turning this house into some sort of mausoleum. If she were ever to lose Molly... Her heart stuttered and a cold sweat broke out on the nape of her neck. No. She would not go there.

"I'm sorry. I didn't realize it was important to you."

He rubbed a hand over his jaw. "It's just that it's my... uh, never mind. I just need it left alone."

"I understand."

The man might be a little rough around the edges and have a few peculiarities, but she wanted to reach out to him and find out what he'd been on the verge of saying. Still, a nagging voice in the back of her mind warned her not to let her defenses down around him. In her experience, men were basically the same—unreliable.

She'd thought the moon rose and set around her father— how could she have been so wrong? She wanted to tell herself that it was because she was a child and didn't know any better. But that didn't explain Chad. She'd utterly and completely fallen for his charm and empty promises. She'd even agreed to his spur-of-the-moment proposal and rushed Las-Vegas-style I dos.

She'd convinced herself that he'd eventually settle down—once they found the right town. But no matter how many jobs he had in this place or that place, none of them suited him.

By the time she became pregnant, she couldn't remember the address of her latest apartment. She was certain when she told Chad about the baby that it would give him a reason to plant some roots. She'd been so wrong.

He'd been enraged and was convinced that she'd tricked him into getting her pregnant. He'd left that night, only to play a sporadic part in their daughter's life while he continued to chase his ever-changing dreams.

And now, at this vital juncture in her life, Kate didn't need any complications. Lucas was one walking string of complications. The first and most important was that he was providing her with the means with which to raise the money for her daughter's surgery. If their relationship didn't last—and relationships never did—the price was just too great.

"Did you see this?"

The following morning, Kate couldn't tear her eyes from the photo of her and Lucas in the paper. If she'd ever had any doubts about whether that kiss in the car had been a dream, she now had proof. But this picture made the kiss appear less than innocent. In fact, the clench appeared quite steamy—on both sides.

Her cheeks flamed as she recalled his lips moving over hers. The way her stomach had filled with a fluttering sensation. And the way he'd left her longing for more. But that wasn't going to happen. She wouldn't let it.

With a frown pulling at her face, she glanced at the photo again. Maybe the photo wasn't an exaggeration, but it had been a private moment—a lapse in judgment, never to be repeated.

Lucas didn't say a word as he sipped his coffee, which added to her frustration.

She smacked the paper. "This headline is outrageous. Carrington Heir Snared?" She set aside her steaming mug, feeling the heat of embarrassment rising up her neck and setting her face aflame. "I thought you said if the picture made the paper, it'd be obscure."

"Don't let it get to you. It's not worth getting worked up over."

"Nothing! How can you call my private life splashed in the news nothing?" Her eyes took in each and every innuendo. She couldn't stop reading any more than she could stop breathing. "This is going to be a disaster. How am I supposed to face everyone much less ask people for money when this article implies you and I are...you know."

"Sleeping together." He supplied the answer so smoothly, so casually as though having the whole world contemplating his sex life was the status quo.

"We have to do something." Her mind frantically sought out an answer. "We should sue them."

He shook his head. "First, it would only make this below-the-fold story bigger. And second, they don't actually lie. We are sleeping together under one roof—"

"But in separate beds."

"And we were seen leaving here early in the morning."

"But it wasn't the wee hours of the morning like they said."

"You're splitting hairs. Besides, did you happen to think

about spinning this publicity around and using it to your advantage?"

"But I don't want publicity. I'm happy with my quiet life."

"Ah, but you're forgetting about the fund-raiser. You know what they say—any publicity is good publicity. Well, maybe not any publicity, but you know what I mean."

The scary part was that she did know what he was trying to say. And she didn't know whether to be angry...or excited.

Maybe she'd misunderstood. "Are you saying we should pose as a happy couple?"

"It's out there now. You might as well capitalize on the news coverage."

"And you're okay with this?"

He shrugged. "I know how to work the press when I need to. It's all an act for the sake of the fund-raiser and the launch of Fiery Hearts. Why not let it play out?"

She crossed her arms and pursed her lips. She noticed how he never said that he was comfortable with this plan, but he seemed resigned to do his part to help their mutual cause. Instead of being angry with him for putting her in this position, she found herself liking him a little more.

"Kate, if you're ready to go, I can drop you off at the hospital on my way to the office."

She shook her head. "I'm not ready to put your plan into action."

"Even so, you can't let those reporters dictate how you live your life. And I promise to be a perfect gentleman and keep my hands to myself."

What worried her more was the thought that she wanted him touching her. She found she liked having him close. Her heart thump-thumped at the memory of him next to her. His finger beneath her chin. His deep, hungry gaze. His lips pressed to hers.

Drawing her meandering thoughts up short, she said the first thing that came to mind. "You should come to the hospital with me. Once I take care of the billing department, we could visit Molly."

He shook his head. "I don't think so."

"Molly wants to meet you. I told her you make the most beautiful jewelry. She wants to know if you make tiaras for princesses."

"I'm sorry. I can't meet your daughter today. My schedule is backed up." He started out of the room. "But I'll make it up to you."

"How?"

"You'll be the first to have a preview of the Fiery Hearts collection."

"I can't wait." She loved jewelry, even if it was only to admire it while window-shopping. "Don't forget to let me know when you have some free time. Molly would really enjoy meeting you."

"I won't forget. Let's go."

Five minutes later, Kate settled into the seat of Lucas's expensive sports car. She loved the buttery-soft leather upholstery, the purr of the powerful engine and most of all, the driver. She watched as Lucas grasped the black shifter. His long, lean fingers drew her attention. Her mouth grew increasingly dry. Why was he getting to her? Was it the tempting thought of what it'd be like to once again be held by those hands? The thought of a mere gentle caress had a sigh slipping past her lips.

"Did you hear me?" Lucas's deep voice jarred her from her ambling thoughts.

"I was thinking about the article." It was that darn paper that filled her mind with…things. Bad things.

He slowed to a stop and glanced her way. "Quit worrying. It'll all be fine."

She was drawn in by his mesmerizing stare. After all,

he was very handsome and very available. Her heart beat faster as heat swirled in her chest and spread out to her limbs. Did he have the heater on in here or what? "Mind if I open the window a crack?"

"Go for it." He chanced a quick glance her way. "Are you feeling okay? You look a little flushed."

"I'm fine." She resisted the urge to fan herself. "Honest."

She eased the window down and savored the cool morning air. What in the world was up with her? Article or not, since when did she let a man get to her?

In an effort to act normal, she said, "You wouldn't believe how helpful your aunt has been. When I'm not at the hospital, she checks on Molly for me."

"I thought your ex was with her."

Kate shrugged. "He's supposed to be, but he isn't exactly reliable. And I don't want Molly to feel like everyone has forgotten her. So Connie and a couple of the nurses promised to call if Chad decides that sitting with a sick kid isn't for him."

"My aunt is very outgoing. She'd help anyone in need. No matter what."

Kate's body tensed. Surely he wasn't implying that she was taking advantage of the woman, was he?

"I didn't ask your aunt for anything—"

"I'm sure you didn't. She never had the opportunity to have a family of her own, and since I'm the only relative she has left, she likes to take in strays—"

"Strays! I'm not a stray." Kate glared at him. "I didn't need to be taken in. Molly and I have been doing fine on our own."

He shifted in the driver's seat. "I didn't mean that like it sounded."

"And how did you mean it?" She wasn't letting him off the hook that easily.

"I just worry. My aunt has a history of taking in the

wrong sort of people—people that take advantage of her naïveté. If you hadn't noticed, my aunt goes through life with rose-colored glasses on. She can't or won't see the bad in people."

Actually Kate had noticed that his aunt was surprisingly trusting and friendly. Lucas didn't seem interested in offering more about his aunt, and she didn't want to probe any further.

They pulled up in front of the hospital and Kate noticed Lucas's shoulders tense as he scanned the area, most likely searching for more photographers. She followed his line of vision, but didn't see anyone paying them the least bit of attention.

"I'd better hurry. After I confirm some details about the fund-raiser with the billing department, I'm going to stick my head in and say good-morning to Molly before heading back to the house."

"Won't your ex be with Molly?"

She nodded. "But it isn't like we're mortal enemies."

"You aren't?"

"We'll never be buddies or anything, but we can tolerate each other…at least for a minute or two."

"And you're okay with him spending time with Molly after being gone so much of the time?"

With anyone else, she wouldn't get into this type of conversation, but something told her this was important to Lucas. "Letting Chad back into our lives is the last thing I want. But this isn't about me. This is about Molly. And she wants him, so who am I to stand between them? But it doesn't mean I trust him to stick around. Old dogs don't learn new tricks, no matter how much they might want to at the moment."

Lucas gazed past her, as though lost in his thoughts.

She got the distinct impression that his relationship with his ex wasn't so amicable. But if that was the case, why was he alone in a dusty house of memories, pining for her? There were a lot of missing pieces to Lucas's puzzle. And though she knew better—knew to keep her distance—she was intrigued by him. What was the real story behind New York City's most eligible bachelor?

CHAPTER NINE

LIFE HAD KATE in the fast lane with no signs of things slowing down.

A week had already passed since Lucas agreed to let her manage the repair work on the house. During that time, they'd fallen into a routine of morning coffee together followed by a late dinner when she got home from the hospital. Sometimes they ate in and sometimes he'd take her out. It was never anything fancy, a little off-the-beaten-path pizzeria or a mom-and-pop diner. She actually enjoyed the warm, inviting atmosphere more than if they'd gone to a high-class establishment where the point was more about being seen than having a relaxing dinner.

But when it came to lunch, she was on her own. Today she didn't have much of an appetite as she arrived at the hospital for an upcoming meeting with Molly's surgeon. They were awaiting test results to make sure the procedure was still an option. Kate had prayed long and hard that there wouldn't be any further complications.

"Kate, did you hear me?" Connie Carrington, Lucas's kindhearted aunt, smiled at her from the other side of the table in the Hospitality Shop. "I said Lucas is lucky you happened into his life."

"I didn't exactly stumble into his life. You had a big hand in that."

"I did, didn't I?" The woman smiled broadly. Her bouncy

personality didn't quite jive with her prim and proper appearance. Her short silver hair was swept off to one side. Her smooth, porcelain complexion had just a hint of makeup and a pair of dark-rimmed glasses perched upon her petite nose.

"You sound quite pleased with yourself."

"My nephew needed his eyes opened before that house collapsed around him. Thank you for making him see sense."

"I don't think it was me as much as the dripping rainwater."

Connie reached across the table and patted her hand. "You, my dear, are good for him."

She highly doubted that. There was an undeniable vibe between them—more like a magnetic force. But he didn't seem any more eager to explore their options than she was to get in any deeper. Experience had taught her that once they crossed that line, there would be no going back.

"Regardless, I have a feeling the house is going to be a huge success. I just hope Lucas likes what I've done."

"I'm sure he will. It's about time that boy lets go of the past and starts living again."

This was a prime opportunity to ask about Lucas's history and the story behind that locked room at the end of the hall, but she couldn't bring herself to do it. She and Lucas were forging a friendship of sorts. If she was going to learn about his past, she wanted it to come from him. She didn't want to sneak around behind his back.

Connie sipped at her coffee and returned the cup to its saucer. "I meant to tell you that splashy headline in the paper was just the publicity we needed."

"It was?"

Connie nodded. "Tickets are going fast. A little more of that free exposure and we should be able to sell out."

Kate lowered her voice. "So you think I should go along

with Lucas's idea to play the happy couple in hopes of gaining more publicity?"

Connie reached out and gave her arm a squeeze. "I do. I really do."

"I...I don't know."

"You've already started quite a buzz. People want to meet the mystery woman caught kissing the Bachelor of the Year. Many women have tried to capture my nephew's attention, but few have ever turned his head. And after the divorce, he's closed himself off. But you—you're making a big difference—"

"What difference would that be?" questioned a familiar male voice.

Kate turned. Her face warmed, wondering how much he'd overheard.

When neither of them replied, his searching gaze moved between the two of them. "Is it some big secret you're sharing?"

Kate's heart pounded in her chest. She was a miserable liar. Her best defense was silence.

Unable to look Lucas in the eye, she lowered her gaze. She noticed his sharp navy suit was tailored to show off his broad shoulders and tapered for his trim waist. Talk about fine packages. Even fully clothed he was definitely Mr. Oh-So-Sexy.

Realizing that she was publicly ogling him, she reined in her thoughts. What was she doing lusting over him? He was here to be a supportive friend. If it weren't for him and his aunt, she didn't know where she'd be or how she'd take care of her daughter.

Lucas and Connie made her feel as though she were no longer alone in this world.

"Heavens, no. We don't have any secrets." Connie's voice wobbled just a bit. "I was telling Kate that even though she isn't doing the guest list and ticket sales that she's making the biggest contribution by pulling together the venue."

"I agree. She's doing a fantastic job." Lucas gave her an approving nod. "The downstairs is all cleaned up and the painting has begun." He smiled, causing the ever-present sadness in his blue eyes to disappear. She wished he looked like that all the time.

"Now, if only the upstairs would go just as fast." Kate finished off the last of her coffee.

"I'm sure it'll all come together."

Lucas's belief in her abilities meant a great deal to her. And the fact he'd shown up today to show his support totally caught her off guard.

She flashed him her best smile. "I'm so glad you decided to take me up on my offer to meet Molly. It'll be a nice surprise for her. Wait until she finds out she has a special visitor. And I see the milkshake I ordered for her is waiting at the checkout."

"But I don't have time—"

"I'll hurry."

Embarrassed by the way she'd nervously chattered nonstop, Kate rushed away. Just because he'd shown up didn't mean she should read anything into his presence. Should she?

Before Lucas could explain that he was there to meet his aunt for their regular lunch, Kate was already across the room.

With a resigned sigh, he sat down across from his aunt. "What's going on here?"

"Kate and I were just discussing the fund-raiser. I'm so glad you agreed to do it at the house. I know that must have been a difficult decision for you, but I'm really proud of you for making the right one. Kate hasn't had many breaks. And at this moment in her life, she can use all of the help she can get."

His aunt might be far too trusting of people she barely knew and might always be looking for the good in everyone, but in this instance he thought she might actually be right. He'd observed Kate this past week, and though he'd given her plenty of chances to take advantage of him, whether by sloughing her work off on someone else or by sponging off him or by leaving him with the bulk of the housework, she'd been a stellar employee.

He shifted positions on the hard plastic chair to get a better view of Kate's slim figure as she stood at the checkout. She was a fine-looking woman. The man who'd walked away from her couldn't be very smart. And best of all, she was as sweet on the inside as she was on the outside.

He jerked his gaze back to his aunt. "And from what I understand, you're helping Kate organize this fund-raiser."

Connie glanced at her wristwatch. "Of course. The girl needs someone to steer her in the right direction. Unless you're offering to take over."

Lucas held up both hands. "Count me out. I'm no party planner. Besides, I have urgent matters to deal with at Carrington. The San Francisco project has hit a snag. More like a brick wall."

His aunt's gaze narrowed in on him. "You aren't thinking of skipping town, are you?"

"Would that be so bad? Or don't you trust Kate after all?"

"I trust Kate. It's you that worries me."

"Me. Why me?"

"How long are you going to keep hiding and putting your life on hold? Why aren't you fighting for custody of your little girl—"

His voice lowered. "You know why. And I don't want to discuss it any further."

He thought if anyone would understand his need to do this, his aunt would. She'd saved him from being a pawn between his arguing parents more than once. He wouldn't do that to his daughter.

"But you are missing so much of Carrie's life—"

"Leave it." He fought back his rising temper. "I thought by agreeing to this fund-raiser, it'd make you happy."

His aunt's gaze needled him. "You only get one go-around in this life and it goes by in the blink of an eye. Please don't waste it."

His palm smacked the tabletop. "I'm not."

No matter how much he missed his little girl, he had to put Carrie's happiness above his own, something his parents had never done with him. And right now his ex-wife was hostile on the phone and argumentative in person. If only he could make her see reason.

Connie got to her feet. "Kate's finished checking out. You better hurry and catch up with her since you two have plans—"

"But we don't have plans. The only reason I'm here is because you insist we meet here for lunch once a week—even though I've offered repeatedly to take you anyplace you'd like."

"And you were late today. Now it's time I got back to work." Connie glanced in Kate's direction. "She's waiting for you. You don't want to disappoint her, do you?"

Before he could argue, his aunt walked away. His gaze immediately sought out the door, but Kate stood between him and the exit. He mentally ran through a list of excuses of why he had to leave. Each excuse sounded more pathetic than the last.

He straightened his shoulders. Time to make a confession. He approached Kate, who was holding a tall cup with a lid and a straw. She'd understand everything once he explained about the mix-up. After all, misunderstandings happened all the time.

She glanced up and a smile bloomed on her face. The color in her cheeks and the light in her eyes touched something deep inside him—a place that had felt dead up until now. He didn't want her to stop smiling, not now...not ever.

"Are you ready to go?" Kate motioned toward the door.

He should speak up...explain that he'd only come here to visit with his aunt. That he had no intention of venturing into the pediatrics unit full of tiny humans—little ones like his Carrie. His mouth opened, but when Kate grabbed his hand, giving him a gentle tug, the words balled up in his throat. He glanced over his shoulder at Connie, but she wasn't paying any attention as she took food orders from customers.

His gut churned. He was backed into a corner with no easy way out. Maybe he could just say a fast "Hi" and then be on his way. In and out. Fast as can be.

"I...I can't stay long."

Kate's eyes lit up. Her lips pursed as though a question teetered on the tip of her pink tongue. His breath hitched in his throat. *Please don't ask any probing questions. Not here. Not now.*

Kate's face smoothed. "We can take the steps if you think it'll be faster."

He exhaled a long-held breath. He understood the strain Kate was under...more so than he'd ever want to admit. He shook his head, resigned to wait for one of the four elevators. As though summoned by his thoughts, a chime sounded and the door in front of him slid open.

Like the gentleman his mother raised him to be, he waited for Kate to step inside. His gut churned with anxiety. On stiltlike legs, he followed her.

"Are you okay?" Kate asked, drawing him out of his thoughts.

They were standing alone in the elevator as it slowly climbed to the fifth floor. He kept his eyes on the row of numbers above the door, watching as they lit up one after the other.

"I'm fine."

"Really? Because ever since we got in the elevator, you look stiff and uncomfortable. And the frown on your face will scare the kids in pediatrics."

He hadn't realized his thoughts had transferred to his face. Willing himself to relax, he tried changing his stance and forced his lips into what he hoped was a smile.

Kate turned to him. "You know you don't have to do this. If you've changed your mind about meeting my daughter, just say so."

Apparently he hadn't done a good enough job of putting on a more pleasant expression because right now, Kate's eyes were filled with doubt. He didn't want to add to her list of concerns. After all, this was a quick visit. Soon it'd all be nothing more than a memory.

"How's your daughter doing?" He was truly eager to hear an update on the little girl, hoping things were improving.

"Today we get the results of her latest scan to see if the treatments are shrinking the tumor."

"Will that make the surgery easier?"

Kate straightened her shoulders. "That's what I'm told."

He wondered if Molly was the spitting image of her mother. Did her eyes light up like her mother's when she was excited? Did her cheeks fill with color when paid a compliment? And when she was concentrating while working with her hands, did the tip of her tongue press against her bottom lip?

Lucas drew his thoughts up short. He couldn't believe in the limited time he'd spent with Kate that he'd gotten to know so much about her.

The elevator dinged and the doors opened. Kate exited the elevator and turned back to him, still leaning against the handrail. "Are you coming?"

He swallowed hard and stepped out onto the pediatrics floor. There was no doubt about which unit they were in as a painted yellow giraffe with brown spots covered the wall, stretching from floor to ceiling, followed by a hippo, tiger and zebra. Large, leafy trees and tufts of grass were painted in the background. Someone had spared no expense in giving the tiny patients the feeling they were anywhere but at a hospital.

His thoughts took a sudden turn back to his own daughter. Would she like the painting? Did she like giraffes? What was painted on the walls of her bedroom?

The fact he knew none of these answers angered him. He should know. Any father worth the name Dad should know this about their child. Yet, Elaina had stolen those moments from him. And worse yet, he'd let her.

He used to think it was the sacrifice he had to make, but being around Kate and listening to her talk about her daughter, he had to wonder if there was another choice he could make.

"Molly's room is at the end of this wing." Kate pushed open one of the double doors.

He followed her past the nurses' station in the center of the floor. A collective buzz of children's voices filled his ears. He'd made sure to avoid kids since he'd come back from California—since he'd confronted his ex-wife.

His steps slowed. The distance between him and Kate widened. The giggle of a little girl filled his head. He paused and glanced as the child sat on the edge of her bed. She had curly blond locks like Carrie's and was smiling at someone. His daughter had never smiled at him like that. The knowledge stabbed him in the chest, robbing him of his breath.

"Lucas," called out Kate.

He meant to keep moving, but he was drawn by this little girl. Her sweet smile threw daggers into his heart. Instead of smiles, Carrie had looked at him with tears in her eyes as Elaina raised her voice, shook a finger in his face and insisted he leave.

Pain churned inside him as though someone had reached down his throat and ripped out his heart. A cold, aching spot remained. He closed his eyes and turned away from the little girl. He shouldn't have come here. This was a mistake. He needed to leave. Now.

Kate reached out and touched his arm. "Molly's room is just a few more doors down this hallway."

The heat of her touch seeped through his suit coat. He glanced at Kate. Her eyes pleaded with him. He wanted to do this for her more than he could say, but the trickle of the little girl's laughter was his undoing. He needed to get out of there. He needed to breathe.

"I'm sorry. I can't."

With that he turned, jerking his arm from her touch. He could feel her lethal gaze shooting daggers into his back. He deserved her anger and so much more.

He'd failed Kate and he hadn't even had the nerve to explain it to her. Although it wasn't as if she'd understand. Her daughter loved her. Looked up to her. Trusted her.

He inwardly groaned as the thought drove home the pain and guilt. If he was doing the right thing for Carrie, why did it feel so wrong?

Unwilling to wait for the elevator, he took to the stairs. He raced down them as though the hounds of hell were nipping at his heels.

Kate would think he was a total jerk. And maybe she was right. Perhaps there was something inherently wrong with him that drove away his ex-wife. And now his child.

CHAPTER TEN

KATE SWUNG THE hammer with more force than was necessary, missing the nail and putting a small half-moon indentation in the plaster. Just what she needed, something else to fix. It'd been two days since the incident at the hospital and she was still fuming. It was Lucas's fault. He'd made a point of avoiding her, rushing off to the office early and receiving an urgent phone call and hurrying out the door just as she returned home for dinner. He assured her it was important business, but she didn't know if she believed him.

Her mind warned her that Lucas was a typical man—unreliable. Why in the world had she let herself believe that he'd be any different than the other men who passed through her life? They said what they thought she wanted to hear and yet when it came to following through with their promises, they never did.

Lucas might clean up nice with his tailored suits and polished dress shoes, but beneath all of that varnish, he was just another lying man. She grabbed a nail, positioned it along the new chair rail and swung the hammer. Hard. Once again, she'd let her guard down and thought she could trust him. She swung the hammer again, hitting the nail dead center. When would she ever learn not to trust men?

She took another whack at the nail, shoving it further into the wall. Not about to ruin the chair rail with a ding from the hammerhead, she looked around for a nail set.

Not finding one handy, she grabbed a scrap piece of wood from the floor, positioned it over the nail and swung again.

"What did that piece of wood do to you?"

Lucas. She'd know his deep, rich voice anywhere. Any other time it'd have washed over her like warm maple syrup—sweetening her up. But not today.

She didn't bother to stop and face him. Another couple of taps and the nail was flush with the wood. "It got damaged from the leaky roof and had to be replaced."

"That isn't what I meant. Seems like you're taking your anger out on that nail. Did something go wrong with the renovations?"

"No." The fact that he was acting all Mr. Innocent drove her nuts. "I have everything under control."

"Listen, I know I've been busy, but it couldn't be helped. With the party coming up, we've had to kick up the media blitz for the new jewelry line."

So that was how it was going to be. Act as if nothing happened. She should have predicted this. Her ex swept any trouble under the carpet and pretended as if it never happened. Well, not today. Something had happened and she wasn't about to forget it.

She set aside the hammer and stood. "Don't do this."

"Do what? Ask about the progress on the house?"

"No. Avoid me and then act like there isn't a problem between us."

A muscle twitched in his cheek. "I wasn't avoiding you. Honest. My marketing director went on an early maternity leave and everyone is pitching in to pick up the slack with the upcoming campaign—"

"Stop. This isn't about your business. This is about you skipping out on me at the hospital without so much as an explanation."

"I…I'm sorry." He looked as though he was searching for the right words. "I wanted to meet your daughter but…"

"But what?" He seemed sincere and she really did want to understand. "Talk to me."

"I can't. Not now. Just please believe it had nothing to do with you or Molly. I'll make it up to you. I promise."

The little voice in her head said not to believe him, but her gut said something else entirely. Not sure which to trust, she decided she needed time to think without him clouding her thoughts with the pleading look in his blue-gray eyes.

"Thank you for your apology, but I don't have time to talk now. I need to finish replacing this chair rail."

"It looks like you'll have this place in tip-top shape in no time."

"I wouldn't jump to any conclusions yet. There's a lot to do and if we're going to showcase the tunnel, we'll need every single minute before the party."

"The tunnel?"

Kate made a point of inspecting her handiwork. Finding a nail that wasn't quite flush, she grabbed the hammer and the scrap piece of wood and gave it a whack. "Surely you know about the prohibition tunnel beneath the house."

"Of course I do. But my family liked to pretend it didn't exist. I'm surprised you know about its existence."

Kate cocked a smile. "You really need to read more often. You'd be surprised what you learn."

"I read the *Wall Street Journal* every day."

"Something tells me that prohibition tunnels wouldn't be of interest to that paper."

"Wait. Are you trying to tell me that you read about my house and my family in the paper?"

"Not exactly. Your aunt mentioned that the place had quite a history. And then I did some research online. You'd be amazed at what is put online these days. This house is just teeming with history."

Lucas raked his fingers through his hair, scattering

it in a haphazard fashion. "Great. Isn't anything private anymore?"

"Quit grumbling and come check it out." She started for the door. When she didn't hear Lucas following, she turned back. "You have to see all of the work the men did on the tunnel—from rewiring the lighting to replacing the rotted wood. Although to be honest, it's more like a long skinny room than a tunnel."

Lucas let off an exasperated sigh, but she knew once he explored the hidden tunnel, he'd be as impressed as the rest of them. She led him to the back stairs that was constructed of stained wood. But it was the small landing that was a beautiful maze of inlaid wood.

"Someone was very clever," she said, coming to a stop by a sunset-inspired stained-glass window. "I'm guessing it was your great-grandfather's idea to create such an artistic floor pattern. If I hadn't known to look, I never would have guessed the center section opens up."

Sticking her finger in a discreet thumbhole, she lifted the wood panel. Inside was a rustic wood ladder.

"Don't worry. The ladder is safe. The men just finished the repairs today and I haven't had a chance to look around. You must be familiar with it."

"Actually, I've never been down there. My grandfather had the entrance sealed. I'm surprised the workmen were able to open it up without damaging the wood."

"Believe me, it took a while and lots of care. But I think they did an excellent job. Let me be the first to give you the grand tour." She didn't bother to wait for him to make up his mind. She started her descent.

Entering this rustic area was like stepping back in time. She let her imagination run wild, thinking of the old-timers trying to outsmart the cops. The Roaring Twenties must have been a very interesting era, especially for the Carringtons with their hidden tunnel.

Kate rubbed her bare arms. There was a distinct drop in the temperature down here. She was certain the goose bumps were from the chill in the air and had absolutely nothing to do with her view of Lucas's long legs or toned backside as he descended the ladder.

She gazed around, imagining the wooden racks lined with bottles. "Back here there's a rack with some very old wine. Seems it was shuffled out of the way and forgotten."

"Interesting. Did you uncover anything else?"

"Afraid not."

He moved closer to get a better look. It wasn't until then that she noticed how tight the quarters were down there. Lucas's broad shoulders filled the space between the brick wall and the wooden shelves. There was no getting around him. And there was no room to back up.

Lucas's spicy cologne teased her senses. How could one man look and smell so good? And why did her body so readily respond to him? She knew better than to let her guard down around him. Perhaps inviting him down here was not the best idea.

"That's all there is. We should go."

Lucas glanced up from the bottle of wine he was examining. His gaze met hers. "If I didn't know better, I'd say you were afraid to be so close to me."

The problem was she liked it too much. If they stayed down here much longer, she was afraid she'd abandon her common sense and cave into her body's lusty desires.

"I...I have work to finish."

"I'm going to look around here a little more."

He returned the dusty bottle to the rack and turned, signaling her to pass him. Anxious to make her escape, she moved. By the time she figured out there wasn't enough room for them to modestly pass, her body was sliding over his. Toe to toe. Thigh to thigh. Chest to chest.

The temperature suddenly rose. Her gaze caught his. Did she stop moving? Or had time slowed down?

"Kate." His voice was raw and full of unmistakable desire.

She'd lied to herself. That first kiss was unforgettable. The memories flitted through her mind every night. What would it hurt to let him kiss her again? Just to see if it was as good as she remembered.

Her heart pounded, echoing in her ears. Her breath hitched. She was playing with fire. She should move. Leave. Run. She didn't want to get burned. But she couldn't turn away from his hungry gaze.

His head dipped. Her eyes fluttered shut. Curiosity and desire collided, holding her in place. And then he was there. His touch was warm and gentle as his lips brushed over hers. No kiss had ever felt so heavenly. Her insides melted and pooled in the center. If she weren't pinned between his hard chest and the wall, she was quite certain her legs wouldn't have held her up.

But all too soon reality rumbled through her dream. The memory of how he had walked away from her at the hospital shattered the moment. She couldn't do this. Not with him.

She couldn't trust him.

Ducking her head, she moved to the ladder. With lightning speed, she rushed up the rungs and hurried back to the library, hoping Lucas wouldn't follow. She willed her heart to slow. For her lips to quit pulsating. Most of all, she needed to think clearly. And with Lucas around, her thoughts became a jumbled heap.

What in the world had just happened?

Had he dreamed that one succulent moment? He ran his tongue over his lower lip, tasting the sweetness of Kate's cherry lip balm. A frustrated groan rumbled in his chest.

He'd given his word that he wouldn't let something that foolish happen again. Yet every time Kate came close and he could smell her fruity shampoo and feel the heat of her touch, logic evaded him.

Now that his ill-laid plan had gone awry, he couldn't leave things like this. He started up the ladder, wondering what he should say to her. "I'm sorry" just didn't seem enough, but he had to try. With the wood plank back in place, he headed for the library.

He rolled his shoulders, trying to ease the tension running through them. He was making too much of this. It was barely even a kiss. No big deal.

When he strode into the library, Kate once again had a hammer in one hand and some trim in the other. He waited for her to turn. When she didn't, he cleared his throat.

"About what just happened, I just want you to know that I shouldn't have overstepped—"

"It was nothing." She kept her back to him, shielding her facial expression. "Now you see why I think the tunnel would hold a lot of appeal for people."

She waved off his kiss as if it was nothing—as if it hadn't meant a thing. The thought that this thing—this growing attraction—was all one-sided pricked him. His jaw tightened and his body tensed. Why was she being this way? He wasn't the only one who felt something.

Kate swung around to face him with the hammer still in her hand. "Do you have a problem with the plans?"

Lucas found himself eyeing the business end of the hammer. If she meant to gain his attention, she'd certainly done that. Not that he couldn't easily overpower her. After all, she was inches shorter than him and looked to be as light as a feather. Only feathers didn't have so many delicious curves. Kate's waist dipped in above the flare of her hips, and his fingers itched to wrap around her and pull her close.

He was tempted to remind her that though the kiss had been brief, it'd definitely ignited a flame.

He straightened his shoulders. "And what if I do have a problem with all of this?"

"You're backing out on me now?" Kate's features hardened and he couldn't help but notice how her knuckles turned white as her grip on the hammer tightened. "You can't do that. I won't let you. We have a verbal agreement. If you even think of backing out now, I'll...I'll..."

He smothered a chuckle as her threat lost steam. Not wanting to add fuel to her rising temper, he willed his lips not to lift into an amused grin. She sure was cute when she was worked up. Maybe it wouldn't hurt to egg her on a little more.

"Should I be worried?"

"You already agreed to this party. It's too late to back out now. I already gave my word to the hospital that I'd have the funds for the operation."

Her words hit him with more sting than any blow from a hammer. She was right. How was he supposed to put up an argument now when faced with a little girl's well-being?

As though remembering the hammer was still in her hand, Kate bent over and placed it on the white drop cloth lining the floor. She straightened and tilted her chin upward. "Besides, your aunt thinks the prohibition tunnel will play in nicely with the 1920s flapper theme."

"That's what I'm afraid of," he mumbled.

As though he hadn't spoken a word, Kate continued, "She also said that at last some good would come from the Carrington history."

He didn't like being ganged up on by his aunt and his... What was Kate to him? A friend? She was closer to him than he let anyone get these days. But *friend* didn't seem to fit what they had either. Especially not after that brief but stirring kiss.

Just then Kate leaned toward him. He froze. What was she planning to do? His gaze slipped down to her lips. They were full and rosy, just perfect for another sweet kiss. Anticipation grew. Was it possible she'd enjoyed his touch more than she'd been letting on?

His breath hitched as she moved closer. Her hand reached out to him. What was she going to do? Pull him down to her?

The thought of her being so bold…of her taking control of the situation turned him on. His eyes drifted closed. All semblance of logic fled his brain. He waited for her to make her move, willing her to keep going.

Long-ignored desires roared through his heated veins. After all, they were alone and it was late in the evening. No one would bother them until morning. And it had been so long since he'd let his defenses down—since he'd been close with anyone.

"There. All taken care of."

Lucas's eyes sprang open. What was taken care of? Certainly not his needs—his desires.

"Don't worry." Kate held out a white piece of fuzz for his inspection. "At first, I was worried that it was some spackling, but it's just lint. Your suit has been saved."

His suit? That wasn't what he was concerned about at this moment. His clothes might be fine, but his mind and body were a jumbled mess. He swallowed hard, working hard to control his wayward thoughts.

"Why are you working so late?" His voice came out much harsher than he'd intended.

Kate's brown eyes flashed with surprise. "I had things to do."

"You're supposed to be overseeing the project, not doing all of the work yourself."

Her hands pressed against her slender hips and her eyes

narrowed in on him. "I'm doing what needs to be done. Unlike some people in this room, I keep my word."

Her barbed comment didn't go unnoticed by him. She was still ticked at him about the episode at the hospital. He should explain to her what had happened. But that would only lead to more questions…questions he didn't want to answer.

Not now.

Not ever.

When he didn't respond, she added, "You know, if you didn't want to meet my daughter, all you had to do was say so in the first place."

"But I wanted to—"

Lucas stopped. His jaw tightened, his back teeth grinding together. What was he saying? This wasn't going to make things better for either of them. But the damage had been done.

An inquisitive gleam showed in her eyes. "What do you mean you wanted to? Why'd you change your mind?"

He glanced away and shuffled his feet. His gut told him that she wasn't going to drop the subject until he fessed up. But how could he do that? He didn't talk about his past with anyone…not even his aunt.

"Surely you have something to say for yourself." Her tone was hard and sharp.

He didn't like being pushed around. His ex-wife had known his vulnerabilities and used them for her own benefit. He wouldn't allow someone else to take advantage of him again.

Kate could push and shove as hard as she wanted, but he wouldn't give in…not until he was ready.

"I'm tired. And I still have reports to go over. There's Chinese takeout on the counter if you want some. And just so you know, I am truly sorry."

He turned away from the confused look in her eyes,

telling himself that he didn't care. This woman meant absolutely nothing to him.

Nothing. At. All.

But if that was the case, why as he yanked the door shut behind him did he feel like a total heel? And why did he want a chance to make things right with her?

CHAPTER ELEVEN

HE'D TOTALLY OVERREACTED.

So what if he'd lost his mind for a moment and kissed her again? It didn't mean he was falling for her big brown eyes or her cherry lips. The whole lack of judgment thing could be written off to a few restless nights and the stress of not bringing in enough money to cover the overages regarding the San Francisco expansion.

Days passed and with each day that went by, Lucas noticed that they were falling back into an easy routine. Pretending they hadn't shared yet another even more intense lip-lock seemed to work during the day, but at night, when he should be sleeping, images of Kate and her tempting kisses filled his thoughts.

"Sorry I'm late." She rushed into the kitchen after returning from her visit to the hospital. "You didn't have to wait to eat. In fact, I'm not really hungry."

"I have plans for us tonight. Instead of the food coming to you, you are going to the food."

She shook her head before sinking down onto a kitchen chair. "I'm sorry. I'm too tired to go anywhere."

Dark shadows under her eyes sent up warning flares. Maybe asking her to work on the house was too much for her.

He realized that in his attempt to avoid his unwanted attraction to her, he'd failed to do his duty as her boss—and, dare he admit it, as her friend. He'd let her work herself into the ground while he'd been busy at the office. He had to fix this, but how?

"No problem. When you get your appetite back, I'll get you whatever you want." He sat down next to her. "Your wish is my command."

With her elbows propped on the table, she rested her chin on her upturned palms. Was it exhaustion that had her so down? Or did she have bigger things on her mind? Was it Molly? Had her health taken a turn for the worse? His chest tightened.

"How's Molly today?"

Kate's eyes widened. "How did you know that's what I had on my mind?"

"What else would you be thinking about?" Unlike him, she probably hadn't fantasized the afternoon away, imagining the temptation of another kiss.

"Molly's refusing the surgery."

This news set him back. "What do you mean refusing?"

"Well, she didn't put it in those terms. But she's moody and depressed. She's insisting on going home and I can't blame her. She's been poked, prodded and examined for months now."

He'd have a hard time dealing with that and he was an adult. He didn't know how a child could put up with visiting doctor after doctor. Children were supposed to be outside, running around in the fresh air playing dodgeball or jumping rope, whatever it was that little girls liked to do.

"I'm sorry. That can't be easy for either of you. Did you tell her that it won't be much longer?"

Kate nodded. Her eyes glistened with unshed tears. "What am I going to do? They say with tricky surgeries that the patient's attitude plays a huge role in the recovery."

He didn't have any experience with sick people or surgeries. He'd been a kid when his grandparents passed on.

And his father died of a massive coronary at his desk at the Carrington offices. So all he could do was try to remember what it felt like to be a kid. And his favorite memories were of the times when he'd been with his aunt.

A thought sprang to mind. "Why don't you give Molly something to look forward to?"

Kate narrowed her gaze on him. "Don't you think that's what I've been trying to do?"

"You aren't understanding me. What if you give her something to dream about? A plan for when she gets out of the hospital?"

"I'm running low on brilliant ideas. And by the time Molly is out of the hospital, I won't have two pennies to rub together much less money for a trip to Disneyland."

This was a small way he could help Kate. "You don't have to spend a lot to make your little girl happy. And you don't have to visit Sleeping Beauty Castle either."

Kate jerked upright. "How would a bachelor like yourself know about Sleeping Beauty Castle?"

He wasn't about to tell her that he too had a little girl and when he used to read her bedtime stories, he'd promised to take her there when she got a little older.

"Who doesn't know about the castle?" he bluffed. "It's in almost every Disney commercial. But what I was trying to say is that you don't need that. You could plan a whole vacation right here in New York City."

"You may not notice the cost, but dinners out and show tickets add up quickly."

"But there are other options."

Kate rolled her eyes. "If you are going to tell me to take Molly window-shopping, save your breath. That will never fly. She'll want everything she sees."

"I can assure you that good times don't have to cost a fortune."

"And what would you know about it? You probably grew up with the proverbial silver spoon in your mouth."

"You might be surprised to know that my childhood didn't have as many silver spoons as you'd imagine."

She paused and eyed him up. "There's no way you're going to convince me that your family sent you out into the world to earn bread money."

Her words pricked his good mood, deflating it. "Money isn't everything. Sometimes I think it would have been better to be born into a different family, one who didn't worry so much about money and appearances. Maybe then my parents wouldn't have…"

"Wouldn't have what?"

He glanced up to find genuine concern in her eyes. He hadn't meant to open this door to his past. Some things were best unsaid. But in this one particular case, his past might show Kate just how good she and her daughter have it.

He sighed. This still wasn't going to be easy. "Maybe without Carrington Gems and the status that came with it, my parents wouldn't have gotten divorced. But even after they got divorced, things didn't get much better. They still fought, mostly over me."

"I'm sorry."

Not about to get into how they'd turned him into a spy for each of them, he continued, "It was during this period that my aunt would whisk me away. She could see that I wasn't happy. So she'd take me on day trips around the city."

Kate waved away his idea. "I'm sure it was nice. But if I want to distract Molly and give her something to look forward to, it's got to be better than a walk in the park and a push on the swings. Besides, when she gets out of the hospital, we'll be heading back to Pennsylvania. This job is great, but it'll be over soon. I have to think about either getting my old position back or finding a new one."

He frowned at the thought that one day soon Kate would be gone. He was getting used to having her around. Not that he was getting attached to her or anything. He just liked having someone at home with whom to share a meal and make conversation.

Still, he'd like to see that Kate and her daughter had good memories to take home with them. His idea would take some convincing. However, seeing something with one's own eyes was always more persuasive than a sales pitch.

Yes, that's what he'd do—show Kate a good time.

The next morning, Kate was back working in the library, mulling over how to cheer up Molly. She liked that Lucas had been there pitching helpful ideas. Most of all, she liked that he'd opened up some about his childhood. Things must have been bad if his aunt felt she had to get him out of the house. Her heart went out to that little boy who'd been in such an unhappy situation.

"Let's go."

Her head jerked up at the sound of Lucas's voice. "What are you doing here?"

"I came to pick you up."

She straightened, not recalling that they'd had any plans. Yet he was standing there midmorning in a dark pair of jeans, which accented his athletic legs, and he'd unbuttoned his blue collared shirt and rolled up the sleeves. What in the world had gotten into him? And why did she find herself staring at him like some starstruck high-schooler? Probably because it should be against the law to look that good.

His blue eyes twinkled with mischief. "Well, are you just going to stand there smearing paint everywhere?"

She glanced down, finding the paint stick she'd been using to stir the white paint for the trim dripping all over the drop cloth. She hurried to set it aside and put the lid back on the can. Something told her that she wouldn't be doing any painting until Lucas left, not if she wanted to get the paint on the walls and not the floor.

That was one thing about this project that she really enjoyed, being able to work with her hands. At her old job she'd done the sketches, consulted with the owners and supervised the transformation. But she hadn't rolled up her sleeves and dived in with the detail work. When she finished with this project, it truly would be the crowning accomplishment in her portfolio. First, though, she had to get it finished. Too many things were riding on her bringing this project in on schedule.

"I can't go anywhere. I have work to do." She pressed her hands to her hips.

"You need a break."

"What I need is a few more hours in the day."

"I thought you might say that so I'd like you to meet Hank and Mike." Two men in white overalls stepped into the doorway. "They can paint or whatever it is you need them to do."

"But I can't just leave."

Lucas grabbed her hand and pulled her toward the door. "We have to hurry—"

"Is it Molly? Did something happen—"

"No. Nothing like that. This is all good. I promise." He sent her a reassuring smile that made her stomach dip. "Go get changed while I make a quick phone call. We have someplace to be."

"I need to have a few words with these guys."

Lucas frowned.

"It'll only take a minute."

"Hurry." He turned and strode away.

Minutes later, dressed in fresh jeans and a pink blouse, Kate stepped outside. The bright sunshine warmed her skin. With just a gentle breeze, it was warm enough to venture out without a jacket.

As they made their way down the sidewalk, she couldn't hold back her curiosity. She stepped in front of Lucas and turned. "I'm not going any further until you tell me where we're headed."

"Didn't your mother ever teach you to wait patiently for your surprise?"

"My mother didn't do surprises. Let's just say she had an active social life and kids didn't really fit into the equation."

Lucas's lips pressed into a firm line. "If it makes you feel any better, I know where you're coming from. My mother wasn't big into the parenting scene either, unless it fit some sort of social agenda."

Their conversation dwindled as they started to walk again. Destination unknown. Kate gave up worrying about it and lifted her face up to the sun. The exercise and the sunshine were working wonders on her mood. The tension in her neck and shoulders eased away.

In no time at all, Lucas was taking her by the hand and leading her through Central Park. "Come on."

This was his surprise? A trip to the park? Her good mood dimmed as she thought of how much Molly would enjoy this adventure. "What are we doing here?"

"I'll show you." He led her over to a beautiful white horse-drawn carriage and held out his hand. "We're going for a ride."

"Are you serious? But why?" She hesitated. "I shouldn't be here."

Lucas's dark brows drew together. "Why?"

"Because it isn't right. Not with Molly in the hospital."

He nodded as though he understood. "I guess I didn't think this through. Would you rather go see her?"

"Yes…but I can't. This is Chad's agreed time with her. And she likes having her dad around. And I…I don't do so well with his occasional snide little comments."

"Well, since you can't see Molly yet, consider this a research project."

"Research?"

"Sure. I'm showing you how to have a good time without spending a fortune. You didn't believe me so I decided to show you."

"This can't possibly be that cheap."

"You'd be surprised. It's actually reasonable. Although the price does go up if you reserve a carriage for a specific time or have some extras thrown in."

Kate was impressed as she climbed in the carriage with a plush red interior. The driver, all decked out in white tails and a hat, closed the door for them. Instead of fighting it and thinking of everything she should be doing, she settled back on the seat and enjoyed the moment.

Now, she truly felt like Cinderella. Wait, that would make Lucas her Prince Charming, and she'd already decided that could never be. As the horses' hooves clipped along, she shoved the troubling thought to the back of her mind. Why ruin this one magical moment with reality?

A few minutes later, Lucas leaned over to whisper in her ear. "Are you enjoying your surprise?"

His breath tickled her neck, sending an army of goose bumps down her arms. "I am." The admission rolled easily off her tongue. "But I don't know if Molly would be excited about a carriage ride."

"Sure she would. What little girl wouldn't want to ride in a horse-drawn carriage?"

"Perhaps."

"I guess I'll just have to work a little harder. I'm sure I can come up with an idea or two sure to impress a little girl and a big one, too."

Kate's stomach fluttered. Maybe it wouldn't be so bad to let herself imagine that Lucas was her Prince Charming and this was the carriage taking her to the ball. After all, fairy tales weren't true. Everyone knew that. This would just be pretend.

When Lucas stretched his arm out behind her, she gave in to the dream and leaned back. Her head rested on him and shivers of awareness cascaded down her spine. She closed her eyes, willing this moment to go on and on. They could just keep going, leaving their troubles behind. A smile tugged at the corners of her lips as she envisioned them riding off into the sunset together. If only fairy tales came true...

"And what has you smiling?"

Kate's eyelids fluttered open. She'd been busted. It was almost as if he could read her thoughts, but even if he could, there was no way she'd confirm how she'd been daydreaming about him pulling her closer and pressing his lips to hers.

She crossed her fingers before telling a fib like she'd done as a child. "Just enjoying the day."

All too soon the ride was over. Lucas gave her a hand down. It was then that she realized they hadn't stopped in the same spot where they'd started.

"It's time for lunch and I know the perfect thing to have on our outing."

He treated her to a hot dog with the works. They settled on a park bench and quietly ate while the world went by without any notice of them. When they'd finished, Lucas took her by the hand and they started walking. He smiled, appearing very relaxed. She hadn't seen him in this good of a mood since...well, ever.

After they'd walked a little ways, she couldn't contain her curiosity. "Where are we going now?"

"You'll see in just a moment."

Soon carousel music lilted through the air, giving the day a surreal feeling as though all was right in the world.

"Come on." He pulled her closer to the colorfully painted merry-go-round.

"Why?"

"You'll see."

How could she resist when he looked like an excited child himself? Laughter bubbled up in her throat, and she let him lead her by the hand. But when he paid for her to ride the merry-go-round, she hesitated.

"I can't ride that."

"Why not?"

"It's for kids."

"Are you trying to tell me that you aren't a kid at heart? Besides, you wanted examples of things you can do with Molly on a budget. This is one of them."

"True." She really did like the idea. She'd been to a carnival as a little kid with her father and she'd loved riding the carousel, especially the horses that went up and down. "But that doesn't mean that I have to ride one."

"Give me your phone."

"What? Why don't you use your own?"

"It will be simpler this way."

"What will?" The man certainly wasn't explaining himself very well today.

"I'm going to take some photos for you to show Molly."

"I don't know." What would Molly think? Her mother off playing without her. Guilt riddled her. "What if it upsets her?"

"You have a good point." Then he snapped his fingers. "I've got it. Just don't show her the pictures with you in them. And make sure you promise to bring her here as soon as she's healthy enough."

Kate wasn't so sure. But so far nothing else was helping to cheer up her little girl. Even the surprise of her father showing up had worn off. Kate was getting desperate to give her daughter hope. Maybe Lucas was right. Maybe this outing would give her the ability to paint a picture in her daughter's mind of the fun things they could do…together.

She wouldn't be an absentee parent like her father…or her mother. Even though they had shared the same house, her mother had been so wrapped up in her own world that she'd never had time for Kate.

She glanced over at Lucas. What would he be like as a father? Probably terrific, if today was any indication. Not that she would be sticking around to find out.

While riding the merry-go-round, she noticed a small crowd forming nearby. Cameras were flashing. It took her a couple of passes to realize they were talking to the city's mayor and his young family, who were most likely campaigning.

A niggling thought started to churn in her mind. Something Connie had said about a little more press coverage and they'd have a sold-out venue. With all of those reporters, it surely wouldn't be that hard to get coverage, but it would have to be something really good.

When she got off the ride, Lucas was waiting for her with a bouquet of balloons fastened to his hand. One of the reporters sent an inquisitive look in Lucas's direction. So his Bachelor of the Year status was still giving him quite a bit of notoriety, or was Lucas Carrington normally that notable of a figure in the Big Apple? Which left her wondering if she should play upon his fame—after all, it was for a good cause.

He smiled, looking proud of himself. "Admit it. You had fun."

"Yes, I did. You've made this an amazing day. Thank you."

He handed over the bouquet of rainbow-colored balloons. "Does this mean I'm forgiven for being a jerk the other day?"

He had really hurt her, but the more she got to know him, the more she realized he truly was a good guy.

"It depends…" When his gaze dipped to her lips, her thoughts scattered.

"Maybe this will help convince you."

Lucas's hands wrapped around her waist, pulling her closer. She willingly obliged. Her breath locked in her chest as she waited. Hoping. Longing.

It that moment, the world slipped away. It was just the two of them on this enchanted day. His head lowered. Her chin tilted upward.

CHAPTER TWELVE

LUCAS SHRUGGED OFF the glances he kept getting from some of the paparazzi. He wouldn't let them ruin this day. Normally he would have quietly slipped away with Kate. But he'd agreed to play up this relationship in public, so there was no need to deny he was enjoying Kate's company. And there was no need to resist what he'd been dying to do all afternoon...

His lips sought hers. The more he tasted her, the more he desired her. When she kissed him back, he forgot their circumstances, their differences and even where they were. The fact she desired him was a powerful aphrodisiac. Her kisses were even more arousing in person than they were in his dreams. A moan swelled in his throat.

Kate startled him when she pressed her hands to his chest and pushed. She broke free of his hold and stared up at him with rosy cheeks and a questioning stare.

"Lucas, people are staring."

So much for staying calm, cool and collected around her. He should probably apologize...again, but this time he wasn't sorry. He'd enjoyed holding her close and he didn't notice her complaining.

"That guy over there," she pointed to a young man who met Lucas's gaze straight on, "I think he took our picture."

Lucas glanced back but the man had disappeared into the crowd. "Good."

"Good?"

"Yes. Remember you and I are playing the happy couple for the press. So turn that frown upside down."

She smiled, but he could tell it was forced. Was she unhappy about the kiss? Impossible. She'd been an active participant. Maybe it was the fact they'd end up making headlines again. She hadn't been too thrilled with it the first time around. It was best not to say anything.

"How about some ice cream before we head back?" He could really deal with something icy cold about now.

A little bit later, they headed back to the house and Lucas couldn't believe what a wonderful day they'd shared. Thanks to Kate, he'd let loose and laughed. He'd truly enjoyed himself.

Kate's hand was wrapped with the ribbons of six helium balloons. A rainbow of colors. All for Molly. In Kate's other hand, she was holding a strawberry ice cream cone. He couldn't turn away as her tongue darted out and slowly made a trail up the creamy surface. There was no point in continuing to deny the chemistry running between them. And he knew by the way she'd eagerly returned his kiss that she felt it too.

He couldn't wait for later tonight. A little dinner after she got home from the hospital. Some conversation. And then, well, he'd let nature take its course.

"What are you grinning about?" Kate shot him a curious stare.

"I'm just basking in the glow of your happiness."

"Seriously? You really do know how to lay it on thick, don't you?"

"Sometimes it works."

"So what you're saying is that you make a habit of seducing women with horse-drawn carriages and rides on the carousel."

He truly enjoyed this playful side of Kate. "Afraid I've been busted. But in my defense, you did enjoy yourself."

She gave a nonchalant shrug, but he noticed the smile she was fighting to hold back. He liked making her happy. He liked it a lot.

She glanced up at him. "Truthfully I haven't had this much fun since I was a kid."

"Did your parents take you to an amusement park?" He was genuinely interested in learning more about her.

"No. But my dad used to take me to the fire department's summer carnival."

"Sounds like a nice memory. Do you keep in touch with your father?"

She frowned and shook her head. "That's all in my past. I learned long ago to keep looking forward. Nothing good comes from glancing back."

"Memories are important." His thoughts drifted back to the time he'd spent with his little girl. "I don't know what I'd do without them. What was your childhood like?"

Kate picked up her pace. What was it about her past that could change her mood so rapidly? Didn't they say that keeping things bottled up only caused them to fester and the only way to heal was to let it all out?

"Talk to me, Kate."

"You aren't going to drop this, are you?"

"Not until you tell me a little about your past...your father."

She stopped suddenly and glared at Lucas. "My father turned his back on a ten-year-old girl who worshipped the ground he walked on, and he didn't so much as say good-bye."

"Surely he didn't just walk away without a reason?"

Kate huffed and started walking again. "Floyd loved surprises. And his biggest surprise of all was disappearing from my life."

"But before he left, you two were close, what with the memory of the carnival and I'm guessing there must be others."

"What does it matter?" When a large black dog on a much too long leash approached them, Kate dodged in front of Lucas, giving the dog a wide berth. Once they passed the overly friendly four-legged canine, she slowed her pace. "I don't know why we're talking about him. I told you, it's ancient history."

Lucas didn't understand why all of a sudden this had become so important to him, but he couldn't let the subject drop. "Are you saying he was a bad parent?"

She stopped and pressed her hands to her hips. With her shoulders squared, she tilted her chin. "Actually it's the opposite—Floyd was a good father. We had a lot of fun together. He made up for my mother's lack of interest."

"I wish my father had been more like yours. He spent all of his time at the office and left me at home with the nanny, unless my aunt took pity on me, dressed me up and took me out."

"I guess we both came up short in the parenting department."

Lucas looked up, spotting a silver car going much too fast. Kate was too busy talking to him to notice. When she went to step off the curb, he grabbed her arm, pulling her back. She lost her balance and fell against him.

Her body seemed to fit naturally against his. He wanted to keep her safe next to him. But more than that he wondered who she leaned on—who watched out for her. He didn't like thinking of her all alone in the world.

Kate glared at him and moved away. "What did you do that for?"

"You almost stepped in front of that car."

"Oh. I didn't see it."

It was probably his fault. He was pushing her too hard

to open up, but he couldn't stop the flow of questions. He needed to know a little more. "So what happened to your father? Why did he just up and leave?"

She sighed. "He and my mother fought a lot, but it was always behind closed doors so I don't know what they argued about that last night. My mother would never talk about it. When I woke up, he was gone. He never came back. And my mother refused to answer my questions. Finally, I quit asking."

As her words sunk in, Lucas's gut knotted. He realized why this conversation was important. He wondered what his little girl would one day say about him. But Carrie wouldn't even have the benefit of good memories. Then again, she wouldn't have the horrid thoughts of being a pawn between her parents—nor the overwhelming guilt from spying on one parent for the other. When his daughter was old enough to understand, she'd realize he'd made a very difficult decision in order to spare her. It was this knowledge that got him through the long, lonely evenings and the depressing holidays. He was doing what was best for Carrie.

He reached for Kate's hand and gave it a squeeze. "I'm sure there has to be a logical answer to what happened—"

"That makes one of us. There's no excuse for just abandoning your child."

The raw edge in her voice cut him deeply. His fingers released her hand. He struggled to keep walking. Was this animosity the way his daughter would feel about him?

Before he could catch his breath, Kate continued. "The only excuse is that he never loved me. He tossed me aside like yesterday's garbage. Men like him are as low as pond scum. No. Lower."

The ice cream churned in his stomach. All Lucas could muster was a nod.

Not love her? Lucas couldn't imagine anyone being able

to resist Kate's smile or her teasing ways. But the firm set of her jaw and the lines between her gathered brows said she fully believed what she was saying. He wanted to put his arms around her and assure her that she was loved, but he couldn't.

He was the last person she'd want holding her. After all, in her book he was lower than pond scum. What was lower than that?

"I don't want to talk anymore about my father. I'd rather think about the beautiful day we had. Maybe it doesn't have to end yet."

Lucas consulted his watch. "Actually, it's almost time for you to head over to see Molly."

It was for the best. He'd already scrapped his plans for this evening—or any evening for that matter. Kate would hate him when she found out that he was an absentee father. And he couldn't blame her. He wasn't pleased about the situation either. He just wanted what was best for his daughter—and now it was going to cost him the respect and friendship of someone who'd given him the gumption to get on with life.

Then again, what if Kate never found out about Carrie? What if he left out that part of his past? But could he do that? Could he deny his own daughter?

Absolutely not. He was not a liar. And he was proud to be Carrie's father. He'd just have to find the right time to tell Kate. Somehow there had to be a way to make her understand. But how?

The next morning, Kate awoke with a definite crick in her neck. She rolled her shoulders, trying to ease the discomfort. Maybe working into the wee hours of the night hadn't been her brightest idea. She'd meant only to sit down on the floor to take a break and the next thing she knew it was morning.

But after that earth-moving kiss in the park during the romantic—dare she say it—date, she'd been full of energy...that was until she'd sat down. She yawned and pushed aside the drop cloth she'd ended up using as a make-shift blanket. Getting to her feet, she stretched her sore muscles.

Heavy footsteps sounded in the upstairs hallway. She glanced at the time on her phone. It was far too early for the workers.

"Kate?" Lucas's voice rang out.

"In here." She smoothed her hair with her palms.

Lucas appeared in the doorway with his hands full. "I thought we'd have something a little different this morning. I ran out for some of that flavored coffee you're always going on about and a couple of blueberry muffins."

"Is this a special occasion?"

He handed over a coffee. "No. I just thought a change in routine might do us good."

She gratefully took a long, slow swallow, letting the warm, creamy coffee fill her mouth with the most delicious flavor. That first sip of the day was by far the best. "I definitely approve."

"When you didn't show up for breakfast, I decided to check on you."

Since when had he started worrying about her? Surely she'd misunderstood. But the fact he'd noticed her missing and tracked her down was something she just couldn't ignore.

"I wanted to start work early. I need to get this done on schedule."

Lucas peered around. With his height and broad chest, he seemed to fill up the room. Awareness awakened Kate's sluggish body. The fresh scent of his cologne wafted past her nose and wrapped around her. Did the man have to smell so good?

He moved, visually examining the balled-up drop cloth on the floor and then taking in her rumpled appearance. "Starting early? It looks more like you never made it to bed."

She shrugged, hoping he wouldn't make a big deal of it. "This coffee sure hits the spot."

He continued looking around before turning back to her. "You're working too hard. If you need more help, just tell me."

"I will." But right now she had something else on her mind. "You know, I was thinking that the night of the fund-raiser would be the perfect time to announce the sale of this place."

He stared at her as if she'd sprouted another head. "Why would I do that?"

"I'm obviously missing something. I know when we discussed it earlier the situation still wasn't clear, but isn't the point of fixing up the house to put it on the market? I mean it isn't like you live here. In fact, you hate being here—"

"I do not." He looked away, studying something on the floor.

"Don't give me that. Every time I turn around, you're running out the door. I get it. This place doesn't hold good memories for you. I have a couple of places like that myself. So why hold on to the house? Let someone else enjoy it."

He ran a hand through his hair, scattering the short strands. "I don't know if I'm ready to make a decision of that magnitude. Lately, I seem to be making one mistake after the other."

"Does that include kissing me?" Kate clamped her lips shut, but it was too late. Her thoughts were out there. Hovering. Waiting.

She should brush aside her careless comment and pretend she was teasing, but she couldn't. She honestly wanted to know how he felt about her.

With every bit of willpower, she lifted her chin and looked at him. Wondering. Hoping.

His Adam's apple bobbed. Their gazes met. And the air around them seemed to crackle with awareness.

"Kissing you is all I've thought about." His voice was deep and thick, sending goose bumps of excitement down her spine. "My only regret is that it ended far too soon."

His intense gaze held hers. She should turn away. She should… She should…

Long suppressed desires swelled inside her and squelched her train of thought. He stepped forward, closing the gap between them. Her stomach fluttered and dipped. The tip of her tongue swished over her now dry lips. He was going to kiss her again, and she wanted him to because for better or worse, she wanted to taste him on her lips.

The breath in her lungs hitched. She'd never anticipated anything this much in her entire life. Her chin tilted upward. And her heart pounded.

Being cautious wasn't all it was cracked up to be. This once she wanted to throw caution to the wind. She wanted to live in the moment.

She shifted her weight to her tiptoes. And then he was there. His warm breath tickled her cheek before his lips pressed to hers. They moved gently at first, tentatively as though questioning her. But that wasn't nearly enough for her. She met his kiss with a hunger that startled her. He tasted like rich, dark coffee and she'd never tasted anything so good.

Mr. Oh-So-Sexy could most certainly kiss. In fact, she'd never enjoyed anything so much in her life. Her needy body leaned into his hard contours. The fact that he wanted her was all too evident and had her insides melting into a liquid pool of desire.

Standing there, wrapped in his arms, her problems and responsibilities temporarily fell away. In that moment, she was the woman desired by the most thoughtful man she'd ever known, who could kiss the common sense from her mind. But one thought came to mind—one very clear and concise thought.

She was in love with Lucas.

She didn't know where or when it had started, but she was falling hard and fast for him. And try as she might, she couldn't stop her heart from spiraling out of control.

Her fingers blindly plucked at his silk tie, pulling it loose. She fumbled with his shirt buttons until enough were undone that her hands could slip over the bare skin of his shoulders and back. Her core temperature climbed with each tantalizing move.

"Tell me now if you want me to go." His voice was raspy as his fingers slipped beneath her shirt.

"Stay. Please."

Her eyes opened for a second, glancing over to the tangle of drop cloths she'd used not so long ago as a makeshift bed. Not exactly the Plaza Hotel, but right now, it didn't matter. His tongue swept inside her mouth, teasing and taunting. Her thoughts scattered.

They stumbled backward, still clinging to each other. Now that she'd found him, she never wanted to let go. She couldn't get enough of him…of his touch. Lucas lowered them to the floor and they landed with a bit of an "oomph" that jarred their lips from each other.

He brushed a few strands of hair from her face. "Sorry about that."

"It's okay. I had a soft landing."

She was half sitting, half lying in his lap while staring into his darkening eyes. They mesmerized her with their ability to change color with his moods. Right now, she was drowning in them.

She was the first to make the move this time. Hungry for more of him, she leaned forward. Her mouth claimed his—needy and anxious. There was no mistaking the passion in his kiss as he followed her lead.

But then he pulled back just enough to start a trail of kisses down over the sensitive skin of her neck. A moan of desire swelled in her throat. She'd never felt such desire by a man. He gave as good as he got and she couldn't wait to find out what else he was good at....

CHAPTER THIRTEEN

THE THUD OF work boots on the steps roused Kate as she savored the way her body still thrummed with utter satisfaction. She lifted her cheek from Lucas's bare shoulder. "Shoot. It's Charlie."

Adrenaline pumped through her veins as she scrambled to grab the edge of the white drop cloth. What had she been thinking to do this here?

Obviously her brain had short-circuited as soon as Lucas's lips had touched hers. Now she didn't know how she'd be able to face the foreman. She pressed her hands to her heated cheeks before combing her fingers through her flyaway hair. One look and Charlie would know what had happened. Soon everyone would know. How in the world would these men ever respect her when they found out she was sharing a bed with the owner?

Lucas jumped to his feet, springing over to the door, pushing it shut. Kate didn't need an invitation. She rushed to locate her discarded clothes.

A knock sounded. "Kate, are you in there?"

She held her breath, hoping Lucas had remembered to catch the lock. The doorknob jiggled. When the door didn't budge, she expelled a pent-up breath. But she still felt the heat on her chest rise up her neck and engulf her entire face.

Lucas was the first to find his voice. "She'll be with you in a couple of minutes."

"Mr. Carrington, is that you?"

"Yes. We are going over some plans."

Is that what he called it? If she'd recalled correctly they'd gone over those "plans" a couple of times…at least she had. A fresh wave of heat rolled over her. She didn't even want to know what was going through Charlie's mind. His imagination was probably painting him a pretty accurate picture of their "meeting."

In a flourish of activity, they dressed. Resigned to the fact she'd done her best to fix herself up without a mirror, she turned to Lucas. She straightened his tie and in turn, he ran his fingers through her hair and tucked a few strands behind her ears.

"Ready?" he whispered.

She wasn't, but she had this feeling Charlie wasn't going anywhere. She nodded and Lucas opened the door.

The foreman ducked his gray head inside. His intense stare took in her not-so-neat appearance, before zeroing in on the scattered drop cloth on the floor next to Lucas's rumpled-up suit jacket.

The man's gaze came back to Kate. "Anything you need?"

She shook her head, not trusting her voice. It took all of her determination to keep from wringing her hands together. She'd never been caught in such a compromising situation. She felt like a teenager, experiencing love for the first time.

A knowing smile pulled at the older man's unshaven face. "Sorry. I didn't know you two were…umm, having a private meeting." He winked. "No biggie. We can go over the discrepancy with the paint order later."

Kate was so hot now that beads of moisture dotted her forehead. She swallowed hard and refused to let on that this thing, this moment of craziness with Lucas, had affected her. There would be time to sort things out later…

much later. First, she had to get her head wrapped around what had happened.

She stepped toward the door. "Charlie, we can go downstairs and go over it now."

"Nah." He waved her off. "You two finish your umm… meeting. I'll go head off the men so they don't disturb you." He started to turn away, then glanced back. "Ya know, the missus was just showing me the picture of you two in the paper this morning. I told her it wasn't any of our business. But thought you should know."

"Thanks." Lucas didn't smile.

Charlie nodded and pulled the door shut. Neither said a word as the foreman whistled a merry tune as he moved down the hallway.

When they were alone again, Kate groaned. "This is awful. I don't know how I missed hearing his approach. The man's footsteps are louder than a stampede of cattle."

"You weren't the only one who was caught off guard. Did you see the unhappy look on his face when he first walked in? I thought for sure I was going to have to defend myself. Looks like you've won him over."

"We're friends. When you work seven days a week with a person, you get to know a lot about them and their family. Just like you and I have gotten to know each other really well. I don't think he'll say anything."

"It won't matter if he does. The whole city thinks we've been doing this all along."

Lucas adjusted his shirtsleeves before slipping on his suit jacket that now had distinct wrinkles. He kept his head lowered as though it took every bit of his concentration to adjust his clothing. But Kate knew differently—knew he had something else weighing on his mind. He was probably just as confused as she was about where they went from here.

No matter what, she couldn't deny that she'd never been kissed quite so thoroughly in her entire life. Nor touched so tenderly and made to feel that her happiness came first. Lucas was a unique man and his ex-wife must have had a few marbles loose to let him slip away. But she couldn't go losing her head over him. She had to keep her focus on Molly and the fund-raiser.

Lucas looked down at the mess of throws on the floor. "I'll just give you a hand straightening up—"

"No. Don't. I've got it."

"Are you sure?"

"Positive."

She licked her dry lips, noticing how they burned a bit. She couldn't remember the last time they'd been kissed raw. But this day—this beautiful day—she wouldn't forget.

With her back to him, she started to fold the cloth. "Besides, I have to hurry. I need to get to the hospital for an update with Molly's doctor."

Lucas slowly moved to the door before turning back. "At least let me give you a lift."

"This," her hand waved around, unsure how to label what had just happened between them, "doesn't change anything. I have a sick daughter and that has to be my focus. Not you and me. Not this moment when we both lost our heads. Just Molly."

His mouth opened as though he wanted to say something, then closed.

When he didn't leave, she added, "As for getting to the hospital, I'll be fine on my own. Always have been. Always will be."

"I never doubted it." There was a strained pause. "But will you have enough time to get cleaned up and walk to the hospital?"

She glanced down at her wrinkled work clothes. Drat. She hated that he'd made a valid point at her expense. "I…I can grab a cab."

"Listen, I'm sorry about what just happened." Another

poignant pause filled the air as she piled the drop cloths in the corner to deal with later. "I lost my head. It won't happen again. You have my word."

He was apologizing? She hadn't seen that one coming. Had their lovemaking been that bad? Was she that out of practice?

Impossible. She knew when a man was into the moment. And Lucas had certainly been into her. So why the regret?

Maybe it had something to do with the ghosts that lurked within these walls? Or more likely he realized that she wouldn't fit into his posh world. She was a nobody from Pennsylvania, who didn't even have enough money to cover her daughter's medical bills.

Certain that she'd be best off keeping as much distance from him as possible, she said, "I've got to go. I'll see you at dinner for your daily update."

Her vision blurred as she walked away. She blinked repeatedly. She'd let herself get caught up in the moment. That had been her mistake. One she didn't intend to repeat—no matter how much her heart said otherwise.

She dashed the moisture from her lashes. Now how were they supposed to continue with their arrangement? Was it possible to move past something this big—this memorable?

Lucas hated that he'd lost control. He'd been a grump all day to the point of scaring his administrative assistant with a snarly response. He'd of course apologized, but she still kept her distance the rest of the day.

Unable to concentrate at the office, he'd come home earlier than normal. He sat at the kitchen table for a long time, staring blindly at the blinking cursor on his computer. His thoughts kept replaying how he'd made love to Kate. What he'd thought would be a chance to scratch an itch had turned into a mind-blowing moment.

From the second he'd laid eyes on Kate that morning,

he'd been a goner. With her hair all tousled and her cheeks rosy, she was a natural beauty. There was nothing phony and artificial about her. He couldn't help but imagine what it'd be like to wake up next to her each morning. That had been his first mistake.

He'd only compounded matters with his second mistake, kissing her. And though he'd savored every delicious moment of their lovemaking—a memory he wasn't likely to forget anytime soon—he couldn't repeat it. For both of their sakes. Once she found out about Carrie, she'd never look at him the same way.

With difficulty, Lucas choked down that last thought. If only there was some way of convincing her that sometimes people made choices they wouldn't normally make in order to spare those they loved.

Lucas's fingers moved over the keyboard, examining the social media campaign planned for the upcoming jewelry launch—Fiery Hearts. He wanted the name on every social media outlet. He was monitoring the Fiery Hearts campaign very closely. Nothing could go wrong.

He didn't really understand the allure of these social sites. He avoided them like the plague. But he was all for different strokes for different folks. And as a businessman, these places were invaluable resources for interactive advertising and research.

He opened a window for MyFriends, keyed in his name and pulled up his personal account that he used to help get the word out about Carrington promotions. He was surprised to find that even with infrequent postings, he'd gained a number of friends.

He moved to the Carrington Gems MyFriends page, which he was pleased to find had a larger following than the last report he'd received. He read over the last few postings, happy to find excitement growing over the launch.

Once he shared the information about the Fiery Hearts

reveal from the Carrington Gems page on his personal page, he also decided to share the announcement about Kate's fund-raiser. The posting included a photo of Kate and her daughter. They certainly looked a lot alike—both beautiful. He smiled.

With his work done on the site, he wondered if Kate had an account. It would be one way to keep in contact with her when this fund-raiser was over and she moved on. For her, he just might become more active on social media. He searched for her name but didn't turn up any results. Then for curiosity's sake, he typed his mother's name and when her face appeared on the screen, his mouth gaped. It seemed MyFriends must be a trendy hotspot.

Then on a lark he typed in Floyd Whitley. Immediately he got a listing. There were three candidates. Lucas knew that he should stop there. But what would it hurt to do a little more digging?

He quickly narrowed the list by nationality and he had one candidate. And Kate resembled the man with her dark hair and her big brown eyes. What were the chances this wasn't her father?

But the man's details were hidden because they weren't friends. So Lucas hit the "Be MyFriend" button. As the message sent, Lucas wondered about Floyd's reason for leaving his little girl. No matter what Kate thought, most people just didn't walk away without a reason.

And then without warning a message popped up on his screen. Floyd had accepted his invitation. Now what? Common sense said he should back away. But when a message appeared on the screen, Lucas was drawn in.

Floyd: Do I know you?

What had Lucas been thinking to contact this man? Had he lost his mind? He didn't have any right to be interfering in Kate's private life just to try and make himself look better in her eyes. For all he knew this man could be nothing but trouble.

"Whatcha doing?" Kate came in the back door.

Lucas slammed his laptop closed. If Kate ever found out he'd opened Pandora's box, she would never forgive him. And he couldn't blame her. He'd let his curiosity get out of hand.

"I...I was just doing some work."

"You look like things aren't going well."

He got up, filled his coffee cup to the top and stared at the rising steam. Shoving aside his near misstep with Floyd, he knew there was something much more important he needed to do—tell Kate about his daughter.

Maybe if he'd done this sooner, he wouldn't have gotten the crazy idea to hunt down her father. He wouldn't have gone off on a lark to prove to her that there are legitimate reasons people walk away from their children.

Lucas turned, finding her still smiling at him. "What has you so happy?"

"I talked to your aunt last night and she said since the second photo appeared in the paper, ticket sales have increased to the point where she thinks we'll sell out. You don't know what a relief that is, but of course, your aunt is insisting we keep up the pretense of being a happy couple until the event. Will that be a problem?"

He shook his head. "Not for me."

"By the way, Molly's excited about the idea of vacationing right here in the Big Apple."

"That's great." He was happy to know that he'd done at least that much right.

As the silence dragged on, Kate sent him a quizzical look. "You know, I was showing Molly the pictures of the carriage and the carousel and she got excited. Except she said when we go for a ride, she wants to pet the horses. Do you think that'll be a problem?"

Lucas shook his head. "Shouldn't be."

Before he could say more, Kate rushed on. "And she made me promise to take pictures of some huge toy store. I don't know how she heard about it, but she wants pictures of the giant piano. So since you're good at playing tour director, what do you say? Want to go with me this week?"

What did he say now? He couldn't refuse Kate anything. Not when she looked at him with those hopeful eyes.

"We'll go," he mumbled.

"You promise? I don't want to let Molly down. So if you aren't up for it, I'll go by myself."

"I promise." He stiffened his shoulders and swallowed. He couldn't drag this out any longer. The truth had to come out now. "I have something to tell you."

CHAPTER FOURTEEN

THE HAIRS ON Kate's arms rose. Something was wrong. Tension rippled off Lucas in waves. And no matter how much she tried to sidestep it with a smile and light conversation, he wouldn't let go of whatever was bothering him. It must be something pretty big.

He stepped closer. "I don't know how to say this."

Say what? Had he changed his mind about having the party here? Surely that couldn't be it. There was no way they could change venues at this late date. The party was only a couple of weeks away.

"Whatever it is we'll work it out."

"I wish it was that easy. The thing is—"

"Excuse me." One of the men Lucas had hired to lighten her workload entered the kitchen. He looked a bit uncomfortable and stuffed his hands in his pants pockets. "Ms. Whitley, we're having a problem. You know that room you wanted us to empty? Well, we're having a problem fitting everything into that smaller room."

"It'll fit. There wasn't that much furniture to move."

"That's the thing—it's not the furniture. It's all of the toys and stuffed animals."

"Toys?" The whole time she'd been working here, she hadn't seen any child's items. None at all. Her gaze sought out Lucas. "Do you know what he's talking about?"

"Damn." Lucas's mug slammed down on the counter, causing Kate to jump.

He moved with long, swift strides as if the house was on fire. She practically had to run to keep up with him. What in the world was going on? Toys? In this place?

Once they made it to the top of the staircase, Lucas turned left instead of right. Suddenly things started to make sense. When she'd told James to clear out the room at the end of the hall, he must have gotten her instructions mixed up and gone to the wrong end—the room with the locked door.

Lucas's shoulders were rigid and his hands clenched. The angry vibes reverberated down the hallway. He'd agreed to the fund-raiser under one condition—that this room not be disturbed. How in the world was she going to make him understand it was an accident?

Lucas came to a stop in the open doorway. "Where are the pictures? The crib?"

"We moved them into the spare room down the hall. One of the rooms that doesn't have any damage like Ms. Whitley told us."

"And did she also tell you to break the lock on the door?"

The man's face paled and he shook his head. "We thought the doorknob was jammed. So we removed the handle. Sorry 'bout that."

"Go. Now." Lucas turned his back on the man.

The workman sent Kate an uncertain look. She waved him away. But Lucas had another thing coming if he thought she could be dismissed so easily. Especially when she didn't have a clue what was going on here.

Lucas's large frame practically filled the doorway. She had to peer around him to get a glimpse into the room. It was painted pink with white-and-yellow flowers stenciled about the white chair rail. There was a gigantic stuffed polar bear with a great big red bow. And a wooden rocking horse. This was definitely a baby girl's room.

Before Kate could formulate any questions, Lucas turned an accusative stare her way. "We had an agreement. You promised not to bother this room."

"I didn't. I swear."

Kate pressed her hands into her hips and pulled her shoulders back. She wasn't about to take the blame for a mistake that obviously wasn't hers. Surely Lucas had to understand that sometimes misunderstandings happened.

He raked his fingers through his hair, scattering the short strands. "I never should have agreed to any of this."

Her curious gaze returned to the nursery. This stuff wasn't old. It was actually quite modern and very expensive, which meant that up until recently there had been a child here.

She turned on Lucas. "Is this your daughter's room?"

Lines etched his face, aging him about ten years. "Yes. Her name's Carrie."

This news shocked Kate. After she'd opened up to him about so much of her life, including the ugly stuff she didn't share with anyone, she felt as if their friendship was one-sided.

"Why is this the first I'm hearing of her?"

"What do you want to know?"

"Everything. Who is she? Where is she?" Then a horrible thought struck her. Was it possible something had happened to his daughter? Was that why he'd reacted so strangely in the pediatric ward? "Did...did she die?"

"No." A moment passed before Lucas spoke up. "Carrie is a healthy, active four-year-old."

"But I don't understand. This room is made up for a baby. Where is she?"

He ran his hand over his face. "I changed my mind. I don't want to talk about her."

That answer wasn't good enough, not after he'd pressed her to dredge up the information about Floyd.

"Obviously you've been keeping this to yourself for far too long. Look at this house. You've kept it locked up like some museum. I'm guessing you did this to hold in all of the memories. If you won't talk to me, you should find someone to talk to."

"Fine." He exhaled a long, weary sigh. "If you want to know the truth, my ex-wife left me and took our daughter."

Kate knew she was missing a piece of the puzzle because she couldn't make sense of his anguish, his need to keep this room locked up. "You must miss her terribly."

"More than you know…"

Kate approached him and reached out, touching his arm. "I'm sure when you have her here for visitation, she sees how much you love her. She won't forget you. You're her daddy."

He jerked away from her touch. "Carrie doesn't know me."

Surely she hadn't heard him correctly. "What do you mean she doesn't know you?"

"I mean she lives in California with her mother."

"And?"

"There's no and. That's it. End of story. They have their life and I have mine."

The jagged pieces of this puzzle fell into place. She knew this picture—had lived out a similar experience. Lucas was just like her father, a love 'em and leave 'em type. And like a fool, she'd gone and opened her heart to him.

Anger, frustration and disillusionment bubbled up in her. "You don't see your own child? But why? How can you just forget her, like she never existed?"

He nailed her with a stern look. "I will never forget her. Ever!"

"Then why isn't she here with you? At least part-time?"

"It's better this way."

"Better for whom? You?"

"Of course not. Do you think I like this?" His shoulders drooped and his gaze no longer met hers. "Do you think I enjoy having my daughter run from me because I'm a stranger to her?"

Kate crossed her arms and angled her chin. "It doesn't have to be that way."

He shook his head. "You don't understand."

"Then explain it to me."

He sighed. "My ex-wife has gone to great lengths to keep me from my daughter. And now that she's remarried, she doesn't want me ruining her picture-perfect family. She's threatened to make everyone's life impossible if I push her on this."

"She can't just keep you from seeing your daughter because it suits her. You have rights—"

"And I also know what it's like to be the pawn between two warring parents—how torn you feel when they want you to take sides. If it wasn't for Aunt Connie looking out for me, I don't know what I'd have done to get away from the fighting." A muscle twitched in his jaw as he stared off into space. "I won't put my daughter through that."

"So instead you'll let your daughter wonder the rest of her life why you didn't love her enough to stick around." Kate's voice wobbled. "You ran instead of standing up and doing the right thing for your daughter."

"I'm doing what's best for Carrie—"

"No. You did what was best for you." Her chest ached as though her heart had been ripped out. "You aren't the man I thought you were."

His head lowered. "I suppose I'm not."

"How could you keep this all a secret after I opened up to you about my father? I started to think we might have a future. I was so wrong."

"And I was wrong to let you in this house. You need to leave." He strode away, leaving her to make sense of things.

"What? But the fund-raiser—"

"Can be held elsewhere. I don't care where you hold it as long as it isn't here. I don't want anything else moved or disturbed. Send those men away."

Lucas stormed off down the hallway. He couldn't be serious. After all the work, all the plans, he was canceling everything? The backs of Kate's eyes stung. She blinked repeatedly. One lousy mistake and her chance to raise the money for her daughter went up in a puff of smoke. She told herself that's what the tears were about—not the fact that Lucas had been keeping this big secret from her.

She swiped her cheeks and sucked in a shaky breath. Things couldn't end like this. He had to be reasonable about the party. They had an agreement. She started after him.

By the time she made it downstairs, Lucas was gone. There was only one thing for her to do. Leave. But this wasn't over. Not by a long shot. But first they both needed to cool down.

Lucas stood alone in the elevator. Just him and a fuzzy pink teddy bear that was wearing a pink rhinestone tiara he'd had specially made for Molly. He hadn't seen or heard from Kate since he'd reacted without thinking and fired everyone. And he couldn't just leave things like this. He wouldn't let Kate or her daughter down. He had to do something to remedy things. Something drastic.

He stared down at the wide-eyed stuffed animal and started to think over what Kate had said the other day about Carrie. Was Kate right? Would his daughter believe he didn't love her? Surely when she was older she'd understand his reasoning. Wouldn't she?

He pushed aside the thoughts of his daughter, though

they were never far from reach. But for these next few moments, he needed to be focused.

"This will all work out." When he realized he was talking to a teddy bear, he moved the stuffed animal behind his back.

The elevator door slid open and Lucas took a deep, steadying breath. A painted giraffe and smiling rhino greeted him, but he didn't smile back. Hesitantly putting one foot in front of the other, he started down the long hallway. The sounds of young children echoed between the walls. The voices still dug and poked at his scarred heart, but he refused to turn around. This trip was more important than his own pain and guilt.

On the ride here, he'd debated how to say what needed to be said. He still didn't have a plan. That in and of itself was so unlike him. He was a visionary. He knew where he wanted his business to go and he took the lead. This time he didn't have a clear vision, only the hope that there was some happy solution to this mess.

He paused outside Room 529. The lilt of Kate's voice followed by a giggle filled the air. He took a deep breath and then rapped his knuckles on the propped-open door before stepping inside the dimly lit room.

"Who's that?" The little girl, who was the spitting image of Kate, pointed at him.

Surprise lit up Kate's face. "Well, that's…umm, was—"

"I'm your mommy's friend. You can call me Lucas."

Molly's gaze swung between him and her mother as though trying to make up her mind whether to like him or not. At last, she smiled. "What's behind your back?"

"Who, me? I don't have anything behind me." He turned around in a circle as though to look behind him, all the while holding the pink bear against his back. "See. I told you there was nothing there."

Molly giggled and Kate smiled.

"Silly, it's right there. Behind you."

Once again he turned around. "I'm telling you, I don't see a thing. Maybe they should check your eyes while you're here."

"I saw it. It's a pink bear."

"You saw a pink bear?" Molly nodded and he stepped closer. "Maybe you better point out this bear that's following me around."

He turned slowly this time and just as he predicted, Molly grabbed the bear. "See, here it is. And it has a crown." Molly pulled the tiara off the bear's head and put it on her own. "Lookie, I'm a princess."

"A very pretty one. Just like your mother." Molly giggled and Kate blushed. "You better keep a close eye on that bear. He seems to like getting himself into mischief."

He winked at Kate and noticed how she fought back a smile. She wasn't as easy to win over as Molly. Oh, well, he'd dug his hole and now it was time for him to pull himself out. But if the gleam in her eyes was any indication, he was making progress, even if she wouldn't admit it.

"I hear you liked the pictures your mother took of the horse and carriage and the merry-go-round."

Molly nodded. "I get to ride them as soon as I get outta here."

"Not quite," Kate corrected. "We have to wait for the doctor to say it's okay."

"And I wanna go play on a giant piano. Have you seen it?"

He really liked this pint-size version of Kate. "I haven't. But it sounds exciting."

"Mommy's going to take me pictures."

"She is?" He glanced over at Kate, hoping to see her stern expression lighten into a smile. No such luck. "Maybe she needs help finding it."

Molly's eyes widened. "You know where it is?"

He nodded. Molly chattered some more before she faded off to sleep while watching a cartoon. Since it was the end of visiting hours, Kate left with him.

When they reached the elevator, Lucas broke the silence. "I'll give you a ride."

Kate's brows lifted. "You don't even know where I'm staying."

"At my place."

She made an indignant sound. "As I recall, I am no longer welcome there."

The elevator door opened and they stepped inside with an older woman and her husband. Kate moved toward the back and he followed.

He leaned near her ear. "I didn't mean for you to actually leave for good. I lost my cool."

Kate's brown eyes flared. "If that's your attempt at an apology, you have a lot to learn."

"Come on, Kate. Surely you've overreacted before and done something without thinking."

She crossed her arms and gazed straight ahead as though he wasn't there.

The older woman turned to him. "Sonny, you need to say you're sorry and buy her some flowers. Women always like that."

Her husband gently elbowed her. "Helen, let the kids work this out on their own."

"I was just trying to help." The elevator stopped and the couple got off.

Alone at last, Lucas moved to stand in front of Kate. "I'm sorry. I shouldn't have said what I did. And I'll buy you a whole flower shop if it'll make you happy again."

"You should know that I have a brown thumb." Her eyes met his. "As for the rest, you're right. You shouldn't have said those things."

The fact she was able to joke around a little about her

brown thumb had to be a good sign. "Please, will you come back and finish the project?"

Kate shrugged. "I'll have to think about it."

"Will you at least come back to the house with me?"

"Seeing as my things are still there, I suppose."

Boy, she wasn't going to make it easy. Then again, he hadn't exactly been easy to deal with either the other day. He could only hope that with time she'd give him a second chance.

CHAPTER FIFTEEN

It certainly wasn't easy. Not at all.

But over the course of the following week, Lucas had convinced Kate he was truly sorry for his outburst. In the end, Kate agreed it was best for everyone to go ahead with the fund-raiser. In return, he insisted on keeping his promise to escort her to New York's grandest toy store. He cajoled her into allowing him to buy Molly a dolly with a few accessories. After all, what was a doll without a wardrobe? Even guys like him knew how important clothes were to both big and little girls.

With only a week to go before the sold-out Roaring Twenties fund-raiser, Lucas was surprised by how well things were progressing with the house. Of course, circumstances could still be better between him and Kate. He planned to work on that, starting with a fancy dinner out.

He was just about to ask her out when her phone rang. As she talked to the unknown caller, her happy face morphed into one of an angry mother bear. "Yes...I understand... I'll be there."

He'd never seen her look so cross. His foot tapped the floor as he waited for the phone call to end. "Is Molly all right?"

"Physically she's fine. Emotionally, that's another story. That was Judy, one of Molly's nurses. She called to let me know Chad was just there to say goodbye."

"But how can he leave now? Molly's surgery is next week."

Kate's hands tensed. "He got a business offer in Tucson. Too good to pass up. He'll supposedly be back as soon as he can."

Lucas watched as Kate paced. He wanted to comfort her, to put his arms around her and pull her close, but he wasn't sure that's what she'd want. Reading women was not something he excelled at. So he sat at the counter, waiting and watching.

"This is classic Chad behavior. Worry about himself first. And the hell with everyone else." She paced back and forth. "This is my fault. My gut said he wouldn't stick it out, but I let him get close to Molly anyway. When will I learn not to count on people to hang around?"

An urge came over Lucas to say she could count on him. He wouldn't walk away. The thought caught him off guard. Was that truly how he felt? Or was he merely sympathizing with her?

She stopped and faced Lucas, her eyes round like quarters. "The house. The men. What am I going to do? Molly needs me. The nurse said she was in tears. But there are still things to do here before the party. I...I..."

He appreciated that Kate took her obligations so seriously. Maybe that was his problem—he took his work way too seriously. It'd cost him dearly. He didn't want Kate to make the same mistakes—putting work ahead of family.

But that would mean he'd have to step up and take over the house renovations. When he'd first met Kate, he'd have never dreamed of working upstairs amongst the memories, but now...

He might not be ready to pledge to Kate forever, but this burden with the house, this was something that he could do for her. It was a chance to show her that not all men were like her father and her ex-husband. He wouldn't cut and run when times got tough. He would be her friend as long as she wanted.

Firm in his decisions, he reached for his keys. "Here. Take the car. And don't worry about things here."

"But it's not finished. The paintings and furniture still need to be placed. And the nursery. I never got a chance to put it back together. I'm sorry." Her eyes filled with tears.

Lucas pulled her close. He rubbed her back while resting his head against hers. "Don't worry. Between Charlie and me, we've got it covered."

Kate pulled away and stared up at him. "But you have your work and the Fiery Hearts launch. And you're already short your marketing director."

"I will take care of everything. I promise. Now go. Be with your daughter. And stop worrying. I've got this under control."

With Kate out the door, Lucas phoned his extremely organized assistant. For the first time in almost two years, he told her he would be out of the office. He relayed what needed to be done in terms of the San Francisco project and the launch of the new jewelry line. He also told her that if she needed him, he'd be at home for the next week—words he'd never said to her at such a critical juncture for Carrington Gems. And he knew he'd made the right choice.

Not so long ago, he wouldn't have believed it...but sometimes there were things more important than work. Kate was counting on him. And he vowed not to let her down.

Lucas changed into a pair of comfy jeans and a ratty old T-shirt. He moved swiftly back to the kitchen where he'd left some rough sketches Kate had done up for him to show him how she planned to stage each room. They'd be his saving grace, but when he sorted through the pile of papers and receipts to locate the drawings, they weren't nearly as detailed as he'd thought.

"How hard can it be?" he muttered to himself as he moved through the hallway.

Taking a deep breath, he started up the steps. He took them two at a time and paused at the top when he came face-to-face with a portrait of his great-grandparents on the opposite wall. They were the inspiration for the Roaring Twenties party. He hadn't seen this part of his past in years…ever since Elaina had decided the mansion needed a more modern look.

He smiled as his gaze moved down the hallway, taking in the paintings that had hung in this house as far back as he could remember. Kate had thoroughly disagreed with his ex-wife's decor, going with a more traditional look. He thoroughly approved of Kate's approach and the use of family portraits and heirlooms.

He felt more at peace in these rooms than he had in a very long time. The tension in his neck and shoulders eased. Kate had worked miracles to turn this place into a home. And now it was time he worked one of his own.

His gaze paused on the open doorway to the nursery. He could put the room back to the way it had been before the workers dismantled it. He recalled the room down to its finest details. But this room wasn't his priority. He pulled the door shut and locked it. He would deal with it another day. There was something more important he needed to do.

A week had passed and Kate couldn't wait to see Lucas's attempt at remodeling. He'd been keeping her bedroom off-limits until he finished.

"Close your eyes." When she didn't move, he lifted her hand over her eyes. "And no peeking."

She shook her head. "You're worse than a little kid."

"It'll be worth it. I promise."

She did as he said while letting him guide her down the hallway. "Okay, you can open them."

Kate smiled as she stood at the doorway of the original bedroom she'd been using up until Lucas had taken over finishing the upstairs. "Wow. I didn't expect you to do such an amazing job."

"I had a great incentive."

She turned to see him staring directly at her. Her heart fluttered and heat rushed up her neck, flooding her face. Had he really done all this for her?

The once bright white walls were now a soothing sandy tan. And the crown molding had been repaired and painted a soft, creamy white that matched the ceiling. She couldn't have done better if she'd picked the colors herself. The furnishings were new. The dark wood of the big sleigh bed fit perfectly in the room.

"Seems you have a hidden talent. I guess you don't need my services after all."

Lucas's head ducked. "The truth of the matter is I sort of…umm…hired the woman at the furniture store to help me get the details right. I know you were making a point of using the furniture that has been in my family for years, but I wanted something new for this room."

She was impressed Lucas seemed to be moving forward and letting go of his tight grip on the past. She wanted to turn and throw her arms around him, but she held back, waiting to hear his reasoning for the new furniture and the impressive makeover.

Lucas took her by the hand and drew her inside. It was only then that she noticed a small table off to the side, all done up with a lace tablecloth, tapered candles and a long-stem red rose. China and stemware completed the impressive setup. No one had ever done anything so romantic for her.

Kate's mouth gaped. "Is this for us?"

"Unless you were planning to have a late dinner with someone else."

"Definitely not. I just wasn't expecting you to go to all of this trouble."

Lucas shrugged. "I thought you might like it, but if you don't, we could go back downstairs."

"Oh, no, this is fine." She glanced down at her jeans and blue cotton top, feeling severely underdressed. "Maybe I should get changed."

"Not a chance. You look beautiful just like that."

Her stomach fluttered.

"Would you like some champagne?" He moved to the table and withdrew a bottle from an ice bucket and held it out to her.

Her gaze strayed over to the bed where the beige comforter was already drawn back. Her pulse accelerated. Lucas was attempting to seduce her. They hadn't made love since that one time, both agreeing that it would be best for their working relationship to keep things casual. So what had changed? Or was she reading more into this than he intended?

"Lucas, I don't understand."

Her stomach was aflutter with nerves as she waited and wondered where this night was headed. Where did she want it to go?

Lucas walked up to her. "I'm sorry things between us have been so bumpy. I'm hoping they'll be better from now on."

He wrapped his hands around her waist. The heat of his touch radiated through her clothing. Her heart thumped with anticipation. He was trying to show her that he could change and she wanted nothing more than to give him a second chance.

His head dipped and she leaned into him, enjoying the way his mouth moved over hers. Each time their lips met, it was like the first time. And she never wanted it to end. Because with each kiss, her heart took flight and soared.

But she couldn't lose control now. She couldn't cave into the desire warming her veins just yet. First, she needed some answers.

With every bit of willpower she could muster, she braced her hands on his shoulders and pushed away. She drew in an uneven breath and willed her pulse to slow. She glanced up, seeing the confusion in his eyes.

"We need to talk." She took a deep breath, hoping the extra oxygen would help clear her thoughts. "This is beautiful, but why have you gone to all of this trouble?"

Her fevered wish was for him to say he loved her. That he needed her. And that he was ready to make peace with the past and reach for the future she knew they could have together.

"I thought it was self-explanatory."

She licked her dry lips, searching for the right words. "Is this the beginning of something? Will you still be interested in me...in us next week? Next month?"

"I...I don't know. You're rushing things."

Kate shook her head. "I'm not rushing anything. This—" she waved her hand around "—was your idea. Are you saying there's room here for me and Molly in your life?"

His brows lifted. "You mean here, in this house?"

She nodded. Inside she was begging him to pick her, to choose a future with her.

"I don't know if I can live here with another family."

His lack of certainty hurt her deeply. She loved him. She'd accepted that fact back when they'd made love. Even though she'd been fighting it, it'd only grown stronger.

"And does that include your daughter? Do you not have room for her here either?"

"You don't know what you're asking."

"Yes, I do. I'm asking you to show your daughter how much she is loved. To keep her from ending up like me, with no family around for the good times and the bad."

"But what if she gets hurt in the cross fire between her mother and me?"

"You'll see that it doesn't happen."

He moved closer, reaching out to Kate. "None of this has to stand between us."

"You never said what it is you want for us."

His hands lowered to his sides. "Why do you need it defined? Can't we just take it one day at a time?"

She drew in a breath and leveled her shoulders. "At the beginning, I thought that something casual would be enough. But it isn't. Soon Molly will be getting out of the hospital and she'll be asking questions about you and me. What do I tell her if I don't even know the answers myself?"

Lucas raked his fingers through his hair and moved to the other side of the room. "I don't know if I can make a new start. Commitments haven't exactly worked out for me if you haven't noticed."

"I'm not asking you for a commitment. I'm just asking if you care enough about me to explore a future together. Can you do that?"

Before he could say a word, her phone buzzed. She wanted to ignore it. Lucas's next words were so important, but if it was the hospital, she had to take it. She held up a finger, stemming off his response. She withdrew her phone from her pocket.

After a brief conversation with Nurse Judy, Kate turned to him. "I have to leave."

CHAPTER SIXTEEN

KATE SAT BESIDE Molly's bed and watched her little girl sleep peacefully. The night before, the hospital had called because Molly had woken up from a nightmare, crying inconsolably for her daddy. Inside Kate seethed over the man being so thoughtless about carelessly dropping in and out of his child's life.

At least Lucas didn't put his daughter through that kind of hurt, but he could do so much more. He could be a reliable part of his daughter's life, if he'd get past his worries. Sure, it might not be easy for him to deal with his ex-wife, but she knew how important it was for a child. And she just couldn't be involved with someone who wasn't there for his family through thick and thin.

She watched her daughter take a late-day nap after one of her treatments. In a couple of hours the fund-raiser was due to kick off. She'd been counting on Chad to watch over their daughter while she attended the event and met with donors. Chad hadn't been thrilled about the idea of being left out of the swanky party, as he put it, but she'd pushed how important it was for Molly and he'd grudgingly relented. So much for him being there for them.

"How's she doing?" came a very soft male voice.

Kate jerked around to find Lucas standing just inside the room. His face was drawn and his eyes were bloodshot as though he hadn't gotten any sleep. She hated how she'd had to run out on their conversation the night before. So much had been left unsaid.

"She's doing better." Kate still got angry every time she thought of how Chad had skipped out, leaving Molly disappointed and heartbroken. "I thought you'd be at the house getting ready for the party tonight."

"Between my assistant and Aunt Connie, they have everything under control. What they really need is you."

Kate's gaze strayed to her sleeping daughter. "I can't leave her alone."

"But you are needed for something very important."

The house was complete. The party was under control. She couldn't think of a single thing that needed her attention. "What is it?"

He pulled a black velvet box from behind his back. "I need you to wear this tonight when you meet your guests."

Excitement pulsed in her veins. "Is this from the Fiery Hearts line?"

"Yes, it is. I know how anxious you've been to get the first glimpse. I only have a few of the pieces, but they are the stars."

"Hurray!" She quietly clapped her hands together in excitement. "Show me."

He flipped open the lid and her mouth dropped open at the heart-shaped ruby and pearl choker with a matching bracelet and earrings. She reached out to trace her finger over them.

"They're gorgeous."

"You approve?"

She nodded, still taking in their beauty. Nurse Judy entered the room to check Molly's vitals.

"Look, Judy." Kate pointed at the sparkling jewelry. "Aren't they gorgeous?"

"They're stunning. Someone sure knows how to pick out great gifts."

"This isn't a gift." Kate shook her head. "These are part of Carrington Gems' newest line."

"Actually," Lucas interrupted, "they are for Kate to wear to the party tonight."

"I couldn't." Kate pressed a hand to her chest, feeling a bit flustered. "You were supposed to have some beautiful model show them off."

He smiled and continued holding the jewelry for her to take. Judy moved over to Molly's bed while Kate tried to figure out what this all meant…if anything.

He gazed deep into her eyes as he pressed the box into her hands. "I can't think of anyone more beautiful than you."

"But…but I can't. I have to stay here."

"This is one party you aren't going to miss. And that's why I'm here. I will sit with Molly."

"You? You're the one who should be at the party. It's your house."

"Ah…but this evening is your creation. And you are the infamous woman in the photo that everyone wants to meet. You will be the star."

She hated that he had a point. This was her party—her idea. The thought that people were going to attend with the interest in meeting her made her stomach quiver.

"And," he added, "I need you to be the face of Carrington Gems."

"Me? I couldn't." She worried her bottom lip. "You need someone beautiful—"

"Someone just like you. And if you need anything my aunt and my assistant will be on hand."

Kate cast a hesitant glance at Molly. She really didn't want to leave her, but this fund-raiser was vital for her surgery. Maybe if she just slipped out for an hour or two…

Judy caught her gaze and smiled. "Go. Molly will be fine. There are plenty of people around here who will keep an eye on her. And I promise we will call you if anything comes up."

Kate stood, still feeling so unsure about this arrangement. She looked into Lucas's steady blue gaze and could feel his strength grounding her. He placed the jewelry case in her hand.

"There's a car waiting downstairs to whisk you off to the ball."

"Just like Cinderella."

"Most definitely."

If only her Prince Charming was going to meet her at the party. But this wasn't a fairy tale. This was reality. She'd been on her own before—why should tonight be any different?

Lucas settled back in the chair, leafing through the financial magazine he'd brought along. He couldn't remember the last time he'd been able to sit down and read something besides sales reports and marketing projections. He glanced over at Molly as she cuddled with the pink teddy bear in her sleep. She was so cute—so like her mother.

"Okay, you can go."

He glanced up, finding Judy standing there. "Go where?"

"Cinderella needs her Prince Charming. So off to the ball with you."

"I can't. I promised to watch over Molly."

"I just got off duty and my husband said he'd entertain our little ones with a pizza and movie so I have the evening free. I know you're dying to be with Kate. So go."

"Is it that obvious?"

She nodded.

"Do you think Kate will mind? I mean, I don't know how this works."

"Kate has become a friend. It'll be okay. Remember, I

am a nurse. Molly will be in good hands." She sent him a reassuring smile.

Lucas prayed that Judy was right. He headed out the door and rushed home, finding the mansion all lit up. It'd been so many years since it'd come to life like this. Instead of the dread he thought he'd feel, he was excited to see Kate. He had something to tell her…something very important.

And what could be better than telling her at the party? It would be a night to remember. Anticipation flooded his veins as he moved with lightning speed through the back door, past the servers dressed in old-fashioned police uniforms. He chuckled to himself at the irony of having police officers serving drinks at a prohibition party. Kate certainly had a sense of humor.

He quickly showered and changed into his tux. By then the party was in full swing. He really didn't want to face the people or the questions. But he had to do this for Kate.

He plastered on a smile and worked his way through the milling guests decked out in 1920s attire from fringe dresses to black pinstripe suits and hats. It was like walking back in time. He smiled and shook hands with people he knew. Some patted him on the back, congratulating him on an excellent party and his choice of such a gorgeous hostess. Lucas promised to stop back later to talk and moved onward.

His gaze searched the crowded living room where a few people were dancing to big-band music. But Kate was nowhere to be seen. He scanned the foyer, followed by the dining room but still no luck. Was it possible she was upstairs showing people around? He started for the steps when he spotted his aunt.

"Do you know where Kate is?"

"Aren't you supposed to be with Molly?"

"Judy got off duty and offered to sit with her so I could

be here for Kate. I really need to talk to her, but I haven't been able to catch up with her."

"Finally came to your senses about her, didn't you?"

He nodded. "If she'll give me a chance."

"I think you'll find her showing some interested guests the prohibition tunnel. But Lucas…"

He didn't have time to chat. He'd been waiting too long for this conversation. Actually, instead of words he intended to show her that he could be the man she needed him to be…the man his family needed him to be.

At last he found her on the landing, talking to an older, familiar gentleman, but Lucas couldn't recall his name. He gazed up at her. A cute black hat was settled over her short bobbed hair. She looked adorable. The Fiery Hearts ruby and pearl choker sparkled on her long neck. His pulse picked up its pace as he imagined replacing the necklace with a string of kisses.

His gaze slid down, taking in every breathtaking detail. In a vintage black dress, her creamy arms were bare except for the matching bracelet. A murmur of approval grew in his throat, but he had enough sense about him to stifle it.

The dropped waist on her dress lent itself to a short skirt, which showed off Kate's long legs in black stockings and black heels. He'd never ever get tired of looking at her. She was by far the most beautiful woman and the ideal choice to wear the Carrington Gems. He gave in to an impulse and let off a long, low whistle.

Kate turned and color tinged her cheeks. He ascended the steps and made a hasty apology to the gentleman before taking her hand and guiding her up the steps.

Kate stopped at the top of the stairs, refusing to take another step. "Lucas, you're supposed to be at the hospital."

"Judy is sitting with Molly. She said I couldn't miss being here for you and I have something to show you."

He couldn't wait to show her the nursery that he'd

changed into a little girl's room—a room for Carrie. If it wasn't for Kate, he might not have understood that letting go of his daughter might hurt her more than fighting to have her in his life. He owed Kate a debt of gratitude.

She withdrew her hand. "Can it wait? I have guests to greet."

"It's important. I've done a lot of thinking about what you said about the future. Just give me a minute to show you what I've come up with."

Her eyes lit up and sparkled with interest. "Since you put it that way, lead the way."

He smiled. This night was going to be unforgettable for both of them. It would be a new beginning full of countless possibilities. His chest filled with a strange sensation— dare it be hope.

"Ms. Whitley." One of the young male servers rushed up the stairs. "Umm...Ms. Whitley." The young man's face filled with color. "I'm sorry to disturb you. I...umm... You're needed downstairs."

She flashed a smile, visibly easing the man's discomfort. "What's the problem?"

"There's a gentleman downstairs. He says he needs to speak with you."

"Please tell him I'll be down in a moment."

The young man shook his head. "He isn't an invited guest. At least I don't think he is. He isn't dressed up. The man says he needs to speak with you right away."

"I'm coming." The young man nodded and hustled back down the stairs while Kate turned to Lucas. "It must be Chad. Seems he came to his senses about leaving. Molly will be so happy. But first I need to have a serious talk with him. Can we finish this later? After the guests leave."

Lucas didn't want to wait. He wanted to show her that he was taking strides to be the man she wanted. But part of that meant having patience—after all, he wasn't going anywhere. Their talk could wait. But that didn't mean he had to like it.

He groaned his impatience and nodded his agreement.

She lifted on her tiptoes and went to press a kiss to his cheek, but he turned his head, catching her lips with his own. He'd never ever tire of kissing her. He went to pull her closer—to deepen the kiss, but she braced her hands on his chest and pushed away. The kiss might have been brief, much too brief, but it promised of more to come.

"Later." She flashed him a teasing smile.

He ran his tongue over his lower lip, savoring her cherry lip balm. He stifled a groan of frustration. He wanted more of her sweet kisses now...and later. Forever.

The last word caught him off guard. He never thought he'd ever use that seven-letter word in terms of a relationship again. But Kate had come into his black-and-white world and somewhere along the way had added all the colors of the rainbow. His heart was healed and ready to fight for those he loved.

How it'd taken so long for him to come to terms with how he felt about Kate was beyond him. Now, he couldn't wait to tell her that he loved her. He was dying to know if she felt the same way. But what choice did he have but to wait? Only a little longer and then he'd have her the rest of the night.

"Let's go greet your ex."

They'd just turned the landing when Kate asked, "So what was it you wanted to show me—"

Her words hung there as she came to an abrupt halt.

"Kate, are you all right?"

When she didn't move, didn't say anything, he followed her line of vision to an older man with white hair standing at the foot of the stairs. He was definitely too old to be Chad. And there was something vaguely familiar about him. In a pair of jeans and a plaid shirt, he certainly wasn't here for the party. The man stared back at Kate with tears in his eyes.

Panic clutched Lucas's chest. The face. The age. The look. It all came together at once. This was Kate's father—her estranged father, Floyd—the man he'd connected with on MyFriends.

A hush fell over the crowd as though they sensed the tension in the room and were checking it out. The paparazzi covering the event for all of the major news outlets moved in closer. Their flashes lit up the room, causing even more people to move in for a closer view. Lucas waved them off and the flashes stopped. But it was too late—the press was going to have a field day with this story. Guilt weighed heavily on Lucas's shoulders.

Floyd placed a foot on the bottom step and Kate took a step back.

"Katie, you look so beautiful all grown up. You're the spitting image of your mother—"

"Don't! Don't say that. There's nothing you could say that I want to hear. Just go."

"Katie girl, I'm sorry—"

Her voice shook. "I don't know why you picked now to pass through my life, but just keep going. You're good at walking away, so don't let the door hit you on the way out."

Floyd's gaze moved to Lucas. A light of recognition filled the man's eyes.

Lucas might not have talked to the man online, but looking back now, he realized even seeking him out and sending a friend request had been too much. The man had already been curious about who he was—all he had to do was look on Lucas's MyFriends page to find a picture of Kate. He'd unwittingly laid out a trail of breadcrumbs that anyone could have followed—including Floyd.

Finding his voice, Lucas said, "You should go. Now."

Kate's shocked look turned in Lucas's direction. He

froze. The breath trapped in his lungs. He wanted to wind back time and change things, but he couldn't any more than he could ease her pain.

"You did this." Her voice vibrated with emotion. "You brought him here, didn't you?"

Her pointed words jabbed at his heart. He wanted to explain and make her understand that he hadn't invited Floyd here. He'd never ever orchestrate a public reunion.

"I didn't invite him—"

Her eyes narrowed. "But you contacted him, didn't you? You couldn't leave well enough alone."

Lucas wanted to deny it, but he couldn't. He was losing the woman he loved and there wasn't a damned thing he could do about it. He merely nodded.

"You had to prove me wrong, didn't you? You had to prove to me that...that he—" she pointed at Floyd "—had some excuse for leaving me just so you could feel better about walking out on your own daughter. I should have never trusted you. When will I ever learn not to trust people?"

"You can trust me—"

Her chin lifted and her eyes shimmered with unshed tears. "No, I can't. You just proved me right. Molly and I are better off on our own."

Lucas could feel the curious gazes boring into his back. He wasn't worried about himself as he was used to providing fodder for the press, but Kate didn't need her private life made public knowledge.

"Kate, this isn't the place for this."

Her brows drew together. "Maybe you should have thought about that before you started poking around in my life. I'm not the one who made it possible for Floyd to be here. You did that all on your own. I should have known I couldn't trust you. I won't make that mistake again."

Kate spun around and sailed up the stairs. Even though he hadn't invited her father here, he had opened Pandora's box. Like Cinderella running off into the night, Lucas knew their fairy tale had just ended.

CHAPTER SEVENTEEN

IT HAD TO BE HERE. It just had to be.

But search as she might, Lucky Ducky was missing.

Kate shoved aside her purse. How could this happen? Ducky was always in her purse. And as Molly's surgery dragged on, Kate was starting to feel nervous. She knew it was silly, but that toy made her feel somehow connected to Molly. She could still envision her sweet smile when she'd handed over the trinket—back before Molly had gotten sick.

With a sigh, Kate slouched back in the stiff hospital chair. Two days had passed since she'd left Lucas at the party. She still couldn't believe he'd stepped so far over the line by contacting her father. She glanced over at Floyd. He sent her a reassuring smile. It was good to have family around. And if it hadn't been for Lucas's meddling, Floyd wouldn't be here. But did that excuse Lucas's actions?

"You've got plenty of time before we hear anything about the surgery," her father said. "Why don't you call that young man of yours and let him know how things are going?"

"I don't see the point. Even if we find a way to get around what he's done, he'll eventually leave."

"I know you don't have any reason to believe me of all people, but not everyone walks away."

"The people in my life do."

"If he really loves you, like I suspect he does, he'll stick." Her father sighed and ran a hand over his day-old stubble. "Don't let my poor decisions color the rest of your life. If you quit letting people into your life, you'll end up old and alone. You know Molly isn't going to stay small forever. Why don't you give him a call and see what happens?"

She hated to admit it, but Floyd had a point. Molly would eventually move on with her own life. But the thought of putting herself out there only to have Lucas reject her scared her to bits.

"I doubt he'll want to talk to me."

"You'll never know until you try. From the sounds of it, you both have some apologizing to do. But he appears to be a good guy. Is he?"

She nodded. "But I can't forget that he went behind my back and contacted you."

"Everyone makes mistakes." Her father reached over and grasped her hand, giving it a squeeze. "If it wasn't for him, I might never have gotten up my courage to track you down. I know we still have a long ways to go, but you are willing to give me a second chance and what I did was so much worse than Lucas's misstep."

But it was more than Lucas contacting her father—it was the way he was willing to back quietly out of his daughter's life. Sure, he had his reasons, but none of them were good enough to walk away from someone you loved. A lump formed in the back of her throat. But wasn't that what she was about to do—walk away from the man she loved without giving him a chance to explain?

The realization that she still loved Lucas even after everything that had happened jolted her. What should she do now? Ignore her feelings and hope they went away?

"Call Lucas."

It was as if her father was privy to her thoughts. Was that even possible after their extended separation?

Just yesterday morning, the day after the party, Floyd had caught up with her here at the hospital. At first, she hadn't wanted to hear what he had to say, but eventually she reasoned that if she ever majorly messed up with Molly, she'd want to be given a chance to explain.

Her father had struggled with the words, but at last he admitted how he'd gotten caught up in gambling and put the family in deep debt. Things continued downhill to the point where he got involved with some unsavory loan sharks. A shiver had run over her skin when he'd described how they'd roughed him up when he didn't have the money he owed. Unwilling to make his family targets, he'd left. It'd taken him years to conquer his addiction, but by then he figured it was too late to fix things.

"The difference is you were trying to protect us." Though she still hadn't made peace with her father's choices, she was willing to give him a chance as long as he was up-front and honest with her. But there was something she'd wondered about. "Mom never spoke of you after you left. I never understood why."

"I hurt her deeply." Her father leaned back in his seat and ran a hand over his aged face. "Things were so messed up back then. I loved her, but love doesn't mean that two people are good for each other. Your mother and I, we were too different. You and Lucas, do you have things in common?"

She thought of the man who could make her heart skip a beat with just a look. They were different, but not to extremes. They liked the same sorts of food. They both enjoyed quiet evenings at home. And they both thought family was important. Secretly she was missing Lucas and wishing he could be here with her now. When he held her close she felt safe and protected—as if nothing could go wrong.

The push-pull emotions raged inside her. But when it came down to the bottom line, she loved him. Nothing had changed that.

And there was something he'd intended to show her. If she didn't talk to him, she would always wonder what it had been. Would it have made a difference?

Oh, what would it hurt to let him know that thanks to his help, Molly was having her surgery? And she would thank him for bringing her father back into her life. She owed him that much.

"I'm going to step out into the hall." Kate got to her feet. "Can you let me know if there's any news?"

"Sure. Go ahead. I'll be right here."

"You don't know how many years I've waited to hear those words." She started to lean down to kiss his weathered cheek but hesitated. They had a long way to go before they'd be that close. "Thanks."

"Things will be different from here on out. I promise." His voice cracked with emotion. "Now go patch things up with Lucas."

"I'll try." But she wasn't getting her hopes up too high. She already missed Lucas terribly. To set herself up for another fall would be devastating.

Lucas waited as the hospital elevator stopped at each floor, allowing people to get on and off. Every muscle in his body was tense. Logic said he shouldn't be here. He didn't want to do anything to upset Kate on such an intense day. But he had something important to give her. He stared down at Lucky Ducky in his hand. He ran his thumb over the toy and prayed some of that luck would rub off on him.

His cell phone vibrated and he retrieved it from his pocket. He was surprised to see Kate's name flash across the screen. "Hello."

"Lucas, it's Kate. I…I needed to talk to you."

"Where are you?"

"At the hospital. Today's Molly's surgery."

"Hang on a sec." He worked his way through the throng

of people and stepped off the elevator into the hallway. "Any word on how she's doing?"

"Nothing yet. We should hear something soon."

He heard the echo of Kate's voice. He took a few steps and peered down the hallway, finding her leaning against the wall with her back to him. He hesitated, not knowing what sort of greeting to expect. He reconciled himself to the fact that he deserved whatever she dished up.

He continued down the hallway. "Kate, turn around."

When she did, surprise lit up her eyes. She looked bone-tired and he wanted nothing more than to wrap his arms around her. But he couldn't. It wouldn't be what she wanted after the way things had played out with her father. If only he'd thought it through and realized how easy it'd be for the man to track them down via the party announcement on his MyFriends account.

But it all came down to the fact that he shouldn't have been meddling. He'd totally messed things up. And the only thing he could think to do was apologize and hope she'd forgive him.

They stared at each other, but he was unable to read her thoughts. Her face was devoid of emotion.

"I'm sorry," they said in unison.

"You are?" Again they spoke over each other.

Kate laughed. Her sweet tones washed over him, easing the tension in his neck and shoulders. Maybe there was a chance she didn't hate him. Maybe it wasn't too late to fix things. But he knew he was getting ahead of himself. First things first.

"Kate, I'm sorry about contacting your father. I just thought… Oh, heck, I don't know what I was thinking." He ran a hand over his tense neck. "Maybe I thought if I could show you that your father was a better man than you thought that I'd have a better chance with you."

"You were that serious about me that you thought you had to go to such lengths to win me over?"

He nodded, fighting back the urge to pull her close and do away with the talking. But something still needed to be said. "Remember how I wanted to show you something at the party?"

She nodded.

"I was wondering how you feel about yellow gingham? At least I think that's what the woman at the store called them—"

"Called what?" Kate's brows drew together as she stared up at him.

"The new curtains I put in the nursery. Well, it isn't a nursery anymore. It's a little girl's room."

Kate's eyes widened. "What are you saying?"

He cleared his throat. "If it wasn't for you, I wouldn't have realized that even though I was working so hard to shield Carrie from seeing her parents fight, she might just be as hurt by the knowledge that I didn't go the extra mile for her. I had a very interesting conversation with my ex-wife's new husband. It seems he's a lot more reasonable since he has kids and an ex-wife. Anyway, he's going to talk to Elaina, and I have my attorney working on a formal visitation schedule. It will be a gradual process until Carrie knows me, but someday I plan to bring her to New York."

"That's wonderful. I'm so happy for you and your daughter."

"And you? Will you be happy, too?"

"That's one of the reasons I was calling you. I wanted to tell you, or I mean, I wanted to thank you for bridging the gap with Floyd. You were right, too. He did have a reason for what he did. As for why he never contacted me later, well, we're working on it."

"Still, I'm sorry I overstepped."

"Is that why you're here? To apologize?"

Then he recalled the trinket in his hand. "Actually, I came to drop off Lucky Ducky. I found him on the floor next to the dresser in your room. I figured today of all days you wouldn't want to be without him."

Kate immediately reached for the keychain and held it close. "Thank you. I was searching for this earlier and I was really upset when I thought I'd lost it. I know it's silly to be so emotional over a cheap toy, but Molly gave it to me and that makes it very special."

And now he had one more important thing to ask her. His gut churned. "I was thinking maybe of starting over and selling the mansion. I'd like to have my new family start in a new home and make new memories." He could see the surprise light up her eyes, but he kept going. He had one chance at getting this right. "Kate, would you consider staying with me and being part of that new future?"

Had she heard Lucas correctly? He wanted a future with her?

Before her brain had a chance to formulate an answer, her father's voice called out to her. She turned and saw Dr. Hawthorne enter the surgical waiting room. Her heart raced. *Please let it be good news.*

"It's the surgeon. Come on," she called over her shoulder to Lucas.

They rushed down the hallway and joined her father. The surgeon sat down and pulled off his scrub cap. "The surgery was a success."

Tears of joy sprang to Kate's eyes. Her baby had made it. She swiped at her cheeks while Lucas gave her a reassuring smile that made her insides flutter.

The doctor continued going over the results of the surgery. "Lastly you should know that there is no guarantee the tumor won't come back. She'll need to be monitored on a regular basis."

His words rang loud and clear in Kate's mind. A guarantee. That's what she'd been looking for with Lucas. She'd been hoping for the impossible—a man who wouldn't ever fail her. And that was asking the impossible.

Life didn't come with guarantees. You simply had to make the best of the good…and the bad times. A step-by-step process. And she couldn't think of anyone that she wanted to be by her side during that journey more than Lucas.

She reached out to Lucas and slipped her hand in his. His touch was warm and strong. Her heart surged with love.

When her father walked with the surgeon into the hallway, she turned to Lucas and wrapped her arms over his broad shoulders and held on tight. She never wanted to let go.

At last, she'd found what she'd been searching for…her home. It wasn't a building with marble stairs and spacious rooms—it was right here in Lucas's arms…in his heart.

She pulled back just enough to gaze up at him. "I love you."

"I love you, too."

She swiped away more tears of joy. "This has been a day of miracles."

"Does this mean that you'd be willing to face the future together?"

She nodded. "And I think the perfect place to start a whole new life is the Carrington mansion."

"You do? You're not just saying that?"

With her fingertip, she crossed her heart. "I love it and I love you."

EPILOGUE

One year later...

"IT'S GORGEOUS. I don't think there's a single cloud in the sky."

Lucas's gaze never left Kate's face. "Definitely gorgeous."

She glanced over at him and rolled her eyes. "I was talking about this spring day. It's so warm and sunny. Makes me feel like I could conquer anything I set my mind to."

The hum of happy voices filled the air as they stood side by side in Central Park. Lucas smiled. He just couldn't help it. Life was good and he was doing his best to savor every moment.

He wrapped an arm around his wife's shoulders, pulling her close. "You know when I brought you here for the first time, I never dreamed this was possible."

"Well, you better believe it, because those are our daughters over there petting that horse. Looks like they'll be wanting a carriage ride next."

His mind tripped back in time. "I remember a certain carriage ride and how it earned me a kiss—"

"And a photo in the paper of us in quite a steamy lip-lock."

"I couldn't help myself. I had to see if your kisses were

as sweet as I remembered. But they ended up being even sweeter. Want to give it a try now?"

She smiled and shook her head. "Do you have spring fever or something?"

"Just a guy in love with the prettiest girl around."

The past year hadn't been the easiest, not by a long shot. But thanks to Kate, he had opened his eyes and realized that caving in to his ex-wife wasn't in the best interest of their daughter. Carrie was very much a part of him and he felt whole with his family around him. And though it'd been tough at first, he hadn't given up. This was Carrie's first visit to New York and she couldn't have been happier having a sister and another family.

"You seem awfully chipper for a workaholic who has been away from the office all week. Admit it, this staycation isn't so bad."

"Maybe you have a thing or two to teach me after all." He still loved his work, but he'd learned to delegate things when his workload became too heavy. Because he'd found something he loved even more than Carrington Gems—his family.

Kate glanced lovingly up at her husband. How was it possible for him to grow more handsome with each passing day? A smile pulled at her lips.

This past Christmas, they'd had a small ceremony with Molly standing tall by her side. The event had taken place at the Carrington mansion with just a few friends and family invited, including his aunt and her father, who hit it off quite well. It was great having people in their lives to create such precious memories.

Kate's gaze moved from her husband to Molly's glowing face as she ran a hand down the horse's side while her grandfather talked with the horse's owner. "It's hard to believe a year ago Molly was in the hospital. Now, she's a smiling, healthy little girl. I know there's still a possibility that the tumor will return, but with lots of hope and prayers, it's gone for good."

Lucas drew her closer to his side and kissed the top of her head. "Molly is going to have a long, happy life."

"I believe you're right. And now I have one more thing to tell you that will make this day even better."

He gazed down at her. "I don't think that's possible."

She pulled away from him so she could look him in the eyes. "Is that a challenge, Mr. Carrington?"

"Yes, it is, Mrs. Carrington."

She smiled victoriously because she already knew that she'd won. "How would you feel about having a baby?"

The color drained from his face. Not quite the reaction she was expecting. Then his eyes grew round like quarters. And she couldn't be certain, but she'd hazard a guess that he'd stopped breathing.

"Lucas, do you need to sit down?"

"A baby?"

"Yes, a baby. You are happy about this? Aren't you?"

"Woohoo!" He scooped her up in his arms and swung her around in a circle. "We're having a baby!"

His lips pressed to hers. Her heart swelled with love for the most amazing man she'd ever known. Their life might not come with a preordained path, but she knew as long as Lucas was by her side, they'd get through the twists and turns—together.

* * * * *

THE TYCOON AND THE
WEDDING PLANNER

BY
KANDY SHEPHERD

Kandy Shepherd swapped a fast-paced career as a magazine editor for a life writing romance. She lives on a small farm in the Blue Mountains near Sydney, Australia, with her husband, daughter and a menagerie of animal friends. Kandy believes in love at first sight and real-life romance—they worked for her!

Kandy loves to hear from her readers. Visit her website at: www.kandyshepherd.com.

To my wonderful husband and daughter
for your love and inspiration-thank you!

Poor Kate.

CHAPTER ONE

As SHE WENT about her lunchtime front-of-house duties at the Hotel Harbourside restaurant, Kate Parker was only too aware of the ill-concealed interest in her. The too-interested glances quickly averted; the undertones; the murmurs.

Poor Kate.

If she heard—or sensed—that phrase one more time, she'd scream.

Her and her big, big mouth.

Why, oh, why had she made such a big deal of her child-hood crush on Jesse Morgan? She wished she'd never told a soul, let alone all and sundry in her home town of Dol-phin Bay, that the next time Jesse was back she'd finally let him know how she really felt about him.

Because now he was home, now she had kissed him for the first time since they'd been just kids fifteen years ago, and it had turned out a total disaster. She'd felt nothing. *Absolutely nothing.* Instead of turning her on, his kiss had turned her off. She'd fought the urge to wipe her mouth with the back of her hand.

And Jesse? He'd been as embarrassed and awkward as she'd been. They'd parted, barely able to look each other in the eye.

She cringed at the memory—as she'd cringed a hundred times already—as painfully fresh today as it had been three days ago when it had occurred.

And now everyone in their small community knew she'd made an utter fool of herself by believing there could be anything more between her and Jesse than the affection due to a family friend she'd known since they'd both been in nappies.

Poor Kate.

The air was thick with pity for her. She looked around the restaurant; many of the tables were already full for Sunday lunch.

She wanted to run out the door, down the steps onto the beach below and get home to lock herself in her bedroom with the music turned up loud.

Instead, she girded herself against the gossip. She forced herself to smile. First, because a warm, confident smile was essential to any role in hospitality. And second, because she couldn't bear for any of those too-interested townsfolk to guess how churned up, anxious and panicky she was feeling inside.

It meant nothing, people, she wanted to broadcast to the room in general. *Less than nothing. I walked away from that darn kiss completely unaffected.*

But that wouldn't be completely true.

Because the Great Kiss Disaster had left her doubting everything she'd believed about who was the right man for her. She'd discovered the man she'd thought was Mr Perfect was not, in fact. So where did she go next? How could she ever trust her judgement of men again?

Smile. Smile. Smile.

The restaurant in the award-winning hotel was one of the best places to eat in Dolphin Bay. More people were arriving for lunch. She had a job she valued. She wanted to be promoted to hotel manager and she wouldn't achieve that by moping around feeling sorry for herself.

She took a deep, steadying breath, forced her lips to curve upwards in a big welcome and aimed it at the next customer—a man who had pushed his way through the glass doors that led from the steps from the beach and into the restaurant.

She nearly dropped the bottle of wine she was holding with hands that had gone suddenly nerveless. He caught her smile and nodded in acknowledgement.

Where the heck had he *come from?*

She'd never seen him in Dolphin Bay before, that was for sure.

Dark-haired, tall and powerfully built, his broad shoulders and muscular arms strained against his black T-shirt, his hard thighs against the worn denim of his jeans. His heavy black boots were hardly seaside resort wear, but they worked. Boy, did they work.

No wonder the two young waitresses on duty stampeded past her to show him to the best table in the house. She had to hold herself back from pulling rank and elbowing them out of the way to get to him first.

His stance was easy, confident, as he waited to be shown to a table. Her heart started to pound double-quick time. When had she last felt the kind of awareness of a man that made her ache for him to notice her?

But, when his gaze did turn in her direction, she quickly ducked her head and studiously read the label on the wine bottle without registering a single word.

She looked up again to see the young waitress who had won the race to get to him first looking up at him in open admiration and laughing at something he'd said. Did the guy realise half the female heads in the room had swivelled to attention when he'd strode in?

Not that he looked like he cared much about what people thought. His dark brown hair was several months away from a haircut—shoved back off his face with his fingers rather than a comb, by the look of it. The dark growth on his jaw was halfway to a beard.

He looked untamed. Sexy. And dangerous.

Way too dangerous.

She was shocked by the powerful punch of attraction that slammed her, the kind of visceral pull that had caused her such terrible hurt in the past. That was so different from how she'd felt for safe, familiar Jesse. She never wanted to feel again for any man that wild compulsion. The kind, when it had got out of control, that had led her down paths she never wanted to revisit.

Not now. Not ever.

She let the smile freeze on her face, stepped back and watched the other girl usher the handsome stranger to his table. She would hold off on her obligatory meet and greet to a new customer until she'd got herself together enough to mask her awareness of his appeal with breezy nonchalance. To use the light, semi-flirtatious tone that worked so well in hospitality.

Because, after all, he was just a stranger who'd breezed into town. She'd overreacted, big-time. She didn't need to fear that rush of attraction for an unsuitable man. He was just a customer she would never see again after he'd finished his lunch and moved on. He didn't even seem the kind of guy who would leave a generous tip.

Sam Lancaster knew he should be admiring the glorious view of the Dolphin Bay Harbour with its heritage-listed stone breakwaters, its fleet of fishing vessels and, beyond, the aquamarine waters of the Pacific Ocean. This stretch of the New South Wales south coast was known for its scenic beauty.

But he couldn't keep his eyes off the even more appealing view of the sassy, red-haired front-of-house manager who flitted from table to table in the Hotel Harbourside restaurant, pausing to chat with each customer about their orders.

Sam wasn't in the habit of flirting with strangers. He wasn't the type of man who always had a ready quip for a pretty flight attendant, a cute girl behind a bar or a hot new trainer at the gym. Consequently, he was stymied by his out-of-the-blue attraction to this woman.

She hadn't reached his table yet, and he found himself willing her to turn his way. In his head, he played over and over what clever remark he might utter when she did.

She wasn't movie-star beautiful, but there was a vibrancy about her that kept his gaze returning to her again and again: the way the sunlight streaming through the windows turned the auburn of her tied-back hair to a glorious, flaming halo. The sensual sway of her hips in the modest black skirt. The murmur of her laughter as she chatted to a customer. All were compelling. But, when she finally headed his way, the warmth of her wide smile and the welcome that lit her green eyes made him forget every word he had rehearsed.

Her smile was of the practised meet-and-greet type she'd bestowed on every other customer in the room. He knew that. But that didn't make it any less entrancing. She paused in front of his table. This close, he could see she had a sprinkling of freckles across the bridge of her nose and that her smile was punctuated with the most charming dimples.

What was a woman as sensational as this one doing in a backwater like Dolphin Bay?

Good manners prompted him get up to greet her, stumbling a little around the compact, ultra-modern chair not designed for a man of his height and build. Her startled step backwards made him realise she was just doing her job and a customer would usually remain seated. He gritted his teeth; he really wasn't good at this. Where was a clever quip when he needed one?

But she quickly recovered herself. 'Hi, I'm Kate Parker; welcome to Hotel Harbourside. Thank you for joining us for lunch.' Her voice was low and throaty without being self-consciously sexy and transformed the standard customer greeting spiel into something he'd like to put on a repeat loop.

He thrust out his hand in greeting. 'Sam Lancaster.'

Again she looked startled. He'd startled himself—since when did he shake hands with waitresses? But she took his hand in a firm, businesslike grip. He noted she wasn't wearing a ring of any kind.

'Hi, Sam Lancaster,' she said, her teasing tone making a caress of the everyday syllables of his name. 'Is everything okay at your table?'

He cleared his throat. 'F…fine.'

That was all he managed to choke out. Not one other word of that carefully thought out repartee.

Damn it.

He was a man used to managing a large, successful company. To never being short of female company if he didn't want it. But he couldn't seem to get it together in front of this girl.

He realised he'd gripped her warm, slender hand for a moment too long and he released it.

She glanced down at the menu on the table, then back up at him, the smile still dancing in her eyes. She knew. Of course she knew. A woman like this would be used to the most powerful of men stuttering in her presence. 'Have you ordered lunch yet? I can recommend the grilled snapper, freshly caught this morning.'

'Thank you, no. I'll order when my friend gets to the table.'

One winged auburn eyebrow quirked. 'Oh,' she said. 'A lady friend?' She flushed. 'Forgive me. None of my business, of course.'

'Nothing to forgive,' he said, pleased he'd given her cause to wonder about the sex of his lunch companion. 'While I'm waiting for *him,* I'm admiring the view of the harbour,' he said. 'It's really something.'

But the view of her was so much more enticing.

'No charge for the view,' she said. 'It's on the house.' She laughed, a low, husky laugh that made him think of slow, sensual kisses on lazy summer afternoons.

He couldn't look at her in case he gave away the direction of his thoughts. Instead he glanced to the full-length windows that faced east. 'I reckon it must be one of the most beautiful harbours on the south coast.'

'Hey, just on the south coast? I say the most beautiful in the whole of Australia,' she said with mock indignation.

'Okay. So it's the very best harbour in Australia—if not the world,' he agreed, playing along with her.

'That's better,' she said with a dimpled smile.

'I like the dolphins too.'

'You mean the real ones or the fake ones plastered on every building in town?'

'I didn't see them on *every* building,' he said. 'But I thought the dolphin rubbish bins everywhere had character.'

She put her hand on her forehead in a theatrical gesture of mock despair. 'Oh, please don't talk to me about those dolphin bins. People around here get into fights over whether they should go or they should stay, now Dolphin Bay has expanded so much. It was such a sleepy town when they were originally put up.'

'What do you think?' he asked.

'Me? I have to confess to being a total dolphin-bin freak. I love 'em! I adored them when I was a kid and would defend them to the last dorsal fin if anyone tried to touch them.'

She mimicked standing with her arms outstretched behind her as if there was something she was shielding from harm. The pretend-fierce look on her face was somewhat negated by her dimples.

In turn, Sam assumed a mock stance of defence. 'I'm afraid. Very afraid. I won't hurt your dolphin bins.'

Her peal of laughter rang out over the hum of conversation and clatter of cutlery. 'Don't be afraid.' She pretend-pouted. 'I'm harmless, I assure you.'

Harmless? She was far from harmless when it came to this instant assault on his senses.

'Lucky I said I liked the bins, then,' he said.

'Indeed. I might not have been responsible for my actions if you'd derided them.'

He laughed. She was enchanting.

'Seriously, though,' she continued. 'I've lived here for most of my life and I never tire of it, dolphins and all. April is one of the best times to enjoy this area. The water's still warm and the Easter crowds have gone home. Are you passing through?'

He shook his head. 'I'm staying in Dolphin Bay for the next week. I'll check in to the hotel after lunch.'

'That's great to hear.' She hit him with that smile again. 'I'm the deputy manager. It'll be wonderful to have you as our guest.'

Could he read something into that? Did she feel even

just a hint of the instant attraction he felt for her? Or was she just being officially enthusiastic?

'Let me know if there's anything you need,' she said.

A dinner date with you?

Gorgeous Kate Parker had probably spent longer than she should at his table. There were other customers for her to meet and greet. But Sam couldn't think of an excuse to keep her there any longer. He was going to have to bite the bullet and ask her out. For a drink; for dinner; any opportunity to get to know her.

'Kate, I—'

He was just about to suggest a date when his mobile phone buzzed to notify him of a text message. He ignored it. It buzzed again.

'Go on, please check it,' Kate said, taking a step back from his table. 'It might be important.'

Sam gritted his teeth. At this moment nothing—even a message from the multi-national company that was bidding for a takeover of Lancaster & Son Construction—was more important than ensuring he saw this girl again. He pulled the phone from his pocket and scanned the text.

He looked up at Kate. 'My friend Jesse is running late,' he grumbled. 'I hope he gets here soon. After a four-hour trip from Sydney, I'm starving.'

Kate's green eyes widened. 'Jesse?' Her voice sounded strangled. 'You mean…Jesse Morgan?'

'Do you know him? I guess you do.'

She nodded. 'Yes. It's a small town. I…I know him well.'

So Kate was a friend of Jesse's? That made getting to know her so much easier. Suddenly she wasn't just staff at the hotel and he a guest; they were connected through a mutual friend.

It was the best piece of news he'd had all day.

* * *

Kate was reeling. Hotter-than-hot Sam Lancaster was a friend of Jesse's? That couldn't, couldn't be. What unfair quirk of coincidence was this?

Despite her initial misgiving about Sam, she'd found she liked his smile, his easy repartee. She'd found herself looking forward to seeing him around the hotel. No way was she looking for romance—not with the Jesse humiliation so fresh. But she could admire how good-looking Sam was, even let herself flirt ever so lightly, knowing he'd be gone in a week. But the fact he was Jesse's friend complicated things.

What if Jesse had told Sam about the kiss disaster? She'd thought she'd fulfilled her cringe quotient for the day. But, at the thought of Sam hearing about the kiss calamity, she cringed a little more.

She should quickly back away from Sam's table. The last thing she wanted was to encounter Jesse not only in front of this gorgeous guy, but also the restaurant packed with too-interested observers, their gossip antennae finely tuned.

But she simply could not resist a few more moments in Sam Lancaster's company before she beat a retreat— maybe to the kitchen, at least to the other side of the room—so she could avoid a confrontation with Jesse when he eventually arrived.

'Where do you know Jesse from?' she asked, trying to sound chirpy rather than churning with anxiety.

'Jesse's a mate of mine from university days in Sydney,' Sam said in his deep, resonant voice. 'We were both studying engineering. Jesse was two years behind me, but we played on the same uni football team. We used to go skiing together, too.'

So that made Sam around aged thirty to her twenty-eight.

'And you've stayed friends ever since?' she said.

She'd so much prefer it if he and Jesse were casual acquaintances.

'We lost touch for a while but met up again two years ago on a building site in India, rebuilding the villages damaged in those devastating floods.'

She hadn't put darkly handsome Sam down as the type who would do active charity work in a far-flung part of the world. It was a surprise of the best kind.

'So you work for the same international aid organisation as Jesse?' she asked.

'No. I worked as a volunteer during my vacation. We volunteers provided the grunt work. In my case, as a carpenter.'

That figured. His hand had felt callused when she'd shaken it earlier.

'I'm seriously impressed. That's so…noble.' This hot, hunky man, who would have female hearts fluttering wherever he went, spent his hard-earned vacation working without pay in a developing country in what no doubt were dirty and dangerous conditions.

'Noble? That's a very nice thing to say, but I'd hardly call it that. It was hot and sweaty and damn hard work,' he said. 'I was just glad to be of help in what was a desperate situation for so many people.'

'I bet it wasn't much fun, but you were actually helping people in trouble. In my book, that's noble—and you won't make me think otherwise.'

He shrugged those impressively broad shoulders. 'It was an eye-opener. Sure made me appreciate the life I have at home.'

'I've thought about volunteering, but I've never actually done it. What made you sign up?'

His face tightened and shutters seemed to come down over his deep, brown eyes. 'It just seemed a good thing to do. A way to give back.' The tone of his voice made her wonder if he was telling her everything. But then, why should he?

Sam Lancaster was a guest—his personal life was none of her concern. In fact, she had to be careful not to overstep the mark of what was expected of a deputy manager on front-of-house duty on a busy Sunday.

It was as well to be brought back to reality.

She returned her voice to hospitality impartial. 'I'm so glad it worked out for you.' She glanced down at his menu. 'Do you want to order while you're waiting for Jesse?' It was an effort to say Jesse's name with such disinterest.

'I'll wait for him. Though I'm looking forward to exploring the menu; it looks very good.' Sam glanced around him and nodded approvingly. 'I like the way Ben built this hotel. No wonder it won architectural awards.'

'Ben, as in Jesse's brother? My boss? Owner of Hotel Harbourside?' She couldn't keep the incredulity from her voice.

'I'm friends with Ben as well as Jesse,' he said.

'Of course you would be,' she replied.

If she'd entertained for one moment the idea of following up her attraction to Sam Lancaster, she squashed it right now. She'd grown up with Ben too. The Morgans had been like family. The thought of conducting any kind of relationship with Sam under the watchful, teasing eyes of the Morgan brothers was inconceivable—especially if Jesse had told him about the kiss.

'Do you go way back with Ben, too?'

'He joined Jesse and me on a couple of ski trips to Thredbo,' said Sam. 'We all skied together.'

'More partying and drinking than actual skiing, I'll bet,' she said.

'What happens on ski trip, stays on ski trip,' said Sam with that devastating smile.

Individually, his irregular features didn't make for handsome. But together: the olive skin; the eyes as dark as bitter chocolate; the crooked nose; his sensual mouth; the dark, thick eyebrows, intersected by that intriguing small scar, added up to a face that went a degree more than handsome.

Jesse or Ben had not been hit with the ugly stick, either. She could only imagine what that trio of good-looking guys would have got up to in the party atmosphere of the New South Wales ski slopes. She knew only too well how wild it could be.

She'd gone skiing with her university ski-club during her third year in Sydney for her business degree. The snow-fields were only a day's drive away from Sydney, but they might as well have been a world away.

Social life had outweighed skiing. That winter break they'd all gone crazy with the freedom from study, from families, from rules. If she'd met Sam then she would have gone for him, that was for sure. Instead she'd met someone else. Someone who in subsequent months had hurt her so badly she'd slipped right back into that teenage dream of kind, trustworthy Jesse. Someone who had bred the unease she felt at the thought of dating men with untamed good looks like Sam.

'So you're friends with Ben, too; I didn't know. We all went our separate ways during the time you guys must have met each other.' A thought struck her. 'Ah, now I get it. You're in Dolphin Bay for Ben and Sandy's wedding on Saturday.'

'Correct,' he said. 'Though I'm not one for weddings and all the waste-of-time fuss that surrounds them.'

Kate drew herself up to her full five-foot-five and put her hands on her hips in mock rebuke. 'Waste-of-time fuss? I don't know if I can forgive you for that comment as I happen to be the wedding planner for these particular nuptials.'

'Deputy manager of a hotel like this *and* a wedding planner? You're the very definition of a multi-tasker.'

'I'll take that as a compliment, thank you,' she said. 'I like to keep busy. And I like to know what's going on. Jesse calls me the self-appointed arbiter of everyone's business in Dolphin Bay.'

She regretted the words as soon as they'd slipped out of her mouth. Why, why, why did she have to bring up Jesse's name?

But Sam just laughed. 'That sounds like something Jesse would say. You must be good friends for him to get away with it.'

'We are good friends,' she said.

And that was all they ever should have been. When they'd been still just kids, they'd shared their clumsy, first-ever kiss. But it hadn't happened again until three days ago when she'd provocatively asked her old friend why it had been so long between kisses. A suggestion that had backfired so badly.

'What Jesse says is true,' she continued. 'He calls me a nosy parker. I like to call it a healthy curiosity about what's going on.'

'Necessary qualities for all your various occupations, I would think,' he said.

'Thank you. I think so too. I particularly need to be

on top of the details of Ben's wedding which is aaargh...'
she mimed tearing her hair out '...only six days away.'
She mentally ran through the guest list. 'Now I think of
it, there *is* a Sam on the guest list; I've been meaning to
ask Ben who it was. I don't know anything about him—
uh, I mean *you*.'

Sam spread out both hands in a gesture of invitation.
'I'm an open book. Fire away with the questions.'

She wagged a finger in mock-warning. 'I wouldn't say
that to a stickybeak like me. Give me carte blanche and
you might be here all day answering questions.' *What was
she saying?* 'Uh, I mean as they relate to you as a wedding guest, that is.'

'So I'll limit them,' he said. 'Five questions should be
all you need.'

*Five questions? She'd like to know a heck of a lot more
about Sam Lancaster than she could discover with five
questions.*

'Don't mind if I do,' she said.

Do you have a girlfriend, fiancée, wife?

But she ignored the first question she really wanted to
ask and chose the safe option. 'Okay, so my first question is wedding-menu related—meat, fish or vegetarian?'

'All of the above,' he said without hesitation.

'Good. That makes it easy. Question number two: what
do you plan to do in the days before the wedding? Do you
need me to organise any tours or activities?'

With me as the tour guide, perhaps.

He shook his head. 'No need. There's a work problem
I have to think through.'

She itched with curiosity about what that problem could
be—but questioning him about it went beyond the remit
of wedding-related questions.

'Okay. Just let me know if you change your mind.

There's dolphin-and whale-watching tours. Or hikes to Pigeon Mountain for spectacular views. Now for question number three: do you…?'

Something made her look up and she immediately wished she hadn't. *Jesse.* Coming in late for his lunch. She swallowed a swear word. Why hadn't she made her getaway while she could?

Too distracted by handsome Sam Lancaster.

Now this first post-kiss encounter with Jesse would have to be played out in front of Sam.

Act normal. Act normal. Smile.

But her paralysed mouth wouldn't form into anything other than a tight line that barely curved upwards. Nor could she summon up so much as a breezy 'hi' for Jesse— the man she'd been friends with all her life, had been able to joke, banter and trade insults with like a brother.

Jesse pumped Sam's hand. 'Sorry, I got held up.'

'No worries,' said Sam, returning the handshake with equal vigour.

'Kate,' said Jesse with a friendly nod in her direction, though she didn't think she was imagining a trace of the same awkwardness in his eyes that she was feeling. 'So you've already met my mate Sam.'

'Yes,' was all she managed to choke out.

'I see you got the best table in the house,' Jesse said to Sam, indicating the view with a sweep of his hand.

'And the best deputy manager,' said Sam gruffly, nodding to Kate.

'Why, thank you,' she said. For Sam, her smile worked fine, a real smile, not her professional, hospitality smile.

Jesse cleared his throat in a way she'd never heard before. *So he was feeling the awkwardness, too.*

'Yes; Kate is, beyond a doubt, awesome,' he said.

Kate recognised the exaggerated casualness of his tone. Would Sam?

'We're just friends,' Kate blurted out. She shot a quick glance at Sam to see a bemused lift of his eyebrow.

'Of course we're just friends,' Jesse returned, too quickly. He stepped around the table to hug her, as he always did when they met. 'Kate and I go way back,' he explained to Sam.

Kate stiffened as Jesse came near. She doubted she could ever return to their old casual camaraderie. It wasn't that Jesse had done anything wrong when he'd kissed her. He just hadn't done anything for *her*. He was probably a very good kisser for someone else.

But things had changed and she didn't want his touch, even in the most casual way. She ducked to slide away.

Big, big mistake.

Sam frowned as he glanced from her to Jesse and back again. Kate could see his mental cogs whirring, putting two and two together and coming up with something other than the zero he should be seeing.

It alarmed her. Because she really wanted Sam Lancaster to know there was nothing between her and Jesse. That she was utterly and completely single.

'Why don't you join us for lunch?' Jesse asked, pulling out the third chair around the table.

No way did she want to make awkward small talk with Jesse. The thought of using her three remaining questions to find out all about Sam Lancaster was appealing—but only when there was just him and her in the conversation.

She pointed her foot, clad in a black court pump, in the direction of the table. 'Hear the ball and chain rattling? Ben would have a fit if I downed tools and fraternised with the guests.'

Did she imagine it, or did Sam's gaze linger on her leg?

She hastily drew it back. 'Shame,' he said. He sounded genuinely regretful.

Not only did she want to walk away as quickly as she could from this uncomfortable situation but she also had her responsibilities to consider. She'd spent way too much time already chatting with Sam. 'Guys, I have to get back to work. I'll send a waitress over straight away and tell the chef to fill your order, pronto. I'm sure you both must be hungry.'

In an ideal world, she'd turn and walk away right now—and not return to this end of the room until both men had gone—but before she went there was wedding business to be dealt with.

'Jesse, will I see you this evening at Ben and Sandy's house for the wedding-planning meeting? We need to run through your best-man duties.'

'Of course,' said Jesse. 'And Sam will be there too.'

'Sam?' Ben had never mentioned that the Sam on the guest list would be part of the wedding party.

Sam shrugged those impressively broad shoulders. 'I've got business with Ben. He asked me to come along tonight.'

She'd anticipated seeing Sam around the hotel, but not seeing him so soon and in a social situation. She couldn't help a shiver of excitement at the thought. At the same time, she was a little put out she hadn't been informed of the extra person. Didn't her friends realise a wedding planner needed to know these things? What other surprises might they spring on her at this late stage?

Ben hadn't mentioned employing a carpenter. Were they planning on getting Sam to construct a wooden wedding arch on the beach where the ceremony was to be held? She wished they'd told her. They were counting down six days to the wedding.

But she would find that out later. Right now she *had* to get back to work.

'I'll see you tonight, Kate,' said Sam.

Did she imagine the promise she heard in his voice?

CHAPTER TWO

SAM DIDN'T WANT to have anything to do with weddings: whip-wielding wedding planners; mothers-of-the-bride going crazy; brides-to-be in meltdown; over-the-top hysteria all round. It reminded him too much of the ill-fated plans for his own cancelled wedding. Though it had been more than two years since the whole drama, even the word 'wedding' still had the power to bring him out in a cold sweat.

If it hadn't meant a chance to see Kate again he would have backed right out of the meeting this evening.

Now he stood on the sand at the bottom of the steps that led down from the hotel to the harbour beach. Jesse's directions to Ben's house, where the meeting was to be held, had comprised a vague wave in the general direction to the right of the hotel. He couldn't see a house anywhere close and wasn't sure where to go.

'Sam! Wait for me!'

Sam turned at the sound of Kate's voice. She stood at the top of the steps, smiling down at him. For a moment all he could do was stare. If he'd thought Kate had looked gorgeous in her waitress garb, in a short, lavender dress that clung to her curves she looked sensational.

She clattered down the steps as fast as her strappy sandals would allow her, giving him a welcome flash of pale, slender legs. Her hair, set free from its constraints, flowed all wild and wavy around her face and to her shoulders, the fading light of the setting sun illuminating it to burnished copper. She clutched a large purple folder under her arm and had an outsized brown leather bag slung over her shoulder.

She was animated, vibrant, confident—everything that attracted him to her. So different from his reserved, unemotional ex-fiancée. Or his distant mother, who had made him wonder as he was growing up whether she had wanted a son at all. Whose main interest in him these days seemed to be in how well he managed the company for maximum dollars on her allowance.

Kate came to a halt next to him, her face flushed. This close, he couldn't help but notice the tantalising hint of cleavage exposed by the scoop neck of her dress.

'Are you headed to Ben's place?' she asked.

'If I knew exactly where it was, yes.'

'Easy,' she said with a wave to the right, as vague as Jesse's had been. 'It's just down there.'

'Easy for a local. All I see is a boathouse with a dock reaching out into the water.'

'That *is* the house. I mean, that's where Ben and his fiancée, Sandy, live.'

'A boathouse?'

'It's the poshest boathouse you've ever seen.' Her face stilled. 'It was the only thing left after the fire destroyed the guesthouse where the hotel stands now.'

'Yes. I knew Ben lost his first wife and child in the fire. What a tragedy.'

'Ben was a lost soul until Sandy came back to Dolphin Bay. She was his first love when they were teenagers. It was all terribly romantic.'

'And now they're getting married.'

Kate laughed. 'Yes. Just two months after they met up again. And they honestly thought they were going to get away with a simple wedding on the beach with a glass of champagne to follow.'

'That sounds a good idea to me,' he said, more whole-heartedly than he had intended.

She looked at him, her head tilted to one side, curiosity lighting her green eyes. 'Really? Maybe, if you don't have family and friends who want to help you celebrate a happy-ever-after ending. Dolphin Bay people are very tight-knit.'

He wondered what it would be like to live in a community where people cared about each other, unlike the anonymity of his own city life, the aridity of his family life. 'Hence you became the wedding planner?'

'Yes. I put my hand up for the job. Unofficially, of course. The simple ceremony on the beach is staying. But they can't avoid a big party at the hotel afterwards. I aim to take the stress out of it for them.'

'Good luck with that.' He couldn't avoid the cynical twist to his mouth.

'Good planning and good organisation, more likely than mere luck.'

'You mean not too many unexpected guests like me?' he said.

Her flush deepened. 'Of course not. I'm glad Ben has invited a friend from outside.'

'From *outside?*'

'I mean from elsewhere than Dolphin Bay. From Sydney. The big smoke.'

He smiled. She might see Sydney as 'the big smoke', but he'd travelled extensively and knew Sydney was very much a small player on the world stage, much as he liked living there.

'My business with Ben could be discussed at a different time,' he said. 'I honestly don't know why they want me along this evening.'

'Neither do I.' She immediately slapped her hand over her mouth and laughed her delightful, throaty laugh. 'Sorry. That's not what I meant. What I meant was they hadn't briefed me on the need for a carpenter.'

He frowned. 'Pass that by me again?'

'You said you were a carpenter. I thought they were asking you tonight to talk about carpentry work—maybe an arch—though I wished they'd told me that before. I don't know how we'd secure it in the sand, and I haven't ordered extra flowers or ribbons or—'

'Stop right there,' he said. 'I'm not a carpenter.'

'But you said you worked in India as a carpenter.'

'As a volunteer. Yes, I can do carpentry. In fact, I can turn my hand to most jobs on a building site. My dad had me working on-site since I was fourteen. But my hard-hat days are behind me. I manage a construction company.'

He couldn't really spare the week away from the business in this sleepy, seaside town. But with the mega-dollar takeover offer for the company brewing, he needed headspace free of everyday demands to think.

The idea of selling Lancaster & Son Construction had first formed in India, where he'd escaped to after his cancelled wedding. In a place so different from his familiar world, he'd begun to think of a different way of life—a life he would choose for himself, not have chosen for him.

'So I'm not in the business of whipping up wedding arches,' he continued.

'Oh,' Kate said, frowning. 'I got that wrong, didn't I?' He already had the impression she might not enjoy being found mistaken in anything.

He threw up his hands in surrender. 'But, if they want a wedding arch, I'll do my best to build them one.'

'No, that's not it. That was only something I thought about. I wonder why they wanted you there, then?'

He smiled to himself at her frown. It was cute the way she liked to be in the know about everything.

'I've got business with Ben,' he said. 'I'm not sure if it's hush-hush or not, so I won't say what it is.'

She glanced down at her watch. 'Well, let's get there and find out, shall we?'

Kate started to stride out beside him in the direction of the boathouse. He noticed her feet turned out slightly as she walked. The financial controller at his company had a similar gait and she'd told him it was because she'd done ballet as a kid. Kate moved so gracefully he wondered if she was a dancer too. He'd like to see her moving her body in time to music—some sensual, driving rhythm. He could join her and...

Kate paused. 'Hang on for a minute. The darn strap on the back of these sandals keeps slipping down.'

She leaned down to tug the slender strap back into place, hopping on the other foot to keep her steady. She wobbled, lost her balance, and held on to his shoulder to steady herself with a breathless, 'Sorry.'

Sam wasn't sorry at all. He liked her close—her face so near to his, her warmth, her scent that reminded him of oranges and cinnamon. For a moment they stood absolutely still and her eyes widened as they gazed into each other's faces. He noticed what a pretty mouth she had, the top lip a classic bow shiny with gloss.

He wanted to kiss her.

He fisted his hands by his sides to stop him from reaching for her and pressing his mouth to hers.

He fought the impulse with everything he had.

Because it was too soon.

And he wasn't sure what the situation was between

Kate and Jesse. Earlier today, he hadn't failed to notice the tension between two people who had professed too vehemently that they were just friends.

Kate started to wobble again. Darn sandals; she needed to get that strap shortened. Sam reached out to steady her. She gasped at the feel of his hand on her waist, his warmth burning through the fine knit fabric of her dress. She wanted to edge away but if she did there was a very good chance she'd topple over into a humiliating heap on the sand.

She didn't trust herself to touch him or to be touched. Before she'd called out from the top of the steps, she'd paused to admire him as he'd stood looking out past the waters of Dolphin Bay to the open sea, dusk rapidly approaching. She'd been seared again with that overwhelming attraction.

But that was crazy.

She'd only just faced the reality that Jesse was not the man for her. That she'd been guilty—for whatever reason—of nurturing a crush for way too long on a man whom she only loved like a brother.

Of course, there had been boyfriends in the time between the two kisses. Some she remembered fondly, one with deep regret. But, in recent years, the conviction had been ticking away that one day Jesse and she would be a couple.

That kiss had proved once and for all that Jesse would never, ever be the man for her. There was no chemistry between them.

Could she be interested, so soon, in Sam Lancaster?

He'd changed to loose, drawstring cotton pants in a sludgy khaki and a collarless loose-weave white shirt—both from India, she guessed. The casual clothes made no secret of the powerful shape of his legs and behind, the well-honed muscles of his chest and arms—built up, she suspected, from his life as a builder rather than from hours in the gym.

Now, as he helped her keep her balance, she was intensely aware of the closeness of their bodies: his hand on her waist; her hand on his shoulder; the soft curve of her breast resting lightly against the hard strength of his chest. The hammering of her own heart.

Somewhere there was the swish of the small waves of the bay rushing onto the sand then retreating back into the sea; the rustle of the evening breeze in the trees that grew in the hotel garden; muted laughter from the direction of the boathouse.

But her senses were too overwhelmed by her awareness of Sam to take any of it in. She breathed in the heady aromas of masculine soap and shampoo that told her he was fresh out of the shower.

She was enjoying being close to him—and she shouldn't be. Three days ago, she'd wanted to kiss Jesse. How could she feel this way about a stranger?

She couldn't trust feelings that had erupted so easily. She needed time to get over the Jesse thing, to plan where she went to next. Not straight into another impossible crush, that was for sure.

Having Sam around was a distraction. He didn't look like the man who had battered her young heart—and a good portion of her soul—eight years ago when she'd been twenty, but he was the same type. Sam had that outrageous masculinity; the untamed, 'don't give a damn' look that sang to something wild and feminine and reckless in her—a part of herself she thought she'd long suppressed.

Panic started its heart-stopping, breath-stealing, muscle-tensing attack on her. She took in a deep breath that came out halfway to a sob.

'You okay?' Sam's deep voice was warm with concern.

She pretended to cough. 'F-fine thanks,' she said. 'Just…just a tickle in my throat.'

She dropped her hand from his shoulder and stepped away so his hand fell from her waist. She immediately felt bereft of his touch. With hands that weren't quite steady, she switched her handbag to her other shoulder.

'Let me carry that bag for you,' Sam said, taking it from her, his fingers grazing the bare skin of her arm. It was just a momentary touch but she knew she'd feel it for hours.

'Th-thanks,' she stuttered.

He heaved the bag effortlessly over his own shoulder. 'It weighs a ton; what on earth do you have in it?'

'Anything and everything. I like to be prepared in case anyone needs stuff. You know—tissues, insect repellent, pain-relievers, tamp— Never mind. My bag's a bit of a joke with my friends. They reckon anything they need they'll find in there.'

'And they probably rely on it. I get the impression you like to look after people.'

'I guess I do,' she said. There was no need to mention the accident that had left her sister in a wheelchair when Kate had been aged thirteen, or how her father had left and Kate had had to help out at home more than anyone else her age. How helping other people run their lives had become a habit.

'So what's in the folder?' he asked.

'The master plan for the wedding. The documents are on my tablet too, and my PC, but I've got backup printouts just in case. There's a checklist, a time plan, everyone's duties spelled out to the minute. I want this wedding to run like clockwork. I've printed out a running sheet for you too, to keep you up to speed, as they've made you part of the meeting.'

Schedules. Plans. Timetables. Keep the everyday aspects of life under control, and she'd have a better chance of keeping errant emotions and unwelcome longings under control.

She couldn't let Sam Lancaster disrupt that.

Sam noticed that as Kate spoke her voice got quicker and quicker. She was nervous. *Of him?*

Had she somehow sensed the tight grip he'd had to keep on himself to stop from pulling her into his arms?

He hadn't been looking for a relationship—especially not when everything was up in the air with the business. Selling it would impact not only on his life but also on the lives of the people employed by his company, including the contractors, suppliers and clients. It was important to weigh up the desire to free himself from the hungry corporate identity that had dominated his life since he'd been a child with the obligations due to those loyal to the company. He owed it to the memory of his father to get such a momentous decision right.

But in just the few short hours he'd been in Dolphin Bay Kate Parker had wiggled her lovely, vivacious way under his skin. He hadn't been able to think of anything else but seeing her again since he'd said goodbye to her at the restaurant.

And now he wanted to take her hand and walk her right past that boathouse—past the meeting she'd scheduled for a big wedding the bride and groom didn't seem to want and onto the beach with him, where she could ask him any questions she wanted and he could ask her a few of his own.

But he would not do that while there was any chance she could be involved with his good friend.

Again, she glanced down at the watch on her narrow wrist. 'C'mon, I can't bear to be late for anything—and especially for a meeting I arranged.'

He liked the dusting of freckles on her pale arms, so different from the orange-toned fake tan that was the standard for so many Sydney girls. He liked that she was so natural and unaffected, unlike the girls his mother, Vivien—she'd never liked him calling her Mum—kept trying to foist on him ever since the big society wedding she'd wanted for him had been called off.

'Let's go, then,' he said, trying to inject a note of enthusiasm into his voice. When they started talking flowers, caterers and canapés, he'd tune out.

Dusk was falling rapidly, as it did in this part of the world. The boathouse ahead was already in shadow, the lights from the windows casting a welcoming glow on the sand. There was music and the light hum of chatter. He thought he recognised Ben's laugh.

As Kate walked beside him, he realised she was keeping a distance away from him so that their hands would not accidentally brush, their shoulders nudge. He didn't know whether to be offended by her reaction to his closeness or pleased that it might indicate she was aware of the physical tension between them.

It was torture not knowing where he stood with her.

As they got within striking distance of the boathouse, he couldn't endure not knowing any longer. He wanted to put out his hand and stop her but he didn't trust himself to touch her again. He halted. She took a few more steps forward, realised he'd stopped and turned back to face him, a questioning look on her face.

Before she had time to speak, he did.

'Kate—stop. Before we go any further, I have to ask you something.'

'Sure,' she said, her head tilted to one side. 'Fire away. We've got a few minutes left before we're late.'

He prepared himself for an answer he didn't want to hear. 'Kate, what's the story with you and Jesse?'

CHAPTER THREE

KATE'S FACE FROZE in shock at his question. For a long moment she simply stared at him and Sam waited for her reply with increasing edginess.

'Me and J…Jesse?' she finally managed to stutter out.

Sam nodded. 'You said you were just friends. Is that true?'

'Yes. It is. Now.'

'What do you mean "now"?'

'You mean Jesse didn't say anything?'

'About you? Not a word.'

Kate looked down so her mass of wavy hair fell over her face, hiding it from him. She scuffed one sandal in the sand. Sam resisted the urge to reach out and push her hair into place. She did it herself, with fingers that trembled, and then looked back up at him. Even in the fading light he could see the indecision etched on her face. 'Do you want to hear the whole story? It's…it's kind of embarrassing.' Her husky voice was so low he had to dip his head to hear her.

Embarrassing? He nodded and tried to keep his face free of expression. He'd asked the question. He had to be prepared for whatever answer she might give him.

Kate clutched the purple folder tight to her chest. 'Our mothers were very close and Jesse, Ben and I grew up together. The mums were always making jokes about Jesse and me getting married in the future. You should see the photos they posed of us as little babies, holding hands.'

Sam could imagine how cute those photos would be, but he felt uncomfortable at the thought of that kind of connection being established between Kate and Jesse at such a young age. He had a vague recollection of Jesse once mentioning a red-haired girl back home. What had he said? Something about an ongoing joke in the family that if he and the girl never found anyone else they could marry each other...

Sam had found it amusing at the time. He didn't find it amusing right now. How difficult would it be to break such a long-standing bond?

'So that's the embarrassing bit?' he asked.

Kate pulled a face. 'It gets worse. When I was thirteen and he was fourteen we tried out our first ever kiss together. It was awkward and I ended up giggling so much it didn't go far. But I guess in my childish heart that marked Jesse as someone special.'

Jealousy seared through Sam at the thought of Jesse kissing Kate, even if they had been only kids. He was aware it was irrational—after all he hardly knew Kate—but it was there. It was real.

He had to clear his throat to speak. 'So you dated?'

She shook her head so vehemently her hair swung over her face. 'Never. We both dated other people. As teenagers, we cried on each other's shoulders when things went wrong. As adults, we lived our own lives. Until...'

Her brow creased as though she were puzzling out loud. 'Until a few years ago—I don't know why—I started to think Jesse might be the one for me. After all, everyone else thought so. I developed quite a crush on him.'

'So what's so embarrassing about that?'

She paused. 'Three days ago we kissed—at my suggestion.'

Now that jealousy turned into something that seethed in his gut. He'd always prided himself on being laid-back, slow to anger. He felt anything but laid-back at the thought of her in another man's arms, even one of his friends. Especially one of his friends.

'And?' His hands were fisted.

'Crush completely over. It was an utter disaster. So wrong that words can't describe it. And I speak for him as well as for me.'

Sam's fists slowly uncurled.

'So Jesse doesn't want you as more than a friend?'

'Heavens, no!' Her voice had an undertone of almost hysterical relief. 'We could hardly wait to make our getaways. And we succeeded in avoiding each other until we met in the restaurant earlier today.'

'It seemed awkward between you. Tense.'

'At first. But it's okay now. We've been friends for so long, seems we can both laugh it off as a monumental mistake and move on.'

With no more kissing, if Sam had anything to do with it.

He stepped closer to her. This time he did reach out and smooth an auburn curl from falling over her cheek. She started but didn't step away and he tucked it behind her ear before letting his hand drop back to his side. They stood as close as they could without actually touching.

'So Jesse's right out of the picture,' he said. 'Is there anyone else?'

Anyone else he had to fight for her?

Her face was half in shadow, half in the dim light coming from the boathouse. 'No one,' she said. 'I…I haven't dated for quite some time.' She paused. 'What about you? Question number three: is there any special lady in your life?'

'I was engaged to a long-term girlfriend. But no one special since that ended.'

He'd smarted for months at the way the engagement had been terminated, the wedding cancelled. In fact, he'd been so gutted he'd taken off to India to get away from the fallout. With perspective, he could see ending the engagement had been the right decision. But, while the wounds had healed, he had been wary of getting involved with anyone. Now he was ready. His ex had moved on, but he hadn't met a woman who had interested him. Until now.

'Oh,' she said. 'Would it count as question number four if I asked about what happened—or would that be part of question number three?'

He grinned. 'I'll allow it as part two of question three—but it might have to wait until I have more time to answer it.'

'I'm okay with that,' she said with a return of her dimples.

The last thing he wanted to do was scare Kate off. He had never before experienced this instant attraction to a woman. He had to work through how he handled it.

Kate was so obviously not the kind of woman for a no-strings fling. It wasn't what he wanted either. But his previous relationships had started off slowly with attraction growing. He understood how that worked, not this immediate flaming that might just burn itself out in a matter of days. The kind of flaming that had seen his parents trapped in an unhappy marriage, the consequences of which he had been forced to endure.

That aside, he realised Kate might not feel the same way as he did. If he wanted to get to know her, he knew he had to take things carefully.

'Before Jesse came into the restaurant, I was about to ask you out on a date,' he said. 'What would you have said?'

'I…I… You've taken me by surprise. I would have said—'

Just then the door of the boathouse opened, flooding them with further light. Ben peered through the door and called out. 'Hey, Kate, what are you doing out there? You warned us all to be on time or suffer dire consequences and now *you're* running late.'

Kate immediately stepped back from Sam so fast she nearly tripped. 'I'm coming!' she called in Ben's direction.

Sam cursed under his breath at the interruption. He wanted to shout at Ben to get lost.

Kate looked back up at Sam. 'Sam, I…'

But Ben was now heading towards them. He caught sight of Sam. 'Sam. Mate. I didn't see you there. Come on in.'

Sam groaned. Kate looked up at him in mute appeal. He shrugged wordlessly in a gesture of frustration. But not defeat; he would get Kate's reply sooner rather than later.

Then he was swept along into the boathouse with Kate, Ben walking between them like an old-fashioned chaperone.

An hour later, Kate was pleased at how well the meeting had gone. Everyone who needed to be there had been there—except for Sandy's sister who lived in Sydney, and her five-year-old daughter who was to be the flower girl. Plans had been finalised, timetables tweaked. Now the bridal party had been joined by a few other friends. Snack platters from the hotel kitchen had arrived and the barbecue was being fired up. There wasn't much more she could do to ensure the wedding went to plan on Saturday.

If only she hadn't been so darned conscious of Sam the entire time. It had been more than a tad distracting. She'd found herself struggling to remember important facts, her mind too occupied with Sam. But no one seemed to have noticed the lapse from her usual efficiency.

She just hoped they hadn't noticed the way she'd found herself compelled to check on him every few minutes. He'd met her glances with a smile, even a wink that had made her smother a laugh. It was only too obvious he was bored by the details of the wedding meeting. He'd crossed his long legs and uncrossed them. He'd not-so-subtly checked his mobile phone. He'd even nodded off for a few minutes until Ben had shoved him awake.

But she hadn't had a moment alone with him since they'd been interrupted on the beach.

She'd been just about to say yes to Sam's suggestion of a date. But would it really be a good idea?

Her fears screamed no. Just the light touch of his fingers on her cheek had practically sent her hurtling to the stars. She'd never felt such strong attraction so quickly. She was terrified that it might lead her into the kind of obsession that had nearly destroyed her in the past. It would be wisest to keep Sam at a distance.

But her loneliness urged yes to seeing Sam. Why shouldn't she go out with him on an uncomplicated, everyday date, with no other agenda than to share a meal, enjoy a movie, find out something about what made the other tick? Flirt a little. Laugh a lot. It didn't have to go further than that.

For so long she'd been on her own. Surely she deserved some masculine excitement in her life—even if only temporary? Sam would only be around for a week and then he'd be gone. Where was the harm in enjoying his company?

It was time to say yes to that date.

She'd lost sight of him—difficult in the space of the boathouse, which was basically just one large room converted into luxury living. He must have escaped outside to the barbecue. She'd go find him.

Before she could make the move, the bride-to-be, Sandy, sidled up beside her. 'Sooo,' she said in a teasing tone. 'You and that gorgeous hunk, Sam Lancaster…'

Kate couldn't help it; she flushed again and Sandy noticed. That was the problem with being a fair-skinned redhead: even the slightest blush flamed. 'What about me and Sam?' she said, knowing she sounded unnecessarily defensive.

'You've hardly kept your eyes off him all evening. And he you. I reckon he's smitten. And maybe you are too.'

'Of course he's not. Of course I'm not.'

'Oh, really?' said Sandy in an overly knowing tone.

Kate narrowed her eyes. 'Are you by any chance paying me back for the way I poked my nose in with you and Ben when you first came back to Dolphin Bay?'

Kate had been overprotective of her friend Ben when Sandy had showed up out of the blue after twelve years of no contact. But she'd very soon warmed to Sandy and they'd become good friends.

'Don't be silly,' said Sandy. 'I'm so deliriously happy with Ben, I want you to be happy too. Sam is really nice, as well as being a hunk. I got the lowdown on him.'

'I only met him today. Nothing is happening there, I can assure you.'

Nothing except her heart starting to race every time she caught a glimpse of him towering over the other guests.

'But it might. You know what they say about what happens at weddings.' Sandy smiled. 'The bridesmaid and the groomsman…'

Kate frowned. 'I don't know what you mean. I'm your

bridesmaid. But Sam isn't Ben's groomsman. I should know, as your wedding planner.'

'Uh, think again. Right now, Ben's asking Sam to be just that.'

'What? I thought he only wanted a best man?'

'He's changed his mind. My sister Lizzie, as chief bridesmaid, will be partnered by the best man, Jesse. That means you'd be coming up that beach aisle by yourself. We thought why not even things up by partnering you with Sam? You'll easily be able to readjust your ceremony schedules. That is, if Sam agrees to it.'

Kate tried to tell herself she was being oversensitive but she could sense that echo again: *poor Kate.*

'Sandy, it's so sweet of you, but is this about what happened with Jesse and me three days ago? If so, I—'

Sandy's hazel eyes were kind. 'Kate, I'm so sorry it didn't work out with Jesse. I know how much you've always wanted him.'

Kate swallowed hard. It was so difficult to talk about it. 'Did I really, though, Sandy? I think maybe I dreamed of a kind, handsome man—so different from the men I'd dated—and Jesse was there. I...I fixated on him. It wasn't real.'

'You could be right. To tell you the truth, I didn't ever see any chemistry between you.'

Kate giggled. 'There was no chemistry whatsoever. I can't tell you how much I regretted it. I couldn't run away fast enough.'

'I bet you wouldn't run too far if you were alone with Sam Lancaster. Doesn't he fit the bill? He's handsome, all right—and he must be kind, or he wouldn't have been off volunteering in India, would he?'

Kate sobered. 'All that. But, Sandy, don't try to match-make, will you? I don't want a pity party. I'm not desperate for a man.'

Sandy put her hand reassuringly on Kate's arm. 'Of course you're not. But is it a bad thing for your friends to look out for you? And for you to let them? You've got to admit, it's more fun being a bridesmaid if you have a handsome groomsman in tow.'

'Of course it is. And you're right; you don't get more handsome than Sam Lancaster. And he's interesting, too.' She found herself looking over her shoulder to watch out for him, only to see him coming back into the room with Ben. 'Here he is. I hope he didn't hear me twittering on about how handsome he is,' she whispered to Sandy.

She watched as Sam and Ben approached. Funny; she'd always found Ben so imposing, Jesse so good-looking. But Sam outshone any man she'd ever met in terms of pure, masculine appeal.

'So did Sam say yes to being groomsman, Ben?' asked Sandy.

'Of course he did,' said tall, blond Ben.

Sam stood shoulder-nudging distance from Kate. She could feel his warmth, smell the hint of bourbon on his breath. 'As if I had a choice, when I heard who would be the bridesmaid I was escorting,' he said with a smile that was just for her. She smiled back, glad beyond reason to have him by her side.

She would ask *him* on a date. ASAP.

Now the planning part of the evening was over and her duties done, she could get the heck out of there and take Sam with her, so they could talk in private away from too-interested eyes.

But Ben had other ideas. He turned to Kate. 'I was going to introduce you to Sam tonight, but as you've already met I'll cut straight to the chase.'

Kate sighed inwardly. All she could think of was being alone with Sam. But she was aware that, while Ben was a long-time friend, he was also her boss. He had his boss voice on now; she almost felt she should be taking notes.

'Yes, sir,' she said flippantly, at the same time wondering how a work thing could possibly involve Sam.

'We've finally got planning approval for the new resort,' said Ben with a whoop of triumph.

'Really?' she said, scarcely able to let herself believe the news. 'Really and truly?'

'Really,' said Ben with a huge grin.

'Congratulations, Kate,' said Sandy, hugging her. 'I know how hard you worked with Ben on the submission.'

Momentarily lost for words, Kate hugged Sandy back. Then she looked from Sam to Ben to Sam again. 'That's amazing. After all the hours we put in, I can hardly believe it's actually happening,' she said.

She grabbed hold of Sam's arms and did a little jig of excitement—then realised what she'd done and dropped her hands. She pulled a face. 'Sorry. I got carried away.'

'Don't be sorry,' he said. 'I can see this means a lot to you.'

Ben put up his hand. 'Wait. There's more. Sam's company is going to build the resort. Lancaster & Son Construction is one of the biggest and the best in the country. We're fortunate to have him on board.'

Kate stared, too astounded to say anything. *Why hadn't she known this?*

When she finally got her breath back, Kate turned to Sam. 'So that was the hush-hush business.'

And she'd thought he was a carpenter.

'Not so hush-hush now,' he said.

'I can't tell you how thrilled I am about this project,' she said. 'A luxury, boutique spa resort nestled in the bush on that beautiful spot. It's on land overlooking Big Ray Beach—that's our surf beach—with incredible views. The resort's a big deal for Dolphin Bay.'

'And a triumph for Kate. It was initially her idea,' Ben explained to Sam. 'As her reward for kick-starting it, she has equity.'

Her ownership was only measured in the tiniest of percentages—a token, really—but Kate intended to be a hands-on manager once the resort was up and running. It would be her dream job, something she wanted so much it hurt.

'Congratulations,' said Sam. 'It's great to hear you're such an entrepreneur.'

Kate basked in the admiration she saw in his eyes. At age twenty-eight, she'd had a few false starts to her career; now she was exactly where she wanted to be. 'I'm still a bit dazed that it's actually going to happen,' she said.

Ben turned to Kate. 'I want you to be our liaison person with Sam—starting from now. I'll be away on my honeymoon after next week and this week too caught up with work at the hotel.'

She blinked at Ben. 'Th..that's a surprise.'

'But it makes sense,' said Ben. 'You know more about the project than anyone else but me. You can start by taking Sam to the site for him to take a look at it. That okay with you, Sam?'

'Of course,' said Sam, though Kate thought he looked perturbed.

'I'll leave you to two to discuss the details,' said Ben, ushering Sandy away.

Finally Kate was left alone with Sam, exactly what she'd longed for all evening. She'd never been more aware of his big, broad-shouldered body, his unconventionally handsome face.

Only now she would value a few minutes on her own to think over what had just happened.

Ten minutes ago she'd been ready to drag him outside and arrange a date. Or two. Except now things were very different. She would have to put all such thoughts on hold. Sam was no longer a stranger blown into town for a week, never to be seen again. He was someone with ongoing links to Dolphin Bay. She'd be working with him as a professional in a business capacity.

How could she possibly think she could have any kind of personal relationship with him?

CHAPTER FOUR

SAM HAD BEEN knocked sideways by the news that he'd be working with Kate on Ben's new resort development. He'd always enforced a strict rule in the company—no dating clients. Without exception. Not for his employees, not for him. He'd amended a number of his father's long-standing edicts when he'd taken over but not that one. It made good business sense.

How ironic that it now applied to Kate—and company protocol was too important to him to have one rule for the boss and another for the rest of the team.

He felt like thumping the wall with his clenched fist, right through the tastefully restored wooden boards. He clenched his jaw and uttered a string of curse words under his breath.

He had to get out of this room. On top of his frustration, he felt stifled by all the wedding talk buzzing around him. When it came to his turn to get hitched—his own derailed wedding hadn't turned him off the idea of getting married one day—he thought elopement would be a great idea.

Then there were the overheard murmurs that had him gritting his teeth. They had all been along the lines of what a shame it was about Kate and Jesse—immediately hushed when he'd come near. Whether that was because they saw him as an interloper, or they could tell he was interested in Kate, he didn't know. But he didn't like it.

Everything he'd heard about the oppressive nature of small-town life was true.

He hated everyone knowing his business. How Kate could bear it was beyond his comprehension. Anything smaller than Sydney, with its population of more than four-and-a-half million, would never be for him.

A middle-aged woman was bearing down on them. No doubt she wanted Kate's opinion on the colour of ribbons on a flower arrangement or some such waste-of-space frivolity.

'I'm going outside for some air,' he muttered to Kate and strode away before the woman reached them.

He realised his departure was being watched with interest by everyone else in the room. Tough. There'd be nothing for them to gossip about now. Kate was strictly out of bounds.

It was dark outside now but the moon was full, reflecting on the quietly rippling waters of the bay. He gulped in the cool evening air, then let out those curse words at full volume as he kicked at the solid base of a palm tree as hard as he could.

His first thought was that after the site inspection tomorrow he would get the hell out of Dolphin Bay. But he'd promised to be Ben's groomsman. He cursed again. He was trapped here—with a woman he wanted but suddenly couldn't have.

The door opened behind him, a shaft of light falling on the deck. He moved away. He was in no mood to talk. To Ben. To Jesse. To anyone.

'Sam?' Her voice was tentative but even without turning around he knew it was Kate.

He turned. There was enough moonlight so he could

see the anxiety on her face. She was wringing her hands together. He ached to reach out to her but he kept his hands fisted by his sides.

'Let's walk out to the end of the dock,' she said. 'You feel like you're on a boat out there. And no one can over-hear us.'

He fell into step beside her. A row of low-voltage sensor lights switched on to light them to the dock. The builder in him admired the electrics. His male soul could only think of the beautiful woman beside him and regret about what might have been.

They reached the end of the dock without speaking. A light breeze coming off the water brought with it the tang of the sea and lifted and played with the soft curls around Kate's face. She seemed subdued, as if the moonlight had sucked all that wonderful vivacity from her.

She turned to him. 'I had no idea you were building the resort.'

'I had to keep it confidential. I didn't know you were involved in any way.'

'It was the first time I heard I was to liaise with you. I hadn't seen that coming.' She looked up at him. Her face was pale in the weak, shimmering light, her eyes shad-owed. 'This…this changes things, doesn't it?'

'I'm afraid it does,' he said, knowing from the regret in her eyes that she was closing the door on him before it got any more than halfway open.

'It…it means I have to say no to that date,' she said.

One part of him was plunged into dismay at the tolling finality of her words, the other was relieved that he hadn't had to say them first.

'It means I have to rescind the offer,' he said gruffly. 'I have an iron-clad no-dating-the-clients rule.'

Her short, mirthless laugh was totally unlike her usual

throaty chime. 'Me too. I've never thought it was a good idea. There can be too many consequences if the dating doesn't work out but you still have to work together.'

'Agreed,' he said. 'There are millions of dollars at stake here.' And his company's reputation—especially at the time of a publicly scrutinised buy-out bid. The company had to come first again—as it always did. This time, it came ahead of him dating the only woman who had seriously interested him since his broken engagement. Again he had that sense of the business as a millstone, weighing him down with protocol and obligation—as it had since he'd been fourteen years old.

Kate laughed that mirthless laugh again. 'Funny thing is, I suspect it's Ben's clumsy attempt at matchmaking and it's totally backfired.'

He gave a snort of disbelief. 'You think so?'

'The groomsman thing? The cooked-up excuse to get me to show you the land when there's no real need for me to?'

'My take on it is that Ben thought you knew more than anyone else about the plans for the new resort. You were the best person for the job. Why would you believe any differently?'

'I guess so,' she said with a self-deprecating quirk of her pretty mouth. 'But the out-of-the blue request to be a groomsman?'

Sam snapped his fingers. 'I get it—you were concerned an extra member of the wedding party would put your schedules out?'

Her smile was forced as she raised her hand. 'Guilty! I guess I *was* a little disconcerted about that. But I mainly felt bad for you being coerced into being a groomsman on such a trumped-up excuse. You don't seem to be comfortable with all the wedding stuff—I saw you yawning during the meeting. Then you get thrown in at the deep end.'

'Ben didn't have to coerce me to be his groomsman. I liked the idea of being your escort at the wedding.'

Wouldn't any red-blooded male jump at the chance to be with such a gorgeous girl? Or had Jesse done such a number on her she didn't realise how desirable she was?

Truth be told, if it hadn't been for the prospect of more time with Kate, he'd rather have stayed a guest and stood apart from the wedding tomfoolery. Now he would have to spend the entire time with Kate, knowing she was off-limits. It would be a kind of torture.

'Thank you,' she said. 'It will be nice to have you there. It might have been awkward with Jesse otherwise. People would have been gossiping. Even though…'

'It has to be strictly business between us now.'

'Yes,' she said. 'I…I realise that.'

The tinkling, chiming sound of rigging against masts from the boats moored in the harbour carried across the water, adding to the charm of the setting. Dolphin Bay was a nice part of the world, he conceded. For a visit, for work—a vacation, perhaps—but not to live here.

'We should be going back to the others,' she said with a notable lack of enthusiasm.

'Yes,' he said, without making a move.

The last place he wanted to be was back in the boathouse. He liked being out here on the dock talking to her, even if the parameters of the conversations they could have had now had been constrained.

Suddenly she slapped her hand on her arm. 'Darn mosquitoes!'

She reached into that capacious shoulder bag, burrowed around and pulled out a can. 'Insect repellent,' she explained.

'You really do have everything stashed in there,' he said, amused.

'Even a single mosquito buzzing its way down the coast will seek me out and feast on my fair skin.' As she spoke, she dramatised her words and mimed the insect dive-bombing her in a totally unself-conscious manner.

Lucky mosquito. Sam could imagine nuzzling into the pale skin of her throat—kissing, nibbling, even a gentle bite…

That was forbidden territory now.

'Want some?' she asked.

Mosquito spray? 'No thanks. They never bother me.'

'Lucky you.' She stood away from him and sprayed her legs and arms with a spray that smelled pleasantly of lavender.

'You're not suited to beach-side living, are you?' he asked when she came close again.

'Not really,' she said. 'Insects adore me and I burn to a frizzle if I'm out in the sun in the middle of the day. But I love to swim, and the mornings and evenings are great for that.'

A moonlight swim: her pale body undulating through the shimmering water, giving tantalising glimpses of her slender limbs, her just-right curves; he shrugging off his clothes and joining her…

This kind of scenario was not on. Not with a client.

He cleared his throat. 'I like to start the day with a swim. Where do you recommend?' he asked.

'The bay is best for quiet water. Then there's Big Ray surf beach—you get to it via the boardwalk. Around from there is an estuary where the freshwater river meets the sea. It's magic. Not many people go there and you can swim right up that river without seeing another soul. Oh, except for the occasional kangaroo coming down to drink.'

'It sounds idyllic,' he said.

'That's a good word for it. I can show you how to get there on the map. I'd offer to take you but that's—'

'Not a good idea,' he said at the same time she did. Not with him in his board shorts and her in a bikini. Or, with that fair skin of hers, did she wear a sleek, body-hugging swimsuit?

A cold sweat broke out on his forehead. Somehow he had to stop himself from thinking of Kate Parker as anything other than a client. She was the Hotel Harbourside client liaison. Nothing more.

'I'll have to have a word with Ben,' said Kate. 'About his matchmaking efforts, I mean—well-meaning but misguided.'

'Ben's an amateur. You haven't seen misguided matchmaking until you've met my mother. She's a master of it.'

Why had he said that?

Why not?

Kate was a client. That didn't mean he couldn't have a personal conversation with her.

'But not successfully?' Kate asked.

What had she called herself? A stickybeak. It was such an Aussie expression but so perfectly summed up a person who couldn't resist sticking their noses into other people's business. He preferred her description of herself as having a healthy curiosity. And right now he could tell it had been piqued.

'I veto all her efforts,' he said. 'I might work in the family firm but I run my own life.'

That hadn't always been the case. His father had been overly domineering. His mother had just wanted him kept out of her hair. There'd been an almighty battle when his mother had planned to send him to boarding school—with his father victorious, of course. As a child he'd had no choice but to go along with the way they'd steered his life. As a teenager he'd rebelled against his father but still had little choice. The real confrontation hadn't come until he'd turned twenty-one, nine years ago.

'Your mother—she's in Sydney?' Kate asked.

An image of his mother flashed before his eyes: whippet-thin in couture clothes, hair immaculate, perfectly applied make-up that could not disguise the lines of discontent around her mouth or the disappointment in her eyes when she looked at her son. Her son who'd chosen to follow his father into the rough and tumble of the construction industry—not a law degree or a specialist medical degree she saw as more socially acceptable. Not that she ever complained about the hefty allowance the company brought her.

He looked at Kate in the moonlight, at her hair, a glorious mass of riotous waves, her simple dress, her eyes warm with real interest in what he had to say. She seemed so straightforward. So genuine. Never had two women been more different.

'Yes. She'd never stray from the eastern suburbs.'

'And your father? I wondered about the "and son" bit in your company name. Are you the son?'

'You realise that's question number four?' he said.

'I guess it is,' she said. Her dimples had snuck back into her smile but now they disappeared again. 'Sorry. I guess I shouldn't ask more questions now...now things have changed.'

'As a business client? Why not? Fire away.'

'And, in fact, it's a three-part question.'

'Well, number two was a two-part question.'

'I start as I mean to continue.'

'So I've got a four-part question to look forward to in the next stage of my interrogation?'

'Maybe. I'll keep you guessing.' Her delightful laughter echoed around the beach. 'But in the meantime, do you want to answer part one of question four?'

'My father died three years ago.'

The laughter faded from her voice. 'I'm so sorry. Was it expected?'

'A sudden heart attack. He was sixty-seven and very fit.'

'How awful for you. And for your mother.'

'It was a shock for her. She was my father's second wife and considerably younger than he was. Didn't expect to be left on her own so soon.'

'And you?' Her voice was gentle and warm with concern. 'It must have been a terrible shock for you too.'

He'd been in Western Australia when he'd got the phone call, a six-hour flight away. He'd never forgiven himself for not being there. He'd been so concerned with proving himself to his father by fixing the problems in Western Australia, he had missed his chance to say goodbye to him.

'Yes. Worse in some ways, because suddenly I had to take over the running of the company. I hadn't expected to have to do that for years to come.'

'That was a truckload of responsibility.'

He shrugged. 'The old man had been preparing me for the role since I'd been playing with my Lego, teaching me the business from the ground up. He was a tough taskmaster. I didn't get any privileges for being the boss's son. I had to earn my management stripes on my own merits.'

'Still, actually taking the reins of such a large company must have been scary.'

'The first day I took my place at the head of the boardroom table was as intimidating as hell. All those older guys just waiting for me to make a mistake.' He had never admitted that to anyone. *Why Kate? Why now?*

'But you won their respect, I'll bet.'

'I worked hard for it.' Too hard, perhaps. He hadn't had time for much else, including his fiancée. That was when she had started accusing him of being an obsessive workaholic who put the company ahead of everything else—particularly her. He'd come to see some truth in her accusations.

'Good for you; that can't have been easy,' said Kate. 'Which brings me back to question four—you're the son in the company name?'

'Actually, the son was my father. My grandfather started the company, building houses in the new suburbs opening up after the Second World War. My dad grew the company far bigger than my grandfather could ever have dreamed. In turn, I've taken it even further.'

'Obviously you build hotels.'

'And office towers and shopping malls and stadiums. All over the country. Even outside the country.'

In the three years he'd been at the helm he'd steered the business through tough economic times. He had pushed it, grown it. He didn't try to hide his pride in his achievements. They'd come at a cost—his personal life.

Kate went quiet again. 'You must have thought I was an idiot for suggesting you were here to build a wedding arch.'

'Of course I didn't think you were an idiot. I'm a builder. I can make arches. Fix drains. Even turn my hand to electrical work if I have to.' He held out his hands. 'With the calluses to prove it.'

She turned away so she looked out to sea and he faced her profile—her small, neat nose, her firm, determined chin. 'But you're also the CEO of a huge construction company. That's quite a contradiction.'

And now she was his client.

He realised the distance their business roles now put between them. Once more his commitment to the company came over his personal happiness. It was a price he kept on paying.

And he wasn't sure he was prepared to do that any longer.

Kate found it difficult to suppress a sigh. *Be careful what you wish for.*

She hadn't wanted to be distracted by Sam while she sorted out her life after the Jesse issue. Now Sam could not be anything more than a business connection.

Her disappointment was so intense she felt nauseous, choked by a barrage of what might have beens. She hadn't been able to get him off her mind since he'd walked into the restaurant. But how did she stop herself from being attracted to him?

Because the more she found out about him, the more she liked him.

Still, she had had practice at putting on a mask, at not showing people what she really felt. At hiding her pain. At being cheerful, helpful, always-ready-to-help-out Kate.

She would simply slip into the impersonal role of client, hide her disappointment that she couldn't spend time with Sam in any other capacity. She must remember to thank Ben for the opportunity to deal with the CEO of the company building her dream hotel.

It was probably for the best, anyway. She wasn't ready for romance, especially with someone who lived so far away. The four hours to Sydney might as well be four hundred as far as she was concerned. One of the reasons Jesse had been appealing was that, although he worked overseas now, he intended to settle in Dolphin Bay.

She looked down at her watch, the dial luminous in the dark.

'We really should be getting back,' she said, aiming for

brisk and efficient but coming out with a lingering, 'don't really want to go just yet' tone that wouldn't fool anyone as smart as Sam.

'I like it out here,' he said. He hunkered down on the very end of the dock then swung his long legs over the edge. He patted the place next to him in invitation. 'No one will have missed us.'

Against her better judgement, she joined him. She was hyper-aware of his warmth, his strength, his masculinity, and she made sure she sat a client-like distance from him so their shoulders didn't touch. The water slapped against the supports of the pier and a fish leapt up out of the water, glinting silver in the moonlight, and flopped back in with a splash.

'You're right; it's like being on a boat,' Sam said.

'Without the rocking and the seasickness.'

'Or the feeling of being trapped and unable to get off exactly when you want to.'

Her eyes widened. 'You feel that way about boats too?'

'I've never much cared for them. Which is at odds with living on the harbour in Sydney.'

'Me neither,' she said. 'I'd rather keep my feet firmly planted on land.'

'*Definitely* not a seaside person.'

'In another life I'd probably live in a high-rise in the middle of the city and go to the ballet and theatre on the nights I wasn't trying the newest restaurants.' Now she did indulge in the sigh. 'Trouble is, I love it here so much. I wasn't joking earlier when I said I thought it was the most beautiful place in Australia.'

'That hasn't escaped my attention,' he said.

'It's familiar and s—' She hastily bit off the word 'safe' and said, 'So relaxed.'

'It's nice, I'll give you that. But have you been to many places to compare?' he asked.

'Do I really sound like a small-town hick?'

'Anything but,' he said. 'I was just interested. I've travelled a lot; we might have been to the same places.'

'Sure, I've been to lots of other places. When I…after I…'

She struggled to find the right words that wouldn't reveal the back story she had never shared with anyone: the reason she'd left university in Sydney without completing her degree. The reason she felt she would always doubt her choice of men. 'I toured all around the country in a small dance company.'

'I thought you might have been a dancer,' he said. She followed his gaze down to where her feet dangled over the edge of the pier.

'Let me guess—because of the duck walk? Years of training in classical ballet tends to do that. Only, we dancers call it "a good turn-out".'

'I was going to say because of the graceful way you move.'

'Oh,' she said and the word hung still in the air.

She blushed that darn betraying blush. She wasn't sure how to accept the compliment. Mere hours ago she might have replied with something flirtatious. But not now. Not when all that was off the agenda.

'Thank you,' was all she said.

'Would I have heard of your dance company?'

'I highly doubt it. It was a cabaret troupe and far from famous. We toured regional Australia—the big clubs, town halls, civic centres, small theatres if they had them. Once we had a stint in New Zealand. We were usually the support act to a singer or a magician—that kind of thing. It was hard work but a lot of fun.'

'Was?'

'A dancer's life is a short one,' she said, trying to sound unconcerned. 'I injured my ankle and that was the end of it.'

She didn't want to add that her ankle had healed—but the emotional wounds from a near-miss assault from a wouldn't-take-no-for-an-answer admirer had not.

During the time the man had had her trapped, he'd taunted her that her sexy dance moves in body-hugging costumes made men think she was asking for it. Coming so soon after her damaging relationship with her university boyfriend, she'd imploded. She hadn't performed since, or even danced at parties.

'I'd like to see you dance some day,' Sam said.

'Chance would be a fine thing. I don't dance at all any more.'

Sadness wrenched at her as it always did when she thought about dance. To express herself with movement had been an intrinsic part of her and she mourned its loss.

'Because of the ankle?' he said.

'Yes,' she lied.

She felt uncomfortable with the conversation focused on her. That was a time of her life she'd sooner forget. She made her voice sound bright and cheery. That was what people expected of her. 'You do realise you've skipped answering part two of question four,' she said.

'I did?'

'You know, about why your engagement ended?' she prompted. 'Unless that's off the agenda now for discussion between business associates.'

'No secrets there,' he said. 'Two weeks before the wedding my former fiancée, Frances, called it off. I hadn't seen it coming.'

'That must have been a shock. What on earth happened?'

Kate really wanted to hear his reply. She couldn't understand how anyone engaged to be married to Sam Lancaster could find any reason to call it off. She could scarcely believe it when—just as Sam was about to answer her—she heard her name being called from the boathouse.

She stilled. So did Sam. 'Pretend you don't hear it,' Sam muttered in an undertone.

She tried to block her ears but her name came again, echoing over the water. Sandy's voice.

'Over here,' she called, then mouthed a silent, 'Sorry,' to Sam.

Sandy rushed along the dock. 'Thank heaven you hadn't gone home. Lizzie, my sister, just phoned. She can't make it to the hen and stag night on Wednesday. We'll have to drive up to Sydney and have it there instead.'

'But I—'

'Don't worry, Kate,' said Sandy. 'I promise it won't be any more work for you.' Sandy turned to Sam. 'Are you okay with the change of plan?'

Sam shrugged. 'Sure.'

Kate cleared her throat against the rising panic that threatened to choke her. She couldn't go to Sydney. She just couldn't. But she didn't want to tell Sandy she wouldn't be going with them. She couldn't cope with the explanations, the reasons. She'd make her excuses at the last minute. They could party quite happily without her.

'Fine by me too,' she said, forcing a smile. 'One less thing for me to have to organise.'

CHAPTER FIVE

UP UNTIL NOW, Sam had never had a problem with the 'no dating the clients' rule. Along the way there had been attractive female clients who had made their personal interest in him clear. But he had had no trouble deflecting them; the business had always come first.

It was a different story with Kate Parker. Kate certainly wasn't coming on to him in any way. In fact, she couldn't be more professional. This morning she had picked him up from the hotel. On the short drive to the site of the proposed resort, the conversation had been completely business-related—not even a mention of the wedding, let alone their thwarted date.

He was the one who was having trouble seeing her purely as a client and not as a beautiful, desirable woman who interested him more than anyone had interested him for a long time. It was disconcerting the way she appeared so easily to have put behind her any thought of a more personal relationship.

The thought nagged at him—if Ben hadn't appointed her as his liaison would she have agreed to that date? Might they have been going out to dinner together tonight?

She was a client. Just a client.

But as she guided him around the site he found her presence so distracting it was a struggle to act professionally.

The way her hair gleamed copper in the mid-morning sun made even the most spectacular surroundings seem dull by comparison. When she walked ahead of him in white jeans, and a white shirt that showcased her shapely back view, how could he objectively assess the geo-technical aspects of the site? Or gauge the logistics of crane access when her orange cinnamon scent wafted towards him?

He gritted his teeth and kicked the sandy soil with its sparse cover of indigenous vegetation, filling his nostrils with the scent of eucalypt leaves crushed underfoot.

Truth be told, he didn't really need to inspect the site. The company had a team of surveyors and engineers to do that. He'd promised Ben he'd take a look more as a courtesy than anything. Now Kate was standing in for Ben and it was a very different experience than it would have been tramping over the land with his old skiing buddy.

'What do you think?' Kate asked.

She twirled around three-hundred-and-sixty degrees, her arms outstretched. Pride and excitement underscored her voice. She'd seemed subdued when he'd said goodnight at the boathouse—thrown by the last-minute change to the stag night. But there was no trace of that today. It appeared she could take change in her stride. He admired that—in his experience, not all super-organised people were as flexible.

'It's magnificent,' he said. *You're magnificent.* 'You're on to a winner.'

The large parcel of land stood elevated above the northern end of what the locals called Big Ray beach, though there was another name on the ordinance surveys. Groves of spotted gums, with their distinctive marked bark, framed a view right out past the breakers to the open sea.

'There was a ramshackle old cottage in that corner,'

Kate said, pointing. 'It had been there for years. It was only demolished quite recently.'

'The great Australian beach shack—that's quite a tradition,' he said. 'No doubt generations of the same family drove down from Sydney or Canberra to spend the long summer holidays on the beach.'

'I wouldn't get too nostalgic about it,' she said. 'It was very basic; just one step up from a shanty. I pitied the mum of the family having to cook in it on sweltering January days.'

'Maybe the guys barbecued the fish they'd caught.'

'You sound like you speak from experience. Did your family have a beach house when you were growing up?'

'We owned a beach house at Palm Beach—it's the most northern beach in Sydney.'

Her eyes widened. 'I know it—don't they call it the summer playground of the wealthy?'

'I guess they do,' he said. 'Our place was certainly no beach shack. And I never went fishing with my father. He was always at work.'

'Your mother?'

'She was partying.'

He shied away from the thinly veiled pity in Kate's eyes. 'Did you have brothers or sisters?' she asked.

He shook his head. 'I was an only child.'

As a little boy he had spent many lonely hours over the long school holidays rattling around the palatial house by himself. Then, when he'd turned fourteen, his father had started him working as a labourer on the company building sites during the holidays. It had been tough—brutal, in some ways, as the old hands had tested the 'silvertail' boss's son from the private school. But he'd been strong—both physically and mentally—and willing to prove himself. He'd won the doubters over.

From then on, the company had dominated his life. And he'd rarely gone back to that lonely Palm Beach house until he'd been old enough to take a group of his own friends.

'I envied the school friends who'd come back from a place like this full of tales of adventure.' He waved his hand towards the demolition site. 'I bet that old shack could have told some stories.'

'Perhaps. But only the one family got to enjoy the views and the proximity to the beach,' Kate said. She looked around the land with a distinctly proprietorial air. 'The owners got a good price for the land and now lots of people will be able to enjoy this magic place.'

'Spoken like a true, ruthless property developer,' he said, not entirely tongue-in-cheek. He had no issue with property developers—the good ones, that was—they were the company's lifeblood.

'I wouldn't say ruthless. More…practical,' she said with an uplifting of her pretty mouth.

'Okay. Practical,' he said.

'And don't forget creative. After all, no one else ever saw the potential of this land.'

'Okay. You're a practical and creative property developer without a ruthless bone in your body.'

'Oh, there might be a ruthless bone or two there,' she said with a flash of dimpled smile. 'But I wouldn't call me a property developer,' she said. 'I just like hotels.'

'Which is why we're standing here today,' he said. 'How did your interest come about?'

'When we were on tour with the dance company we stayed in some of the worst accommodation you could imagine.' She shuddered in her exaggerated, dramatic way that made him smile every time. Her face was so mobile; she pulled faces that on anyone else would be unattractive but on her were disarming.

'Let me count the ways in which we were tormented by terrible bedding, appalling plumbing and the odd cockroach or two. In one dump out west, we found a shed snakeskin under the bed.'

That made Sam shudder too. He hated snakes.

'Whenever we could manage it, a few of the girls and I scraped together the funds to lap up the luxury of a nice hotel where we lived the good life for a day or two.'

He nodded. 'I did the same thing in India. While we were working, we didn't expect accommodation any better than the people's homes we were rebuilding. When we were done, I checked in for a night at an extraordinary hotel in an old maharajah's palace.'

Her eyes sparkled green in the sunlight. 'Was it awesome? I would so love to see those Indian palace hotels.'

'The rooms were stupendous, the plumbing not so much. But I didn't care about that when I was staying in a place truly fit for a king.'

'That's it, isn't it? It doesn't have to be bandbox perfect for a good experience.' She bubbled with enthusiasm. 'It can be something more indefinable than gold-plated taps or feather mattresses. On those tours, I really got to know what made a good hotel or a bad one—regardless of the room rate. When the chance came to work with Ben at Harbourside, I jumped at it. I had to train from the ground up, but knew I'd found the career for me.'

'You've never wanted to work at a different hotel? A bigger one? Maybe somewhere else—one of those Indian hotels, perhaps? Or even Sydney?' He fought a hopeful note from entering his voice when he spoke about the possibility of her moving to his home city. There was no point. She was off-limits.

She shook her head emphatically. 'No. I want to work right here in Dolphin Bay. I couldn't think of anything else I would rather do than manage the new hotel. I want to make it the number-one destination on the south coast.'

She looked out to sea and he swore her dreams shone from her eyes.

But he was perturbed that her horizons seemed so narrow. In his view, she was a big fish in a small pond, too savvy to be spending her life in a backwater like this. And yet, despite that, her vision had been expansionary.

'What gave you the idea for this kind of resort?' he asked, genuinely interested.

She gave a self-deprecating shrug but he could tell she was burning to share her story. 'I saw friends flying to surf and yoga resorts in Bali. Others driving to Sydney to check in for pampering spa weekends. I wondered why people couldn't come to Dolphin Bay for that. We're well placed for tourists from both Canberra and Sydney: we've got the beach, we've got the beautiful natural environment. Get the eco credentials, and I reckon we could have a winner. Ben thought so too when I talked it over with him.'

'You've obviously done your research.' But as he thought about it, he realised there was something vital missing from her impassioned sell.

'You haven't actually visited the surf and spa hotels in Bali and Sydney yourself, by way of comparison?'

'Unfortunately, no.' Her face tightened and he could tell he'd hit a sore spot. 'I'm more of an armchair traveller. I know the best hotels' websites backwards, but I don't have the salary to afford overseas trips.'

He would enjoy showing her the world. The thought came from nowhere but with it the image of showing her some of the spectacular hotels he'd stayed in. Of taking her to the ones she'd dreamed of and ones she'd never imagined existed. But that went beyond the business brief of liaising on the hotel build.

'Maybe you should talk to Ben about your salary.' He couldn't imagine his old mate Ben would rip Kate off. But he knew only too well how tight-fisted some business people could be. His father had believed in rewarding people properly for their work and he'd followed suit. It was one of the reasons the company had so many loyal, long-serving employees.

Those people were why he hadn't immediately accepted the takeover offer. The owners of Lancaster & Son Construction had always prided themselves on being a family company, not only in the sense that it was owned by a family, but also because the people who worked for them were a family of sorts. Many of the staff would see a sale as a personal betrayal on his part. Worry about that was keeping him awake at night.

Kate shook her head. 'You probably know hospitality isn't the highest paying of industries, but Ben pays me fairly. And I've had the opportunity to learn the business from the ground up.'

'Soon you'll get the chance to see a hotel built from the ground up.'

'I can't wait to see it come to life,' she said, bubbling again with the enthusiasm he found so attractive.

She reached down for the clipboard she'd left on the bonnet of the small white van with the Hotel Harbourside logo. 'That's a cue to get down to business.'

'Fine by me,' he said. 'Fire away with any questions you might have.'

'Okay.' She looked up at him. 'Do I have to include the business questions in the questions I've got left with you?' She hastily amended her words. 'I mean, those questions wouldn't be about the actual building but about you. Uh... about you as our builder, I mean.'

'Fair enough,' he said. Her series of questions indicated

that underneath her businesslike attitude she might still be interested in him as a person, not just a contact. Though he doubted they'd be in one another's company long enough for her to ask them all.

'How long do you think it will take to build the resort?' she asked.

'From breaking ground to when you greet your first guests?'

She nodded.

'At least a year, maybe longer. This site is out of the way with a section of unsealed road to complicate matters in bad weather. That might pose problems with transporting equipment and materials. Then there's the fit-out to consider. You've specified a high standard of finish.'

'But you'll give us dates for commencement and completion in the final contract?'

'Of course. But we'll err on the side of conservative.' It was difficult to stay impartial and businesslike when the look of concentration on her face was so appealing; when the way she nibbled on the top of her pen made him want to reach over, pluck it from her hand and kiss her.

She scribbled some notes on her notepad. 'I'll include that in my report.'

Going on what he already knew about Kate, Sam had no doubt the report would be detailed and comprehensive.

'Talking like this makes it all seem very real,' she said. 'I'll be out here every day after work impatiently watching it go up. Will…will you be here to supervise it?'

He shook his head. 'There will be a construction manager on site. The team here will report back to Sydney.'

'So…you're just here for the one week?'

'That's right,' he said.

He wasn't sure whether he saw relief or disappointment in her eyes.

This was just one of many jobs for him but to her it was a big deal. He knew she wanted to do her best for Ben as well as make a mark for her own career. It would be best to be honest with her.

'Actually, there's a chance I won't be involved at all with the company by the time construction starts.' He kept his voice calm, not wanting to reveal the churning angst behind his words.

His obsession with the company had turned him into the worst kind of workaholic. Someone who, once his headspace was on the job, had pushed all other thoughts aside—family, friends, even his fiancée. His obsession had meant he had not been present at his father's deathbed. It had led his fiancée to dump him. To sell the company might free him to become a better person. But it could never be an easy decision.

Kate's eyes widened in alarm. 'What do you mean?'

'There's a serious offer on the table for the company.'

'You mean you're going to sell your family company?' The accusation in her eyes made him regret that he had opened the subject.

'It's an option. A decision I still have to make,' he said, tight-lipped.

She frowned. 'How could you do that when your father and grandfather built it up?' Her words stabbed like a knife in his gut. *Betrayal*—that was how people would see it. Like Kate saw it.

'Businesses are bought and sold all the time. You must know that.'

The words sounded hollow to his own ears. He knew what his father would have said—would have shouted, more like it. But he'd spent too many years trying to live up to his father's ambitions for him. The business was his now, to make the best deal as he saw it.

Her frown deepened. 'But surely not family concerns? It's…it's like the business has been entrusted to you, isn't it?'

What was she, the voice of his conscience?

'You could say that, but a company becomes an entity of its own,' he said. 'The multi-national company making the bid would grow it beyond what I could ever do in the current climate.'

'Bigger isn't always necessarily better, you know.'

He had no answer for that. Not when he couldn't understand why she wanted to lock herself away in a small town. But he *could* cut this conversation short, stop her from probing any further into the uncomfortable truths he had to deal with.

'That's beside the point,' he said. 'What I do with the company is my concern.'

Her mouth twisted. 'So you're telling me it's none of my business?'

'That's right,' he said.

Kate didn't know why she was shocked by Sam's revelation, or his blunt dismissal of the ensuing conversation. After all, her first impression of him was that he looked a tough, take-no-prisoners type of guy.

But then she'd seen a different side to his character with his talk of his volunteer work in India.

Who was the real Sam? Was she not the only one with lurking, unresolved issues?

She had to keep in mind he was a successful businessman. Could he have got where he was without elbowing other people aside, trampling over them, focusing only on the end goal no matter who might get hurt along the way?

But she didn't like the idea of him trampling over someone she cared about. 'What about Ben? That *is* my business. Ben trusts you to build this hotel. How could you be so…so disloyal to him?'

She didn't expect loyalty to her—after all, they were barely strangers—but the fact he could walk away so easily stung just a little.

His face was set rigid. 'There's nothing disloyal about it. It's business, pure and simple. Ben's a businessman himself, he'd understand that.'

'Don't be so sure of that. Ben wants you to build this hotel. Now I've met you, I…I want you to build the hotel. I call it disloyal if you hive it off to some other company we don't know.'

That scowl was back, his eyes bitter chocolate, dark and unreadable. 'Correction,' he said. 'You want the *company* to build your hotel. Not me personally.'

'That's not true. It's the personal connection that won you the tender.'

He towered above her. 'And I thought it was because of my expertise in building hotels.'

'That too, of course.' His glare made her fear she'd overstepped the mark. 'I'm sorry. I should back down.'

She was surprised that he didn't agree with her, remind her again it was none of her business. But she got the impression he carefully considered his next words. 'If—and it's still an "if"—the company is sold, the new owners will honour existing contracts and do exactly the same job as the company would have done under my direction.'

She exclaimed in disbelief. 'How can you say that? When our local deli was taken over by a bigger company, the first thing they did was sack people and the quality declined. Same thing happened with our garden centre. They were never the same. How can you be sure that wouldn't happen with your company?'

He paused. 'I can't be sure. If I sold, the new company would make certain assurances. But once new management was in charge they would do things their own way.'

'As I thought,' she said slowly. She dreaded having to bear this news to Ben.

'But as yet, I haven't made any decisions,' Sam said. 'That's one of the reasons I'm here, to take a break and think about the issue with a clear mind.'

Was that a crack in his armour of business speak?

'I still don't get it,' she said. 'Why would you consider selling, with all that family history invested in your company?'

'Try I'd never have to work again in my life?' His voice was strong and certain but the conviction was missing from his eyes.

She was probably totally out of line but she persisted. 'I don't know you very well, but I wonder if never working again would really satisfy you. What purpose would you have in life? I have the feeling you're not the kind of person who would be happy doing nothing.'

Sam's mouth tightened and his jaw tensed. She got the feeling she'd prodded a raw spot.

'Let me rephrase that,' he said. 'Selling would give me freedom to make my own mark, rather than carry on my father's vision for the company. To forge something new of my own.'

She paused. 'I guess there's that,' she said. She looked up at him. 'I might be speaking out of place here but—'

'But you're going to say it anyway,' he finished, with the merest hint of a smile that gave her the confidence to continue.

'Please think about it really carefully. Not just for Ben's

sake. Or mine. Or, I guess, the people who work for you. But for you.'

'I'll keep that in mind,' he said, his voice studiously neutral.

'Good,' she said. 'I don't know why, but I care about the effect it might have on you. You seem like a good person. And I reckon you might never forgive yourself if what makes your family company so special was to be destroyed.'

Sam swore under his breath. Every word Kate had said had hit home hard where he felt most vulnerable—and then hammered at his doubts and insecurities. How did she know how much he feared wrecking everything that was unique and good about his family company?

He'd known her for barely twenty-four hours yet straight away she seemed to have tuned in to the dilemmas that nagged at him regarding the sale. Yes, he'd seen moral outrage in those green eyes. But he'd also seen genuine understanding.

Frances, his ex-fiancée, would have advised sell, sell, sell. Not for the money, but to rid him of the business that she'd seen as a greedy mistress that had taken him too often from her side.

'You're a workaholic who doesn't care about anything but that damn company, and there's nothing left to give me.' Frances had said that on any number of occasions, the last when she'd flung her engagement ring at him. She'd never understood his compulsion to work that Kate had figured out within hours of meeting him. The compulsion he scarcely understood himself.

But he didn't welcome Kate's naive assumptions about the nature of the company deal. He didn't want to keep the business because of misplaced loyalty to an outmoded 'one set of hands on the steering wheel' management model. *He had to be one hundred per cent sure.*

'Thank you, Kate. You've made some good points and I'll certainly take them on board,' he said in a stiff, businesslike tone. As if the deadline for his decision wasn't already making his gut churn and keeping him awake at night.

'I'm glad you're not offended,' she said. 'I don't want to get off to a bad start for our working relationship.' Her brows were drawn together in a frown and her eyes were shadowed with concern.

'Not offended at all. What you said makes sense. I'm not the type of guy who deals well with time on my hands. I like to be kept busy. A day out from the office and I'm getting edgy already.'

He had started to pace back and forward, back and forward, in the same few metres of ground in front of Kate. It was a habit of his when he was stressed. He was scarcely aware he was doing it.

In silence, she watched him, her head swivelling each time he turned, until eventually she spoke. 'Do you realise you're wearing a groove in the sand?'

He stopped. 'Just making a start on digging for the foundations,' he said in a poor attempt at defusing his embarrassment with humour. As a CEO, as the child of a dominant father who had expected so much of him, he didn't like revealing his weaknesses.

She stared at him for a long moment then laughed. 'Okay. I get it. But if this is what you're like when you're meant to be taking a break, I'd hate to see you when you're on a deadline,' she said.

He halted. 'I need to hit the gym. Or the surf. Get rid of some energy.'

'If you really want to keep busy, I have a job for you that could fill a few hours.'

'A job?'

She shook her head. 'No, sorry, forget I said anything. You don't like waste-of-time wedding things.' She looked up at him, green eyes dancing. 'Do you?'

CHAPTER SIX

SAM GRITTED HIS TEETH. Kate so obviously wanted him to cajole her into telling him about the job she wanted him to do. If he played along with her girly game he could end up with some ghastly wedding-related activity like tying bows on frilly wedding favours, or adding loops and curls to his no-nonsense handwriting on place cards—all activities he'd managed to avoid for his own cancelled wedding. On the other hand, if he called her bluff and didn't cajole her, he'd always wonder if it was a job he might have enjoyed, that would have helped take his mind of the looming deadline for his decision.

'Tell me what you'd like me to do and I—'

'Okay,' she said with delight. 'I'd like you—'

He put up his hand to stop her. 'Before you go any further, please let me finish. I reserve the right to pass on any excessively frivolous wedding duty.'

She pulled one of her cute faces. 'Oh dear. I'm not sure if what I was going to ask you to do would count as frivolous or not.'

He tapped his booted foot on the ground. 'Try me.'

She gave an exaggerated sigh. 'Okay, then. That wedding arch.'

'The wedding arch you thought I'd come here to build?'

'The very same. Only there was never a wedding arch. That was me jumping to conclusions.'

'But now there *is* a wedding arch.'

'The more I thought about it, the more I thought Sandy would love a wedding arch. And, as you told me you could build one, I thought it might be a good idea. As a surprise for the bride and groom.'

He shrugged. 'Why not?'

'You mean you'll do it?'

'Yep.'

'Really?' Her face lit up and for a moment he thought she was going to grab his hands for an impromptu jig, like she had last night. But then she turned away, aware, no doubt, as he was, that it was inappropriate behaviour for a business relationship.

He realised that, again, his devotion to the company and company rules was squashing the development of a potential relationship with a woman. Did it have to be that way? Was there a way he could keep the company and conquer the workaholic ways that had led him to be single at thirty when he had anticipated being happily married at this age? Maybe even with a family?

'But won't it be quite difficult?' she said. Kate's words brought him back to the present.

'For a simple wooden structure? Nah. I reckon I could get everything I need at your local hardware store. Just give me an idea of what you've got in mind.'

'I've looked on the Internet and downloaded some images of beautiful arches for inspiration. I'll show you on my phone.'

'Okay,' he said. He liked to work with his hands. He found the rhythm of sawing, sanding and painting relaxing. Kate's 'little job' might be just what he needed to get the takeover offer into perspective.

'But I'd have trouble getting flowers and ribbons at this stage,' she said.

He frowned. 'Ribbons?'

'Sorry, I'm thinking out loud,' she said.

'Do you need all that stuff? I can paint the arch white.'

'Nice. But not enough. Not for a wedding.' She thought some more. 'I've got it—lengths of white organza draped around the poles. Simple. Elegant. Sandy would love that.'

Sam wasn't too sure what organza was. 'That's some kind of fabric, right?'

'Yes. Fine, white wedding-like fabric.'

'Then we'll have to make sure the arch is anchored firmly in the sand. If it's windy we don't want the fabric to act like sails and pick it up.'

'Oh no. Can you imagine the whole structure taking off and flying into the ocean?' She gracefully waved her arms in her long white sleeves, miming wings, and he could see the dancer in her.

He had been dragged along with his mother to see *Swan Lake* for some charity function; he was struck by the image of Kate in costume as an exquisite white swan. He wished he'd seen her dance on stage.

'Yep. I can see the headlines in the *Dolphin Bay Daily*,' he said. '"Bridal Arch Lost at Sea".'

'Eek! Please don't tease me about it. A wedding planner's nightmare.' She frowned. 'That really would be a disaster, wouldn't it? Maybe we should forget the whole idea of the arch."

'I'll make it work. I promise.' He liked it that his words of reassurance smoothed away her frown.

'Thank you, Sam. You're being such a good sport about this.'

She looked up at him and smiled and there was a long moment of complicity between them.

Working on the project meant more time spent with Kate. He shouldn't be so pleased at the idea but he was. He usually looked temptation in the eye and vanquished it. Not so when it came to the opportunity to spend more time with this woman.

Building a wedding arch was the last thing he wanted to do. Correction—the frilly wedding favours would have been the last thing. But he'd happily make ten wedding arches if it meant seeing more of Kate. He couldn't have her. He couldn't date her. He couldn't think of her in terms of a relationship. But that wouldn't stop him enjoying her company in a hands-off way.

'Okay, now that you've reassured me it will work, I'm so excited we're doing this,' she said. 'I can't wait to see the look on Sandy's face when she walks onto the sand and sees it there.'

'Let's get on with it, then,' he said.

And try not to think about what it would be like to have a hands-on *relationship with Kate.*

'So, show me the pictures on your phone,' he said.

'Sure.' She burrowed into that oversized handbag and pulled out her phone. 'Here they are,' she said, holding it up. He moved towards her so he could stand behind her, looking over her shoulder to her phone. He ended up so close, if she leaned backward she would nestle against him, as if they were spooning. *Not a good idea.*

He took a step back but then he couldn't see. He narrowed his eyes. 'The sun's reflecting off the screen,' he said. 'All I can see is glare.' He reached around her shoulder so he could cup her phone with his hand and shade it from the sunlight.

Bad move. It brought him way too close to her. He had to fight to ignore his tantalising proximity to her slender back, the curves of her behind.

Was she aware too? Her husky voice got even huskier as she chattered on, which made him suspect she was not as unaware as she was trying to seem. 'This one's made with bamboo but I think it looks too tropical,' she said. 'I like the wooden ones best; what do you think?'

She scrolled through the images of fancy wedding arches, but he was finding it too hard to concentrate when he could only think of the way-too-appealing woman so close to him.

'Can you see it?' she asked, swaying back. Now they were actually touching. He gritted his teeth.

'Yes. The wooden one is good,' he said in a strangled voice.

'Might the bamboo be easier for you to make?' she said.

'The wooden is fine. Easy.'

'So you don't like the bamboo?'

'No.' He couldn't care less about the arch. He could easily look up some designs later himself when he got back to the hotel.

'Can you figure out the measurements you need?'

There was only one set of measurements on his mind, and it wasn't for a wooden wedding arch.

'You have to allow room for both bride and groom,' she nattered on, while he broke out in a cold sweat. 'Ben's tall, but Sandy isn't wearing a big skirt, so...'

He couldn't endure her proximity for a moment longer. 'I've got the measurements,' he said abruptly as he stepped back.

He wanted to forget every rule he'd ever made and gather her into his arms.

But he couldn't. She was a client. And, while he still owned the company, he still followed its rules. He was stuck here in Dolphin Bay until after the wedding. He had to get through his friend's ceremony without there being any awkwardness. Kissing Kate right now would be ill-advised. Unwise. Irresponsible.

And he just knew it would be utterly mind-blowing.

He took another step back so she was more than arm's length away, so he could not be tempted to reach out to her.

She turned to face him. 'Are you okay with that? Do you need to see more?' Her face was flushed, her eyes wide, her mouth slightly parted. *She felt it too.* He was sure she did. Maybe she was more disciplined than he was. Because all he wanted to do was kiss her. Claim that lovely mouth, draw her close to him.

'No. I've got it,' he said.

'So, now we've settled on the style we—I mean you—need to start making it happen.'

'I won't be able to do it by myself. You'll need to consult. Approve.'

The flush on her cheeks made her eyes seem even greener. 'Of course,' she said. 'If we want to keep the arch a secret, we'll have to work on it away from the bride and groom. There's a big shed at home. It…it used to be my father's; there are tools in there.'

'Sounds good,' he said.

'I'll give you the address and you can have the timber delivered there.'

She looked around her and then at her clipboard. 'Have we done all we need to do for the site inspection?'

'For the moment.'

'Let's go, then. I'll drop you at the hardware shop. I'll look for the organza but I don't think I'll find it in the quantity we'll need in any of the shops here. I might have to ask Sandy to get it for me in Sydney on Wednesday. I'll tell her it's for the table decorations. She won't question that.'

'Hold on,' Sam said. 'Why wouldn't you buy it in Sydney yourself?'

Kate stilled and didn't meet his gaze. 'Because I...I won't be going to Sydney.'

'What?' He was astounded. 'For the stag night? Hen night? Hag night? Whatever they're calling it.'

Her freckles stood out from her pale skin. 'No.'

'But you organised it.' He'd been looking forward to getting her on his home territory. He'd even been going to propose they all stay at his apartment instead of a hotel. He'd bought the large penthouse in anticipation of getting married. It was way too big for one person; sometimes he felt as lonely there as he had in the palatial Palm Beach house. Kate could have her own room; there would be no question of any more intimate arrangement.

She shook her head. 'I organised a night out in Dolphin Bay. Not Sydney.'

'You're upset that your plans were changed?'

Colour rushed back into her face. 'Of course not. If Lizzie can't come here, you should all go to Sydney. But not me, I'm afraid.'

He drew his brows together. 'I don't get it. Don't you want to be with your friends?' He paused. 'Is it because you don't want to spend time with Jesse? He's the best man. It would be difficult to avoid him.'

'No. Jesse and I are fine with each other now. It's as if the...the incident never happened. He's as relieved as I am.'

'I was going to suggest I show you around the Lancaster & Son headquarters while we're all in Sydney.'

'That would have been nice. Perhaps another time?'

The stubborn tilt of her chin and the no-nonsense tone of her voice made him realise she had no intention of coming to Sydney. To party, to visit his office, even for a change of scene.

'Sure,' he said. 'But this would be a good time for a visit to the office.'

'You mean while you still own the company?'

It felt painful to think there could very well be a time when he had no connection to the company. But how could he keep the business and stop making the mistakes that had blighted his life because of it?

'That too. But at the beginning of the job. You could meet the team who'll be working on the resort build. That way they won't be strangers when they come to Dolphin Bay.'

'By the time we got up to Sydney and back the next day, I'd be away for too long. I'm needed here.'

'At the hotel? Surely Ben can organise someone to replace you?'

'Maybe. But it's late notice. I'm also learning how to look after Sandy's bookshop while she's away on her honeymoon. I love Bay Books.'

Everything she loved seemed to be in Dolphin Bay.

He remembered how she'd referred to Sydney as 'outside'. It had seemed odd at the time.

'I can't believe Ben and Sandy would want you to stay here working and not go to Sydney with them. You're their bridesmaid.'

'It's not just them. I have…other commitments here.'

'Commitments?' He suddenly realised how little he knew about her. She could be a single mother with kids to support. She could have an illness that required regular hospitalisation. She could belong to some kind of sect that didn't allow partying. Who knew?

'I live with my mother and sister,' she said.

Okay, it was unusual to be living at home at twenty-eight years old, but not unheard of.

'And they don't let you leave town?' he quipped in a joke that immediately fell flat.

'Of course they do. I don't let myself leave town because I'm needed here.'

He frowned. He didn't think he was particularly obtuse but he didn't know what she was getting at. 'I don't follow you,' he said.

'My mother and I share the care of my sister,' she said. 'She was injured in a car crash when she was eleven and left a paraplegic. She's confined to a wheelchair.'

For a long moment, Sam was too stunned to speak. That was the last thing he had anticipated. 'I'm sorry,' he eventually managed to say.

'No need to apologise,' said Kate. 'You weren't to know. Mum's a nurse and often works night shift at the Dolphin Bay Community Hospital. My sister, Emily, says she's fine on her own, but we like to be there when we can.'

'I understand,' he said.

Did he really? Sometimes Kate didn't understand herself how she'd ended up at her age living at home with her mother and her twenty-six-year-old sister.

Sam's brow was furrowed. 'But you lived in Sydney and travelled with your dance troupe. Who looked after your sister then?'

She wished he wouldn't ask the awkward questions that made her look for answers she didn't want to find. The more he spoke, the more she could see herself reflected in his eyes. And she wasn't sure she was at ease with what she saw.

'My mother. Then she broke her arm, couldn't manage and asked could I come home for a while.'

'How long ago was that?'

'Five years ago.' Right when she'd fallen apart after the near-assault and had left the dance troupe. She'd been glad for an excuse to run home.

'And you never left again?'

'That's right.'

'That's when you started to work for Ben?'

'Yes. Though it was only casual hours at first. You see, I'd dropped out of university in the final year of my business degree.'

'To join the dance troupe?'

'Yes.' There'd been so much more to it than that. But she wasn't ready to share it with Sam. With anyone. 'So when I came back, I finished my degree part-time at a regional campus not far from here.'

'And here you've stayed.'

'Put like that it sounds so grim. Trust me, it isn't. I'm happy here. This is a fabulous community to live in. And I love my job.' She tried not to sound overly defensive.

'If you say so.' He didn't look convinced. Who would blame him? Even her mother urged her to get more of a life. 'I'm not one for small towns,' he said.

'Dolphin Bay might not be for everyone but it suits me.'

'Sure,' he said. 'But I'm sorry you're not coming to Sydney for the party. Have you told Sandy?'

She shook her head. 'No, I haven't, and I'd appreciate it if you didn't tell her. I'll make an excuse at the last minute so she doesn't waste time trying to convince me to change my mind. Because I won't.'

'*I* can't make you change your mind?'

If anyone could, it would be him. 'Not even you.'

The knots of anxiety that could tie her up for hours were starting to tighten. She could lose control. She had to stop thinking about the trip to Sydney, not get caught up in that vortex of fear.

But right now she had to be cheerful Kate and put a bright face on it.

'Let's get moving, then, shall we? We've got a top-secret wedding arch to build.'

CHAPTER SEVEN

SAM NOTICED THREE things about the home Kate shared with her mother and sister as he approached it the next afternoon. The first was the wheelchair-friendly ramps that ran from the street to the house. The second was the riotously pretty garden and tubs of bright flowers everywhere. The third was the immediate sense of warmth and welcome that enveloped him when Kate opened the door to him.

'Come in,' she said with a smile that sparkled with dimples. 'The delivery from the hardware store has arrived. I got them to stack it in the shed out the back.'

She had only recently finished her shift at the hotel but had already changed into faded jeans and a snug-fitting T-shirt. The simple clothes did nothing to hide her shapely body. That was going to prove distracting. And yet even if she were dressed in an old sack he'd find her distracting.

It was getting more difficult with every moment he spent with Kate to think of her only as a business contact. He shoved his hands in his pockets so he wouldn't be tempted to greet her with a hug.

Inside, the open-plan house was nothing special in architectural terms, comfortably furnished with well-worn furniture in neutral colours. What made it stand out was that it had obviously been redesigned to accommodate a wheelchair—plenty of space left between furniture and the kitchen benches set much lower than was usual.

Framed photographs propped on practically every surface caught his eye: a wedding photo from thirty-odd years ago, baby photos—the adorable infant with the fuzz of ginger hair and gummy smile with tiny dimples already showing must surely have been Kate. There was another of Kate wearing a checked school uniform with her wayward hair tamed into two thick plaits. Kate with her arm around a younger girl with strawberry-blond hair. Kate, graduating in a cap and gown.

But the picture that held his attention was a large, framed colour photograph hanging on the wall of a young Kate in a classical ballet costume. The slender teenager was wearing a white dress with a tight, fitted bodice with gauzy wings at the back and a full translucent skirt. She balanced on pointed toes in pink ballet slippers. Her pale graceful arms were arched above her head to frame her face. Her hair was scraped right back off her face but glowed with fiery colour, and her green eyes sparkled with irrepressible mischief.

Sam gestured to it. 'That's nice.'

'When I was thirteen I was embarrassed when Mum hung it up so prominently. Now I look at that girl and think she was kinda cute.'

Sam's mother didn't like family photos cluttering up the house. There was just one of him as a baby framed in heavy silver on her dressing table. There had been photos of him in the formal blazer and striped tie of his private school, others of him playing football. They used to be in his father's study. He had no idea where they were now. He was gripped by a sudden, fierce desire to get them back. One day, when he had his own family, he wanted the living room to look like this one—not the stark, empty elegance of his mother's.

'You were lovely,' he said, then quickly amended, '*Are* lovely.'

'Thank you,' she said, looking wistfully at the photo. 'It seems so long ago now. I thought I was going to be a prima ballerina. So much has happened since.'

The time the photo was taken must have been around the time she'd shared her first kiss with Jesse. Again jealousy seared him. Unwarranted, he knew; he had no reason to doubt Jesse or Kate. Jesse had taken him aside and explained that, while he loved Kate like a sister, there was absolutely no romance between them. But still he felt uncomfortable at the thought of them kissing.

There was another equally large framed photo of an attractive, strawberry-blond teenager playing wheelchair basketball. 'Is this your sister?' She was holding the ball up ready to shoot a goal with strong, muscular arms, her expression focused and determined.

'Yes. Emily's a champion basketball player.'

He looked around the room. 'She's not home now?'

'No. She's an accountant at the bank in Dolphin Bay, so won't be home until this evening. Though you might meet Mum; she'll be knocking off from the hospital early today.'

'I'll look forward to that,' he said. He was curious about the dynamic between three adult women sharing a house.

'Come on,' said Kate. 'I'll take you out the back to the shed. I'm looking forward to getting started on the *amazing arch*.' She said the last two words with typical Kate exaggeration.

'So it's to be an *amazing* arch now, is it?' he asked as he followed her.

'Of course. After all, you're making it,' she said with that unconsciously flirtatious lilt to her husky voice.

'I'm flattered you're so confident in my abilities,' he said.

She laughed but, as she neared the old wooden shed at the bottom of the garden, her laughter trailed away. She stopped outside the door. 'I…I don't go in here often.'

'You said it was your father's workshop. He's not around?'

Kate looked straight ahead rather than at him. 'He…he was driving the car when Emily was injured. Another car was on the wrong side of the road. Dad swerved to avoid a head-on collision but smashed into a tree.'

For a long moment Sam was too shocked to speak. 'I'm sorry.'

'Emily was trapped inside the car. He…Dad…walked away uninjured. But Emily… Her spine was broken.' Kate's mouth twisted. 'Dad never forgave himself. Couldn't deal with it. Started drinking. Eventually he…he left. Six months later, he died.'

Sam found it hard to know what to say as Kate's family tragedy unfolded. 'When did that happen?'

Her arms were tightly folded across her chest. 'The accident happened not long after that photo of me at my ballet concert was taken.'

'That must have been tough for you.' He knew the words were inadequate but they were the best he could come up with. He had lost his father but it had been to a quick heart attack. He'd gone too soon, and he still mourned him, but the loss hadn't been in the tragic way of Kate's father.

She nodded. 'For me. For my mum. Most of all for Emily. She was in hospital for more than a year. Our lives changed, that's for sure.'

He longed to reach out and draw her into his arms but couldn't bring himself to do it. It would change things between them and he didn't know that she would want that. Or if he did.

Instead he pushed open the door to the shed. Inside it was neat and orderly. Hand tools were arranged on shadow boards. Nails and screws were lined up by size in old glass jars. He whistled his appreciation. 'This is a real man cave. Your dad must have liked spending time here.'

Kate hesitated, only one foot past the doorway. 'He liked making things. Fixing things. I…I spent lots of time in here with him. He taught me how to be a regular young handywoman.'

Just as his father had decided to make a man of him and introduce him to building sites.

Kate adept with hammer and saw? She continued to surprise him. 'That's a good attribute in a girl.'

'He wanted me to grow up as an independent woman who didn't need a man to change a tap washer for her.'

'And did you?'

'He left before he completed my workshop education.' Her voice was underlined with a bitterness he hadn't heard from her before.

'I'm sorry,' he said again. He realised that while he could handle disputes on building sites, or argue the fine points of a multi-million-dollar contract, he was ill-equipped to deal with emotion. Frances had accused him of being so tied up with the company he couldn't care about anything—or anyone—else. Perhaps she'd been right.

'He changed so much,' said Kate. 'Changed towards me. Became angry when he'd always been so even-tempered. I was okay, he was okay, but Emily was lying broken in her hospital bed. Survivor's guilt, I suppose now. But as a kid I didn't know about all that. In a way…in a way I was glad when he went.'

Sam stood silent, not knowing how to comfort her in her still-present grief, raging at himself that he couldn't. He was relieved when she changed the subject.

'Anyway, enough about that,' she said with a forced cheerfulness to her voice. We've got an *amazing* wedding arch to make.'

Kate found it disconcerting to have another man working in her father's shed—and totally distracting because the man was Sam in jeans, work boots and a white T-shirt. Strong, capable and utterly male.

For a moment it seemed like the past and present collided. Yesterday, she was the little girl revelling in being allowed to work with Daddy in his shed, her father kind and endlessly patient. Today the grown-up Kate was acutely aware of tall, broad-shouldered Sam dominating the restricted space. Sam, the successful—and possibly ruthless—businessman. Sam, the man who spent his vacation helping people in need. Sam, who had been so good-natured about agreeing to make the arch she was sure would delight her friends on their special day.

Her dad would have liked him.

She forced the thought away. For so long, her memories of her father had been bitter ones. Not that he had caused Emily's accident—his action in the car had saved her sister's life—but the way he had changed afterward. Had become someone so different he had frightened her.

But being here with Sam was bringing back the happy memories, memories of being loved and cherished.

Sam checked the delivery from the hardware store. 'It's all here,' he said. He looked around him. 'Your dad had a good collection of tools. That orbital saw is in good nick. I'd like to use it.'

'Help yourself,' she said. 'And anything else you need. Nobody else uses the tools.'

'Not even you? Not after what your father taught you?'

'No,' she said, her tone letting him know she didn't want to talk any further about her father.

She stepped back from Sam, though there wasn't much room to move in the confined space of the shed. Wherever she stood, she wasn't far from him. She was aware of his proximity, the way his muscles flexed as he hauled the timber into place, the way he looked so good in those jeans.

She liked the assured way he handled the pieces of timber as he showed her how he intended to construct the arch. 'There will be four sturdy supports and four corresponding brace supports across the top,' he explained, running his hands along the length of the timber. 'Building it with four supports instead of just two will make it much more stable.'

His hands were large and well-shaped, strong but deft. She refused to let herself think about how they would feel cradling her face, stroking her body…

'Tell me where you want to drape your fabric and I'll insert a series of pegs you can wind it around to keep it in place,' he said.

'That sounds perfect,' she said. 'Clever you.'

'The actual structure will be quite big and cumbersome,' he said. 'I'm going to use hinges so we can easily dismantle it to get it to the beach in your van and put it together again.'

'Good idea,' she said. 'We'll have to work on the logistics of that. Like, when do I attach the fabric, and how do we get it to the beach early enough so it's a surprise? We might have to let someone else in on the secret.'

Sam paused and looked searchingly at her. 'Have you spoken to Sandy about getting the fabric yet?'

She couldn't meet his gaze. 'I'll do that tomorrow.'

'Are you sure you won't change your mind about going to Sydney?'

'No,' she said firmly so he wouldn't be aware of the fear thudding through her at the thought of getting in a car and driving to Sydney. 'As I said, it's too inconvenient.'

'You'll be letting your friends down—'

She spoke over him. 'Don't you think I know that?' She wanted her voice to sound firm, even a little angry, at his interference but it came out shaky and unsure.

She turned her back on him and picked up one of her father's pliers from the shadow board. She remembered it was one of his favourite tools and hung it back again on the exact spot where he had so carefully outlined its shape.

She tried to avoid the empty section of shadow board where her set of child-sized tools had hung. Her dad had bought them for the birthday she'd turned eleven. After he'd left, in a fit of anger and grief she'd pulled them down and hurled them to the ground, wanting to destroy them. She didn't know what had happened to them after that.

'I see where you got your organisational skills from,' Sam said in a voice that was too understanding.

A voice that made her want to rest her head on his broad shoulder and confess how confused and scared she was. Tell him she didn't know what was wrong with her, that she was letting her friends down. How she was dreading letting Sandy know she wouldn't be going to Sydney.

Instead, she pasted on her bright, cheery smile and turned back to face him.

'Can I tell you again how much I appreciate you doing this for me?' she said.

'You're welcome,' he said gruffly and she knew she hadn't fooled him one bit. 'Now you've told me your dad taught you some handywoman skills, I guess I can count on you to help.'

'I'm not that great with saws or drills. But I can hammer and use a screwdriver, and I'll put my hand up for sanding.

I'm very good at sanding.' She picked up a sanding block from the bench to prove the point. 'The surface will have to be really smooth. We don't want Sandy's gown catching on it and snagging. Can't have a bride with a snagged gown—not on my watch.'

She was aware she was speaking too rapidly. Aware that it wasn't just from nervousness but acute awareness of Sam—his perceptive brown eyes that saw right through to her innermost yearnings; the heat of his powerfully muscled body that warmed her even without them touching. Just looking at his superb physique and so handsome face made her feel wobbly at the knees.

Towering above her, he seemed to take up every bit of the confined space. When he took a step closer it brought him just kissing distance away. She would only have to reach out her hand to stroke that scar on his eyebrow that she found so intriguing, to trace the high edge of his cheekbone, to explore with trembling fingers his generous, sensual mouth.

Looking intently into her face, and without saying a word, he took the block from her suddenly nerveless fingers and placed it on the bench. 'No need for that right now,' he said. Her breath caught in her throat in a gasp that echoed around the walls of the small space.

She didn't resist when, without another word, he drew her close, cupped her chin in his hand and kissed her. She sighed with pleasure and kissed him right back, her heart tripping with surprise, excitement and anticipation. Hadn't she wanted this from the day she'd first seen him?

His lips were firm and warm and, when his tongue slipped into her mouth, passion—so long dormant—ignited and surged through her. She quickly met his rhythm with her own, slid her hands up to rest on his broad shoulders, delighted in the sensation of their closeness.

This was how a kiss should be. This kiss—Sam's kiss—consigned any other kiss she'd ever had into oblivion.

His breath was coming fast and so was hers. Desire, want, need: they all melded into an intoxicating hunger for him.

He pulled her close to his hard chest and his powerful arms held her there, her soft curves pressed against him. His kiss became harder, more demanding, more insistent. She thrilled to the call of his body and her own delirious response.

They kept on kissing. But the force of his kiss pushed her backwards against the wall of the shed so it pressed hard into her back with no way of escaping the discomfort. Suddenly her mind catapulted her back to the farmer forcing his unwanted attentions on her. He'd backed her into a boot cupboard, confined, airless—like the shed she was in now.

Sudden fear gave her the strength to put her hands flat against Sam's chest and push him away. 'No!' she cried. He released her immediately.

Swaying, she gripped on to the edge of the bench beside her.

His breathing came fast and heavy; her own was so ragged she could barely force out words. 'I'm sorry. I'm so sorry, I—'

'I rushed you,' he said hoarsely.

'No. It wasn't that. Things moved so quickly. I was… scared.'

He drew his dark brows together in a frown. 'Scared? I would never hurt you, Kate.'

'I…I know that. It's just…' There was no easy explanation for her behaviour.

'Just what? Is there something wrong?' His voice was rich with concern, which only made her feel worse.

'No. Nothing wrong,' she lied. But she knew she should tell him that it was nothing he'd done. That it was old fears, old hurts, that were tethering her. 'Sam, I—'

At that moment her mobile phone rang. She picked it up and swore silently at the voice of the panicking staff member at the other end. She put the phone back in her bag and turned to Sam, unable to meet his eyes.

'Th…there's an emergency at the hotel they seem to think only I can solve.' She didn't know whether to be relieved or annoyed at the interruption.

'Go,' he said.

'What just happened—I'm sorry.'

'Nothing to be sorry about,' he said. 'You're needed at work. You have to be there. No one knows that better than I do. Work comes first. It…it always has with me.' There was an edge to his voice that made her wonder what was behind those words. Again she wondered if she wasn't the only one with secret hurts in her past.

'Are you sure you'll be okay here?'

'Sure. It will be good to get stuck into working on the arch. I want to get as much as I can done before I leave for Sydney tomorrow.'

Saying goodbye was awkward. Now there could be no denying their mutual attraction. They were not friends, so no casual kiss on the cheek. Not just business contacts, so shaking hands would be inappropriate.

The kisses they'd shared had changed everything, had broken the barrier of business that they had constructed between them and had left her wanting more kisses—wanting *more* than kisses. But she'd freaked out and pushed him away. What must Sam think of her?

The emergency at work took longer than Kate expected. The glitch in the online reservation system had required rather more than the tweak she'd initially thought. It was more than two hours later before she returned home. She headed for the shed but was disappointed to find it empty.

The pieces of timber Sam had been working on lay across her father's pair of old wooden sawhorses. Wood shavings and sawdust had fallen to the floor and their sharp fragrance permeated the room. Sam's leather work gloves, moulded to the shape of his hands, sat on the bench top. She picked one up. It still felt warm from his body heat. She couldn't resist the temptation to put it to her face and breathe in the scent of the leather and Sam. It was intoxicating.

Where was he? She was surprised at the depth of her disappointment that he hadn't waited for her. Had her reaction to his kiss made him leave?

Her mobile phone rang from her handbag. Her mum. 'We heard you come in. Sam's in the house with me and Emily.'

Of course.

Why hadn't she realised that would happen? She'd told her mother that Sam would be using the shed. Mum, in her hospitable way, would have popped in to see how he was and next thing she'd probably have invited him in for a cup of tea.

Sam looked quite at home on the sofa drinking tea, as predicted, with her mother and Emily. His big boots were propped by the door and he was in socked feet. She drank in the sight of him, looking so relaxed and at ease in her home. Her heart seemed to swell with the pleasure of it.

'Sorry, I got held up, Sam,' she said.

He immediately got up to greet her. His eyes connected with hers, probing, questioning. But his voice was light-hearted. 'As you can see, I'm being well looked after. Dawn's chocolate fudge cake is the ideal fuel for a hungry man.'

There was a tiny smear of chocolate on the top of his lip that she found endearing. She fought the impulse to lean over and wipe it off with her finger. Tried to fight the thought of what it might be like to lick it off, then follow it with a kiss that would show him how much she wanted him and negate the awkwardness of their earlier encounter.

'Sam was working so hard out there, I thought he needed feeding,' said her mother.

'Thanks, Mum,' she said. 'You always think people need feeding.'

'You mean you're going to pass on a piece of chocolate cake?' said her mother.

'Of course not,' Kate said, affecting horror. 'Bring it on, please.'

'Sam's been filling us in on your project,' said Emily. 'I love the idea of the wedding arch.' She laughed. 'Sandy's plan to have just her and Ben and Hobo on the beach with no one else sure isn't going to happen.'

'It will still be simple and intimate, but with just a few more guests and a lot more to eat afterwards,' said Kate, unable to prevent the defensive note that crept into her voice.

'Sandy won't regret it,' said Dawn. 'Your wedding day should be something really special you can always look back on with joy. Sandy will thank you, sweetie, for taking it in hand for her.'

'Did you say Hobo was going to be part of the wedding?' asked Sam. 'You mean Ben's dog?'

As a guest at Hotel Harbourside, he would be familiar with the big, shaggy golden retriever who was often to be found near the reception desk.

'Yes,' said Kate. 'He'll be wearing a wide, white bow around his neck.'

'If he doesn't chew it off first,' said Emily.

'How well trained is Hobo?' asked Sam. 'I'm thinking about the arch.'

'Oh no, you don't think he…?'

Sam shrugged. There was a definite twinkle in those dark eyes. 'Dogs and lamp posts. Dogs and trees. Why not dogs and wedding arches?'

Kate stared at him. 'Noooo! Hobo lifting his leg on our beautiful wedding arch in the middle of the ceremony? Not going to happen. Someone will have to make darn sure he stays on his leash.'

'Another job for the wedding planner,' said Sam. 'Better appoint an official dog minder and write them out a schedule of duties.'

There was a moment of silence. Kate saw her mother and Emily exchange glances. Did they really think she would take offence at Sam's teasing?

Emily laughed, which broke the tension. 'Sam, have you ever got Kate sussed out already.'

Her mother laughed too, then Sam, and Kate joined in. It was warm, friendly, inclusive laughter.

'Kate, we've invited Sam to stay for dinner,' said Dawn. 'If that's okay with you.'

Sam caught her eye. She could see he liked being here, liked her family. But he was waiting for her to give her okay. Had the kiss they'd shared made any difference?

'That's fine by me,' she said.

But she knew she'd have to be on guard all evening. Their passionate encounter had made a difference to her. She could no longer deny how strongly she was attracted to him. And she knew beyond a doubt she was in serious danger of developing deeper feelings for Sam.

CHAPTER EIGHT

TELLING SANDY SHE wouldn't be going to Sydney for the bridal party's night out was every bit as difficult as Kate had dreaded it would be. And then some.

Kate cringed at the hurt in her friend's eyes. Her excuses for why she was dropping out of the trip were weak and didn't stand up well to interrogation.

'I totally don't believe Emily needs you to be here with her tonight,' Sandy said.

Neither would her fiercely independent, mobile sister if she'd known she'd been used as an excuse. In fact, Emily would be furious.

'Is this about Sam?' Sandy asked. 'Are you mad at me and Ben for throwing you together with him?'

'Not at all. I really like him. Seriously, I do.' The cursed blush crept into her cheeks.

'Then *why?*'

I don't know! Tell me and we'll both know.

Kate bit down on her bottom lip to stop it from betraying her with an about-to-cry quiver. She felt so bad about letting Sandy down. But she'd suffered enough humiliation over the Jesse disaster not to want anyone—even Sandy—to know she couldn't even explain to *herself* why she was staying behind.

'I'm sorry but I just can't go. Can we leave it at that?'

Sandy eventually gave up her questioning. But Kate felt more and more miserable by the minute.

The wedding party had decided to go up to Sydney in one car. Kate stood in the driveway of Hotel Harbourside, perilously close to tears, as she watched Sam throw his overnight bag into the boot of Ben's big SUV.

Just as she thought he was about to leave, Sam turned and strode towards her. 'Last chance. Are you sure you won't come with us?' he said in a voice lowered for her ears only.

There was nothing she wanted more than to go with him. To throw herself into his arms and say 'yes.' But she was terrified of what might happen when she tried to get into the car.

Poor Kate.

In her mind, she could hear the shocked exclamations as if they were really happening.

No way would she ruin this moment for her friends, or endure further humiliation for herself.

She looked back up at Sam and mutely shook her head.

He met her gaze for a long moment, then frowned, obviously perplexed by her behaviour. 'Okay,' he said and turned away. 'I'll see you tomorrow when we get back.' He made no attempt to touch her, to kiss her goodbye. But then why would he, when she had so soundly rejected his last kiss?

Would he ever want anything to do with her again?

Shoulders slumped, she watched him head to the car. Ben and Sandy sat in the front and Sam climbed in with Jesse in the back. If she'd gone with them, would they have expected her to sit in the middle between Sam and Jesse? She wouldn't have let that happen. She would have wanted it to be just her and Sam.

As the car pulled away from the hotel driveway she

turned her back on it and dragged one foot after the other, away from the hotel. No way did she want to wave them off. She wished she could have gone with them to celebrate the wedding of two people she cared about, who both deserved their second chance at happiness.

But something she didn't understand was holding her back with a grip she seemed powerless to resist. She knew what would have happened if she'd tried to get into that car—pounding heart, nausea, limbs paralysed.

What was wrong with her?

She left the hotel behind her and kept walking, away from the harbour and along the boardwalk that led to Big Ray beach.

Had she become such a small-town hick she'd developed an aversion to fast traffic and bright lights?

She walked slowly along the beach, mid-week quiet with only a few people enjoying the surf, not taking her usual joy from the sight of the aquamarine water. She didn't even look out for the big, black manta rays for which the beach had been unofficially named.

At the north end of the beach, where the sand ended, she clambered over the rocks that divided Big Ray from the next beach. It was low tide and the rocks were fully exposed, smelling of salt and seaweed and the occasional whiff of decay from some poor stranded sea creature. She climbed down the final barrier of rocks onto the sand of the neighbouring beach, Wild Water, which had waves so violent and rips so dangerous only the boldest of adolescent surfers braved its waters.

Was it because she feared being alone with Sam?

With the rocks behind her, ahead of her was a stretch of white sand, bounded by rocks again at its northern end. To her right was the vast expanse of the Pacific Ocean. To her left was the freshwater river with its clear, cool water.

She slipped off her sandals and scuffed her feet in the sandbar that blocked the estuary of the river from flowing into the sea. The sandbar had appeared after the last big storm to hit the coast. It would just as likely disappear in the next one. In the meantime, the thwarted river pooled into a wide stretch of safe, shallow water. Her parents had taught her and Emily to swim here. She remembered again her father's endless patience and encouragement.

On one side were sand dunes, on the other bush straggled down a slope right down to the banks of the river, stands of spotted eucalypts reflected in the still waters of the lagoon. The beach bordered national park and there wasn't a building in sight. Sometimes kangaroos came down to the surf and splashed in the shallows, much to the delight of visitors, but there weren't any today.

This was one of her very favourite places. When she'd been on tour, tossing and turning in yet another uncomfortable hotel bed, she'd closed her eyes and envisaged its peace and beauty. In the first rapturous weeks of her romance with R—she could only bear to think of him by his initial—she'd told him about this place and suggested he come with her to see it. Thankfully he had scorned the idea, and that meant it was untainted by memories of him.

She inhaled a deep breath of the fresh salt-tangy air. And another. And another. Somehow she had to get herself together. If she couldn't get her thoughts in order here, she couldn't anywhere.

Dolphin Bay was her safe place. This place was her safest of the safe. But had she somehow transformed a safe place into a trap from which she could never escape?

Sam sat in the back seat of Ben's car, headed north to Sydney on the Princes Highway. There should have been laughter and banter as they started to celebrate in time-honoured style Ben and Sandy's last nights of 'freedom' from matrimonial chains.

But an uncomfortable silence had fallen upon the car. Kate.

No one wanted to mention her. No one wanted to express their worries about why their friend had reneged on part of the wedding arrangements she had so wholeheartedly thrown herself into. He, who had known her for such a short time, was eaten up with concern about her.

How had she become so important, so quickly?

The car passed the last petrol station on the far outskirts of town.

'Stop the car,' Sam said. 'Can you pull over here, please, Ben?'

Ben did as directed, bringing the car to a halt on the side of the road.

'Do you need to visit the little boy's room, mate?' asked Jesse.

'No,' said Sam. 'I'm going back for Kate.'

The sound of the combined intake of three sets of breath echoed through the interior of the car.

'Good,' said Sandy at last. She twisted around from the front seat to face Sam. 'There's something wrong. I'm worried about her. Really worried.'

'Me too,' said Jesse. 'It's unlike Kate to pass on the chance of a party.'

'She wouldn't come to Sydney with me to help me choose my wedding dress, either,' added Sandy. 'At the time I thought she wanted me to have time just with Lizzie. Now I'm not so sure that was her reason.'

'Should we all go back?' asked Ben.

'No,' said Jesse. 'It should be Sam. When it comes to Kate, Sam's the man.'

As he got out of the car, Sam nodded to Jesse in unspoken male acknowledgement of what his words had meant.

'Tell her how much we want her to come,' Ben called after him. 'Kate's been so good to us. It won't be the same without her.'

Sam didn't have to wait long to hitch a ride back into town. Once back at the hotel he dumped his bag and went to look for Kate. Her mobile went to voice mail. Neither her mother nor sister answered the phone at their home. Finally, the girl at the hotel reception told him Kate wasn't on duty but that, after the boss and his fiancée had taken off for Sydney, she had seen her heading in the direction of the beach.

Sam strode out towards the boardwalk to Big Ray beach. The surf beach was practically deserted. He spied a lone set of small, female-looking footprints just above the waterline. The footprints tracked along the length of the beach right to the end where the rocks took over. Shallow, swirling waves were encroaching and starting to obliterate them. He remembered Kate telling him about the idyllic place she loved on the next beach. The footprints turned out slightly, ballet-dancer style. He took a punt they were hers.

Kate sat in the shade of a grove of overhanging gum trees set back from the water's edge. She wished she could have a swim but the one thing her capacious handbag didn't hold was a swimsuit. When she was younger she wouldn't have hesitated to strip off her dress and swim in her underwear in the welcoming waters of the lagoon. She would even swim nude on a day like this when there wasn't another soul in sight.

She wouldn't risk that now, not since R had insinuated into her psyche such doubts about her body, her sexuality, her desires. Not since her attacker had taunted her about her provocative dance moves and her immodest stage out-fits.

These days she kept everything buttoned up: her emotions, her desires, her needs. She realised, with a sharp stab of despair, that she had barricaded herself against intimacy, against love, against feeling.

Against allowing herself to admit the depth of her attraction to Sam and enjoy to the full the pleasure of being in his arms.

She sat hunched over with her arms wrapped around her knees, lost in the thoughts that spun around and around in her brain. How had she come to this, sitting alone on a beach, when the life she wanted went on around her?

When she was younger the restrictions of small-town life had chafed her. She'd thought the best view she'd ever see of Dolphin Bay would be in the rear-view mirror as she'd left to go to university in Sydney. Back then, she'd been full of hope and ambition and dreams of seeing the world. She'd never imagined she'd come back to Dolphin Bay as anything other than a visitor to catch up with her family and old friends.

She shut her eyes. The muted rhythm of the waves crashing on the nearby sand was near-hypnotic. A breeze gently rustled the branches of the trees above her. It was like she was going deep inside herself to dark places she had never wanted to see again. Deep. Deep. Deeper.

She didn't know how much time had elapsed before the sound of dried twigs crunching underfoot and a shadow falling across her made her snap back out of the trance and her eyes flew open.

She blinked at the light and then focused on the unex-pected intruder in her solitary reverie.

'Sam? What are you doing here?' She shook her head

to clear her thoughts, pasted on her best smile. 'This is a surprise.'

He smiled back—that heart-wrenchingly wonderful smile—as he towered above her, his strong, muscular legs planted firmly in the sand. 'What did I want to go to Sydney for? I live there. I can party in the city any old time.' He'd rolled up his jeans; he was barefoot.

'But…I saw you leave with the others…'

He shrugged. 'So I came back. I thought I'd rather stay in Dolphin Bay and count the seagulls—or whatever you do for fun in this part of the world.'

In spite of herself, she giggled. 'Stay still for a moment and you might see a goanna running up a gum tree. That's nearly as much fun.'

'Yeah. Right,' he said with a grin. 'I forgot to tell you, I don't care much for reptiles, especially huge lizards.'

'So you just happened to come upon me here?' she said. Her heart leapt at the thought he might have sought her out.

'I remembered you told me about this place when I asked you about good spots to swim. I figured I might like to see it for myself.'

'So where's your swimsuit and towel?' she said in mock interrogation.

'If I hadn't encountered a certain redhead, I'd planned on diving in without the benefit of swimsuit or towel.'

She couldn't help a swift intake of breath at the thought of Sam stripping off his clothes and plunging naked into the water. She had to mentally fan herself. 'Oh, really?' she said when she thought her voice would work again.

He threw up his hands in surrender. 'Okay. You got me. I came back for you.' His tone was light-hearted but his eyes were very serious.

'For me?' Her heart started to thud at twice its normal rate.

Now he dropped all pretence at levity. 'To see if I could talk you into driving with me to Sydney. Just you and me. We could join the others later.'

'Why would you do that when I'm just…just a business contact?'

He looked down at her and for a long, still moment their gazes connected so there was scarcely a need for words. 'I think you know we're more than that,' he said finally.

'Yes,' she said. 'I believe I knew that from the get-go.'

She went to get up but she'd been sitting in the same position for so long, her right foot had gone numb and she stumbled. He caught her by both hands and pulled her to her feet. When she regained her balance, he kept hold of her hands. She was intensely aware of his nearness, his scent, his strength. There was no terror, no overwhelming urge to break free from his hold. Not in this safe place. Not with Sam.

'Wh…what did the others think about you coming back for me?'

'They couldn't understand why you didn't want to go with them.'

She gasped and the gasp threatened to turn into a sob. 'Sam, can't you see it's not that I don't *want* to go to Sydney? It's that I *can't*.'

She tried to twist away from him, embarrassed for him to see the confusion and worry that must be only too apparent on her face. But his grip was strong and reassuring and he would not let her go.

Slowly, he nodded. 'I think I can see that now. Can you tell me what's really going on, Kate?'

The concern in his brown eyes, the compassion in his voice, made her long to confide in him, though she scarcely knew him. She couldn't lie to *herself* any longer that there was nothing wrong, so why should she lie to *him*?

She took a deep, steadying breath. 'I've been sitting here for I don't know how long, wondering what the heck has happened to me.'

'You mean, the way you're too frightened to go to Sydney?'

'Is the…the fear that obvious?' So much for her 'nothing bothers me' facade.

'Not immediately. But as I get to know you, I realise—'

'How constricted my life has become?'

'The way you don't seem to want to leave Dolphin Bay.'

She took in a deep intake of breath and let it out as a heavy sigh. 'As I sat here, I came to terms with how my life has become narrower and narrower in its focus. The truly frightening thing is that I realised I hadn't left Dolphin Bay for more than two years.'

He frowned. 'What do you mean?'

She disengaged her hands from his, turned to take a step away so she could think how to explain without him thinking she was a total nut job, then turned back to face him. There was no other way than to state the facts.

'Not just to go to Sydney but to go anywhere outside the town limits. I haven't been to any of the places I used to enjoy. Every time someone wanted me to go to Bateman's Bay for dinner, or to Mogo Zoo to see the white lion cubs, I'd find some excuse. I never made any conscious decision not to leave, it just *happened*.'

'Have you thought about why?'

She could see he was carefully considering his words. Something twisted painfully inside her. Did he think she was crazy? *Maybe she was*…

'I was beginning to suspect I might have some kind of…of agoraphobia. I…I looked it up at one stage. But I don't have full-blown panic attacks, or need someone with me just to go out of the house. I feel absolutely fine until I think about leaving Dolphin Bay.'

'It's not a good idea to label what you're feeling from looking it up the Internet,' he said, more sternly than she had ever heard him speak.

She managed a broken laugh. 'You're right, of course. Self-diagnosis is kinda dumb. But one thing that did give me a light-bulb moment was that agoraphobia—even in its mildest forms—can have had some kind of triggering event.'

'That makes sense. Have you thought back to when your fear started?'

'Yes.'

'Want to tell me about it? I've got broad shoulders.'

She shook her head, unable to speak. Ashamed of how she'd behaved, what she'd become, not so many years ago. 'It's…it's personal. We don't know each other very well.'

'Maybe this is one way to get to know each other better.' That damaged eyebrow gave him a quizzical look. If she ever got the chance, she'd like to ask him how it had happened.

'You might not want to know me better after I've cried all over your shoulder,' she said, trying to turn it into a joke, but her voice betrayed her with a tremor.

'Let me be the judge of that,' he said. 'We've all done things we've regretted, Kate. I certainly have. I reckon whatever it is that's causing your fear could be like a wound that's got infected. You have to lance it to let the poison out or it will continue to fester.'

'Maybe,' she said but didn't sound convinced even to her own ears.

'Look around us,' said Sam, with an all-encompassing wave of his arm. 'There's no one else to hear but me. And I won't be telling anyone.'

She'd held everything inside her so tightly. It might be a relief to let it all out. To Sam. 'Can we sit down? This might take a while.'

'Sure,' he said, casting his gaze around them. 'How about a comfy rock?'

She giggled again, aware of the trill of nervousness that edged it. 'This grassy ledge here might be more comfortable.'

'Much better,' he said, flattening the tall grasses that grew there before he sat down.

She sat down next to him, trying to keep a polite distance, but his shoulders were so broad, his arms so muscular, it was impossible for hers not to nudge them.

'C'mon,' he said. 'Spill.'

She still wasn't at all sure it was a good idea to talk to a man she liked so much about her time with another man. But maybe Sam was right—she needed to release the poison that had been seeping into her soul.

'I…I had a bad experience in Sydney, when I was at university.'

'With a guy?'

She shuddered. 'I can't bear to think about it. I can't even think about his name. In my mind, I only refer to him by his initial.'

Sam tensed. 'Did he… Was it…?'

'No. Not that. I was more than willing to go along with him. That's what makes it so bad, that I could have been so stupid.'

'Or innocent?'

'Maybe that too. I was in my third year of university in Sydney. We met on a vacation ski trip where we were all acting a little wild. He was the handsomest man I'd ever seen.' She snuck a sideways glance at Sam. 'Until now, of course.'

Sam snorted. 'You don't have to say that.'

'But it's true. Seriously.'

'Huh,' he said, but she thought he sounded pleased. 'Go on.'

'I fell for him straight away. Not only was he good-looking, he was funny and kind. Or so I thought.'

'But it was all an act?' Sam's face was grim.

She nodded. 'It was a…a…very physical relationship. I…I hadn't had much experience. He got me well and truly hooked on him and how he could make me feel. I became obsessed with him. It was like…like a drug. Being with him became more important than anything else. I started missing classes, being late with assignments.'

'And then he changed?'

She liked the way he seemed to understand, the way he listened without judging as she finally let it all out. 'It became a…a sexual power game. I wanted love and affection but he wanted something much…much darker than that. He…he had me doing things I'd never dreamed I'd do. Humiliating things. Painful things. But he threatened me that if I didn't go along with what he wanted I'd lose him.'

'And you couldn't bear that,' Sam said slowly.

She looked down at the ground between their bare feet, not wanting to see on his face what he must think of her. 'I thought I loved him. That I couldn't live without him.'

'And you thought he loved you too.'

'That didn't last. He'd been so full-on, but then he became distant. Unavailable. Not answering my calls. But when we saw each other, he'd reassure me nothing was wrong.'

'It was all about control. He wanted to keep you under his thumb.'

She gritted her teeth. No matter what Sam thought about her, she had to tell him the truth. 'I became so anxious that I turned into a person I didn't want to be. I became hysterical if he didn't reply to my texts. Stalked him to see if there was someone else. I dropped out of uni, didn't finish my final semester, just to be at his beck and call. What a fool I was.'

If that wasn't guaranteed to scare Sam off, nothing would be.

He shook his head. 'You were young and vulnerable, he was manipulative.'

'And sadistic,' she said, spitting out the word. 'My suspicions weren't unfounded. I discovered him with another girl. He laughed at my distress.'

'And that was the end?' Sam's voice was gruff.

'He still thought he could pick me up and put me down as he chose. But seeing him with someone else finally knocked some sense into me. To let him get away with that would have been a step too far on a path to self-destruction. I…I walked away.'

'Good for you to find the courage to do that.'

She managed a shaky laugh. 'Oh, I wasn't very courageous. I was scared of how far down I might let myself be dragged. I didn't want to go there.'

'But you did it. You broke the chains. You took the control back.' There was a dark intensity to his eyes as they searched her face.

'Yes. But university was a complete wipe-out. I couldn't stay there to repeat the subjects I'd failed, not when I'd see him around the campus. When the offer came to join the dance troupe, I jumped at it. I got away from Sydney and him and I didn't have to crawl home with my tail between my legs. People thought I'd moved on to something more glamorous and exciting than finishing a business degree. Only I knew what a failure I was.'

He frowned. 'You didn't tell anyone about what had happened?'

'There was a girl at uni who was very supportive. But we lost touch. I didn't really want to be reminded of the person I'd been when I was so obsessed.'

'You didn't tell your mother or your sister?'

'I couldn't bear to tell them I'd failed uni. They thought I'd dropped out because I wanted to dance. They still don't think any different. Still think I threw away my degree.'

'But that meant you didn't ever have to face up to what had happened?'

'That's right. I can't tell you how many times I wished I'd gone home then. Got some help. Because I didn't, it meant I didn't know how to cope with the next situation that made me doubt myself.'

She took a deep breath and edged away from him. 'But I think you've heard enough of my history for one day.'

He put his hand out to draw her back to him but then he hesitated, his dark brows drawn together, and dropped his hand back to his side. She couldn't bear it if he thought she didn't want his touch, his kisses, *him*. She took a step that brought her closer to him, her gaze locked with his. 'Hold me, Sam,' she said. 'Please?'

He put his arm around her shoulder and drew her back closer so her head rested on his shoulder. It was, indeed, broad. And solid, warm and comforting. 'You need to get all that poison out. If there's more, I want to hear it,' he said.

CHAPTER NINE

Sam had always scorned the concept of love at first sight. In his book, instant attraction was all about sex, not love. The proof had been his parents' disastrous 'marry in haste, repent at leisure' marriage. And yet, although he wanted to kiss her, hold her, make love to her, he felt more than physical attraction for Kate—something that had been there from the first time they'd met. A feeling that was so strong, it made any further pretence at a business-only relationship seem farcical.

He was surprised and pleased, after the way she had pushed him away from their kiss the previous day, that she had actually sought his touch. He held her close to him, her bright head nestled on his shoulder, the folds of her blue dress brushing his legs, her hand resting lightly on his knee. He breathed in her heady, already so familiar scent. And he didn't want to let her go.

But this was no simple boy-meets-girl scenario.

Beneath that open, vivacious exterior Kate seemed to be a seething mass of insecurities, far from the straightforward person he'd thought she was. She'd been hiding secrets for years. Were there more? Could he deal with them?

With every fibre of his being he wanted to help her. But he didn't know how he could, other than being supportive. Nothing in his life experience had prepared him for this.

She shifted back from him, not so that she eluded the protective curve of his arm but so he could see her face.

'Can I tell you how good it is to talk to you like this?' she said.

Shadows from the overhanging trees flickered across her face. It made it difficult to read her eyes.

'If it helps, I'm glad.' He wasn't sure what else he could say. He risked dropping a kiss on her bare, smooth shoulder. She didn't flinch from him—that was progress.

'Are you sure you want to hear more? The second incident wasn't such a big deal. Not nearly as traumatic. I mightn't even mention it if I wasn't trying to find what triggered my aversion to leaving the city limits.'

'Bring it on. Did something happen while you were on tour with the dance troupe?'

Her hair was pulled back in a tie and he could see every nuance of her expression. She pulled a puzzled 'Kate' face. 'How did you know that?'

'Lucky guess,' he said, not adding that as soon as she'd started to talk about it her stilted words had become a dead giveaway.

'The injured ankle wasn't how my career as a cabaret dancer ended,' she said. 'Though I did hurt my ankle in a triple pirouette that collapsed in a less-than-graceful stumble.'

After the story of her abuse at the hands of her university lover, he wasn't at all certain he wanted to hear this double whammy, but he asked anyway. 'So how did it end?'

'After the injury healed, I joined the troupe again. They were about to go to Spain. I was so looking forward to it.'

'You would have gone overseas?' He couldn't keep the surprise from his voice.

'Yes. That's the crazy thing. I was so looking forward to it. Not a trace of this…this current affliction. We'd done a few weeks in New Zealand and I'd loved it. I'd even bought myself a "teach yourself Spanish" CD.'

The best thing, he figured, was to let her talk. 'So what happened to change things?'

'We had an extended stay at a club in a big country town in western New South Wales. There was a guy.' She rolled her eyes. 'Yeah, I know—another guy.'

'I should imagine there were a lot of guys interested in you,' he said drily. Smart. Beautiful. A dancer. She must have been besieged.

'Maybe,' she said with a wobbly smile. 'But I wasn't interested in *them*. In fact, after my experience at uni I'd sworn off men. I…didn't feel I could trust anyone.'

'Understandable,' he said, while thinking of a few choice words to describe the creep who had treated a vulnerable girl with such contempt and cruelty.

'There were often men at the stage door hoping to meet the dancers but I never took any notice of them. This guy seemed different. A gentleman. The Aussie grazier with the Akubra hat, the tweed jacket, the moleskin jeans. Older than the guys I'd dated. We had a drink after the show one evening and he was charming. He bred horses on his property and showed me photos. His historic old homestead, quite a distance out of town, looked amazing. And there were photos of foals. He asked me would I like to come and see the foals.'

'And of course you said yes.'

'Who could resist foals? They looked adorable with their long, baby legs. I couldn't wait to pet them.'

'You let down your guard.'

'He…he seemed so nice…'

'I can hear an "until" in your voice.'

Kate reached down to pick up a fallen eucalypt leaf. She started to tear it into tiny strips, releasing the sharp tang of eucalyptus oil to mingle with the salt of the breeze that wafted over them. 'Until he tried to kiss me and wouldn't take no for an answer. He wanted more than kisses. Got angry when I refused. Told me I was asking for it by dressing in sexy costumes and dancing provocatively onstage.'

Sam surprised himself with the growl of anger that rumbled from his throat and the string of swear words directed at her attacker.

'I used some of those words, too,' she said. 'But I got away, thank heaven. Luckily some sense of caution had made me refuse his offer of a ride to his place. I'd borrowed a car to get out there, so was able to get back under my own steam. The troupe left town the next day. I've never been so glad to get out of a place.'

'Did you report him?'

She shook her head. 'I was strong and agile and very angry—he didn't get anywhere near me.'

'You were lucky.' If he could get his hands on him, the guy would know not to go anywhere near her again.

'I know. I shook for hours when I got back when I thought about how differently it might have ended. He... he'd backed me into a boot room and closed the door.'

'That's why you reacted the way you did in the shed yesterday?'

Mutely, she nodded.

'Please tell me you confided in someone about the attack.'

'I didn't tell anyone. It made me look so stupid. The more experienced girls would never have gone off alone with a stage-door stalker.'

'He was cunning to use baby horses as a lure.'

'I know, which made me look even stupider for falling for it. And again, I began to doubt myself.'

'What do you mean?'

She got up from the ledge, threw the shredded leaf to the ground. 'The farmer guy was right in a way. Our dance costumes *were* form-fitting. Modern dance moves *can* be provocative. For one of our routines we had to dress as white poodles and bark as we danced. Can you imagine?'

She seemed determined to put a light spin to her story. She even took a few graceful, prancing steps on the sandy ground, mimed a dog's paws held out in front of her, her head alert to one side.

'You had to bark like a dog?' It took an effort not to laugh.

'Not just any old dog. A poodle. I listened to how a poodle barked in the interests of authenticity.' She paused. 'Go on—you're allowed to laugh. I get quite hysterical when I remember it. You'd be hysterical too if you saw us in those skin-tight white costumes with pompom poodle-tails on our butts and fluffy poodle ears on our heads.'

'I don't actually think I'd be laughing. It sounds very cute to me.' And very sexy. It wasn't difficult to see how a guy in the audience had got obsessed with her.

'There was a circus ringmaster cracking his whip as we danced and barked, which was kinda weird.'

This time he couldn't stop the laugh. 'I'm sure you made a gorgeous poodle.'

She pulled another of those cute Kate faces. 'You never know, I might do my poodle bark for you some time. I got quite good at it.'

He could only imagine. 'I'd like to see you dance.'

'Wearing a poodle costume?'

'Maybe. Or a white dress, like in that photo in your living room.'

This time the face she pulled was wistful, her eyes shadowed with regret. 'We danced *Swan Lake* that year for the end-of-year concert. I was Odette.'

'How fortunate that *Swan Lake* is the only ballet I've ever seen. So I actually know what you're talking about.'

'You won't see me perform it again. I stopped dancing soon after that near escape, even social dancing. The farmer guy's words kept going around and around in my head. Even though I'd been dancing since I was a child, I suddenly lost it. Became self-conscious, too aware of how I looked. How the men in the audience might perceive me. Scared, I guess.'

'Scared?'

'Scared of the next incident when some weirdo guy might think I was asking for it.' She paused. 'Now you know all my secrets. All my disasters updated.'

Sam jumped up from the ledge and took the few steps needed to reach her. But he didn't hug her close like he wanted to. Not when she'd just been remembering an assault.

'Kate, what that guy did was not your fault. What the guy in Sydney did wasn't your fault.'

Slowly, she nodded. 'I know. But, no matter how many times I told myself that, I didn't quite believe it. Was it something about me that attracted creepy guys? Why didn't I see them for what they were? Whatever; I couldn't get out there onstage and dance any more. I blamed it on my ankle but that didn't fool people for long. When Mum called to say she'd broken her arm and could I come home for a few weeks, I quit the dance company before they had a chance to sack me.'

'And you haven't danced since.'

'Sadly, no. I came back here where I know everyone and they know me. There were no opportunities to dance professionally. I'm qualified to teach dance but I didn't even want to do that.'

'And here you stayed.'

'No one knew what had happened to me—the abusive boyfriend; the scary experience with the farmer guy. Mum and Emily were glad to see me back. I was wanted, I was needed, and I just settled back into life here.'

'You didn't talk to anyone when you got back? Your family doctor, maybe?'

She shrugged. 'There was nothing to talk about. I blamed everything that happened on being away from home. Once I was home, it was okay.

'So you pretended it hadn't happened.'

'That's right. I felt safe here. Unthreatened.'

'I told you, small-town life is not for me. But, after dinner at your place last night, I can see the attraction for you. Your mum is such a nice lady—not to mention an incredible cook. And Emily is delightful. If I had a family like yours, I'd be tempted to stay here for ever too.'

But Kate was of an age when she should be making her own home. Thinking about starting her own family. *So should he.*

He realised with a sudden flash of clarity that the reason he spent so much time in the workplace was that it had become a substitute for family. At work he got recognition, admiration, companionship, security.

'Your family isn't like that?' she said, frowning.

'My family was so far removed from yours, there isn't any comparison. Home was like a battlefield where both sides have made a truce but occasionally resume hostilities. My mother was my father's second wife. He was still grieving his first wife when he met Vivien and—'

Kate put up her hand to interrupt him. 'Who is Vivien?'

'My mother. She doesn't like be called Mum or Mother—says it makes her feel too old.' He hated explaining it, as he'd always hated explaining it. Sitting in Kate's house, with her mother fussing over him with tea and home-baked cake, he had felt a tug of envy. His mother had not been the cake-baking, cosy type.

For once, Kate seemed lost for words. 'That's, uh, unusual. Even when you were a little boy?'

'Even when I was so little I had trouble pronouncing "Vivien".' He made a joke of it, but he'd never liked calling his mother by her name. If she hadn't wanted to be thought of as a mother, what had that meant to his identity as a son?

'You poor little thing,' said Kate. 'I mean you *were* a poor little thing. I don't mean you're a poor little thing *now*. In fact, you're rather big and—'

'I get it,' he said with a laugh.

Kate was back in full stickybeak mode but he had the distinct impression she was using it to distract him. 'You have to tell me more. We should shut up about me now. I still have one more question to go, you know; I've been saving it to find out about—'

He cut across her. 'We can talk about me later. Right now, we need to concentrate on you.'

She fell silent. 'Try to sort me out, you mean?' Her mouth turned downward so far it was almost comical.

'Don't be so hard on yourself. You were young, you had some traumatic experiences. You retreated to the safe place you needed to get over them.' She started to wring her hands together, something he noticed she did when she was upset.

'That safe place seems to have become a comfortable prison,' she muttered.

Without a word, he reached out and stilled her hands with his. 'That you now realise you have to release yourself from.'

He didn't know where these words of comfort came from other than a deep need to connect with her—maybe from his management training. It certainly didn't come from the tough love dished out by his parents. But it seemed to be helping Kate and that was all that counted.

She sighed. 'I'm angry at myself that I took the comfortable option instead of confronting my problems. Problems that, as you said, must have festered away.'

'Don't beat yourself up about it. Sounds like you've had a good life in Dolphin Bay.' He looked around him. 'Idyllic' really was the right word to describe their surroundings. 'There are worse places to be holed up while you heal.'

She slammed one fist into another. 'But it's not enough any more. I feel like I'm in a science fiction story where some big, transparent dome is over the town that only I'm aware of and I can't get past it. Meeting you has reminded me of what I'm missing out on.'

'True. For one thing, there's a whole, wide world of fabulous hotels out there for you to explore.' He kept his tone light, teasing, to defuse the anger she was turning on herself.

'You're right,' she said, after a long pause. 'Starting with that fabulous palace hotel in India. I looked it up after you told me about it. I so want to see it for myself.'

'I studied engineering at university, not psychology. But that seems to make sense. To go see a maharajah's palace is as good an incentive as any for you to break out.'

'I'm going to aim for it—something to focus on.' She looked up at him, her face still and very serious. Then she reached up and touched his cheek with her cool, eucalyptus-scented fingers. 'Sam, thank you for being the first person I've ever told anything about all this.'

Knowing he had helped her felt good. He caught her hand with his. 'Don't let me be the last. Talk to your mother. Perhaps even seek professional help,' he said. 'We really don't want you trapped inside that dome.'

'But only *I* can get over it. No one can do that for me.' She kept hold of his hand as she spoke.

'You've taken the first step by realising you need help,' he said.

Her eyes widened. 'Sam Lancaster, how did you get to be so wise?'

'I'm not wise. I…I just like you.' Maybe that was all it took—to care enough about another person to help her. It might transcend everything.

'I'm glad to hear that. Because…because I like you too,' she said.

Her eyes were in shadow but amazingly green, the pupils very large as she looked back at him. Again, there was that long moment of silent communication between them. She swayed towards him. Before he could think any further about it, he caught her and lowered his head to kiss her, first on each of those delightful dimples, then her pretty mouth. But this time, now he understood where she was coming from, he held back so the kiss stayed tender and non-threatening.

She gave a gasp of surprise followed by a murmur of pleasure as she relaxed into the kiss. Her arms slid up around his neck and she pulled his head closer. The kiss started as a light brushing of lips, returned tentatively at first as if she were wary, then more passionately, perhaps as she realised she was safe with him. Her warm lips, the cool taste of her tongue, ignited his hunger for her. A shudder of want ran through him as he deepened the kiss. But as it became more urgent she broke away, gasping, her face flushed.

'Sam. Wow. That…that was wonderful. Yesterday was wonderful. And…and I wasn't scared.'

'You will *never* have cause to be frightened of me,' he said.

He would do all he could to make sure she trusted him. But the confusion and doubt on her face made him realise it would not be plain sailing.

'Thank you,' she said and squeezed his hand. 'But I…I don't know that I'm ready for…for more yet. I…I haven't got anything to give you when I'm such a mess.'

He had trouble keeping his voice even, still reeling from the impact of her kiss. From knowing he wanted so much more. 'You're not a mess. You're a smart, special woman who just has the one problem to deal with.' He dropped a light kiss on her cheek. 'And I've got the takeover bid for the business looming.'

He should take his cue from her—the last thing he needed right now was the complication of a relationship. Not when he only had a few days to make a decision that would impact on so many other people.

Though wasn't he doing what he always did—using work as an excuse for keeping his distance?

'I guess we both have issues to deal with,' she said. She looked up at him. 'Sam, you've been such a help to me today, I'd love to be able to help you. If you want someone to talk over your business stuff with, well, I'm your girl. Not that I know anything about construction, but I could be a sounding board.'

'Thanks,' he said. He was touched by her offer, but the decision whether or not to sell the company his grandfather, his father and then he himself had invested their lives in rested firmly on his own shoulders.

She made a game of fanning herself with one graceful, elegant hand. 'I'm going to dip my feet in the water to cool off. Want to come with me?'

She walked into the ankle-deep shallows at the river's edge and he fell into step beside her.

Cooling off seemed like a very good idea.

* * *

Sam had kissed her again and Kate had loved every moment of it. There'd been no panic, no fear, just pleasure, comfort and excitement. But now wasn't the time for further kissing—though there was nothing she'd rather be doing. She knew, deep down, that until she sorted out her agoraphobia—if that was what it was—kissing Sam would only complicate things.

When she'd first seen him, her instincts had told her he was dangerous. Now she was convinced he wasn't dangerous in the way she had feared. The real danger was to her heart.

It would be only too easy to fall in love with Sam.

And she couldn't handle that right now.

To talk about all that stuff she'd kept bottled up inside her for so long had been truly liberating. Sam was a wonderful listener and seemed to have an instinct for drawing out her most painful memories. What she'd liked most was that he had given her good advice without judging her.

'When did you realise that Dolphin Bay had become a prison?' he said now as they walked hand in hand in the ankle-deep water at the edge of the lagoon.

'Only recently. The wedding has brought it all into focus. And…and it's only today, here by myself in this place that I love, that I realised how restricted my life had become. That…that it isn't enough any more.'

'You might have to dig down deeper under the scars from the past to find out how to fix it,' he said, obviously choosing his words carefully.

She turned away. 'You must think I'm a neurotic wreck.' She tried to make a joke of it, but her words came out as sounding anything but funny. With a tug to her hand, he pulled her back to face him.

'Of course I don't think you're a neurotic wreck. In fact, I don't know how you've held it together this long.'

'Obviously I didn't hold it together. I'm a recluse.'

'Where do you get these labels from? You're far from being a recluse. You have family and friends who all care for you.'

'I haven't dated for years, you know.'

'That I find very difficult to believe.' The admiration in his eyes took the sting out of her admission.

'I didn't trust my judgement. I couldn't tell the bad guys from the good guys.'

'Have you made a judgement of me?'

'You're…you're definitely one of the good guys.' Of her intuition, she was absolutely certain.

'Good,' he said. 'So where did Jesse fit in?'

'I've been thinking about that too. Trying to analyse how I got it so wrong.'

'Seems to me you got attached to Jesse about the same time as your dad moved out.'

She thought back to that traumatic time. 'Maybe. Everything else got turned upside down but my friend was still there. Stable. Secure. Maybe I got to believe all those family jokes about if we didn't each meet someone else we'd end up together.'

'Maybe that stopped you from getting serious about someone else.'

'You mean, after I came back here I used a crush on Jesse to protect myself from taking risks with other guys?'

'Could be.'

'It…it makes a strange kind of sense,' she said slowly.

Sam glanced down at his watch. 'Talking of Jesse, Ben and Sandy—if we leave now we can meet our friends in Sydney in time for dinner. What do you think?'

She swallowed hard at the sudden constriction in her

throat. 'I want to go. I really do. I feel sick that I've let them down—feel even sicker that I've let myself down with this stupid fear.' She forced bravado into her voice. 'Maybe…maybe I'm ready to try again. With you to hold my hand, that is.'

'I can drive us. But are you sure you want to go?'

She wasn't at all sure. But she was determined to give it a try. For Sandy. For Ben. For Sam, who'd been so patient with her.

She held on to his hand as they made their way back via the quicker route up through the bushland and along the pathways that led past the site for the new hotel. But, as they got closer to the town centre where she'd parked her car, Kate dropped his hand.

'I know it's ironic, as I'm the biggest gossip in town myself, but I've had enough of people talking about me,' she explained. 'I want to keep our…our friendship to ourselves.'

'Fair enough. I don't like people talking about my business either.' He stopped. 'But I do like holding your hand,' he said with a grin that warmed her heart.

Kate was okay getting into her car and driving home with Sam seated next to her. She was okay packing an overnight bag while Sam checked on his carpentry work out in the shed. She only started to get shaky as she drove back to the hotel to transfer to Sam's sports car.

'You okay?' he asked.

'Yep,' she said, pasting on that cheerful smile, hoping it would give her the courage and strength she so severely lacked.

But as soon as Sam opened the passenger door for her to get in she was again gripped by fear. As she went to slide into the seat, her knees went to jelly. Nausea rose in her throat and she started to shake.

She gasped for air. 'I can't do it, Sam. I thought I could, but I can't.'

He pulled her out of the car and held her to him, patting her on the back, making soothing, wordless sounds until the shaking stopped. She relaxed against him, beyond caring who saw her or what they might say.

'Too much, too soon,' he said.

She pulled away. 'Maybe,' she said. 'But I'm so angry with myself, so disappointed…'

'So we don't go to Sydney. What's the fuss?'

'You could still go. You've got plenty of time to get up there.'

'What's the point of a groomsman going out on the town without his bridesmaid?'

'You can still have fun in Sydney. Lizzie booked a really nice venue.'

'No arguments. I can go out in Sydney any time. I'm staying here with you.'

'But—'

He placed his index finger over her lips. 'No buts. We're going to look at this afternoon like it's a bonus. It gives us more time to spend working on the arch.'

She took a few more deep breaths, felt her heart rate returning to normal.

'I haven't shown you yet how good I am as a handy-woman.'

'Now's your chance,' he said. 'Then we're going to go on that date.'

'Wh-what about your no dating rule?'

'I own the company; I make the rules. I say to hell with that rule—as least, as it applies to you. I'm taking you out to dinner. We'll have our own party.'

She laughed with relief and a bubbling excitement. 'As Ben so obviously tried to set me up with you, I don't think there's a "no dating Sam" rule in place. It was more my own…my own fears giving me an excuse.'

'Let's book the best restaurant in Dolphin Bay.'

'The Harbourside is the best restaurant,' she said loyally.

'Okay—the second-best restaurant in Dolphin Bay,' he said. 'Or Thai take-out on the pier. Or fish and chips at the pub. Your choice.'

She smiled, relieved she could feel normal again, excited at the thought of dinner with Sam. 'I'm overwhelmed by the responsibility of the decision. But Thai does sound kind of tempting.'

'Thai it is—and lots of it. I'm starving.'

'Are you always hungry?'

'Always,' he said.

She laughed. 'I'm really getting to know you, aren't I?'

While she kept a happy smile pasted to her face, inside Kate wasn't so happy. The more she got to know Sam, the more she liked him.

But what future could there be for a man who travelled the world and a girl who was too scared to go further than the outskirts of her home town?

CHAPTER TEN

SANDY HAD BEEN RIGHT, Kate realised on the day of the wedding. A wedding *was* more fun for a bridesmaid when she had a handsome groomsman in tow. It was also more fun for a wedding planner when that groomsman had volunteered to be her helper—not only with the construction of the bridal arch, but also with other last-minute jobs along the way.

Not that Sam and she had spent much time together since their Thai take-out dinner. She'd still had her shifts at the hotel. And Sam had seemed to be in one conference call or video call after another. So much for that break from his business.

But, despite his grumbling about waste-of-time wedding fripperies, Sam had not only finished the arch but had also helped Sandy and her with writing the place cards and Emily with counting out the sugared almonds to put in the tulle-wrapped wedding favours. He had, however, point-blank refused to tie pretty pastel ribbons on them.

Now Ben and Sandy's big day was here. Dolphin Bay had, thank heaven, put on its finest weather for the last weekend of daylight saving time—although Kate didn't take the good weather for granted. With a ceremony being held outdoors on the beach, she'd planned alternative arrangements to cover all contingencies, from heatwave to hailstorm.

At noon she was still in the function room at the Hotel Harbourside, where the reception was to be held, making final checks on the arrangements for the buffet-style meal.

Sliding doors opened out onto an ocean-facing balcony that gave a good view of the ceremony site on the beach below. Every few minutes she dashed out to see if the sky was indeed still perfectly blue and free of clouds, the wind still the gentle zephyr that would not make an organza-adorned arch suddenly become airborne as the bride and groom exchanged their vows. Not unnecessary anxiety, she told herself, for a wedding scheduled to start in just four hours.

Everything that could be checked off on her multiple pages of lists had been checked off. Everyone who had needed to be briefed on their wedding duties had been briefed. Now it was time for the hotel staff to take over. And for her to start having fun.

But, as she headed for the door that led into the hotel corridor, she couldn't resist turning back and picking up a silver serving platter to see if it had been polished as directed. She peered closely at it, fearing she saw a scratch.

'Ready to stop being an obsessive wedding planner and start being a bridesmaid? I've been dispatched to find you.' Sam's deep, resonant voice coming from behind her made her jump so she nearly dropped the platter. She hadn't heard him come in.

She turned to face him and halted halfway. Her heart seemed to stop as it always did at the first sight of this man who took up so much space in her thoughts. He'd shaved and had had his hair cut. She smiled. 'You look different,' she said, after a long moment when her heartbeat had returned somewhat to normal. 'Just as handsome, but different.'

And even hotter than when she'd last seen him.

'I'm taking my groomsman duties seriously,' Sam said. 'Ben wanted me clean shaven, so I got clean shaven.'

She was unable to resist reaching up and tracing the smooth line of his jaw with her fingers. She would have liked to kiss him, but two of the waiting staff were polishing champagne flutes at the other end of the room. 'You look more corporate than carpenter and that takes a little getting used to. But I like it. And the haircut. Though, I have to say, I really liked the stubble.'

'I guarantee that'll be back by morning,' he said with a grin.

"Good," she said.

She put her hand on his arm. 'Are you okay with all this wedding stuff? I mean, it isn't weird for you when your own wedding was cancelled? I hate to think it might bring back sad memories.'

'I'm good with it. I wasn't actually there for all my own wedding preparations. I was working in Queensland or Western Australia, or Singapore or somewhere else far away.'

'Your fiancée mustn't have been too happy about that.'

'She wasn't. To the point she accused me of being so uninvolved with the preparations, she didn't think I was interested in the wedding or, ultimately, truly interested in her.'

Kate didn't know what she could say to that other than a polite murmur. 'I see.'

'Her tipping point was when I couldn't make the rehearsal because it clashed with an important business engagement.'

Suddenly Kate felt more than a touch of sympathy for

Sam's unknown fiancée. 'I would have been furious if I were her.'

'She was. That's when she threw her engagement ring at me and told me the wedding was off.'

'And you were surprised?'

'Well, yes.'

'Now that you've had time to reflect about it, are you still surprised?'

He grinned. 'No.'

'Good. I would have had to revise my opinion of you if you had said yes.'

'I've had plenty of time to reflect that I was a selfish workaholic, too obsessed with proving myself to my father to be a good boyfriend or a good fiancé. Certainly, I wouldn't have been a good husband.'

'So you weren't really ready to get married?'

'Probably not. But I've also had time to think about whether Frances was right. Maybe…maybe I just didn't love her enough to make that level of commitment and subconsciously used work as an excuse.' He paused and she could see remembered pain in his eyes. 'I was gutted at the time, though. We'd been together for years.'

'Would you say you're still a selfish workaholic?' Kate asked, unable to stop a twinge of jealousy at the thought of the woman who'd shared Sam's life for so long.

'Probably. That's one reason I'm considering selling the company. I suspect I've given too much of my life to it—given it too much importance at the cost of other more important things.'

Kate was just about to reply when a tall, slender girl with a mop of silvery blonde curls poked her head around the door. 'There you are, Kate. The hairdresser, make-up artist and manicurist are all waiting for us.' Lizzie scowled at Sam. 'You, Sam, were charged with getting Kate up to

Sandy's suite,' she scolded. 'We've got secret bridesmaids' business to attend to.'

Kate put up her hand. 'Just one more minute, Lizzie,' she said.

Lizzie folded her arms in front of her chest and ostentatiously tapped her foot. 'I'm going to wait right here to make sure you don't disappear.'

Kate leaned up to whisper in Sam's ear. 'Is everything okay with the arch?'

'Yes,' he murmured. 'Your mother and a friend from the hospital—some guy named Colin—are going to drive the van down to the beach. I'll slip out at the time we arranged and they'll help me install it.'

'Fantastic. Thank you,' she whispered. 'I can't wait to see it.'

'Hurry up, Kate,' urged Lizzie.

'Okay, okay,' said Kate and fled the room.

Sam hadn't been one hundred per cent honest with Kate. The frenzied wedding activities *had* brought back memories of his own abruptly terminated nuptials nearly two years ago.

Seeing at close quarters the levels of planning that went into even a simple ceremony like Ben and Sandy's made him realise how badly he'd neglected Frances in the months leading up to their big, showy wedding. On many of the times she'd asked for a decision, he'd brushed her aside with his stock replies: 'You decide,' or 'I'll leave it to you.' He hadn't cooperated with his mother, either, who had thrown herself into the elaborate preparations with great gusto. With hindsight, he realised his mother had done a lot to help Frances when it should have been *him* doing the helping.

Thinking about how he'd behaved made him feel

vaguely ashamed. At the time, he had paid lip service to an apology. But, feeling aggrieved, he hadn't really been sure what he had done to deserve the cancellation of his wedding and the dumping by his fiancée.

Being around Kate, her family and friends made him realise exactly what he'd done wrong. And that he'd be damned sure he got it right the next time round.

Being around Kate was also making him question how he'd felt about his former fiancée. After several years together, he had never felt for Frances what he already felt for Kate. If he were about to marry Kate—and of course that was purely a hypothetical situation—no way would he be away in another country. He would want to be with his bride-to-be every minute, working alongside her to plan their future together. *Hypothetically, of course.*

Now he stood barefoot on the sand, lined up with Ben and Jesse under the arch he had built with Kate in her father's shed. It held firm in the breeze coming off the waters of the bay. Ben, in that jesting way of good mates, had told him that he had a bright future ahead of him making gimcracks for weddings. Because it was Ben's day, he had let him get away with it.

The three men waited for the bridesmaids and then the bride to walk down the sandy aisle that had been formed between rows of folding white chairs and delineated with two rows of sea shells.

Suddenly the guests swivelled around to a collective sigh. 'Oohs' and 'aahs' greeted the sight of Lizzie's five-year-old daughter, Amy. But, by the time Amy was halfway down the aisle, Sam only had eyes for the beautiful red-haired bridesmaid who followed her.

He'd never understood the expression 'took his breath away' until now. In bare feet, Kate moved like the dancer she was, seeming to glide along the sand towards him.

Her strapless peach dress showed off her graceful shoulders and arms, and clung to her curves before it ended just below her knees. Her hair, pulled up off her face with some of it tumbling down her shoulders, shone like a halo in the afternoon sun.

Her glorious smile captivated him as it had the first time he'd seen her. Only this time her smile seemed only for him. Somehow, with just a glance, she seemed to convey how happy she was to be sharing this day with him. He smiled back, unable to take his eyes off her. When she reached the arch, he stepped forward to offer her his arm to guide her to the bride's side of the area. He had to resist a strong impulse to gather her to him and keep her by his side, an arm planted possessively around her waist.

Kate couldn't help a moment of self-congratulation at how well the shades of the sunset colour-scheme worked. She herself wore apricot, Lizzie a shade that veered towards tangerine and little Amy's white dress had a big bow in a pale tint of magenta. The three men were handsome in chinos and loose white shirts. But Sam was the one who made her heart race, who made her aware of where he was at all times without her even having to look.

She kept sneaking sideways glimpses at him, glances that were often intercepted and ended in secret smiles. Every minute she knew him, he seemed to grow more attractive. Not just in his looks but also in his personality, which was funnier, kinder and more thoughtful than she could have imagined—though she didn't let herself forget there must be a ruthless side to him too.

For a moment, when he had stepped forward to take her arm, she had indulged in a fantasy of what it might be like if she'd been walking up an aisle to meet him as her groom. She had immediately dismissed the thought as impossible but its warmth lingered in her mind. How was she going to endure it when he went back to Sydney the next day?

She forced her gaze away from Sam and straight ahead to where Sandy was about to commence her walk down the aisle.

But first it was Hobo's turn. Ben's mother Maura—officially appointed by Kate as dog-handler—had spent days training Hobo to sedately stroll down the aisle and take his place with Ben under the arch. The big, shaggy golden retriever—wearing a white ribbon around his neck, slightly chewed around the ends—started off fine, sitting as directed at the head of the aisle, giving the guests a big, doggy smile. There was a furious clicking of cameras.

'Good boy, Hobo,' Kate heard Maura whisper. But her praise was premature. Hobo caught sight of Ben, lolloped off down the aisle and came to a skidding halt next to his master's feet, spraying sand around him as he landed.

The guests erupted into laughter and Sandy was laughing too as she started her walk down the aisle. It was a perfect start to the ceremony, Kate thought, the laughter vanquishing any last-minute nerves or tension.

When Ben and Sandy exchanged their vows in front of the celebrant, there wasn't a sound except their murmured 'I do'—and the occasional muffled sob and sniffle from the guests.

As she watched them, Kate was tearing up too. She couldn't help an ache in her heart—not from envy of the bride and groom but a longing for the same kind of happiness for herself one day. She'd never really let herself imagine being married, having children, but of course she wanted all that one day.

She just had to get the man right.

She stole another surreptitious glance at Sam, to find

him looking to her too. Did she imagine a hint of the same longing in his eyes? *If only...*

Weddings seemed to dredge up so many deeply submerged emotions and bring them to the surface. She had to be careful she didn't let her imagination run riot and believe Sam felt in any way the same as she did.

But, when the newlyweds moved off to the small table they had set up for the signing of the official papers, Sam was next to her the first second he could be. He interlinked his fingers with hers and drew her to him for a swift, sweet kiss. 'You outshone the bride,' he murmured.

She protested, of course, but was deeply, secretly pleased. She wondered if anyone had noticed their kiss but decided she didn't care. Forget the 'poor Kate' whispers. She reckoned there was more likely to be whispers of 'lucky Kate'.

She *was* lucky to have met him. And, if tonight was the only time she ever had with Sam, she was going to darn well enjoy every minute of it.

CHAPTER ELEVEN

SAM FELT A certain envy at the newlyweds' obvious joy in each other. Being part of the wedding ceremony had stirred emotions in him he'd had no idea existed. Above all, it had forced him to face up to what he could not continue to deny to himself: he was besotted with Kate. No matter how much he fought the concept, he had fallen fast and hard for her.

From his seat at the bride and groom's table he watched Kate as she flitted her way around the wedding reception like a bright flame; her hair, her dress, her smile made her easy to pick out in the crowd.

'She's a great girl, isn't she?' said Lizzie, who was sitting next to him. Was it so obvious that he couldn't keep his eyes off Kate?

'Yup,' he said, not wanting to be distracted.

Lizzie laughed. 'Don't worry, your secret is safe with me.'

He twisted to face her. 'What do you mean?'

'That you're smitten with Kate.' He started to protest but she spoke over him. 'Don't worry. I don't think too many other people have noticed. They're all still determined to pair her off with the home-town favourite, Jesse Morgan. I don't know how Kate feels about that. I thought that might have been the reason why she didn't come up to Sydney on Wednesday.'

A tightness in her voice made Sam look more closely at Lizzie. 'Kate likes him as a friend, almost a brother, that's all.' He was surprised by the flash of relief that flickered across Lizzie's face. 'But you—you like Jesse?'

She flushed. 'Of course I don't. He's arrogant. A player. Much too handsome for his own good and way too sure of himself.'

Sam stored her excessive denial away to share with Kate later. In the meantime, he had to stick up for his friend. 'Actually, Jesse is a mate of mine and a really good guy. He's confident, not arrogant. And he's not a player.'

Lizzie snorted. 'I'll have to take your word for it.'

Lizzie had an acerbic edge to her and possibly too many glasses of champagne on board. Sam decided he didn't want to engage in any further discussion about Jesse. He was relieved when she excused herself to go and have a word with her sister.

He drummed his fingers on the tabletop and wished Kate would come back to her chair. Ideally, he wanted her to be by his side all evening, but that wasn't going to happen—not with the number of people who were waylaying her for a chat. She knew everyone and they knew her. No wonder she had found it so easy to stay in this town for so long; there was no denying the sense of community.

But could he live here?

Despite his aversion to small-town life, it was a question he had to ask himself. What if Kate was unable to get over her problem, to get out from under that invisible dome? The way he felt about her, he would find it untenable for them not to be in the same town if anything developed between them. If she couldn't come to him in Sydney, might he have to come to her in Dolphin Bay?

If it meant being with Kate, he had to consider it.

When his father had had one too many drinks, he'd

sometimes decided to give his son advice on women. It had always been the same—telling Sam to be sure he knew a woman really well before he considered commitment. The old 'marry in haste, repent at leisure' thing would inevitably come up. His dad had adored his first wife, the only blight on the marriage being the fact they hadn't had children. He had been devastated when she'd died, had not been able to handle being on his own. Quite soon after, he'd met Vivien and had married her within months. By the time they'd realised it was a mistake, Sam had been on the way. They'd never actually said so, but he'd come to believe his parents had only stayed together for their child's sake.

Sam wasn't ready to propose to Kate after only a week. That would be crazy. But he didn't want to wait for ever to have her beside him, sharing his life.

He wanted what Ben and Sandy had, and he wanted it with Kate.

Kate slid into the chair beside him and hooked her arm through his. 'My mouth is aching from smiling so much and I'm not even the bride,' she said. 'Are you having fun?'

'Now you're back with me, the fun is back on track,' he said.

'The perfect reply,' she said, with the full-on dimpled smile that was getting such a workout. This was the vivacious, bubbly Kate everyone knew. Looking at her flushed, happy face, it was difficult to believe she had secrets that haunted her.

'You must be pleased at how well everything is going,' he said. 'Congratulations to the wedding planner.'

'Congratulations to the world's best wedding-arch builder,' she said. 'It was a big hit.'

'I'm glad we made the effort.' He realised he had fallen into talking about 'we'—and he liked the feeling.

'Clever us.' She sighed. 'I can't believe how fast it's gone. All that work and it's over in a matter of hours. But now the speeches are done, the band is starting up and we can all relax.'

On cue, the band started to play and the MC announced it was time for the bride and groom to dance the first dance to a medley of popular love songs.

Sam noticed Kate go so pale, her freckles stood out. She looked anything but relaxed. 'Are you okay?'

He noticed she was wringing her hands together under the table. 'I didn't think this through,' she said in an undertone. 'According to the order of the reception, the best man and chief bridesmaid will get up to dance next. Then they'll expect you and me to get up.'

'I'm okay with that, if you don't mind my two left feet.'

'It's not that. It's me. I can't dance—I don't dance—especially not in front of all these people.'

Her panicked voice reminded Sam all over again of the way Kate's fears had paralysed her. Lizzie had been correct—he was smitten with Kate. But would he be able to help her overcome those fears so she could move on to a less constricted life? If she couldn't, would there be any chance of a future for them?

He covered her hands with his much bigger ones to soothe their anxious twisting. 'No one is going to force you. But I do think, as you've been such an important part of this wedding, you're expected to get up on the dance floor. I'll lead you on and we can shuffle.'

'Shuffle?'

'Stand there and sway to the music. That way you don't have to dance, I don't have to dance—and you won't let your friends down.'

She took a deep breath and Sam could see what an effort it was for her. 'All those years of dance training and it comes to this,' she said with that bitter twist to her mouth.

'You're in a room full of friends,' he said. 'And do you know what? None of them know you're afraid to dance.'

'You're right,' she said, not looking at all convinced.

But when the MC invited the bridesmaid and grooms- man to get up onto the dance floor, Kate let him pull her to her feet. She was a little shaky but Sam didn't think anyone but he noticed it. He took her by the hand and led her onto the dance floor. She rested one hand on his shoul- der and the other around his waist. Only he could feel her shivers of nervousness.

'Now we can shuffle,' he said. 'Just think of it like an ambulatory hug.'

'That's a Sam way of putting it,' she said, but she laughed. And he was glad he could make her laugh.

Kate had dreaded the dancing part of the evening. But standing there with Sam in the circle of his arms she felt safe, protected by his closeness. She trusted him not to let her make a fool of herself.

'I'm stepping my feet from side to side,' he said in an undertone she could only just hear over the music. 'We have to look like we're making an effort to dance. The people who know you're a professional dancer will be feel- ing sorry for you for being stuck with a shuffler grooms- man like me.'

Wrong! No woman in her right mind would ever pity her for being in Sam's arms. They'd envy her, more like it. She held on to him just a little bit tighter.

After the barefoot wedding ceremony, the bridal party had changed into high-heeled strappy sandals for the girls and loafers for the boys. She felt Sam's shoe nudge her toes.

'Hey, I felt that,' she said. 'Crushed toes aren't part of the deal.'

'I warned you I had two left feet.'

But she did as he suggested and stepped lightly from side to side. Securely held by Sam, as she tentatively started to move, the rhythm of the music seemed to invade her body. First her feet took off in something that was much more than a sideways shuffle, then her body started to sway. The old feeling came flooding back, the joy of her body moving—not just to the beat of the music but in step with Sam, who was also doing more than stepping from side to side.

Before she knew it, he had steered her into the centre of the dance floor and they were whirling around with the other couples. With a start of surprise, she realised she was being expertly led around the dance floor by a man who was light on his feet and perfectly in rhythm. She felt flushed with a relieved triumph that she had overcome her debilitating fear, and warm delight that she was back in the swing of things.

'I thought you said you couldn't dance,' she said to Sam.

'I said I had two left feet. But years of dancing instruction at my private boys' school beat a bit of coordination into them.'

'You had dance lessons at school?'

'It wasn't all rugby and cricket—though I was a far better football player than I ever was a dancer. We had to learn so we could dance with the girls from our corresponding girls' school. And take our place in Sydney society, of course.'

'I wish I'd known you when you were a schoolboy. I bet you were the hottest boy in your class.'

'I wouldn't say that,' he said, obviously uncomfortable

at such flattery—warranted though it was. She couldn't resist teasing him.

'I can imagine all the girls were after you.'

'Think again. I was this tall when I was thirteen. Big, awkward and shy.'

'I don't believe that for a moment.'

'Seriously. The other boys had way better chat-up lines than I did. By the time I'd thought about what I'd say, the girl had danced off with one of them.'

'Who needs chat-up lines when you're as handsome as you? Trust me, you would have been breaking girlish hearts all over the place. You could probably have had three at a time.'

'I hope not,' he said with genuine alarm. 'I'm a one-woman kind of guy.'

Suddenly the conversation had got kind of serious. And important.

'Really?' she said. Her breath caught in her throat.

'I met my first serious girlfriend in the final year of high school. She took a gap year in Europe and we broke up. Then there was a girl I dated at university and then Frances after that.'

'You…you don't have to give me your dating résumé,' she assured him.

'I want you to know you can trust me,' he said. Those bitter-chocolate-dark eyes searched hers.

'I think…I already know that,' she said.

'Good,' he replied and expertly twirled her around the floor until she was exhilarated and laughing. She couldn't remember when she'd enjoyed herself more.

Kate had been dancing for so long the soles of her feet were beginning to burn. All evening she'd regretted she hadn't worn her new shoes in—but then she hadn't anticipated she'd dance every dance. When the band took a break, she was hot and breathless and fanning herself with her hands.

'Some fresh air?' asked Sam.

'Absolutely,' she said, panting a little.

She followed Sam out onto the balcony away from the stuffiness and high chatter levels of the ball room. They virtually had the balcony to themselves, with only one other couple right down the other end.

The full moon reflected on the water of the bay. She took a deep breath of the cool night air. Sam leaned on the railing and looked out to sea. She slid her arms around his waist and rested her cheek against his broad back.

'Thank you for your help back there,' she murmured. 'I can't tell you how it feels to be able to dance again. I wouldn't have dared get up without you. Well, I might have, but maybe not for a long time and maybe—'

He turned around to face her. '*You* did it. Not me. But I'm happy I was able to help. Do you think, now you've danced once, you'll be able to do it again?'

She looked up at him. 'To be honest, I doubt I'll ever again dress up in a white leotard and bark like a poodle.'

He laughed. 'Sorry, but I wish I'd seen you. Do you have any photos?'

'*No.* And, if I did, no one would ever see them. It was hardly the highlight of my career as a professional dancer. A career I won't be reviving any time soon. But now it's not because I *can't,* but because I don't want to.'

'Sounds good to me.'

'It gives me hope I'll be able to get out of Dolphin Bay, too. I finally told Mum some of what happened in Sydney. She gave me the name of a psychologist at the hospital—someone I can speak to in confidence. I've made an appointment to see her next week.'

'That's a step in the right direction,' he said. 'I'm proud

of you. I know how difficult it's been for you to talk about it.'

'It's a small step. You're the one who can take the credit for helping me to get me this far.'

'I was just the shoulder you needed—'

'You were so, so much more than that, Sam.' She reached up and traced a line down his cheek with her fingers. Already his beard was growing and was rough under her fingertips. 'I...I hope I might be able to come and see you in Sydney before too long.'

He caught her hand and briefly pressed his lips to it. 'I wish you could come with me tomorrow.'

Joy bubbled through her that he should suggest it when deep down, in spite of her growing trust in him, she'd feared these few days might be all they'd ever have.

'Me too,' she said with a catch in her voice. 'But I can't. Not just because of...because of the dome but also because I'm looking after the hotel for the next ten days while Ben is on his honeymoon.'

'And helping out at Bay Books in your—' he made quotation marks with his fingers '—spare time.'

'It...it won't give me any time to mope around missing you,' she murmured, turning her head away, not wanting him to see the truth of how deeply she felt about him in her eyes.

With his index finger, he gently turned her chin back so she faced him. 'I'll miss you too,' he said. 'If I didn't have to go back to Sydney tomorrow morning, I wouldn't. But you know it's decision time at the meeting on Monday.'

'I know,' she said. 'I have every faith in you to make the right choice.'

His dark brows slanted. 'What happens if you don't get out from under that dome? If I sold the company, I could live anywhere I wanted. Even here.'

'In Dolphin Bay?' She shook her head. 'I don't think so.'

He cleared his throat. 'What I'm trying to say is that I want to spend more time with you, Kate. If that means moving to Dolphin Bay...'

She could hardly believe what she was hearing. 'I couldn't—wouldn't—ask that of you. You'd hate it here.'

'How can you be so sure of that?' he said. 'It...it's kind of growing on me. The community. The beach. The—'

'The way you'd be bored out of your brain within weeks?'

'I couldn't imagine ever being bored with you,' he said.

'Oh,' was all she managed to choke out in response.

He cradled her face in his two large, warm hands. His deep, brown eyes searched her face. 'Kate, in such a short time you...you've become...important to me.' Behind the imposing adult, the man who was gearing up to do battle in the boardroom over a multi-million-dollar deal, she saw the schoolboy, uncertain of the words he needed to find to win the girl.

'Oh, Sam, you've become so important to me too. But I...I... Until I get myself together I...'

He silenced her protest with a kiss. After a moment's surprised hesitation, she kissed him back and she gave herself up to the sheer pleasure of the pressure of his mouth on hers. Her lips parted on a sigh of bliss and his tongue slipped between them to tease and stroke and thrill. Her breath quickened. She met his tongue with hers and she pulled his head closer, her hands fisting in his hair. His hands slid down to her waist and drew her closer to his hard, muscular body. She could feel the frantic thudding of his heart, answered by the pounding of her own.

As the kiss flamed into something deeper and more passionate, desire ignited in delicious flames of want that surged through her, her breath coming hard and fast and broken. Sam groaned against her mouth and she answered the sensual sound by straining her body tighter to his.

She wanted him desperately—so desperately, she forgot she was on a balcony in close proximity to family and friends. Every sense was overwhelmed by her awakened need for him, the utter pleasure coursing through her body. Making her want more, making her want him at any cost.

She stilled. Her heart pounded harder, now from fear rather than passion as she realised the direction her thoughts had taken. This hunger for him would have her do anything he wanted. It could have her enslaved. It might transport her on a tide of need to an obsession where she lost all sense of herself. She felt like she was choking.

She wrenched away from Sam's arms and staggered backwards. He put out a hand to steady her. 'I…I can't do this,' she said.

He dropped his hand from her arm. His jaw clenched and his dark scowl was back, overlaid with both disbelief and pain.

'Because people can see us?' he growled. 'Because *Jesse* might see us?'

She shook her head. 'Because I want you so much and… it scares me.'

'This is about the guy at university,' he said flatly.

Mutely, she nodded.

His expression was grim as he seemed to gather his thoughts. Her heart sank to somewhere below her shoes. Had she scared him off with her endless fears?

'Kate, do you realise that this might scare me too? I've only known you a week and you're all I can think about. My feelings for you have become an issue in the most important decision I've ever had to make. This…this is new to me. I've laid it on the line for you. But are you ever going to be able to trust me?' He turned so his shoulder was facing her and his face was shrouded by shadow. Terror grabbed at her with icy claws.

He could walk away.

And that would be worse than anything else that could happen.

'Sam, I'm sorry. I...I've been so caught up in me and how I'm feeling, I...I didn't think enough about how it was affecting you.'

To her intense relief, he turned back so she could see his face, illuminated by the pale moonlight. 'I wouldn't break your spirit in the way that guy did. Your feistiness and independence are part of your appeal for me. I'm strong, Kate. I want to be there for you. You need time to sort through your issues and I know that. But it has to be two-way.'

She needed time. But it had been years since she'd fallen into that dark tunnel. Years when she'd hidden herself away, protecting herself against any real relationships by her fixation on Jesse, letting fear inhibit and stultify her emotional growth. She'd been a girl then, now she was a woman. She had to grow up. She had to come to Sam as an adult who considered his emotional needs as well as her own. Be aware that *she* could hurt *him*.

'Sam.' Urgently, she gripped his upper arms to keep him with her. She looked up into his eyes and her heart twisted painfully at the wariness that clouded them. No way could she lose him. 'You're right; I've been so focused on myself. I want a partnership. Me looking after you, as well as you looking after me. My shoulders aren't nearly as broad as yours, but I want them to be there for you like yours are for me.'

He started to say something but she rose up on her toes and silenced him with a kiss. She murmured against his mouth, 'And I want you. Tonight, when the party is over, I want to come with you to your room.'

He pulled back. She could see it was an effort for him but he managed a lopsided imitation of his usual wide grin. 'I want you too, believe me. I can't tell you how tempted I am to pick you up and carry you up to my room right now. But it wouldn't be right. It's too soon. And the whole of Dolphin Bay will know you've stayed with me. Neither of us wants that, especially as I'm going in the morning.'

Her body was still warm with want for him. But, in a way, she was relieved. It *was* too soon. The growing up she needed to do wasn't going to happen overnight. 'Yes. You're right.' But she twined her arms around his neck and drew him down for another kiss. 'But making love with you isn't an easy thing to say no to,' she murmured as she kissed him again.

'Woo-hoo!' Lizzie's voice interrupted them.

Kate pulled away from the kiss, flushed, her breathing erratic. Not only Lizzie, but also Jesse was standing in the doorway. Jesse caught her eye and winked. She knew Jesse so well, she realised that meant he approved of her and Sam getting together. What really surprised her was the knowing look Lizzie sent to Sam and the sheepish smile he sent her in return. What was that about?

'C'mon, you two, Sandy's about to toss her bouquet,' said Lizzie, ushering her and Sam back into the room. 'I'm staying right out of range but you, Kate, might want to be within catching distance.'

Did she?

After the encounter she'd just shared with Sam, was it weird to entertain the thought of marriage for even the briefest moments of wedding-fuelled madness? The groom in her 'walking to the altar' fantasy was tall, dark-haired and with a scowl that transformed into the sexiest of smiles...

For all they'd come to tonight, there was still much

both she and Sam needed to consider before she got carried away by dreams. Even if she did break her way free from the dome, what happened next?

Still, she had to admit to a twinge of disappointment when Sandy's bouquet went sailing over her, and the outstretched arms of all the other single ladies vying to catch it, to land fairly and squarely in Emily's lap. Kate was surprised by Emily's blushes and protests at the chants of, 'You're next,' 'Emily is next.' Hmm. She might have to quiz her little sister on the reason for those blushes.

But she forgot all about that as Sam put his arm around her to lead her over to the table that was serving coffee and slices of chocolate wedding cake.

'I hate fruit cake,' he said, picking up the biggest piece on the platter. 'When I get married, I'll want a chocolate cake.'

He said it so casually, seemingly without even being aware of the significance of his words, it made her wonder if Sam had a few dreams of his own.

CHAPTER TWELVE

SAM WOKE UP and for a long moment wasn't sure where he was. Then he realised he was sprawled across the sofa in Kate's living room. Kate was asleep, snuggled into his side, her head resting on his chest, her sweetly scented hair spilling over his neck. She was breathing deeply and evenly.

There were sooty smudges around her eyes where her make-up had smeared. Her lips were free of lipstick—it had been thoroughly kissed away. Her bridesmaid dress was rumpled up over her slender thighs. She'd kicked off her sandals and he noticed her toenails were painted the same pretty colour as her dress. He was fascinated by how pale her skin was, how he could see the delicate traceries of veins. Such a contrast to his own olive skin.

With her colouring, she certainly hadn't been made to live by the sea where so much activity was played out on the water or the sand under the blazing Australian sun. She loved her home town, but he suspected she was a city girl at heart. He thought she'd be happy in Sydney.

His Sydney was very different from the student haunts where she'd played out the relationship that had so traumatised her. The waterfront penthouse apartment he owned was part of a redeveloped wharf complex and was right next to some of the best restaurants in town. It was only a walk into the centre of the city. He reckoned she'd love it.

His arm was around her shoulder and he cautiously adjusted it to make himself more comfortable. She made a little murmur of protest deep in her throat and nestled in tighter, one hand clutching on to his chest. He dropped a light kiss on the top of her head.

He knew he should go, but he could not resist a few more moments of having her so close to him.

After the bride and groom had left the reception last night, he and Kate, along with Jesse, Lizzie and a group of their other friends, had adjourned to the bar at the Harbourside. Eventually it had ended up with just Kate and him left. There'd been nothing he wanted more than to take her up to his room and make love to her. But he had known, much as he'd wanted her, that wasn't going to happen. That *mustn't* happen. Instead he'd taken her home, she'd invited him in for coffee and they'd made out like teenagers on the sofa until they must have fallen asleep.

Sam smiled as he remembered how they'd kept talking until the time between each other's responses had got longer and longer until finally there had been silence. He hadn't wanted to let her go, hadn't wanted to say goodnight. And he didn't want to now.

The pale light of dawn was starting to filter through the blinds. He couldn't stay any longer. Not only would it be awkward for Dawn and Emily to come in and find him there, but he had to get on the road.

He edged his way into a sitting position and pulled Kate upright. He stroked her hair. 'Kate,' he whispered. 'I have to go.'

Her eyes opened, then shut again, then finally opened wide. She blinked as her eyes came into focus. 'Sam! Wh-where…? Oh. I remember now.' She stretched her arms languorously above her head, which made the top of her breasts swell over the edge of her strapless dress. She put her hand over her mouth as she yawned.

He averted his eyes to look over her head. Waking up with her pressed so intimately close was bad enough; seeing her skirt all rucked up around her thighs and the top starting to slide right off was more than a man could be expected to endure.

'C'mon, Kate.'

She planted her arms around his neck and pouted. 'No. Don't want you to go.' Her hair was all tousled and the smudged make-up around her eyes gave her a sultry air. The effect was adorable. She kissed him, her mouth soft and yielding, her tongue teasing the seam of his lips.

He groaned softly and kissed her back. Then he summoned every ounce of self-discipline he had to push himself up from the sofa, which in turn tipped her back against the cushions. She still looked groggy, a little bewildered and quite possibly half-asleep. Leaving her there was one of the most difficult things he had ever done.

He slipped into his shoes and picked up his car keys from the coffee table. Then he crouched down to the level of the sofa. 'Kate, listen. I'm leaving for Sydney as soon as I pick up my bag from the hotel. Do you understand?'

Her eyes widened and she nodded. 'Yes.' She pulled a sad, funny Kate face. 'I don't know when I'll next see you, but I hope it will be soon.'

'Me too,' he said. He kissed her gently on the mouth. 'Bye, Kate. You try to get some more sleep.'

''Kay,' she murmured.

He pulled a throw over her and tucked it around her bare legs. Then he let himself out of the door. He suspected she was asleep again before the door had closed behind him.

He forced his brain to change gears from thinking about making love to Kate to corporate responsibility and business pros and cons. And what would be the decision he would communicate to the potential purchaser of his company.

Her lingering perfume and the imprint of her body against his made his old workaholic tricks the least effective they'd ever been.

Kate had to put up with much teasing from her sister and mother when they discovered her dishevelled and asleep on the sofa, with two empty cups on the coffee table.

'I don't have to ask who you had here until all hours,' said Emily, her eyes dancing.

There was no point in denying it. Half of Dolphin Bay had probably seen her kissing Sam on the balcony of the hotel. And Emily had been among the group who'd congregated in the bar after the wedding reception. Kate and Sam had held hands the entire time.

As she showered, she thought that over breakfast might be a good time to talk through a few things with her mother and Emily.

The thought of their Sunday favourite of scrambled eggs and bacon made her gag. Not that she was feeling ill; it was just that her stomach was tied in knots of tension. She missed Sam already. It was devastating to think that when she started her shift at the hotel this afternoon he wouldn't be there. And she was also coming down from the high of all those frantic wedding preparations.

She waved away the eggs and instead nibbled on the platter of fruit Emily had cut up. Clearing up and doing the dishes was her breakfast task for today. As three adults sharing a house, they also shared the chores.

'So,' said her mother, sipping a cup of tea. 'Have you got something you want to say to us?'

'Something about someone?' said Emily. She broke into

the childish chant the sisters had used since they'd been tiny and still did. 'Someone whose name begins with *S*?'

Kate put down her own cup of herbal tea. 'Yes. I do. And it *is* about me and Sam.'

'Tell all,' said Emily, leaning forward on her elbows, her eyes avid.

'There's not a lot to tell yet, but there might be,' said Kate.

'We really like Sam, don't we, Mum?' asked Emily. Her mother nodded.

'I like him, too,' confessed Kate, the accursed blush betraying her. 'But he lives in Sydney and I live here. Which could be a problem.'

'Sweetie, there is that major issue for you to overcome before you can think about going to Sydney,' said her mum, raising her eyebrows in the direction of Emily. 'You know…'

'Don't worry, Mum, I've told Emily about the dome,' Kate said. She'd found visualising her issue as 'the dome' made it easier somehow to imagine herself breaking out of it. She wondered if the psychologist she was seeing on Tuesday would think it was a good idea.

'Good,' said her mother.

Kate took a deep breath. 'But there's another problem— one that doesn't just involve me. When I'm able to, I'll want to drive to Sydney fairly often. Who knows, I might end up living there one day before too long so I can date Sam, if I can afford exorbitant city rents. But…but I know I'm needed here. With you two.'

Her mother and Emily exchanged glances that Kate couldn't quite read.

She hastened to reassure them. 'Don't worry. If you want me to stay, we can work things out and—'

'Don't even *think* of giving up Sam for my sake,' said

Emily. 'A guy like him only comes along once in a million years. Grab on to him and don't let him go.'

'Er, Emily, that's not quite the way to put it,' said her mother. 'But we know what you mean and I echo the sentiment.'

Dawn reached out to give Kate a comforting pat on her arm. 'Don't worry about us, sweetie. It's been wonderful having you here with us all these years, and don't think I don't appreciate it. But things change. For all of us. You need to get your wings back and start to fly.'

'Actually, I have something to say too, Kate,' ventured Emily, an edge of excitement to her voice. 'I'm moving out next month. I didn't want to announce anything until it was certain. I've only just told Mum.'

Emily had talked about moving out on her own often enough but it was a big step. Kate was disconcerted it was actually happening. 'Where are you moving to?'

'To Melbourne. I'm going to share with some other basketball players in a house that's set up for wheelies. The bank has organised a transfer for me to a branch down there. I'm all set.'

Kate narrowed her eyes. 'And are all your new roomies female?'

'Um, no,' said Emily. 'But that's all very new and I don't want to jinx it by talking about him.'

'Okay,' said Kate, determined she would get all the details out of her sister before the end of the day. 'I'm really pleased for you. And visiting you will give me a good excuse to get to Melbourne.' Another reason to get out from under that dome.

She could feel her major tie to Dolphin Bay stretching and snapping. Emily didn't need her any more—though, if she was honest with herself, Emily hadn't needed her for a long time. *Had she needed to be needed?*

'So that just leaves you and me, Mum,' Kate said.

'I'm not pushing you out, Kate, but it will do you good to go when you're ready. I never imagined I'd have my great big girls of twenty-eight and twenty-six still living at home with me. It's time for me to have my independence too.'

Kate had inherited her tendency to blush from her mother and she was surprised at the rising colour on her mother's cheeks.

'I didn't know Colin's other name was "independence", Mum,' teased Emily.

Kate looked from her mother to Emily and back again. 'Colin?'

'My friend from the hospital—he's new in the admin department. He was the one who helped me and Sam put up the wedding arch. He…he's very nice.'

'And why didn't I know this?' demanded Kate.

'You're losing the plot, sister dear,' replied Emily. 'Too caught up with handsome Sam to keep your finger on the pulse of everyone else's business as you usually do.'

'And the wedding planning. And the resort stuff…' began Kate, and realised she was being overly defensive. She laughed. Maybe she didn't need to keep such a rigid control on things any more. Maybe there were fewer fears to keep at bay.

She'd ask Sam what he thought.

CHAPTER THIRTEEN

ON MONDAY MORNING, Sam sat behind the imposing desk that had once been his grandfather's in his office at the Sydney headquarters of Lancaster & Son Construction. He was aware if he went ahead with the sale of the family company that the name Lancaster & Son, founded by his grandfather, carried on by his father and then nurtured by him, would disappear into the history books.

That would be inevitable. But if he didn't have a son— or had a son who didn't want to go into the construction industry—would the name be such a loss?

In many ways it would be a relief—the burden of living up to that name and to his father's expectations would be finally lifted. He remembered back to the day he'd turned twenty-one when he'd demanded some autonomy from his father. Grudgingly, it had been given. But, even though his father had gone, there was still that feeling of having stepped into his shoes without having forged shoes of his own. He'd worked for the company since he'd been fourteen years old. Surely he deserved the chance for some cashed-up freedom?

Still, it was gut-wrenching to think of pulling the plug on so much of his family's endeavours. Thanks to his canny management, the company had been successful through all the ups and downs of the market. The balance sheet was very healthy with profits consistently rising—which was what made it so attractive to the company wanting to buy it. And the Lancaster reputation for quality and reliability was unsurpassed.

The money the sale would earn him was a mind-boggling amount, more than enough for him to start a business that was just his own. As well as the luxury of time to decide what that new venture might be.

It was a compelling reason to sell.

Again he flipped through the document that answered his questions about what the multi-national company intended to do if he accepted their offer. With the turn of each page, his gut clenched into tighter and more painful knots. Whatever labels you put on a business strategy, be they 'process re-engineering', 'shifting paradigms' or 'amalgamating cost centres', the truth of the matter was that the sale would result in downsizing. And not one member of his crew deserved to lose their job. There were the clients to consider too—clients who trusted him. Clients like his friend Ben Morgan.

He thought about what Kate had said—and knew there was much truth in her words. With his inheritance had come responsibilities. His father had been fond of that old-fashioned word 'duty'. In the contemporary world of dog-eat-dog business, did words like 'responsibility' and 'duty' have a place—or were they just remnants of a more honourable past?

Then there was his personal life to consider. His workaholic devotion to the company had lost him a fiancée. Now he'd fallen for a woman who might not be able to leave her small, coastal home town in the short-term; perhaps not for a long time. If he wanted to be with her, he might have to live there too. What had she said? *You'd be bored out of your brain within weeks.*

He'd started to be seduced by Dolphin Bay but now he was back in Sydney the thought of living in a backwater became less and less appealing. Even with Kate by his side, a ton of money in the bank and freedom from corporate responsibility, he suspected he would find it stifling.

If he took that path, might he come to resent her? Might that resentment become a poison that would destroy their relationship before it would have time to flourish?

There was such a short time left for him to make his momentous decision. He leaned back in his big leather chair, linked his hands behind his head, closed his eyes and reviewed again his options.

It seemed like no time at all had elapsed before his PA buzzed him that his meeting was about to start.

He picked up the folder with all the relevant documents and headed for the boardroom.

Kate was on edge all morning. From the time Sam's meeting was scheduled, she had started checking her mobile phone for messages. Whatever decision he made it would be life-changing for him—and possibly for her.

When the call finally came, she found her hands were shaking as she picked up her phone. 'Well?' she asked him. She held her breath for his answer.

'I didn't sell,' he said. 'The company is still mine.'

She let out her breath in a sigh. 'Congratulations. I'm proud of you. It must have been difficult but I think you made the right decision.'

'Me too. I did that "make a choice and live with it for an hour" exercise—and decided to sell. But as I headed to the meeting, and realised it would be the last time I would have a say in the business, I knew there was nothing I'd rather do than run Lancaster & Son Construction. I finally understood that my inheritance had never been a burden but a privilege. And that it was entirely up to me how I chose to direct it—my vision, my future. So I changed my mind.'

'Which means everyone gets to keep their jobs and Ben gets to keep his builder.'

'All that.'

'I'd like to give you a big hug.'

'A big Kate hug is just what I need right now. I didn't realise just how stressful the whole process would be.' She could sense the weariness in his voice.

'I wish I...'

'You wish what?'

'Oh, I wish I could hop in the car and drive up to Sydney to be with you to celebrate. But obviously that can't be.'

'You'll get there, just give it time,' he said. It still amazed her that this big, sexy hunk of a man could be so considerate.

She took another deep breath. 'I've got a new goal to aim for—besides seeing the Indian palace hotel, that is. When Ben comes back from his honeymoon, I plan to drive up to Sydney to see you.'

There was silence at the other end of the line. 'You're sure that's not too ambitious?'

She shook her head, even knowing he couldn't see her. 'No. I'm going to drive a little further every day until I can point that car in the direction of Sydney and go for it. And hope I don't drive smack into the dome, of course.'

'Okay. But don't beat yourself up about it if the practice proves more difficult than the theory.'

'I won't,' she promised.

There was a pause on the line before Sam spoke again. 'Unfortunately, the decision to hold on to the company means it's unlikely I'll make it down to Dolphin Bay. Not before the time Ben gets back, anyway.'

Disappointment, dark and choking, constricted her

voice but she forced herself to sound cheerful. 'That's okay. I'll...I'll be so flat out with everything here. Not to mention the daily get-out-of-town driving goals I've set myself that—'

'It's not okay,' he said. 'But because I've been away for a week, and because I've got to be seen to be taking the reins with confidence, that's the way it's got to be. There are changes I want to make straight away. This is seen as a turning point for the company.' She suspected his words were accompanied by a shrug. 'I'm sorry,' he added.

Her voice was too choked to reply immediately and she nodded. But of course he couldn't see that. She donned her 'everything is just fine' voice. 'Sure. We can call or text. Maybe even video calls.'

'It won't be the same as seeing you but, yes, that's what we'll do. Now, I have to go for the first of a long line-up of meetings. The start of the new era.'

'Where the company is truly yours—in your mind, anyway.'

There was silence at the end of the line and Kate thought he might have hung up. But he spoke again. 'You're very perceptive. That's exactly what the decision has meant to me.'

When Kate put down the phone she was more than ever determined to get out of that dome so she could take more control of her life—and choose when she wanted to see Sam, rather than waiting for him to come to her.

By Wednesday afternoon, Kate had driven further away from Dolphin Bay town centre than she had for two years. While being aware there was such a thing as overconfidence, she felt buoyed by the knowledge that she had got into the car without shaking or nausea. By the end of the ten days, she was sure she would make it onto the Princes Highway and away.

The initial meeting with the psychologist had gone well. She'd been surprised that the thoughtful, middle-aged woman hadn't wanted to talk much about the past. Rather, she'd acknowledged that Kate—thanks to her talks with Sam—already had a level of insight into what had caused her problems. Then the psychologist had gone straight into examining and challenging Kate's thoughts and feelings. At the second session on Wednesday morning, she'd given her strategies for coping in trigger situations, like getting into cars. Kate had found the breathing techniques and visualisations particularly helpful.

She'd been amazed that she could progress so quickly when she'd thought it might take months—even years— to get to the bottom of things. Why on earth hadn't she admitted to herself long ago that she'd needed help, when the solution seemed so straightforward?

By the following Tuesday, on her morning off, she drove all the way south to the larger town of Bateman's Bay nearly an hour away. She strolled up and down the water-front, revelling in her freedom. Then she sat in a café right on the water and congratulated herself for having pushed the boundary of the dome so far back. She was confident that by Friday she'd be on the road north to Sydney, count-ing down the minutes until she saw Sam.

After she finished her coffee, she decided to phone Sam on her mobile to share the good news. She'd be in Sydney on Friday in time to meet him for dinner.

'I'm so proud of you, you're doing amazingly well,' he said. 'But there's going to be a change of plan.'

Kate swallowed hard against that same lump of disap-pointment that seemed to rise in her throat when she talked to Sam about her plans to visit him in Sydney. But she refused to listen to the nagging, internal voice that taunted her that she had, once again, been a bad judge of a man's character. That maybe, just maybe, Sam would hedge and defer and change dates until it ended up that she would never see him again.

Trust him, trust him, trust him, she chanted to herself.

'A change of plan?' she repeated, desperately fighting a dull edge to her voice.

'Not such a bad one,' he said. 'At least, I don't think you'll find it so bad. In fact, I'm sure you'll think it's good news.' There was a rising tone of restrained excitement to his voice that made her wonder.

'Okay, so enough with the torture,' she said. 'Tell me what it is.'

'I have to fly to Singapore tonight for a series of meetings that will go on until the weekend.'

'And that's good news?' she said, her heart sinking.

'The good news is I want you to meet me there. Now that you've told me you'll be in Sydney, I'm confident you can do it. I'll send you an email with the details.'

She had to pause to get her thoughts together. 'In Singapore? You want me to meet you in Singapore?' She wasn't sure if the churning in her stomach was dread or excitement.

'Yes.'

'When I've only just managed Bateman's Bay?'

'You can do it, Kate. I know you can. Especially when you hear where we'll be staying in Singapore. Remember the hotel you told me about that shared top spot with the Indian palace one on your list of must-see hotels?'

'The huge new one with the mammoth towers and the world's highest infinity pool, fifty-seven floors up?'

'The very one.'

'The one with the amazing spa on the fifty-fifth floor?'

'Yup,' he confirmed.

'And the luxury shopping mall underneath, and the casino, and what they say are the best views in Singapore?' By now she was practically screeching with excitement. A couple at the next table looked at her oddly and she lowered her voice.

'I've booked a suite on the highest floor I could,' he said. 'With a butler.'

'A butler? You're kidding me.'

'No. Nothing short of the lap of luxury for Ms Parker.'

'But...but you'll already be there and I'll have to get there by myself. I don't know that I—'

'If you can get to Sydney, all you have to do is get to the airport. There'll be a first-class ticket waiting for you. You'll hardly know you're in the air.'

She lowered her voice to a note above a whisper. 'But, Sam, what if I can't do it? What if I don't get as far as Sydney?'

'Then we cancel it all and wait until I can get down there to see you.'

'Okay. So I have an escape route.'

'If you like to see it as that, yes,' he said. 'But Kate, here's the deal: to make it easier for you, I'll send down a chauffeur-driven limo to pick you up from home. He'll drive you to Sydney International Airport so you don't actually have to worry about driving. That will be one less pressure on you. The driver—who is on my staff—will escort you into the first-class lounge where you can check in. Then I'll meet you at the other end.'

'Sam, I so want to see you. I...I miss you. And this all sounds terribly exciting. Like a dream, really.'

'So you'll do it?'

'Just give me a second.' She took a few of the controlled, calming breaths she had been practising. 'Yes. I'll do it.

Mum told me I needed to get my wings back but I didn't know that she meant aeroplane wings.'

'Great,' he said and she was surprised at the relief in his voice.'

'Sam?' she ventured. 'Thank you. This might just be the incentive I need to get me out of that dome once and for all. I'll see you in Singapore.'

CHAPTER FOURTEEN

I CAN DO THIS. Kate kept repeating the words like a mantra as the ultra-smooth limousine, way too big for one person, left Dolphin Bay behind. She realised she was sitting rigidly on the edge of the seat and she made herself sink back into its well-upholstered comfort.

She'd only had a light breakfast, but felt a little queasy, so she made herself take the controlled, calming breaths the psychologist had taught her. Buried deep in her handbag was some prescription medication she'd got from her doctor, as insurance in case she got overwhelmed by panic. But she was determined it would not come out of its wrapping. She wanted to be with Sam. To be with Sam, she had to stay in this car and not beg the driver to take her home. She was determined to find the strength to turn her life around. *I can do this.*

She pulled out her phone from her bag and flicked through to the photos of the wedding. There was a lovely one of Sam and her, she smiling up at him, him with his dark head bent to hear what she was saying. She pressed a kiss to her finger and transferred the kiss to the photo. All this was worth it.

It didn't seem long before coastal bushland made way for rolling green farmland. She gazed out the window and marvelled that she had not been along these roads for five years. But that self-imposed isolation was behind her now. She'd smashed through the dome.

The previous night she'd had a broken sleep, kept awake by alternate bouts of churning excitement and worry. Three times she'd got out of bed to check that her passport and travel documents were packed. By the time the car was driving through the picturesque town of Berry, she was fast asleep.

The driver woke her as they approached Sydney International Airport. She looked around her, bewildered, until she realised where she was. A wave of exultation surged through her. *I've done it!*

The last time she'd flown, it had been with the dance troupe. That had involved a bus ride to the airport and the cheapest of bargain airline seats right down the back of the plane.

Being ushered into the first-class lounge was a different experience altogether. She tried not to look too awe-struck at the level of elegant luxury that surrounded her. Customers waiting for their flights could enjoy anything from a snack to a three-course meal. There was even a day spa where she could book in for a facial—all part of the service. It was like a six-star hotel on a smaller scale. But she couldn't enjoy it—even if she tried looking on it as research.

Everyone else seemed to know where they were going, what they were doing. The staff bustled around, greeting frequent flyers by name but not paying her any attention. Kate felt awkward and alone and unable to pretend she fitted in. She sat huddled on the edge of an ultra-contemporary leather sofa with a plate of gourmet snacks uneaten on the small table beside her.

She was wearing slim black trousers, a silk tank top and a loose, fine-knit black jacket trimmed with bronze metallic studs. Teamed with black ballet flats, she thought her outfit looked fine and would be comfortable for the flight.

But there wasn't a designer-label attached to any of it.

And this was designer label territory.

Was this Sam's world? She hadn't thought of him being super-wealthy but the personal chauffeur and the first-class travel indicated otherwise.

How well did she actually know him?

Every so often, boarding calls went out over the sound system. Each time she thought it might be for her. Each time she realised she'd forgotten her flight number and had to fumble in her bag to pull out her boarding card. Each time she got more and more flustered.

She began to dread the thought of actually boarding the plane—seven hours cooped up with no possibility of escape. Seven hours of escalating worry. What if Sam wasn't there to meet her at the other end? What if she had to find her own way to the hotel in a foreign city? What if she got lost?

Dread percolated in the pit of her belly. She started to shake and tried to control it by wringing her hands together. Her heart thudded wildly. Perspiration prickled on her forehead. *She couldn't do this.*

She used her breathing techniques to slow down the panic—then started to feel angry. This wasn't about an unresolved issue in her past. It was about Sam.

Sam should not have expected this of her. This was forcing her to run before she was even sure she could walk. He knew her problems only too well—and she'd thought he understood them. She should not be expected to fly to Singapore on her own. This was the first time she had been able to venture out of her home town for five years. To pop her on a plane all by herself like a first-class parcel and expect her to cope was nothing short of cruel.

It dawned on her that, not only hadn't she seen Sam since he'd gone back to Sydney, she hadn't really talked to him that much either. He was always preoccupied with the company he had taken charge of with renewed vigour. What had he said about the reason for his cancelled wedding? *I was a selfish workaholic.*

Obviously things hadn't changed. *He* hadn't changed.

Maybe Sam in Dolphin Bay and Sam in Sydney were two different people. Away from stress and the pressure of his job, he'd been the kind, thoughtful man she'd fallen in love with. But back on the city treadmill he'd become that ruthless, selfish person she'd always suspected might be there beneath the surface—a man whose woman would always come second to his business, who would have to fit in around him when it suited him.

She didn't want that kind of man.

It had been a classic holiday romance, she supposed with a painful lurch of her heart. Only he had been the one on holiday and she had been the one left behind when he'd gone home. He had been more than generous with dollars in organising this trip for her. But he had been exceedingly stingy with his time.

Sure, she'd wanted to see that wonderful hotel in Singapore. But most of all she'd wanted to see *him.* Now, on top of the shaking and shivering and cold sweats, she felt tears smarting. *She could not get on that plane.*

No way could she risk a public meltdown high in the sky somewhere between Sydney and Singapore. Only to be met at the other end —if he wasn't too busy in a business meeting—by someone she was no longer certain she wanted to see.

Kate swallowed the sob that threatened to break out, got up from the sofa and picked up her bag. She couldn't go home, that was for sure. Instead she'd march out to the taxi rank and get a ride to one of the glamorous new Sydney hotels she'd explored only on their websites. There she'd lock herself away for a few days, cry her eyes out, order room service and figure out where she went from there.

But as she headed towards the exit she was blocked by a tall, dark-haired man wearing a crumpled business suit, sporting dark stubble and an expression of anguish. 'Kate. Thank heaven. What was I thinking of, to expect you to fly by yourself?'

Her heart starting pounding so hard she had to put her hand to her chest. Sam. Gorgeous, wonderful, sexy Sam. She desperately wanted to throw herself into his arms. But that wouldn't work.

Kate looked at him with an expression of cold distaste in her beautiful green eyes. How could Sam blame her? He'd been nothing short of inept in the way he'd gone about this whole trip, a trip that was supposed to give her a treat and cement their relationship.

He could blame the pressures of the sale decision and subsequent reassurances to the staff, many of whom had been unsettled by the reports in the press about the potential takeover. But that was no real excuse.

By the time he'd finally got some time to himself on the plane to Singapore, he'd realised what he'd done. He'd reverted to the same old bad, work-obsessed ways that had destroyed his relationships before. After all that angst over the sale of the company, the new direction he wanted to take, he hadn't changed a bit. He'd expected a girl struggling to overcome a form of agoraphobia to do what must have seemed impossible to her. What kind of fool was he?

Kate went to move away from him and he realised she was heading towards the exit. 'Kate, where are you going? We have to board the plane in ten minutes.'

She spun back on her heel. '*We?* Sam, what are you doing here? I'm confused, to say the least.' He realised she was dangerously close to tears—tears caused by him. The knowledge stabbed him with pain and guilt for hurting her.

'I got to Singapore and realised what an idiot I was to expect you to get on a plane by yourself. So I got another plane back here as soon as I could so we could fly together.'

Her brow furrowed. 'You *what?*'

'I just flew back from Singapore. My plane landed here at this terminal. I wanted to be here to meet you when you arrived by limo, but the plane was late and there was a hellish crowd in the arrivals hall. Thankfully, I got here in time.' He would never have forgiven himself if he had missed her.

A smile struggled to melt her frosty expression. 'I don't believe what I'm hearing.'

'I booked another ticket for me so we could fly together, like we should have in the first place.'

'But what about your meetings in Singapore?'

'I rearranged them.'

'Weren't they important?' she asked.

'Nothing is more important than you, Kate.'

He didn't blame her for the scepticism that extinguished that nascent smile. He put his hands on her shoulders and this time she didn't move away. 'Seriously. I had a lot of time to think on that plane coming back to Sydney. I realised I had to change my obsessive, destructive, workaholic ways or I'd lose you. And I couldn't bear that.'

'So what do you intend to do?' she asked.

'Delegate. Give some of the really good people I have in my organisation more chance to manage. My father's old right-hand man has been seriously under-utilised because I saw him as a threat rather than a help. Most of all, I'm going to build in time for the woman I love.'

Her eyes widened with astonishment. 'Did…did you just say you…?'

'That I loved you? Yes, I did. And I'll say it again—I love you, Kate Parker.' He gathered her into his arms and kissed her on the mouth.

After the frantic dash from the plane to the lounge, Sam had been so engrossed with making sure Kate would be getting on the plane with him that he had completely forgotten about his surroundings. He was brought back to reality by a polite smattering of applause and turned around to see that they had attracted a smiling audience.

He looked at Kate and she blushed and laughed, her dimples flirting in her cheeks. She turned to face the people applauding and dipped a deep, theatrical, dancer's curtsey. He joined her in a half-bow of acknowledgement. Then he took her hand and tugged her towards him. 'C'mon, we've got a plane to catch.'

Travelling first class was an adventure all on its own, Kate thought as they disembarked in Singapore. She'd enjoyed a fully flat bed, pillows, blankets, luxury toiletries, even pyjamas. And the food had been top-class-restaurant standard delivered with superlative service.

The best thing of all had been Sam's company. After his frantic dash from Sydney to Singapore and back again, he'd drowsed for much of the flight, but every moment they'd both been awake they'd been together. She'd even managed to ask her final question, number five—how had he got that scar on his eyebrow? The prosaic answer related to an unfortunate encounter with a sharp metal window frame being moved around on a building site. She would have preferred something more romantic but, as he'd said in his practical way, he was lucky he hadn't lost an eye.

And now was her first sight of exotic Singapore.

Another limousine was there to pick them up. As she waited for her suitcase to be loaded into the boot, she sniffed the warm, humid air, tinged with a fragrance she didn't recognise. She asked Sam what it was.

'I call it the scent of Asia—a subtle mix of different plants, foods, spices. I find it exciting every time I smell it—and it's intoxicating when it's the first time.'

She couldn't agree more. *She was in Asia!*

It was night-time, and Singapore was a city sparkling with myriad fairy-tale lights that delighted her. As they drove across a bridge, her first sight of their hotel made her gasp. Brightly lit, its three tall towers seemed to rear up out of the water, the famous roof-top pool resort slung across the very top.

'I can't wait to get up there and swim on the top of the world,' she said. She clutched Sam's arm. 'Oh, thank you for bringing me here. This is the most amazing place I've ever seen.'

'I'm happy to be sharing it with you.' He smiled his slow, sexy smile. 'Around here is the really modern part of Singapore. Most of this area is built on reclaimed land—it's an engineering marvel. Tomorrow I'll take you to the old part. There's a mix of gracious buildings from the colonial past and temples I think you'll find fascinating.'

'I'll look forward to it,' she said. 'You know, I'm having to pinch myself to make sure this is all real and I'm not dreaming.'

He laughed. 'It's real, all right.' He looked down at her. 'But the best part is having you here with me.'

'Agreed,' she said happily, squeezing his hand.

Thank heaven, she thought, as she had thought a hundred times already, she hadn't walked out of that exit back at Sydney airport.

Inside, the hotel didn't disappoint. The atrium was so

mind-bogglingly spacious she got a sore neck from look-ing upwards. And the interior design was like nothing she'd ever seen—upmarket contemporary, with Oriental highlights that made it truly unique.

'Considering your interest in hotels, I've arranged for you to have a private tour,' Sam said as they went up in the elevator to their room. 'You just have to decide on a time that suits you.'

'You've thought of everything,' she replied with a con-tented sigh.

'Except the most important thing,' he said with a wry twist to his mouth. 'I'll never forgive myself for expect-ing you to get on that plane by yourself.'

Kate silenced him with a halt sign. 'I've forgiven you, so you have to forgive yourself. Really. You realised your mis-take and remedied it with the most marvellous of gestures.'

'So long as you're okay with it,' he said. 'I shocked myself at how easily I relapsed into work-obsessed ways.'

'So, I'm going to police this workaholic thing,' she as-serted more than half-seriously. 'It's not good for you. Or me.'

'You can discipline me whenever you like,' he shot back with a wicked lift of his eyebrow.

'Count on it,' she said, smiling as the elevator doors opened on their floor.

The first thing she noticed when they walked into their spacious suite wasn't the smart design or the view across the harbour. It was the fact that in the open-plan bathroom the elegant, free-standing bathtub was full of water and had sweetly fragrant rose petals scattered across the sur-face. When she looked across to the bed, rose petals had also been scattered across it.

'How romantic!' she exclaimed, clapping her hands in delight. 'Did you organise this too?'

'I can't take the credit,' he said. 'The hotel staff…uh… they seemed to think we were on our honeymoon.'

'Oh,' she said. 'Well, I hope… That is, I'd like to think this will be a…a honeymoon of sorts.' She wound her arms around his neck. 'Sam, this hotel is wonderful. Singapore is wonderful. All the stuff you've got planned for us is wonderful. But just being alone with you is the most wonderful thing of all.'

She kissed him, loving his taste, the roughness of his beard, the hard strength of his body pressed close to hers. 'I'd have to argue that you're the most wonderful of the wonderful,' he murmured against her mouth.

'I've never been so lonely as those days in Dolphin Bay after you went home. I ached to be with you,' she confessed.

'One night, after a business dinner, I got into the car and decided to drive down just to see you for an hour or two,' he said.

'So why didn't you?'

'Because I figured I'd end up driving home at night without sleeping at all and thought there was a good chance I'd crash the car.'

She stilled as she thought of the accident that had injured Emily and ultimately, because of its repercussions, taken her father's life too. 'I'm so glad you stayed put,' she said. 'Although I probably wouldn't have let you go back if you'd come.'

He kissed her and she eagerly kissed him back. Then she broke away to plant hungry little kisses along the line of his jaw, and came back to claim his mouth again in a deep kiss that rapidly became urgent with desire.

Without breaking the kiss, he slid her jacket off her shoulders so it fell to the floor. She fumbled with his tie, and when it didn't come undone easily she broke away from the kiss with a murmur of frustration so she could see what she was doing.

'Did I tell you how incredibly sexy you look in a suit?' she asked, her breath coming rapidly as she pulled off his tie and started to unbutton his shirt so she could push her hands inside. His chest was rock-solid with muscle, his skin smooth and warm. 'But then you look incredibly sexy in jeans too. Maybe you look incredibly sexy in anything— or maybe nothing.'

Her body ached with want for him. And this time there was no reason to stop—except *he* stopped. 'Wait,' he said.

'I don't want to wait,' she urged breathlessly. 'We're in the honeymoon suite.'

He stepped back. 'Seriously. I have to tell you something,' he said, the words an effort through his laboured breathing.

'Okay,' she replied, thinking of the bed behind her and how soon she could manoeuvre him onto it.

'Kate, listen—I can see where this is heading.'

'Good,' she said.

'And I don't think you're ready for it.'

Her eyes widened. 'Let me be the judge—' she started to say.

'Please,' he broke in. 'This is important. I've told you before, I want you to be able to trust me.'

'Yes,' she said.

'I want you to be sure of me before we…we make love.'

She wasn't certain what he was trying to say but she sensed it was important. Very important.

'What I'm trying to say is that if we wait until we're married you'll have no doubts about how committed I am to you. And it will give you the security I think you really need.'

She stared at him, lost for words, but with a feeling of intense joy bubbling through her.

'I'm asking you to marry me, Kate,' he said hoarsely.

'And…and I'm saying yes,' she whispered.

He gathered her into his arms and hugged her close. They stood, arms wrapped around each other for a long moment, when all she was aware of was his warmth and strength, the thudding of his heart and their own ragged breathing.

'I love you, Sam,' she said. 'I…I couldn't say it at the airport in front of all those people. It's too…too private.'

'I didn't mean to say it there; no one was more surprised than I was. I was just so relieved you hadn't flown away already, never to speak to me again, when you discovered I wasn't in Singapore to meet you.'

Then and there, she resolved never to tell him that she'd been on her way out of the airport when he'd found her.

'There's another thing,' he said, reaching into his pocket and pulling out a little black velvet box. 'I want to make it official.'

She drew a sharp intake of breath. It couldn't be. *It just couldn't be.* That would be too, too perfect.

With a hand that wasn't quite steady, she took the box from him and opened it. Inside was an exquisite ring, set with a baguette-cut emerald surrounded by two baguette-cut diamonds. 'Sam. It's perfect.'

'I thought it went with the colour of your eyes,' he said, sounding very pleased with himself in a gruff, masculine way. 'There's a good jewellery shop in the shopping arcade attached to the hotel.'

'I love it,' she whispered as Sam slipped it on to the third finger of her left hand. 'I absolutely love it.' She held her hand up in front of her for them both to admire. 'It's a perfect fit.'

'Lucky guess,' he said. 'Though, we builders are good with measurements.'

'Clever you,' she said, kissing him.

'I'd like to get married as soon as possible,' he declared. 'So we can…?'

'Not just because of that. Because I want you to be my wife.'

'And I love the idea of you being my husband,' she murmured. 'My husband,' she repeated, liking the sound of the words.

'Obviously, with the business, there's no way I can live in Dolphin Bay—though we can buy a holiday house there if you like. We'll have to live in Sydney. If that's okay with you.'

'Yes,' she said. 'I'd like that. Though, there are things we need to sort out. Like Ben. My job.'

'I don't think Ben will be at all surprised to be losing you, and you'll still be involved with the new resort as a part owner.'

'And through my connection with the owner of the construction company,' she said.

'I was thinking of setting up a hotel development division in the business,' he told her. 'What do you think?'

'That I could work with?' she asked.

He nodded. 'Of course, that would involve necessary research visiting fabulous hotels all around the world with your husband.'

'That seems a sound business proposition,' she said.

'Starting with a certain palace hotel in India where we can have our real honeymoon.'

'And write it off on expenses,' she said with a giggle.

'I like your thinking,' he said. 'Welcome to Lancaster & Son Construction, Mrs Lancaster-To-Be.'

'We…we might have a son,' she said. 'The name would live on.'

'Or a daughter. Or both. I want at least two children, if that's okay by you. I hated being an only child.'

'Quite okay with me,' she said on a sigh of happiness.

She wound her arms around his neck, loving it when her ring flashed under the light. 'Sam? I feel like I really trust you now. And I'm very sure of your commitment.'

'Yes,' he murmured, kissing the soft hollow at the base of her throat.

'And I want you to be sure of my love and commitment.'

'Thank you,' he said.

'We're officially engaged now, aren't we? You're my fiancé, right?'

'Yes,' he replied, planting a trail of little kisses up her neck to the particularly sensitive spot under her ear. It was almost unbearably pleasurable.

'So do you think we could start our practice honeymoon now?'

She looked meaningfully across at the enormous bed, covered in pink rose petals.

'Good idea,' he said as he picked her up and carried her towards it.

* * * * *

SWEPT AWAY
BY THE TYCOON

BY
BARBARA WALLACE

Barbara Wallace is a lifelong romantic and daydreamer, so it's not surprising that at the age of eight she decided to become a writer. However, it wasn't until a co-worker handed her a romance novel that she knew where her stories belonged. For years she limited her dreams to nights, weekends and commuter train trips, while working as a communications specialist, PR freelancer and full-time mum. At the urging of her family she finally chucked the day job and pursued writing full-time—and she couldn't be happier.

Barbara lives in Massachusetts with her husband, their teenage son and two very spoiled, self-centred cats (as if there could be any other kind). Readers can visit her at www.barbarawallace.com and find her on Facebook. She'd love to hear from you.

To Kumkum Malik.
Without your help and advice I would never
have started my publishing journey.
Thank you.

CHAPTER ONE

PLEASE SAY SHE was not watching her boyfriend hit on another customer.

Okay, perhaps *boyfriend* was too strong a word. After all, she and Aiden had never said they were exclusive. Still, Chloe Abrams figured they were, at the very least, serious enough that he wouldn't pass his number to other women *while she was standing six feet away*!

Wasn't as though he couldn't see her. Last time Chloe checked, between her height, her heels and her hair, she stood above the crowd by a good couple inches. Yet there he was, flashing his heavy-lidded smile at some blonde on the other side of the coffee bar, and Chloe would bet it wasn't because the woman had asked for an extra shot of syrup.

From behind her, she heard a chuckle. "I wondered when you'd catch on."

Great. As if the moment wasn't humiliating enough, the resident slacker decided to chime in.

"You know she's not the first one, right? Dude gives out his number more than directory assistance."

Chloe dug her nails into the strap of her designer handbag and pretended not to listen. A difficult task, since the slacker's voice had a silk-over-sandpaper quality that made him hard to ignore.

"Funny, he always gives out his number. He never asks the women for theirs. I can't figure out if it's because he thinks his company is that desirable or if it's because by having them call him, he gets off the hook for paying. You wouldn't want to weigh in, would you, Curlilocks?"

The strap on her bag crumpled, Chloe was squeezing so tightly. Problem with narrow city coffee shops was that it was hard to escape the crowd. In this case, the owner had crammed tables along the brightly colored walls, which meant that during the morning rush the patrons in line stood on top of those sitting down.

The slacker had first appeared shortly after the new year. If she was being honest, *slacker* wasn't the right word, but she couldn't come up with anything better. Every time Chloe came in—which was obscenely often—she would see him nursing a cup of coffee. A permanent ginger-haired fixture. Sometimes he read. Other times, she'd spy him bent over a pile of paper, scribbling away. Rugged, unshaven, bundled in a worn leather jacket, his no-nonsense presence jarred with Café Mondu's trendy atmosphere. Usually he kept to himself.

Until today, anyway.

"If you ask me," he continued in his quiet growl, "a woman like you could do a lot better."

Not really, Chloe thought, but she didn't feel like arguing the point.

"Your iced coffee is ready." In an obvious show of female solidarity, the other barista called out Chloe's order in an overly loud voice. First the slacker, now Aiden's coworkers. Was there anyone who hadn't noticed her humiliation?

"Thanks," she replied. If the slacker wanted to assume the acknowledgment was for his comment, too, let him. Stepping toward the counter, she loosened her grip on her strap, the motion causing the leather satchel to slide downward slightly and brush the blonde's hip. The woman stopped flirting long enough to glance over her shoulder. *That* got Aiden's attention. He immediately looked in Chloe's direction.

And winked.

Winked! Un-freaking-believable. He could have at least looked embarrassed over getting caught. No, the jerk winked, as if she was in on the joke.

"You okay, Curlilocks?" the slacker asked.

Okay? Try furious. Discovering Prince Charming was a jerk, she could handle. She was used to jerks. But to have him make a fool of her in front of the slacker and everyone else in the place? No way.

"Excuse me," she said, tapping the blonde on the shoulder, "but you're going to want stand back."

"Why?" the woman asked.

"Because of this." She raised her drink over Aiden's head and poured.

"What the—?" Coffee and ice streamed down the sides of the barista's face, plastering his shiny black mane to his cheeks. He looked like a long-haired dog after a bath.

Satisfaction gave a way better jolt than caffeine. "He's all yours, sweetie," Chloe said, tossing a smile to the blonde. "I've got better things to do." Turning on her heels, she marched to the front door.

The slacker rewarded her with a slow clap as she passed. "Well played, Curlilocks. Very well played."

At least someone enjoyed the performance.

"You did not." Larissa Boyd stared at her with wide-eyed admiration. "The entire iced coffee?"

"All twenty ounces," Chloe replied. "I've got to tell

you, those bangs don't look nearly as sexy when dripping wet." She sat back in her office chair, smiling with a boldness she didn't truly feel.

"What did he do?"

"Nothing. He and his new friend were too stunned to speak. I think everyone in the shop was." Except, that is, for the slacker. She could still hear his applause.

"Too stunned to speak about what?" Delilah St. Germain's ponytailed head poked around the cubicle wall. "I got your text. What happened?"

"Chloe caught Aiden passing his number to another woman, and dumped an iced coffee on his head."

Delilah's eyes widened to match Larissa's. "You did not."

"Is there an echo in here? Yes, I did. Blame temporary insanity."

"No, insane was when you started dating the jerk. This, on the other hand… I'm impressed. You've got guts."

Guts or really poor judgment? Chloe's rebellious high had started to fade in favor of foolishness.

Based on her friends' awestruck expressions, they disagreed, so she kept up the facade. She was good at that: pretending to be unaffected. "I prefer to say I struck a blow on behalf of misled females everywhere."

"Use whatever term you want. If I had been in your shoes, I wouldn't have had the nerve."

"Me, neither," Larissa said.

They needn't worry; neither of them would ever be in her shoes, and that wasn't simply because they were both engaged to be married. To begin with, her friends attracted a different kind of man. Nice men who believed in calling women back. Neither of them would be impulsive enough to dump a cup of coffee over a guy's head, because neither of them would be involved with a man jerk-offish enough to warrant the behavior.

Not that Chloe resented her friends' happiness. On the contrary. She couldn't be more happy. From the moment the three of them met at CMT Advertising's new employee orientation, Chloe had recognized her two best friends were different than her. They were soft and lovable, with a smiling optimism she couldn't muster if she tried. The two of them deserved all the happiness in the world.

"When you think about it, Aiden's the one with the nerve." Larissa's voice dragged her back to the present. "Giving his number out when you were standing right there? What kind of guy does that?"

The kind of guy Chloe dated. "Apparently it wasn't the first time, either. The slacker told me he's a regular directory assistance."

"Wait, who?" Delilah asked. She had a habit of tucking her hair behind her ear, a motion that caused her sinfully large diamond to sparkle as it caught the fluorescent lighting.

"The slacker. You've seen him. He sits at the front table every day." She was met with blank looks. "Leather jacket? Buzz cut?" How could they not have noticed him? "No matter. He's the one who told me Aiden writes his number on a lot of coffee cups."

"You believed him?"

Oddly enough, yes. "No reason for him to lie."

Delilah ran a hand around her ear again. "All the better you dumped his sorry behind, then. We never did think he was good enough for you."

"Delilah's right. Any guy who doesn't appreciate you is a jerk. You can do better."

"The slacker said the same thing," Chloe muttered.

"The slacker has good taste," Delilah stated.

She smiled. Naturally, her friends would rush to her defense, same as they did whenever her latest relationship went belly-up. Only Chloe knew the truth. That the betrayal wasn't all Aiden's fault. How could it be when she was the one genetically programmed to pursue doomed relationships? Short-term Chloe, good for a few laughs, but not worth sticking around for. Good thing she didn't expect more, or she'd have serious depression issues.

"Jerk or not, he was also my date for your wedding, Del." The brunette's wedding was two weeks away. She was marrying the head of their advertising agency in a black tie ceremony that would be filled with colleagues and society people. All of whom would have plus ones now, except for Chloe. She sighed. "Damn, but he would have looked good in a tuxedo."

"A tuxedo you were paying for," Larissa pointed out, placing a comforting hand on her shoulder. "Don't worry; we'll find you a proper date. One who can afford to pay his own way. I'm sure Tom has a friend."

"Or Simon…"

"Absolutely not." She'd rather go solo than take a blind date. Scrambling to find some stranger to take simply so she had a dance partner? Thanks, but she didn't need another short-term deal right now. "In fact," she said, thinking aloud, "not having a date is a good thing. Now I don't have to worry about entertaining anybody, and can focus on being the maid of honor. What if you have a bridal emergency? I'm supposed to be at your beck and call for anything you need."

"You're not funny," Larissa said, narrowing her eyes. "Beck and call" had been an inside joke for months. Ever since Larissa got engaged and turned planning her wedding into her life's work.

"Actually," Chloe replied with a grin, "I am very funny."

"Wait till you start planning your own wedding. You're going to want my help, and I'm not going to give you any."

"Oh come on, La-roo, you and I both know I plan on being one of those inappropriate cougars who dates your son's friends."

Larissa folded her arms across her chest. "You would, too, just to get me, wouldn't you?"

"You know it," Chloe said with a cheeky grin. When discussing her love life, she was very good at playing the irreverent, cavalier friend. Only after Delilah and Larissa returned to their desks did she let herself give in to the hollowness plaguing her chest.

She'd liked Aiden, dammit. So what if their relationship consisted mostly of meeting up at parties and clubs? Enough time had gone by that she'd started to think maybe he might be a guy who stuck around awhile. She should have known better. Sooner or later all men left. After all, a person had to be worth sticking around for.

"Well, well, well, look who's back. Should I grab my umbrella?"

The slacker's gravelly greeting seemed to inch its way up Chloe's spine, causing her to stiffen. Looking over at the front table, she saw him leaning back in his chair, a smile on his ginger-stubbled face. *You really need to find a better nickname,* she thought to herself. Smug Bastard might work today.

"I wouldn't want to waste a good coffee," she told him.

"Again," he replied.

"Excuse me?"

"You mean you wouldn't want to waste a good cup of

coffee again. Though now that I think about it, you didn't really waste yesterday's drink, did you?"

Chloe narrowed her eyes. She was so not in the mood.

"Not a morning person, are we, Curlilocks?"

"Depends on the company."

"Ouch." He clutched his chest. "You wound."

If only. She looked away, hoping he'd get the hint and stop talking. Being here was awkward enough without the commentary.

He didn't. "I've got to admit, I'm impressed. I wasn't sure you'd be back."

Neither was she, until she'd walked through the door. In fact, she'd stood on the corner for a good ten minutes, debating the decision, convinced the manager would toss her on the sidewalk the second she entered. Or worse, Aiden would throw an iced coffee in her face.

In the end, pride won out. Stopping for her morning iced latte had been part of her routine long before Aiden came into the picture. No way was she letting some two-timing coffee jerk change that.

"Why wouldn't I come back?" she asked Slacker. He didn't need to know about her indecision. "Like I said, they've got good coffee here."

"Better than good, if you ask me." To prove his point, he took a sip. Chloe noticed the side of his left hand already had ink smudges. Today was a note writing day, apparently.

"Although," he added, once he'd swallowed, "if I were you, I'd ask another barista to wait on me. In case."

"I'm not you," she reminded him.

He surprised her by raking his eyes up and down her entire length. "That you're not, Curlilocks," he said with a rough-sounding growl meant to make her insides take notice.

Chloe's hand flew to her abdomen. Something about the man's voice managed to get beneath her skin. He knew it, too; his eyes gleamed with cockiness.

Keeping her head high, she headed to the register, where Aiden waited. "Hey," she greeted.

"Good morning. May I take your order?"

That was it? Where was the glare? The terse words? *The recognition*? Surely she was worth some kind of reaction beyond a bland, generic greeting? "About yesterday..."

"Did you want a coffee?" The bland smile didn't slip. He was, for all intents and purposes, treating her like a complete stranger. As inconsequential as an out-of-state tourist. Punching her in the stomach would have hurt less. "The usual."

"Which is?"

The cut deepened. Chloe's eyes started to burn. She quickly blinked. He did not deserve the satisfaction.

"The lady drinks iced peppermint mocha latte."

Looking over her shoulder, she got a shrug from the slacker. "You know my order?"

"What can I say? Sit here long enough, you hear things."

"Don't you mean eavesdrop?"

His lips curled into a crooked smile. "Only on the interesting customers."

"No offense, but that's a little creepy." Even if her stomach did flutter at the idea that she qualified as interesting.

"You say creepy; I say observant. Sort of a potato-pot*ah*to kind of thing. I like people watching."

"Let me guess. You're a writer."

"If I am, then literature as we know it is in trouble," he said, punctuating the remark with a low chuckle.

How on earth did Del and La-roo not notice him sitting there every day? Even as possibly crazy slackers went, the man stood out in a crowd. What, at first glance, looked like street scruff was really very controlled. His hair was shortly cropped, and his not quite red, not quite blond stubble looked more like he simply couldn't be bothered with pulling out the razor than a lack of grooming. His battered jacket was similarly deceptive. Looking closer, she recognized what had been a very expensive piece of leather that had been worn till the thing molded to his broad shoulders. It reminded her of the basketball sneakers she couldn't give up even after she could afford better ones.

"See anything you like, Curlilocks?"

Crap. Chloe turned back to the register, hoping she didn't look too flustered. "I was admiring your jacket."

His chuckle was low and raspy. "This old thing? I've had her for years."

Her? Much as she knew she shouldn't, Chloe took the bait. "You gave your jacket a gender?"

"Sure. Why let the big ticket items have all the fun?"

"Interesting point," she conceded. "I supposed you named her, too."

"Don't be silly. That would be crazy."

As opposed to this whole conversation. Fortunately, Aiden chose that moment to return with her drink. "No need," he said, when Chloe reached for her wallet. "It's on the house."

"Seriously?" Didn't she feel like a heel now. Maybe she'd misjudged him *and* yesterday's situation. "That's really sweet of you."

"Don't thank me. I didn't do anything."

Her smile fell. "You mean you're not trying to apologize for yesterday?"

"Why should I apologize? I'm not the one who acted like a raving lunatic for no good reason."

No good reason? Chloe tightened her grip on the cup. He was lucky she didn't give him a repeat performance. "Who did then?" she asked, forcing herself to step back from the counter before she could give in to impulse.

The barista raised and lowered a shoulder. "Beats me. Note on the register says the next time you came in, your drink was free. Apparently someone appreciates acts of lunacy."

Chloe took another step back. The only people who knew what had happened were Larissa and Delilah, and as of last night, they'd vowed to boycott the café until "Aiden came to his senses."

"Must have been one of those random acts of kindness."

No, it couldn't be. A glance at the front table showed a definite sparkle in the slacker's ice-blue eyes.

"Why would someone pick me?" Particularly when she'd been rude to him? Regret stole at her insides.

Slacker leaned back, letting the hood of his sweatshirt become a gray cotton cowl around his neck. "Maybe that someone enjoyed seeing Don Juanista there get his come-uppance. I hear it took a couple hours to get the pepper-mint smell out of his luscious locks."

A snort escaped before she could stop herself. Aiden was so vain about his hair.

"Too bad I didn't snap a photo for the front bulletin board. I'm guessing there's an awful lot of women who wished they could have seen karma bite ole' Aiden in the rear."

"I'm guessing you're right." The realization brought back yesterday's humiliation in force.

Meanwhile, back at the register, Aiden had turned his

sights to another woman in line, his grease pencil seconds away from marking his digits at the base of her cup. "Doesn't look like karma bit all that hard," Chloe noted.

"Oh, but it will. You just wait. Ten years from now, that suffering musician look will have morphed into a receding hairline and a beer gut. Let's see how many women want him writing his number on their cup then."

Chloe swallowed another snort. "You paint an interesting picture."

"Interesting? Or Satisfying?"

"Maybe a little of both."

"Then my work here is finished." Slacker grinned broadly, revealing a row of bright perfect teeth. He had freckles, too, Chloe realized. The slightest dusting across the bridge of his nose, along with a couple of faint scar lines. Rugged, weather-hewn. He'd had a run-in with karma himself, hadn't he? Did he win or lose? Chloe wasn't sure why, but she had a feeling he would come out victorious in any battle.

A jostle from behind brought her back to reality. The gathering crowd meant eight-thirty was getting close. "I better get going," she told him.

"Already? The conversation was just getting interesting. Sure you can't stick around?"

"Unfortunately, some of us have to work for a living." As soon as the words left her mouth, she winced. Man buys her a cup of coffee and she insults him. *Insensitive, thy name is Chloe.*

"Just as well. I've got a meeting myself."

Chloe didn't call him on the obvious lie. "Do me a favor and if you see the 'stranger' who bought me the coffee, thank him, okay?"

"Sure thing. Enjoy drinking it—this time."

He winked.

Chloe squeezed her cup. Why'd he have to go and spoil a perfectly pleasant moment with a comment like that? Worse, why did her insides have to tap dance in response?

She'd retort, but the words didn't want to come out. Snapping her jaw shut, she marched to the door, barely avoiding a collision with a cashmere overcoat as she rushed past.

Ian Black watched her exit with amusement. Kid was trying so hard not to look flustered. She had swagger, that's for sure, although Ian had known that long before she'd tipped coffee over the Irish Casanova's head. The way she strutted in here every morning with her high heels and that long curly hair every morning, as if she owned the damn shop... Bet she walked into the Empire State Building the same way. You had to admire her display of confidence, whether it was real or strictly for show.

Her cacophony of curls blew back from her face as she slipped through the front door, treating him to a glimpse of her tawny-skinned profile, a golden flash amid the early spring gray. For a tall woman, she had surprisingly delicate features. Like a Thoroughbred horse, she was lean and leggy. A damn attractive girl, and the barista was an idiot for not treating her better. Ian had been watching the two of them flirt for weeks, disappointed when he'd heard Aiden say they were "hooking up." Ian had hoped the swagger meant she knew better. Thankfully, she'd come to her senses. Then again, let he who wasn't guilty of bad judgment cast the first stone. Sure wouldn't be him, that's for certain.

"One of these days, I'm going to insist on meeting somewhere less crowded," Jack Strauss grumbled as he unbuttoned his cashmere coat.

"Excuse me for frequenting my own business." Ian

nodded at the girl behind the register, who immediately moved to get Jack a coffee. "And you're late."

"Stop confusing me with one of your employees. Traffic was a bear."

"Driving wouldn't be such a problem if you lived in the city."

"Not everyone can afford the rent."

"Good grief, you're a laywer. Of course you can pay the rent."

"Okay, not everyone can afford your kind of rend. Did I say something funny?" he asked when Ian chuckled.

"Inside joke." He was wondering what Curlilocks would make of the conversation. She thought he was a bum. The color on her cheeks when she'd made the remark about working betrayed her. He would have corrected her if he didn't find her mistake so damn amusing. Ian wondered if, when she did find out, he should duck for cover. She looked as if she had quite an arm.

"Must be a good joke, whatever it is. I haven't seen you smile in a long time."

Draping his coat along the back of the chair, the silver-haired man sat down in the chair opposite Ian just as his coffee and pastry arrived. He took a large drink, then let out a breath.

"Feeling better?" Ian asked.

"Aren't I supposed to be asking you that question?"

Yes, he was. Much as Ian wanted to believe Jack's concern was as much out of friendship as it was obligation as his sponsor, he knew better. "Same as always. One day at a time.

"You're not…"

He shook his head. "No worries. These days I'm all about the coffee."

"So I see." Jack took another sip. "Although you didn't

have to go to such extremes. Most recovering addicts settle for buying cups of coffee, not coffee shops."

"I'm not most guys in recovery."

"No kidding. One of these days I expect to walk in here to find you bought a coffee plantation so you can grow your own beans."

"Don't think the thought hasn't crossed my mind." Ian never did believe in doing things halfway. Military service, business, alcohol abuse.

Hurting people.

Jack nodded at the stack of stationery by his elbow. "Still writing letters, I see."

"Told you when we first started meeting, I had a long list." He ran a hand across the stack. Twenty years of being a rat bastard left a long tail. "Don't suppose you have those addresses I wanted tracked down?"

"Again, stop confusing me with an employee."

"Are you planning to bill me for your law firm's time?"

When Jack's look said "of course," Ian stated, "Then technically, you are an employee. Now, do you have the names?"

"I'm beginning to see why your board of directors ousted you. You're an impatient son of a gun." The lawyer reached for his briefcase. "My investigator is still trying to locate a few people." He held up a hand before Ian could comment. "You gave him a pretty long list."

"Could have been worse. Tell him to be glad I stuck to Ian Black, the business years."

"Thank heaven for small favors. You do realize that when the program says you need to make amends, you don't need to literally contact every single person who ever crossed your path."

You did if you wanted to do things right. "You make amends your way, I'll make amends mine," Ian told him, snatching the papers. He didn't have the heart to tell Jack the list didn't begin to scratch the surface.

Quickly, he ran his eyes down the top sheet. Three pages of ex-girlfriends, former friends, employees and associates, all deserving of apologies.

And one name that mattered most of all. He glanced up at his friend. "Is—"

"Last page. At the bottom."

Of course. Save the worst offense for last. Flipping pages until he got to the last one, he found the name immediately. His biggest mistake.

And the hardest of all to make amends for.

CHAPTER TWO

"WHAT DO YOU mean, don't call him?" Ian slapped his empty coffee cup on the table. Since they'd started meeting, Jack had done nothing but talk about the twelve steps. Make amends to the ones you hurt, ask forgiveness, etc., etc. Now here Ian was, doing exactly that, and the man was saying he shouldn't? What the hell?

"I didn't say you should never call him," Jack replied. "I'm simply suggesting you slow down. Amends aren't made overnight."

"They aren't made sitting around doing nothing, either."

"You aren't doing nothing. He answered your letters, didn't he?"

"Yeah," Ian replied, "but…" But letters could say only so much. It was too easy to censor what you were writing. Too hard to read what wasn't being said. In the end, everything sounded flat and phony.

"Some conversations should be face-to-face. I need him to hear my voice, so he knows I'm sincere."

"He will, but I think you still need to go slow. You can't push the kid if he's not ready."

"Who says he's not ready? It's not like I'm suddenly appearing in his life unannounced."

"Then why didn't he give you his phone number?"

"Because I didn't ask," Ian quickly replied. Truthfully, he should have called long before this. During those early months of sobriety, however, he'd been shaky—and all right, a little scared—so he'd let Jack and the counselors talk him into writing a letter instead. But he was stronger now, more himself, and he needed to face his son. "I'm tired of wasting time," he told Jack. "I've wasted enough."

Thirteen years, to be exact. Thirteen years during which his ex-wife, Jeanine, had no doubt filled his son's head with garbage. Even if a good chunk of what she said was true, it wouldn't surprise Ian if she went overboard to make him look as bad as possible. His ex-wife was nothing if not an expert at deflecting blame. Her influence made repairing his mistakes all the more difficult. He could already sense her lies' effect in the way Matt phrased his letters. So polite and superficial. Again, it was too easy to read between the lines. The only way he would loosen Jeanine's grasp was for them to talk face to face. "I'm not expecting us to plan a father-son camping trip, for crying out loud. I simply want to talk."

On the other side of the table, Jack shook his head. "Still think it's a bad idea."

"I didn't ask what you thought," Ian snapped. He already knew the older man's opinion, and disagreed with it. Jack didn't have children. He wasn't sitting here with the window of opportunity growing smaller and smaller. A year ago Matt was in high school; now he was in college. Three years from now he'd be out in the world on his own. Ian didn't have time to take things slow.

"Maybe not." The lawyer didn't so much as blink in response to the rude reply. Ian suspected that's why Jack had been assigned as his sponsor; he was one of the few people who didn't back down at the first sign of temper.

"But I'm giving it to you, anyway. I've seen too many men and women fall off the wagon because they tried to do too much too fast too soon."

"How many times do I have to remind you, I'm not your average addict." He was Ian Black. He believed in moving, doing. Too many people wasted time analyzing and conferring with consultants. Sooner or later you needed to pull the trigger. Getting to yes meant getting things done.

Which was why, as soon as Jack left for his office, Ian reached for his cell phone. The call went straight to voice mail. Hearing the voice on the other end, he had to choke back a lump. He'd heard it before, but never this close, never speaking directly to him. Hearing his son sound so grown-up… All the milestones he'd missed rushed at Ian. So many lost moments. He had to fight himself not to call back and listen to the message again. They'd speak soon enough.

Eleven hours later, though, his phone remained silent. He told himself to relax. Kid was probably in class or doing homework. For all he knew, they had lousy reception in the dorms and Matt hadn't even gotten his message. Ian came up with a dozen reasons.

None made him any less agitated.

Letting out a low groan, he scrubbed his hands over his face.

It didn't help that he spent the day writing letters of apology. A stack of envelopes sat by his elbow. One by one he'd addressed and ticked off names on the list Jack had supplied.

So many names, so many people who hated his guts and probably—rightfully—danced when they heard he'd been ousted from Ian Black Technologies. As he'd told

Curlilocks, nothing beat a healthy dose of karmic blow-back. *Curlilocks*. Aiden said her real name was Chloe, but he thought the nickname suited her better.

He probably shouldn't be thinking of her at all considering the shocking number of women he finished apologizing to. So many wronged women. Some, like his ex-wife, were women he never should have gone near in the first place. Others were opportunistic bed partners who'd hoped to become more. But many were simply good women who'd offered their affection and whom he'd let down. Their names stung the most to read. Business casualties he could rationalize as part of the industry; personal betrayals showed how toxic a person he could be.

Ian ran his finger across Matt's name and felt an emptiness well up inside him. The head roads he'd made in this relationship weren't nearly enough.

To hell with waiting. Patience was overrated. He grabbed his phone and dialed. Voice mail again. He slammed it down on the table, the force causing his empty coffee cup to rattle.

When he'd bought the coffee shop, the first thing he did was order new drinkware, replacing the cutesy china cups with sturdier, heavier stoneware. The kind that, when hurled, would leave their mark rather than shatter. What, he wondered, would happen if he tossed one right now? Would his employees duck in fear as they used to? The new and improved Ian Black vowed not to be a bully. But damn, did he want to heave something right now....

"Should I get out my umbrella?"

He looked up to find Curlilocks looming over his table. Even with his black mood, a rush of male admiration managed to pass through him. At some point during the day she'd corralled her curls into a high ponytail that controlled, but didn't completely tame them. She must have walked a few blocks because her nose and cheeks were bright pink from the harsh winter air that had taken up residence in the city that night.

"Little late for you to be roaming the streets, isn't it?" It wasn't like him not to notice her entrance. He wondered how long she'd been standing by his table. Long enough to witness his little meltdown?

"Working late. Came here for a refuel, because the office coffee stinks." For the first time, he noticed she was holding two coffee cups, one hot, one cold. She slid the hot one in his direction. "Here."

"What's this?"

"Call it a random act of kindness."

Ian stared at the white cardboard cup. Kindness didn't suit him at the moment. "No, thanks."

"Seriously, go ahead. I owe you for spending your money on me this morning."

Right, because she thought him down on his luck and was probably worried that he didn't have the money to waste. This morning he found her mistake amusing, but tonight it merely emphasized his current position, and the mistakes he'd spent the last eleven hours trying to amend. "I don't need your coffee. You want to feel charitable, try the guy on the corner." Someone who deserved the gesture.

Her eyes widened, their chocolate warmth replaced by humiliation. Ian immediately regretted his response. "Look, I just meant—"

"Forget it!" She held up her hand. "I was paying you back for this morning, is all. You don't want the coffee, then you give it to the guy on the corner."

"Chloe—" A blast of cold air killed the rest of his apology.

So much for the new and improved Ian Black. Why didn't he go kick a kitten, too, so he could really be a jackass?

Chloe strode from the shop as fast as she could. You try to do a guy a favor. Jeez, she'd bought him a cup of coffee. No need for him to make a federal case out of it. What did he think she wanted to do? Save him? Only reason she bought him the drink was because the café was about to close, and he'd looked a little lost staring at his empty mug. He didn't have to toss her good deed back in her face.

What had caused his sudden mood shift, anyway? The guy had been happy-go-lucky enough this morning. Did the day just wear him down? Lord knows sitting alone in a coffee shop all day would do that to her. Such a waste of what looked like a strong, capable man. More than capable, really.

Not that she studied him all that closely.

The wind bit her cheeks, reminding her that, at the moment, she was the one braving the cold, not her slacker. She flipped up the collar on her coat. It wasn't much protection against the wind, but at least she could bury her chin a little. With her eyes focused on the sidewalk, she dodged the sea of homebound commuters, wishing she could be one of them. Stupid slacker. It was his fault she was dodging anything. If she hadn't wasted half her day wondering about his story, she'd be on her way home, too, instead of heading back to the agency.

The attack came out of nowhere. One minute she was rushing down the sidewalk, the next her shoulder was being ripped backward. A pair of hands slammed into her back, hard, knocking the air from her lungs and her body off balance. Before she could so much as gasp she was pitching forward, face-first onto the sidewalk. Stars exploded behind her eyes as her hands and chin struck the cement.

From behind her, she heard a shout, followed by the scrambling of feet and a second, deeper cry of pain. A second later, she felt an arm around her waist.

"You all right, Curli? Damn, look at your chin."

"Wh-what?" Chloe was too dazed to answer. The arm around her waist felt warm and safe, so she leaned in closer.

"Your chin," her savior repeated, his voice soft and rough. "It's bleeding."

She touched her face, flinching when she felt sticky wetness. The dampness trailed down her scarf to the front of her coat. She tried to look down, to see the damage, but everything was dark.

"It's mostly coffee," he told her, but we should make sure your chin doesn't need stitches. Do you have anything in your bag I can use to wipe the skin clean?"

"I don't think—my bag!" She sat up a little straighter. That had been the tug she'd felt on her arm. The jerk had stolen her pocketbook.

"Right here." The soothing arm disappeared from her waist. A second later, a brown leather bag appeared in her lap, minus the strap. Chloe fingered the jagged end where the mugger cut the strap free. The bag had been her twenty-fifth birthday present to herself. Now it was ruined. Because some thug had got close enough to...

Her lower lip started to quiver. That made her teeth and chin hurt more.

"Shh, don't cry, Curlilocks. It'll be all right."

No, it wouldn't. "I—I was m-m-mugged." The word hurt to say. She felt dirty and violated.

"I know. I know." His whisper reached through the

cold, calming her. "If it's any consolation, they're hurt worse than you."

"They?" There were two? She started to feel nauseous. "I didn't see them."

"That's how it works. They find someone who's not paying attention and grab the bag from behind."

Fingers brushed the hair from her face. Tender fingers, but they made her tremble nonetheless. "You stopped them," she said.

"Right place, right time." The fingers found their way to her jaw. Tilted her face until she could see his pale blue eyes. Under the streetlight, his stubble looked more blond than red, the freckles across the bridge of his nose more prominent. "We really need to treat that cut," he said. "Do you have anything in your bag?"

Chloe shook her head. "Afraid not. I cleaned the thing out this morning." Thank goodness, too. Any heaver and the force of it being ripped away might have dislocated her shoulder.

"Lucky for you, I'm good at improvising." Before she could ask what he meant, he'd shed his jacket and begun peeling the sweatshirt over his head.

"What are you doing?"

"Relax. The shirt's fresh from the laundry." He mopped at the cut with one of the sleeves.

Chloe caught his wrist. "You're ruining your sweat-shirt."

"A sacrifice for a worthy cause," he replied.

By now, they'd attracted curiosity and several people had stopped to check on them.

"We'll be fine," the slacker told them. "Doesn't need stitches."

"How do you know?" She hated to admit it, but with

the gentle way he was dabbing at her wound, she wouldn't care one way or the other.

"Let's say I've seen my share of cuts and wounds. How are your hands?"

She turned them over. Road burn marred her palm. "I'm betting your knees match," he said. "Come on, I'll take you back to the coffee shop and clean you up properly. We can call the police from there, too. Chances are there's not much they can do at this point, but you should file a report, anyway—just in case."

Chloe could do little more than nod. The way her insides were shaking, she couldn't think straight if she tried.

Meanwhile, the slacker took charge, effortlessly. Letting someone else carry the load for a change felt good. When his arm returned to her waist, and he helped her to her feet, she couldn't help curling into his body. He smelled of coffee and wood. Strong, masculine, solid scents that filled her insides with a sense of security.

"I don't even know your name," she said, realizing that fact almost with surprise. "Slacker" definitely no longer applied.

He paused a moment before answering. "Ian Black."

Ian Black. The name sounded familiar, but she couldn't figure out why. Didn't matter; her rescuer finally had a name. "Thank you, Ian Black," she said, offering a grateful smile.

"You're welcome, Chloe." Hearing him use her proper name only made her smile wider.

They held each other's gazes, not saying a word. Finally, Ian stepped back, his arm slipping away from her waist. "What do you say we get you cleaned up?"

Right, her chin. Unbelievably, Chloe had forgotten. "I'm not sure what I would have done if you hadn't happened along when you did," she told him as they walked slowly back.

With the immediate drama over, adrenaline had kicked in, causing her legs to shake. She was afraid her knees would buckle beneath her if she moved too quickly. Ian kept pace a few inches from her elbow, not touching, but close enough to grab her should something happen. He held her bag tucked under his arm. The big leather satchel looked ridiculous, but he didn't seem to mind.

"I'm only sorry I didn't arrive a minute earlier. I might have spared your chin," he said.

Which throbbed. To make walking easier, Chloe had taken over the job of pressing it tight. She was pretty sure the bleeding had stopped long ago, but Ian insisted she maintain pressure. "I don't care about my chin." She'd suffered worse playing college ball. "I'm more bummed out about my bag."

"Pocketbooks can be replaced."

"Not at that price," she muttered.

"Then on behalf of your bag, I'm sorry I didn't move faster."

"You showed up. Better than nothing."

Why did he show up, though? He'd been sitting at his table when she'd left. She started to frown, only to have pain cut the expression short. "Were you following me?"

"Yes, I was."

"Oh." At least he scored points for honesty. She scooted an inch or two to the right. "Why?"

"To apologize," he told her. "I had no business being so rude to you earlier. You bought the coffee to be nice. I was wrong to bite your head off."

Had all that taken place tonight? The exchange seemed like eons ago. "Be pretty rude of me not to accept now, wouldn't it?"

"You wouldn't be the first person."

It was such a strange response, Chloe couldn't help frowning again. "What do you mean?"

She didn't get an answer. They'd rounded the corner to the coffee shop. A Closed sign hung in the window. "Shoot," Chloe muttered. "I'd hoped we'd get here before they locked up for the night."

"No worries."

There was a female barista wiping down the counter. Ian rapped on the window to draw her attention. Her chin must have looked pretty bad because the woman immediately stopped what she was doing and unlocked the door.

"Oh my God, what happened?"

Once again, Ian took charge, steering Chloe straight to the table in the corner. "We're going to need the first aid kit, Jesse."

Now, Chloe knew she had to be a mess, because the woman obeyed without a word. On the other hand, Ian's demeanor didn't exactly invite discussion.

While the barista disappeared into the back room, Ian made his way to the sink behind the coffee bar. Reaching into an upper cabinet, he retrieved a fresh towel. Then, grabbing a stainless steel bowl that was drying on the counter, he filled it with water.

"You look pale," he said when he returned. No surprise there. The shaking in her legs had spread to the rest of her body. Took all she had not to fall off the chair.

"Hold on." He crossed the room again, this time to help himself to a bottle of water from the display case. "Here. Drink some of this."

"Thank you." Drinking and keeping the sweatshirt pressed to her chin proved difficult, especially with her free hand trembling. Some of the water dribbled past her lips and onto the shirt.

"You're really making a mess tonight, aren't you Curli?"

Chloe was about to comment when she caught the twinkle in his eye. A smile tugged the corners of her mouth. "Good thing you didn't give me coffee. I might have stained your sweatshirt."

"Heaven forbid. Coffee's such a bitch to get out."

As opposed to blood. "I hope this wasn't your favorite shirt."

"A worthwhile sacrifice," he said again, then ran his index finger down the bridge of her nose before giving the tip a playful tap.

Fighting to keep to the color from flooding her cheeks, Chloe looked away. Maybe it was the change in temperature after being outside, but her chill had begun to fade, replaced by an odd fluttering deep in her muscles. Like shivers, only more intense and without the nervous edge.

"Here's the first aid kit. I can't vouch for the contents. Been awhile since we've had to use anything in it." Jesse's return removed some of the electrical charge from the moment. "I grabbed some plastic bags, too. In case you want to make an ice pack."

"Good idea. Could you make me a couple? You might want them for your knees," he added to Chloe.

As soon as he mentioned them, she lifted her skirt for a peek. Sure enough, both knees had quarter-size scrapes right below the kneecap. Dark red marred the outer skin, the beginnings of what would be large purple bruises. The cuts didn't hurt now, but they would soon. She looked around for a way to prop her legs so she could balance the ice bags. Finding none, she left her feet dangling. She'd ice the bruises later.

Meanwhile Ian was sorting through the first aid kit. "I see what you mean about the contents," he said tossing a half a roll of gauze on the table. "Better make an extra ice pack for her chin, too."

"Sure thing, boss."

Boss? The sweatshirt pressed against her chin was the only thing keeping Chloe's jaw from dropping. "You work here?" she asked Ian.

"Something like that."

"Define something." She'd caught the look Ian and the barista exchanged. Either he worked there or he didn't. Why the evasive answer?

Ian didn't reply. "We're going to be here awhile, Jess," he told the other woman. "Will you be all right getting home?"

"I'm meeting my boyfriend up the street for drinks."

"Be careful. We don't need a second incident."

Chloe waited until Jesse said goodnight before resuming her questioning "You could have told me you were an employee here." Might have saved her an afternoon of speculating if she'd known there was a perfectly logical reason for him to be hanging around. Not to mention saving her from being mugged.

"Could have, if I was an employee."

"But she called you boss."

"Uh-huh."

The answer hit her like a ton of bricks. Good Lord, but she could be dense, "You're the new owner."

"Guilty as charged. Ow! What was that for?"

She'd kicked him in the shin. If her knees didn't hurt, she'd kick him someplace else. "For making me think you were down on your luck," she snapped.

"I didn't make you think anything. You drew your conclusions all on your own."

"You still could have said something. Do you have any idea how much—" *Time I spent thinking about you?*

Thankfully, she caught herself before the rest of the sentence left her mouth. The hole she'd dug herself was deep enough, thank you. "Why didn't you correct me?"

"Let's say I found the misconception entertaining."

"Glad I could amuse you."

"Trust me, Curli, you did." His eyes met hers, their sparkle so bright and smug Chloe would have glared in return had her stomach not chosen that moment to do a somersault. She felt like an idiot. Her and her big grand gesture. "No wonder you told me to give the coffee to the man across the street."

"Figured he could use the warmth more than me." Moving closer, Ian lifted the sweatshirt from her chin. The fabric tugged the skin where the cloth had dried in place, causing her to wince. "Sorry," he said, tossing the garment aside.

"For the chin or for misleading me?"

"Both. Now, tip your head back so I can clean you up."

Although annoyed, Chloe did what she was told. A second later, Ian's fingertips brushed across her throat. She jumped, her frazzled nerves making the touch feel far more intimate than it was.

Ian sensed her discomfort. "Shhh." His thumbs stroked her pulse points. Again, intimate, but soothing. "I need to see how deep the cut goes."

As he spoke, he leaned in tight. Once again, Chloe found herself breathing in coffee and wood, strong, manly scents that calmed her nerves. His hands were softer than she expected. Given his gruff exterior, she would have guessed them to bear signs of exposure and hard labor. These fingers, however, had the surface of silk, with a touch to match. Hard to believe they belonged to the same strong hands she'd seen gripping a coffee mug this morning. Until he fanned his thumbs along the base of her throat, that is. Then she felt every ounce of their strength thrumming below. Controlled but ever present.

"You know," he said, his breath ghosting warm across her skin, "that was one of the reasons I ran after you. I wanted to set the record straight."

The sting of a wet cloth pressing against her cut kept her from responding. "Wasn't fair to keep stringing you along the way I was, especially after you made such a nice gesture."

"Nice, but irrelevant."

"Being irrelevant doesn't erase what you were trying to do." He rinsed out the towel and began dabbing at her chin again. "Good intentions should be acknowledged."

His answer brought back the odd fluttering sensation from earlier. She wanted to press her hand to her stomach, but their position made doing so impossible. Somehow, while cleaning her cut, he'd moved so close his knee had wedged itself between her legs. Or had her legs parted for his knee? She felt the seam of his jeans pressing against her flesh, making annoyance increasingly difficult to maintain.

"One," she said suddenly, grabbing the first distraction that came to mind. "You said setting the record straight was only one of the reasons you ran after me. What was the other?"

"I already told you, I wanted to apologize for being a jerk. I had no business biting your head off."

"Why did you?"

The only sound was that of water being wrung from the towel. "Long story."

And guessing from the sour way he spoke, not a very pleasant one. "Want to share?"

"Ever wish you could turn back time?"

Having expected him to say no, his question caught her off guard. "Beyond tonight?"

"Yeah," he replied, tossing the cloth into the bowl. Water splashed over the sides, leaving a puddle on the table. "Beyond tonight. Muggings don't count."

Then what did? Relationships? Bad decisions? "All the time," she answered. More than he could possibly know. She gave a soft laugh, trying to inject a little humor into what was otherwise a pathetic situation. "You met Aiden."

"True enough. What on earth did you see in him, anyway?"

"A really sexy Irish accent. What can I say?" she added, when Ian arched a brow. "I'm shallow."

"Aren't we all?" he replied with a smile.

Right now, the shallow part of her had noticed the shadows behind his eyes. The darkness alternately marred and enhanced their blue color, giving his gaze depth. "So why are you turning back time?" she asked him. "Don't tell me you have relationship issues."

"I've got issues up the ying yang, Curlilocks." His hands cradled her jaw again, tilting her head backward. "Let's see what we're dealing with."

"Will I live, Doc?" She really wanted to ask what he meant, but those were the words that came out.

Ian was quiet as he studied the wound. Amazingly, his touch was even more gentle than before. Between the featherlight contact and his breath blowing warm at the base of her throat, Chloe found herself fighting not to break out in a warm shiver.

"You already have a scar," he said after a moment.

"Took a header going in for a layup. College ball," she added for clarification.

"A six-foot-tall woman playing basketball. There's a stereotype."

"Six feet and a half inch, thank you very much." She lowered her chin, a mistake, since she found herself nose to nose with him. The shiver she'd been fighting broke free. "And playing ball helped pay for school."

"Lucky you."

"Suppose that's one way of looking at things." If you call being born with pterodactyl-length arms lucky. "I didn't really have a choice."

"We all have a choice," he said.

"What does that mean?"

Busy pawing his way through the bandages, Ian didn't answer right away. "Exactly the way it sounds. We always have a choice. We don't always make the right ones."

"You can say that again," she replied. "I've made enough bad decisions to qualify as an expert."

"Nonsense, you're just a baby. Talk to me when you've made as many mistakes as I have." He tore open a Band-Aid. "Then you can call yourself an expert."

Chloe recalled her thoughts this morning, about whether Ian had battled karma. Apparently he had, although not as victoriously as she'd supposed.

"All done," he announced, stepping back. He was referring to bandaging her cut, but intuition told her he meant the conversation, as well. The abrupt end left her as unsettled as his touch.

Made her wonder if she wasn't dancing around a mistake herself.

CHAPTER THREE

"Do you lie to everyone you meet, or did I win some special kind of prize?"

Engrossed in letter writing, Ian almost missed the question. He looked up to find Chloe towering over his table. She'd dressed for dramatic effect today, with her hair pulled back and a pair of large sunglasses accentuating both her cheekbones and her bandaged chin. Instantly, the memory of her skin beneath his fingers sent awareness rolling through him, and he had to squeeze his pen to keep from reaching out to touch her again. She was too attractive for her own good. The type of woman the old Ian would have pursued with a passion. Wined her, dined her and charmed those boots right off. On second thought, he'd charm off everything *but* the boots.

Damn the conscience that came with sobriety.

"Would you mind starting the conversation again?" he asked her. "I missed the beginning."

"Ian Black Technologies."

Ah. His not-so-secret identity. "Someone's been playing on the internet." He wondered how long it would take for her to dig up his story.

"Your name sounded familiar, so I went online to find out why, and there you were, larger than life. Ian Black, technology entrepreneur extraordinaire."

"*Extraordinaire*'s a pretty strong word. More like a guy who had the right idea at the right time. Still doesn't explain how I lied to you."

Her sunglasses rose and fell, signaling an arched eyebrow or two. "You said you owned a coffee shop."

"I do."

"Conveniently leaving out the part about the global defense company. A lie of omission is still a lie."

"Maybe I like keeping a low profile." The sunglasses moved again; an eye roll this time, he suspected. "Besides, I didn't omit anything. Or didn't you read the part where I got kicked out of my own company?"

"My ad agency works with a lot of large companies. CEOs get replaced all the time. Corporate politics, change in culture. Doesn't alter the fact you're hardly as down-and-out as you led me to believe."

Fascinating. She might the first woman he'd ever met who was annoyed because he was rich. She was also terribly naive if she thought his eviction was solely because of politics or culture change. "If you work in advertising, you know there's also such a thing as corporate spin. Believe me, I earned my ouster." Given how bad things got, he was lucky he'd held his office as long as he did. "As for the omission…I already apologized for misleading you. Defense contracting is part of my past. I prefer to focus on fixing my present."

"Fixing?" she asked.

"Told you, I made a lot of mistakes." He pointed with his chin at the two paper cups in her hand. "One of those mine?"

A blush made its way up those cheekbones, adding a shade of pink to the tawny color. "Apparently I didn't learn my lesson last night."

"Last night was sweet."

"Don't you mean naive?"

"Never apologize for doing something nice. So was buying coffee today." Regardless of whether he owned the place or not. "Besides, profits are always appreciated." He motioned for her to sit down.

"I wanted to do something to thank you for saving me," she said, settling into the place across from him. "I thought about buying you a new sweatshirt, but that was when I learned you were a big-time tycoon."

"Meaning I can buy my own."

"Meaning you could buy me one."

Ian laughed. She was a spunky one.

"From the looks of things, I'm going to assume you made it home okay, too."

"More than okay. I've never had a police escort before."

"I have," he told her. "Although they weren't as friendly." Nor did any of them check out his legs the way Officer Kent did hers.

"You didn't need to ask him."

Yes, he did. Curlilocks might put on a good show, but she wasn't as tough as she liked people to believe. Beneath all the spunk and saucy comments lurked a whole lot of vulnerability. If you looked close enough, you could see it flashing behind her eyes. Lord knows, he'd looked close enough last night. Exactly why he had asked the police officer to take her home. Talking, touching her.... he'd pushed his luck far enough. For a man who hadn't been with a woman in over a year, taking her home would have been way too tempting. He had enough mistakes to fix without throwing into the mix a one-night stand with a woman just out of a bad relationship.

"Don't sweat it," he said. "Part of the perks of being semi-famous is you feel okay asking the police for favors."

"No, I meant he'd already offered."

Oh. How considerate of the man. "Does this mean poor Aiden's been replaced?"

"No way," she replied with a wave of her gloved hand. "Not that Aiden's irreplaceable, because believe me, he isn't. I'm simply not looking to do any replacing. I wasn't kidding when I said I had a bad track record. I'm not what you'd call the best judge when it comes to people, as you know."

All the more reason he'd made the right decision last night. "How do you know Officer Kent wasn't the exception to your track record?"

Leaning forward, she lowered her sunglasses as if about to share a secret. "Because there is no exception."

"You sell yourself short."

"I'm not selling anything short," she said, wrapping her lips around her straw. "I know I'm a prize. It's the men that fail to meet expectations."

"Present company included?" Ian couldn't help himself; she'd left the door wide open. When she didn't answer right away, he laughed. "I'll take that as a yes."

"Seems to me a guy who lied about being poor shouldn't ask stupid questions."

Ian laughed again. No sense arguing, as she'd only reboot her lie-of-omission argument. Given neither of them were likely to concede ground, the argument would last all day.

They were alike in a lot of ways, weren't they? Stubborn, quick with the verbal cut. It's why he knew she wasn't as cavalier about men as she made out to be. The sunglasses might hide her eyes, but you couldn't kid a kidder. Last night's vulnerability tinged her voice.

Of course, she'd deny the charge to her dying day. Ian knew, because he'd do the same. Better to face the world with bravado. Hide the scars and fears, lest your weakness show.

So why did he talk about his mistakes last night? Reaching across the table, he pulled the other coffee close and peeled off the lid. The aroma of fresh brewed arabica greeted his nostrils. Hot, steaming and black. The one habit from his drinking days he never planned to drop. Closing his eyes, he inhaled deeply. *Heaven.* "What did man do before the invention of coffee?"

"Killed each other."

"In that case, I'm starting a petition to award the man who brewed the first cup the Nobel Peace Prize. I'm not sure, but I think his name might have been Starbuck."

This time Chloe was the one who laughed. Ruby-red lips parting to release an indulgent lilt. The sound wound through his insides, warming places long dormant.

He took a long drink, reveling in the relaxation. It had been a long time since he'd dropped his guard around someone—someone besides Jack and his rehab counselors, that is. No wonder he'd backed off last night. Subconsciously, he recognized the potential friendship and didn't want to screw things up.

"I should let you get to work," he said, setting his coffee down. "Going out on a limb, I'm going to guess you didn't show up early just to buy me a cup of coffee."

"If only. That is—" her eyes dropped to her cup "—I have to make up the work I didn't stay late and finish last night. I don't like leaving things hanging."

Me, either, he thought, glancing down at the letter he'd started and restarted a half dozen times. Another ex-lover whose feelings he'd crushed. Every apology he wrote was a reminder of how many "things" he still needed to address. "You have a good excuse, though," he told Chloe.

"I'm sure your boss will understand. Especially when he sees your chin."

"Why do you think I kept the bandage on?"

Damn, but he wished she wasn't wearing sunglasses. He liked the way her eyes sparkled when she got cheeky. "If you really want to ratchet up the sympathy, add a limp. Nothing tugs on an employer's heartstrings like a little hobble."

"Did the tactic work for your employees?"

"Hell no. Why do you think they were happy to see me go? I was a major hard-ass."

"So I read last night."

"And yet you still talk to me."

"Today, anyway." She started to leave, only to stop suddenly. When she spoke again, it was without the saucy edge. "In case I didn't make myself clear earlier, I really do appreciate everything you did last night. This probably sounds silly, but if there's anything I can do for you…"

"Don't sweat it. And you don't owe me a thing. Believe me, the good karma points are more than enough."

"Trying to avoid a receding hairline and beer gut?"

"You're onto me, Curli."

The corners of her mouth curled into a playful smirk. "I don't think you need to worry too much, *Ginger*. Man your age? The damage is already done."

Didn't he know it. Exactly why he forced himself not to watch her behind strut out the door. His blood was stirred up enough for one day. Stir it any further and he'd have to add another letter to the pile.

The transition from toasty coffee shop to the harsh outdoors hit hard. Chloe shivered and hugged her bag tight. She might have acted all laissez faire to Ian, but the truth was last night still had her feeling vulnerable. She couldn't imagine how she'd feel if he hadn't been there to lean on. His steady presence was the only thing keeping her from falling apart. If she concentrated, she could still smell his scent. Twelve hours later, the memory alone warmed her nerves. He'd been so strong, so dependable. She wasn't used to dependable.

Of course, you could have knocked her over with a feather when his photo popped up during her internet search, and she found her slacker slash coffee shop owner was none other than the CEO of a major defense company.

Former CEO, she corrected. A fact Ian had been quite keen on emphasizing this morning. Something to do with his abrasive management style leading to a power shake-up. She'd been too shaky to do more than skim the story last night.

Wonder where the ouster fell on his list of "issues"? She'd ask, but feared opening a wound. Especially recalling the pain he'd so clearly tried to mask when speaking. And here she thought knowing the slacker's story would end her speculating.

Up ahead, she spotted a familiar blonde head wrapped in miles of dark blue scarf and moving slower than the rest of the pedestrians. La-roo didn't do cold weather well.

"Trying to dial the phone by telepathy?" she asked when she caught up to her friend.

Larissa frowned at the cell phone in her hand. "I could have sworn Tom said he would be in the office early this morning. We're supposed to talk about groomsmen gifts. Oh my God, what happened to your chin?"

"I got mugged last night." Chloe did her best to sound casual, but her friend stopped short anyway.

"You're kidding! Are you okay?"

"Other than the chin and a few scrapes on my hands and knees, I'm fine. My bag suffered the brunt of the damage. Two hundred dollars down the drain."

"Thank goodness. You must have been terrified." Larissa took a step, then stopped short again. "What about your stuff! Are you going to have to cancel everything?"

"Fortunately, no. Ian tackled the guy before he could get too far, and saved my credit cards."

"Who's Ian?"

Chloe told her the whole story, including Ian's true identity, although she left out the part about last night's odd sense of closeness. Knowing La-roo, she'd get all romantic over what was nothing more than an overblown reaction to Ian's heroics.

When Chloe finished, her friend shook her head. "Unbelievable. This guy sits around a coffee shop all day? Why? I know running a small business takes a lot of time, but moving in seems extreme."

"No clue. Maybe he likes being idly rich." Which was doubtful. Ian didn't strike her as a man who liked being idly anything. He was more the man of action type. Like last night. She got a hot thrill just thinking about how he'd taken down the thug.

"Whatever the reason," Larissa said, "you're lucky he was there."

"Yeah, I was."

They pushed their way through the revolving door into the office building lobby. After three blocks of cold, the rush of warmth was almost tropical. Not as cozy feeling as at the café, but definitely welcome.

"I hate this weather," Larissa said, unwinding her miles of scarf. "I thought it was supposed to be spring."

"Early spring," Chloe reminded her. "You know as well as I do, that doesn't necessarily mean warm."

"No kidding. Did you hear they are predicting rain this weekend? If I don't see some sunshine soon, I'll go crazy."

"Cheer up. Another few weeks and you'll be in Mexico sipping champagne."

"The trip can't come soon enough. I only hope Del gets good weather for her wedding."

"Somehow, I don't think Del and Simon care, so long as they get married."

"True. Those two are so in love it's sickening."

Chloe had to agree. Both Delilah and their boss had worked late last night themselves. She wondered if they'd noticed she didn't return from her coffee run, or if they were too caught up with each other. Simon's door had been shut tight. She pressed a fist to her midsection. Inexplicably, thoughts of Simon and Delilah dissolved into an image of her and Ian, causing the fluttering sensation to return.

"You're one to talk. You've got Tom," she said, focusing her attention back where it belonged. Outward.

"I guess." Busy pressing the elevator button, Larissa sounded distracted. "Hey, is this Ian guy cute?"

Cute was the last word she'd use to describe Ian Black. "He's attractive. Why?"

She didn't have to answer; Chloe knew the reason as soon as she asked the question, and it was a bad one. "I'm not interested in getting involved right now."

"He's a step up from the men you usually date. A lot better than Aiden, that's for sure."

Was he? At least with Aiden, what you saw was what you got. Ian, on the other hand.... She barely knew the man and she already could tell he ran deeper and stiller than most waters. There was a reason she preferred shallow. Men with depth left bigger scars when the relationship ended. The nicks and cuts caused by guys like Aiden hurt bad enough. Why invite bigger pain?

"You know, there's no law that says people have to be in a relationship," Chloe said as soon as the doors closed. Thankfully, no one joined them, meaning they could finish this conversation in private.

"No one ever said there was."

"Then why do you keep pushing me to have one?"

"I'm not pushing anything. All I did was ask if this Ian person was good-looking. You're the one who went off."

Chloe looked at her shoes. Her friend was right. She had flown off the handle prematurely. "Sorry. Last night might have made me a bit oversensitive."

"Can't blame you there. If I'd been mugged, I'd be touchy, too. Although…" Larissa hesitated.

Glancing over, Chloe noticed her friend had literally bit her lip to keep from saying more. "Although what?" Might as well finish the whole discussion. When it came to certain subjects, Larissa could be relentless. Chloe's love life was frequently one of those subjects. "Spit it out."

"Fine," she said. "You're always so adamant about not wanting a serious relationship."

"I happen to like being single."

"So you say." Arms folded, lips drawn in a tight line, her friend was a five-foot-two-inch block of doubt. "I can't help wondering, who you're trying so hard to convince with your argument. Me? Or yourself?"

Under normal circumstances, Saturday morning meant sleeping in and drinking coffee in her pajamas. This Saturday, however, the bridal salon called to say her dress for Delilah's wedding was ready, so instead of being happily curled up under her comforter, Chloe found herself making the trek uptown. She wanted to run her errands before the rain started.

And she wanted to avoid Larissa. Chloe was still annoyed with her for that comment on the elevator. Who was she trying to convince, indeed. What a stupid question. Why would she need to convince herself of something she'd known for years? La-roo's problem was that she had an overdeveloped sense of romanticism. Her whole world consisted of brides, weddings and babies. Chloe was far more practical. She'd much rather preserve her self-esteem than chase some useless fantasy.

Thankfully, Larissa didn't notice how she'd dodged the original question: whether Ian was attractive. Big fat yes there. Even a dead woman would think so. For crying out loud, his voice alone qualified as sex on a stick. Add in the rugged features and obvious rock-solid torso, and who wouldn't be...intrigued?

Intrigued, though, didn't mean interested. If she happened to find herself walking three blocks out of her way to visit Café Mondu, it was only because she had a craving for a well-crafted iced peppermint mocha latte.

Just as it was surprise, not disappointment tightening her stomach when she discovered a pair of middle-aged women occupying the front corner table.

"Good morning," the barista at the counter said in greeting. It was Jesse, the woman from the other night. "Looks like Ian did a good job."

"Excuse me?"

"Your chin. The cut's healing nicely."

"Thanks." Chloe ran her fingertip along the scab. She still had a bump from smacking the sidewalk, but the redness had started to fade. "Lucky for me your boss has a knack for first aid."

"Must have been the army training," Jesse said.

"You knew about that?"

"I overheard him talking to a couple servicemen one day, why?"

"No reason." For a second Chloe worried that she was the only person in New York who didn't recognize the man. She'd learned online that his military service was an important part of the Ian Black corporate story. It was his experience as a medic that inspired him to invent the Black blood clotting patch that launched the company's success. "I only recently found out, is all. He's not here today, is he?" she added. Only because it would be rude not to say hello.

Jesse didn't have to answer, for at that moment Ian's stage whisper reached her ear. "For crying out loud, Jack, you make it sound like I'm popping in on the kid out of the blue. We've been in contact."

He walked through the storage room door, cell phone tucked under one ear, a coffee cup clutched in the other. Chloe nearly dropped her dress bag. Today was the first time she'd seen Ian without his vagabond clothes, and the result was breathtaking. He'd shed the sweatshirt and ratty jacket in favor of khakis and a sweater the same light blue as his eyes, making him look every inch the successful entrepreneur he was purported to be. He'd pushed the sleeves of his sweater to the elbows. Chloe tried hard not to stare at his exposed forearms. She'd never been one to care about arms and hands before, but Ian's were extraordinary. So hard and lean you could see the muscles playing with every move. A jagged scar ran down his right arm. It began beneath the cuff and traveled to his wrist. As Chloe followed the line with her eyes, she recalled how capable his hands were. Strong yet tender. The consummate male touch.

A flush washed over her. Why on earth did this man waste himself on baggy sweatshirts?

"Because some things can't be said long distance, and the longer I wait…" He pinched the bridge of his nose, clearly unhappy. "My gut says different."

"Three eighty-five," Jesse said. Chloe handed her a five dollar bill and waved off the change. She was far more interested in the conversation behind the counter.

"Fine. Your opposition is duly noted." Heaving a sigh loud enough to be heard across Manhattan, Ian slammed the phone onto the counter.

Chloe spoke without thinking. "Problem?"

He'd been staring at his cell and didn't hear her come around to his side of the counter. Her question caused him to look up suddenly, revealing a look of such weariness, it tore her insides in two. "Difference of opinion," he replied. He looked back down at the phone and sighed. "Damn. Now I'm going to have to call back and apologize at some point for hanging up."

"Sounded like this Jack person ticked you off pretty good."

"Nah, more like me taking my frustrations out on him. A habit I thought I had a handle on."

"Sorry," she replied.

Ian frowned. "What are you sorry about?"

To be honest, she wasn't quite sure. The lack of sparkle in his eye made her want to say something. "You being frustrated."

"No need to be sorry there. It's my own damn fault."

"Anything I can do?"

As expected, he shook his head. "If only, Curlilocks. Afraid this is a problem only I can fix. I just wish people would stop giving me advice I didn't ask for."

"I hear ya there," Chloe said, thinking of Larissa. "My

friends are very big on advice. I wish I could make them understand that when it comes to my life, I know best."

"Exactly." A fabric of understanding wove them together as he gave her the first smile of the day. A half smile, with a hint of sadness, but a smile nonetheless. "I keep trying to explain to him these are my mistakes. I need to fix them my way. Especially this one."

Must be one helluva mistake for him to react so strongly, but then, some events marked you more than others.

"I take it this Jack disagrees."

"To put things mildly. I swear, if he had his way, I'd still be on step one."

"Step one?"

"Yeah, out of twelve. I take it that that fact didn't show up during your internet search.

"What fact?"

He reached for the nearby coffeepot and poured himself a cup. "That I'm a drunk."

CHAPTER FOUR

"Technically, functional alcoholic would be a better term, since I preferred to keep a steady day-long buzz rather than get rip-roaring drunk. Enabled me to—"

"Function?" The remark came out far more sardonically than Chloe meant it to.

Ian saluted her with his cup. "Couldn't build a company otherwise."

Following his pronouncement, the two of them moved their conversation to a nearby table. In a way, Chloe was surprised he wanted to talk with her about such a personal subject. On the other hand, she wouldn't deny being curious. Not so much regarding his alcoholism as the shadow crossing his features. She'd seen the same shadow the other night. The slip suggested that while Ian spoke matter-of-factly, he felt far from casual about his past. His mistakes, whatever they were, struck him hard. If he wanted or needed a sympathetic ear, then she was willing to listen.

"What happened?" she asked him. A naive question, but she didn't know where else to start.

"I drank. A lot," Ian replied. "You mean how did the drinking get out of hand, though, don't you?" He shrugged and focused on stirring his coffee. "There wasn't any kind of traumatic event or anything. Started out with a few drinks to de-stress. As the stress grew, so did the drinks. Before I knew it, I was drinking all the time."

There was more to the story; Chloe could tell by the way he avoided her eyes. She was willing to bet that missing component caused the shadows, too. "What about work?"

"Functional, remember?" He laughed over the rim of his coffee. "Work was everything. Well, everything other than alcohol. The rest of the world took a backseat.

"People especially," he added in a soft voice. This time Chloe caught the shadows.

"Anyway, about eighteen months ago, I started the program, and I've been busy working on step eight—making amends to the many, many people I hurt."

Fixing his mistakes. Understanding clicked in, setting off a swell of admiration in her chest. She'd been right, he did beat karma. Leading her to the puzzling phone call she'd overheard a few minutes earlier. "Is your friend Jack one of those people you have to apologize to?"

Ian offered another mirthless laugh. "Jack's my sponsor. I deep-sixed my friends, good, bad and otherwise, a long time ago. In case you didn't guess by the fact I'm sitting here pouring out my guts to you."

So he did need someone to talk to. "I don't mind." If anything, she was flattered to make the cut. Meaningful conversation didn't happen with the men who usually crossed her path. Ian's inclusion made her feel substantial.

"You've only just met me. Give me time."

Meaning what? That he'd deep-six her, too? The comment made her nerves flare onto to quickly extinguish when she saw the melancholy in his eyes. Reminding her that his story was far from over. "I'm confused. Why doesn't your sponsor want you to make amends? Isn't he supposed to be encouraging you?"

"This is where we come to the unsolicited advice," Ian replied. "Jack thinks I'm moving too quickly. I need to 'move with caution' to use his favorite phrase. He doesn't get that I can't afford to move slowly. I've already wasted thirteen years."

A long time. Chloe watched Ian sip his coffee, trying to hide the expression she knew matched his voice. Her own drink had grown lukewarm long ago. She didn't care. His story was far too engrossing.

"This person must be pretty important to you, to want to reach out after a decade and a half," she noted. Or else the crime so egregious he couldn't forget.

"He is," Ian said. "He's my son."

His son. Her insides froze, killing the sympathy she had regarding Ian's pain.

"You abandoned your family?" She didn't bother hiding the edge in her voice. A man who abandoned his child didn't deserve consideration. To think she'd actually thought Ian was different. Better.

"Not entirely. I gave financial support. Paid his and Jeanine's—ex-wife's—bills. Made sure he lived well, but otherwise I kept my distance. Figured he was better off."

Oh yeah, the kid was so much better off. All those years, wondering what he'd done to chase his father away. Thinking he must be horrifically damaged if his own parents couldn't love him.

"You get what you deserve," she murmured.

Ian mistakenly thought she meant him. "You won't get an argument here. I wrote to him once I thought sobriety was going to stick. We've been corresponding for about a year now."

"Letters and money," Chloe repeated. More than she

ever got from her father. Still, the kid deserved better. Apologies were as flimsy as promises. More often than not the child still ended up with her nose pressed against the picture window, waiting in vain.

"Not enough, I know," Ian agreed. "I wish I had an excuse, but the truth is I was a miserable son of a bitch and a drunk. He *was* better off without me around."

"Do you honestly believe that?"

"I know it." He washed a hand over his face, leaving an expression of regret behind. "I was not a nice person, Chloe. I stepped on and hurt a lot of people to build my company. I would have hurt him, too."

"And a lifetime of being without a father didn't?"

"Hurt him a lot less." Ian sounded so resolute, Chloe decided not to argue. Perhaps he had a point. Drive-by visits certainly didn't do her any good other than trick her into hoping again.

Shaking off the memories, she returned to the topic at hand. "So what is it Jack doesn't think you should do?"

"I got Matt's number, and I called him. There are things that can't be said in a letter."

Yes, there were. "What did Matt say?"

"He hasn't returned my call yet. I told Jack I wanted to drive out to see Matt in person. That's where you walked in."

Ian's long fingers played with the cup handle, tracing the top curve again and again. Disappointed as she was, Chloe still watched the movement, remembering how those fingers had drifted across her skin. It hurt to think a man capable of such tenderness could hurt people.

"He thinks I should stick with letter writing," he continued. "But Matt's my son. He needs to hear the apology out loud. So he knows I'm serious."

A kernel of sympathy worked its way toward Chloe's

heart. It was clear Ian regretted his behavior. Pain clung to every word he spoke. And he was trying to repair the damage. Letters, a phone call. Driving to see the boy. What she wouldn't give for one of those efforts.

"I know I forfeited my rights as a parent a long time ago," he continued. Chloe couldn't tell if he was making his argument to her or himself. "All I want is five minutes so I can let Matt know I didn't forget him. My staying away was for his own good."

He reached into his wallet and handed her a photograph. "His high school graduation picture. I asked him to send me one."

Chloe saw a handsome boy with tight auburn curls and a wary smile. She could identify with the wariness. It was the fear that the camera would capture the inner flaws. "Handsome boy. Looks like his father."

"Smart, too. Salutatorian of his class. You should have heard the speech he gave at graduation."

"You were there?" In her surprise, Chloe nearly dropped the picture. "Why didn't you go see him then? Were you…?"

He shook his head. "Not at graduation."

"Then why not let him know?"

"I didn't want to ruin his day. His mother and I can't be in the same room without killing each other. I always made a point of flying under the radar so he wouldn't get caught in the middle."

Always? "You attended other events?"

"As many as I could. Just because I wasn't visible in his life didn't mean I didn't care."

A lump rose in Chloe's throat. Ian couldn't say more magical words if he tried. During how many basketball games, art shows and teacher nights had she fantasized about her father hiding in the back? Ian had done exactly that for his son.

How she envied Matthew Black. Ian was offering his son the gift of a lifetime—the chance to know he mattered.

She reached across the table and grabbed Ian's hand. "Jack's wrong. Your son deserves to hear your apology in person. Don't let him talk you out of going."

Ian stared at the fingers resting on his arm, soft and golden against his own pale skin. Comfort seeped from her touch, warming places inside him he hadn't realized were cold. Common sense said he should pull away, but his selfish side wanted to enjoy the sensation. "Sweetheart, did you read any of those internet articles? Once I make up my mind, you'd need an atomic bomb to move me from my position."

"So you're going to see your son."

He nodded. "Today. He's attending the state university in Pennsylvania." The trip couldn't be more than three or four hours. With luck, he could be there by late afternoon, and home before midnight.

Chloe was smiling. "Good. The sooner the better, if you ask me." She spoke emphatically, with an unreadable emotion behind her words that didn't fit the situation. From the glow in her eyes, you'd think she was the one receiving the apology.

"No offense, but for a woman who heard my story only five minutes ago, you sound pretty darn invested." Reluctantly removing his arm from her grip, he sat back so he could better see her face. "How come?"

"No reason." Her darkened cheekbones disagreed. "You're doing a good deed. I'm showing support."

"Good deed? Hardly." This apology was as much

for him as it was for Matt. Guilt over his many sins had driven him to drink in the first place. If he didn't atone for his mistakes—or at least make every effort he could—how long before the face he saw in the mirror drove him to drink again?

So no, his actions weren't good. Like everything he did, they were underscored by selfishness. The last thing he needed was a beautiful young woman looking at him with stars in her eyes.

Much like Chloe was looking at him right now. As though he was about to climb Mount Everest or cure cancer. A man could live on a look like that for days. If he deserved the admiration. "I'm no hero," he said. Reminding her and himself.

"At least you're reaching out to your son and letting him know you care. Some fathers couldn't care less."

Hers, perhaps? The way the sparkle faded from her eyes suggested as much. Ian's insides hurt at the thought. Then again, maybe it was his own guilty conscience needling him.

He could ask her, but the mood had already grown far too somber and serious. Funny how he opened up around her. Even after pulling back the other night, here he was, sharing his biggest secrets. It wasn't as though he couldn't stop himself, either. He simply felt comfortable around her in a way he never felt around anyone else.

Looking for a lighter topic, he spied the black garment bag draped over the spare chair. "Shopping?"

"Excuse me?" Chloe pulled her thoughts out of whatever fog they'd disappeared into.

"The dress bag."

She shook her head. "Maid of honor dress. My friend Delilah is getting married next week. To our boss, if you can believe it."

"That's one way to get a promotion."

"Aren't you cynical?"

Ian laughed. "Occupational hazard." For as many women whose hearts he'd broken, there was an equal number who'd been after the money.

"I didn't realize coffee vendors were such a catch," Chloe replied.

He laughed again. This was why he enjoyed talking with her. "Haven't you heard? Caffeine's the new sexy."

"Thanks for the tip."

"As for your friend...?"

"Delilah. In this case we're talking real, honest-to-God true love. If there is such a thing as soul mates, it's Simon and Delilah."

"Now who's sounding cynical?" There was a definite weariness in her last sentence.

"I'm not cynical. I'm broke. Both of my best friends are getting married this spring, and I'm maid of honor at both ceremonies. Although, on the plus side, I do get some completely useless dresses out of the deal."

There she went, acting cavalier again. Without the sunglasses to shade her eyes, the act didn't work as well. "You can always pay them back by getting them a completely useless wedding gift," he suggested. "Gold-plated salt and pepper shakers, pearl-handled shrimp forks. Just make sure you stay away from silver candlesticks. I still have the scar from when my ex-wife tossed one at my head."

Chloe winced. "Ouch."

"Ouch indeed." She didn't know the half of it. "In fairness to the candlesticks, the injury wasn't their fault. Jeanine and I were the equivalent of gasoline and a match. Some people aren't meant to have relationships."

"No, they are not."

Referring to himself, he didn't expect to hear her agree so quickly. Or with so much bite. "You're bitter because your boyfriend cheated on you." Which reminded him, he needed to stick Aiden on a few more late-night Saturday shifts.

Chloe reached for her coffee. "For your information, I am completely over Aiden," she told him.

"You sure?"

"Honestly? Other than the embarrassment factor, I wasn't all that into him."

Then what caused the shadows behind her smile? Something—or someone—had given rise to her jadedness. If not the Irish barista, then who?

Ian's thoughts returned to her earlier comments regarding parents. Fathers could screw up so much, he realized with sudden despair. What if Matt felt the same way about relationships? Jeanine had never married again. Ian…well, his dating history was well documented. Had he doomed his child to a life as cold and meaningless as his own?

"What's wrong?"

Ian shook his head. "Nothing. I was thinking I should get on the road soon, if I'm going to make it to the school before dark."

"I didn't realize the time," Chloe said, glancing down at a watchless wrist. "I'm sorry to keep you."

"Don't apologize. I'm glad you stopped by. It was nice having someone to listen." He stared at the hand resting on the table, his own itching to entwine their fingers. To physically connect as they had moments before. Needing a distraction, he grabbed his cup, hoping coffee replaced needs besides "Like I said, I don't have many friends anymore."

"You have at least one now."

She meant her. The declaration settled over his shoulders, solid and warm, like an invisible embrace. Friendship was a luxury he hadn't afforded himself in a long time.

"A very sweet one, too." How long before he let her down? If he listened to the ache pulsing through his limbs, it was only a matter of time before he turned a touch into another mistake.

No reason to make the mistake today, he decided, and stuffed his hands in his pockets. "Rain's getting heavier. I better grab a cup of coffee and hit the road. Next time you come in, the coffee's on me."

"Again?"

"Again," he repeated with a grin. "We're developing a pattern."

"Might be easier to buy our own and call it even."

"Might be."

He was dragging his feet. As soon as he left the coffee shop, he would be on his own, and while he normally didn't mind solitude—had grown used to it, even—he wasn't quite ready to leave Chloe's warm presence.

"Would you like some company?"

Focused on walking to the counter, Ian almost missed the question. When he finally realized what she'd said, he had to stop and repeat the question in his head, to make sure he heard correctly. "You want to come to Pennsylvania?"

"Why not? I don't have anything planned. Plus I could help distract you if you get nervous."

"I don't get nervous," he told her. "I get focused."

She shrugged. "Hey, if you don't want the company, just say so."

"I didn't say that."

"Then what are you saying?"

"I…" This wasn't a conversation he felt like having from opposite sides of the coffee shop. Making his way back to the table, he stopped short of her crossed legs. "Why?" he asked her.

"I don't understand."

Yes, she did; she was dodging the question. Ian leaned in. The fact that Chloe had stayed seated gave him a height advantage, and he had to admit he enjoyed the way her chin tilted upward. "Do you always offer to go away with men you barely know?"

She jutted her chin higher. "A day trip isn't exactly going away. Besides, barely knowing me didn't stop you from telling me your life story."

"Curlilocks, I haven't come close to telling you my life story." Nor, he realized, had she told him hers. Other than knowing she'd played college ball, worked in advertising and had lousy taste in boyfriends, he knew very little about Chloe Abrams. Hell, the only reason he knew her last name was because of Aiden.

"You still haven't answered my question. Why would you want to drive to Pennsylvania with me?"

"Because I owe you for the other night. You were there when I needed you. This is my chance to be there when you need someone."

"And?" he asked, digging.

"Does there have to be an 'and'? Isn't wanting to pay back your kindness enough?"

"Sure, for some people." Something, though made him think her offer wasn't totally out of obligation, even if she did sound sincere. After all, while he might not run a major corporation anymore, he was still a very wealthy man. An enterprising woman might easily think his recent spiral made him especially vulnerable.

"I'm simply trying to be a friend," she said, reading his mind.

"A friend, huh?"

"You don't believe me."

"I've been sold that line before."

"Trust me, it's not a line this time."

"Well, I could use a friend...." His eyes swept up the length of her. Along the mile-long legs, the squared-off shoulders, every inch a study in indifference. Until, this is, he reached her eyes. There, despite her best effort to hide it, he caught a flash of vulnerability. A little-girl-lost quality that could wrap a stranglehold around his insides if he let it. Any kind of relationship with this woman was a bad idea.

At the same time, they were talking about one day. Ten hours tops. It would be kind of nice, having an ally for once.

"All right," he said, his better judgment kicking him. "But I'll give you fair warning. I don't do pit stops or side trips, and I pick the radio station."

CHAPTER FIVE

"LAST CHANCE TO change your mind," Ian said, placing Chloe's garment bag over the backseat of his SUV. "I can still drop you off at your apartment instead."

It was the third such offer he'd made, the first one coming as they were leaving the coffee shop, and the second issued in the parking garage elevator. "Are you trying to make me change my mind?" she asked.

"Just trying to be certain. Never let it be said I didn't give you the opportunity to back out."

"Or that you know how to accept a nice gesture."

"Been a while since anyone's made one, so I'm out of practice."

The comment made her sad. No friends, no kindness. Ian had painted a pretty lonely picture of his existence this morning. No wonder he'd turned to drinking. Unless the drinking had caused the isolation. Chloe suspected a little bit of both. One big, lonely circle. At least she had Larissa and Delilah in her life.

Speaking of which, both of them would completely overreact if they knew about this field trip. Delilah would sigh and make some comment about impulsiveness, while Larissa would, of course, bring up Chloe's comment about never having a relationship. Her friends wouldn't understand that her offer was neither impulsive nor one of her short-term flings. Her reasons were far more personal. A part of her needed to witness Ian's apology, to prove that fathers who deserved redemption existed, even if she never experienced the phenomenon herself.

"You think we'll be back by midnight?" she asked, sliding into the front seat.

"Why? Will you turn into a pumpkin if we don't?"

"You'll have to wait and see."

The grin he flashed her while shutting the door was nothing short of knee-buckling. "Lucky for you I like pumpkin."

The wiper blades made a soft swishing sound as they pulled out into traffic. At some point between their entering the garage and driving to the first level, the sky opened up, and the rain began falling heavier than ever. "Hope you weren't planning on a sunny Saturday drive," Ian said.

"I wasn't planning on a Saturday drive, period, remember?"

"True. You act on impulse a lot, don't you?"

She was pretty sure every inch of her skin blushed. "What gives you that idea?"

"No reason. You'll notice I brought extra napkins, though, in case your coffee accidentally flies out of your hand."

Pour one drink over one person's head... "I'm never going to live the other morning down, am I?"

"No way. Far as I'm concerned, the other morning will live in infamy," he told her. "Not that I'm one to judge anyone's bad behavior, given my history."

No, he wasn't. At the same time, Chloe had a nagging sensation that perhaps he judged himself too harshly. Granted, he'd made a killer mistake when it came to his son, but what other mistakes was he atoning for? Dammit, she wished she'd read those articles more closely.

She watched Ian navigate the New York traffic, noticing how the skin around his knuckles pulled taut as he squeezed the steering wheel. Who could blame him? This reunion meant a lot, and their current conversation led straight to his failing.

"What's he studying?" she asked, hoping the change in subject would distract Ian. "Your son. Do you know?"

There was no mistaking the pride in his voice. "Engineering. Got a full ride, too."

"Sounds like he got his father's head for technology."

"Better that than any of my other habits. Sorry, bad joke." His smirk held a shadow. "I should be glad. Seeing as how money and genetics were my only two contributions, I'm glad he got the good parts."

"Could be worse," she shot back. "All I got from my father was a seventy-eight-inch wingspan."

"Beg your pardon?"

"Sorry, basketball term. My arms measure seventy-eight inches fingertip to fingertip. The bigger the span, the better the rebound potential."

"I take it seventy-eight inches is good."

"Definitely. I'm terrific at rebounding." The phrase's dual meaning hit her then and she started to laugh.

"What's so funny?"

"Inside joke."

"I see." His attention stayed on the road as he spoke, but he might as well have stared straight at her the way her skin prickled, each hair standing on edge. His *I see* sounded way more like *What are you hiding*? What on earth had made her mention her father in the first place?

"Did your dad play basketball?" Ian asked. Again, might as well have been *tell me your secret.*

"So I heard. Do you mind if we turn on the radio?" Running the two sentences together as she reached for the power button, she prayed he would focus on the latter question and miss the first half. She had barely touched the knob when his fingers closed around her wrist.

"What do you mean, so you heard?"

Chloe sighed. So much for her prayers. She stared at the dials, afraid to look upward.

Meanwhile, the car was stopped at a red light, allowing Ian to turn in her direction. The entire left side of Chloe's face warmed from the scrutiny.

Might as well confess the entire sad truth and get things over with. "My father wasn't around when I was born. I've seen him maybe twice, three times in my life."

It took a little courage, but she managed to look Ian in the eye for her next remark. "Needless to say, he never tracked me down to apologize."

Ian let the sympathy in his eyes speak for him. Chloe hated the look. She didn't want his sympathy or his pity. What she wanted was to forget the past. That's all she had ever wanted. To pretend she wasn't the flawed little girl her parents created.

Ian's thumb swept across the top of her wrist, the touch dangerously gentle. "Avoid talk radio, hip-hop, classical, easy listening or love songs and we'll be fine," he said, voice low.

In other words, he would let her share at her own pace. Tightness, sudden and thick, squeezed her throat. "That leaves us with country music," she said, once she managed to find her voice.

"So it does."

Chloe turned on the radio. Seconds later, the sounds of steel guitar filled the interior. It wasn't until she leaned back in her seat that she realized Ian's hand still had her wrist. Jeez, but his grip was sure. So sure it practically melted her bones. Ever since seventh grade, Chloe had been the large one, the girl who loomed over her class-mates and took up more space than she should. Ian's hands, with their large, manly grip, made her feel dainty. Feminine. More feminine than she could ever remember. Worse than that, his touch made her feel significant. It was an unusual and heady sensation. One she could get very used to.

Not to mention scared her to death.

Two hours west, the weather shifted. What had started as heavy rain turned first to sleet, then to freezing rain. All the changes turned the highway into a parking lot. If the odometer could be believed, they'd traveled ten miles in half an hour. "For crying out loud, you'd think people never saw bad weather before," Ian said as the car in front of him flashed its brake lights—again. Thank God for four-wheel drive.

"Funny how icy conditions bring out the caution in people, isn't it?"

Chloe's sarcasm took some of the fight out of him. Some. "I hate wasting time," he muttered.

"Big talk from a man who spends his days sitting around a coffee shop."

"Not sitting, observing," he shot back. "I'm learning the business."

There was a time when he'd barked off people's heads for less. But Chloe's comments simply amused him. He liked how she continued to treat him like a bum. It kept him grounded.

He risked a glance in her direction. Ten minutes into the drive, after he suggested she get comfortable, she'd kicked off her ankle boots and pushed the seat all the way back. Now she sat with her long legs folded beneath her in the bucket seat, her plaid wool scarf draped across her hands and lap like a blanket. His Thoroughbred had become a kitten.

"Cold?" he asked her.

"A little."

He reached for the thermostat, catching the faint scent of peppermint as he shifted to the right. He remembered being amazed by her smell the other night, and wondered if her skin tasted as minty. The speculation caused his jeans to tighten.

"Better?"

"Yes. Thank you."

"No problem." Reluctantly, he grasped the wheel again. He'd much rather keep his hand on the control panel and continue breathing in the mint, but that would only lead to trouble. They were friends sharing a drive, nothing more. "Why didn't you tell me you were uncomfortable?"

"I was told by the driver that he chose the interior temperature."

So he had, right around the time she'd asked if she could switch the radio station. "No one touches the control panel but me," he'd told her.

Mint drifted past him again as Chloe shifted in her seat. Unfolding her legs, she stretched them out as much as she could and wiggled her toes. No woman should have such long legs. Between them and her enticingly-scented skin, how was a man supposed to concentrate on the road?

Ian suddenly felt her eyes on him, making concentration worse. "Clearly, the media profiles told the truth," she said. Out of the corner of his eye he saw her wave her phone. "Caught up on my internet research."

"I was going to ask what you were doing.... So, what were the articles right about?"

"You having control issues."

"You're only coming to that conclusion now? Wow."

"I had my suspicions before I began reading," she told him. "The article confirmed them."

Confirmed and elaborated, more likely. "I know the picture they painted. Hotheaded micromanager who wouldn't relinquish control."

"Are the articles right?"

"Yeah." And no, too, but he didn't want to get into the whole psychobabble about how he needed to stay on top—stay one step ahead—so he wouldn't screw up and prove his father right. How, little by little, he'd morphed into the old man himself, until he couldn't stand looking at himself in the mirror. Chloe was far too sweet and innocent to dump his dirty past on. Besides, she had her secrets; he might as well have his.

Dammit! When did the driver ahead put on the brakes? Ian slammed on his. At the same time, he shot his arm out to keep Chloe from moving forward. With a loud grinding noise, the antilock brakes kicked in, bringing the vehicle to a stop inches from the other car's bumper.

"You okay?"

"Fine," Chloe told him. Perhaps, but he could feel her chest rising and falling against his forearm. He should have paid closer attention. "You're right about the other drivers being skittish," she said. "It's getting rough out there."

Much as he hated to admit it, she was correct. The farther west they drove, the more conditions deteriorated. Seemed like for every mile the wind velocity gained, visibility lost one. Ian didn't want to say anything, but he'd seen more than one set of lights fishtailing as vehicles swerved on the slippery surface. It served him right for failing to check the regional weather forecast before leaving New York. Stupidly, he'd thought that, it being spring, the frozen weather was behind them.

"Regretting your decision to come along?" he asked

"For the last time, no. If anything, the storm adds to the adventure."

"Interesting attitude. That why you're squeezing your seat belt?" He could feel her arm muscles tensing beneath the cloth.

Too bad the traffic demanded his attention and he couldn't enjoy the color he knew bronzed her cheekbones. "All right, so maybe I'm a little nervous."

He gave her leg a reassuring squeeze. "We'll be fine."

"I know." The surety in her voice made his heart catch.

"Read a few more articles and you might not feel so confident," he replied.

"I've read enough. Besides, why would you being a bastard in business affect your ability to drive?"

"You'd be surprised." Knowing more about his sins would erase some of the faith from her voice. Her confidence unnerved him. He'd become far more comfortable with people's disdain.

Give her time. Seriously, how long could he keep her friendship? Even now, while she smiled trustingly in his direction, he was focused on how her leg muscles tensed and released. Every blessed shift made his groin twitch. A better man would lift his hand away. He wouldn't contemplate sliding it down toward her knee and back along the inside of her thigh, measuring her length by the reach of his fingers. What kind of friend did that?

Just then, a gust of wind shook the car. Mother Nature ordering him to keep his hands to himself. Squeezing the leather as tightly as possible, he silently thanked her for the intervention. "On second thought," he said aloud, "do you still have cell service?"

"Barely. The storm's cutting into my signal, why?"

"Dial 511 and see if you can get a traffic update. I'm wondering if there's more than weather slowing us down."

While Chloe fiddled with her cell phone, he played with the radio tuner. With luck he'd find a local station and get an update on the weather. Learn whether or not they'd be stuck with these conditions all the way to the state university. He'd already ditched any plan of arriving midafternoon. Late afternoon was more likely. Hopefully not much later than that. After all, it was Saturday night. College kids went out on Saturday nights, right? Frat parties and all. Maybe Ian should call his son again, let him know they were coming. For that matter, he should check to see if Matt had returned yesterday's call yet.

"No luck," Chloe announced. "I can't get any signal."

He wasn't having much luck finding a local broadcast, either. The few stations that didn't have static were out of either New York or Philly. "Hope you were serious about adventure, Curlilocks," he said, "because we're about to have one."

He nodded toward the emergency vehicles in the distance.

Oh, yay. Chloe shivered and tucked her scarf tighter around her legs. It wasn't the approaching accident that had her on edge, however, but the way her nerves came to life when Ian's palm rested on her thigh. The touch he'd meant to be reassuring burned through two layers. She swore a palm imprint marked her skin.

Over in the driver's seat, Ian tapped out an impatient

message on the steering wheel. "A lot of flashing lights up there," he said. "Explains the backup."

"Hope it's nothing serious." Chloe spotted red and blue, indicating a variety of rescue vehicles. Tucking her hands beneath her scarf so Ian wouldn't notice, she returned to squeezing her seat belt. It wasn't that she worried about Ian's driving skills—she really did have confidence in his abilities. After watching him take down her mugger, how could she not?

No, she was more nervous that they would stop abruptly and he would fling his arm across her body again. Stupid, getting anxious over a man's touch. But the protectiveness and strength felt so damn good, it scared her.

Drawing closer, they discovered four police cruisers parked facing oncoming traffic. Beyond them, a set of fire trucks surrounded an overturned 18-wheeler. "Looks like she lost her cargo," Ian remarked.

Sure enough, dozens of plastic water bottles were being blown across the pavement, lodging under truck wheels and jamming up against the guardrail. One rolled under the feet of the police officer routing traffic. Poor guy could barely keep his balance in the wind as it was. When the bottle struck his leg, he literally slid several inches. Chloe swore she saw icicles forming on the brim of his hat, as well.

"What do we do now?" she asked, as if she didn't know.

"Follow along and get back on the highway at the next exit," Ian said. "We don't have much choice."

Nothing a control freak hated more than an unplanned game change. While Ian looked calm on the outside, Chloe didn't miss the way his jaw muscles twitched.

"Look on the bright side," she said, "at least the traffic's moving now."

Except the traffic *didn't* move. Half an hour later they hadn't gone more than three miles. Outside her window, Chloe watched as a dead branch fell from a nearby tree. The wind pushed it end over end until it smacked the base of a brightly colored sign. While the limb struggled to break free, Chloe shifted in her seat with a sigh. She knew how the branch felt. No telling how long they'd be stuck in this line. Making matters worse, Ian had turned off the radio, plunging the car into silence. She understood why—he wanted to eliminate distractions so he could concentrate on the stop-and-go traffic. Unfortunately for her, the silence had the opposite effect. Without noise, every breath Ian took became like thunder, every crinkle of his leather jacket a reminder of his proximity.

"La-roo would be miserable," she said. Even if Ian didn't answer, at least her voice made some noise.

"Who?"

"My friend Larissa. She hates cold weather. Put her in a storm like this and she'd never stop complaining."

"Lucky me I'm not with Larissa then. I prefer your attitude."

He was giving her points for not complaining, nothing more. Still, Chloe warmed from the inside out. "How are you doing?" She hadn't forgotten the real reason for their trip: to see his son. All these setbacks delayed their reunion.

"Me? I'm dandy. Nothing I like better than crawling along a country road behind the slowest drivers in America."

"Really? I'd never guess," she said, biting back a smile. "If you like we can switch places. I'll drive and you can be the passenger."

"You're kidding."

The look on his face was priceless. Half horror, half utter disbelief. Chloe let out a laugh. "Don't worry, I'm completely fine with you fighting the roads. I'll just curl up here and enjoy the scenery."

"Such as it is."

She smiled again. Petulance and impatience worked to make his voice rougher. "Are *you* kidding? Have you looked outside?" She pointed to where the same tree branch continued waging war on the same roadside sign. "Where else would you see an advertisement for a place called the Bluebird Inn and—" Ian had flung his arm across her chest again, cutting off the rest. "What…?"

"Another rear end collision. Four cars up. We're stuck while the drivers check out the damage."

"Oh." She'd take his word for it. At the moment, all she could think about was the forearm pressed against the underside of her breasts, and whether or not Ian could feel her heart racing. "What do you want to do?"

He didn't answer. He didn't move his arm, either. Too deep in thought to notice, probably. Taking a slow breath, Chloe gently lowered his hand to her lap. The new position wasn't much better—she'd stupidly let his fist rest between her knees but it beat being wrapped in a faux embrace. "Ian?"

Finally, he shook his head. "This isn't going to work."

"What isn't? The trip?" He wasn't turning back, was he? After they'd come this far?

Rather than answer, he pulled to the right and began inching his way along the side of the road. Ice crunched beneath his tires as they moved up and over frozen mounds of dirt. "Sign back there says there's a restaurant two miles from here."

The Bluebird Inn and Restaurant, the sign she'd been

reading before they stopped. "You want to go to lunch?" Whatever plan she expected, stopping at a cozy country inn didn't come close. "What happened to the no side trip rule?"

"That was before we got stuck in the highway death march. I figure we'll grab something to eat, and if we're lucky, by the time we're finished, the traffic will have eased up."

"And if it hasn't?"

"Then hopefully the inn has internet service so we can look up an alternate route." He flashed a broad grin. "See, I can roll with the punches as well as the next guy."

No quick answer came to mind. Chloe was too busy recovering from his smile.

The Bluebird Inn and Restaurant turned out to be a large stone farmhouse atop a hill. It took Ian two tries before their rental car made it up the wooded drive to the parking lot. "Guess we're not the only ones with the idea," he said, pulling next to an oversize pickup truck. Sure enough, there were several other cars in the lot. A few, like the truck, were covered in ice, indicating they'd been parked for a while. But the others looked like more recent arrivals.

"Ready to brave the storm?" he asked.

"I thought that's what we'd been doing?" Chloe replied, reaching for her ankle boots. The insides were warm from being near the heating vent, causing the rest of her body to shiver in comparison. "These shoes might have been a mistake, though." The stylish heels were made for city walking, not ice storms. "Do you promise to catch me?"

"Why, you planning to fall?"

"I'll try not..." What was that about falling? In the

gray of the rental car, Ian's eyes shimmered like icicles on a sunny day, the pale blue bright and beautiful. Far warmer than their color implied. Chloe found herself thrust back to the other night, as the familiar warmth wrapped tightly around her, the closeness sending her pulse into overdrive. She felt light-headed and grounded at the same time.

Ian's eyes searched her face. Looking for what, she didn't know. Whatever it was, the inspection caused his pupils to grow big and black. A girl could fall into such eyes.

Falling. Right. She blinked herself back to reality. "We—we should probably get moving," she stammered. "Waiting won't make the storm go away."

"No. No it won't." Must have been the left over brain fog making Ian's voice sound rougher than normal as he backed up to the driver's side door.

Snatching her scarf, she tied the square into a make-shift head cover. "I'm ready. And don't worry, I'll do my best to keep my feet on the ground."

A sign on the building said the structure was over one hundred years old. In better weather, Chloe would have been more appreciative of the building's old-world charm. Things like the bright blue storm shutters and matching farmhouse door. As it was, she was too busy trying to keep her promise to Ian. An icy crust covered everything. Only the fact that the parking lot was loose gravel saved her from wiping out completely. Chloe managed to keep her balance by jamming her heel through the crust into the stones beneath. Her shoes would be ruined, but at least she wouldn't land on her bottom.

They were halfway to the door when Ian's arm wrapped around her. "You look like you're going to topple over any second," he said, his breath warming her dampened skin. Chloe fought the urge to curl up close and wind her arms around him in return. Funny, but if she'd been with Aiden or someone else, she wouldn't have thought twice about holding tight.

The front door was painted a vibrant blue. A pair of potted pines decked with white lights stood sentry on either side. Thanks to the overhang, they were the only three items not covered in ice. Ian opened the door and guided her inside.

It was like stepping into another time and country. With its exposed beams and stenciled walls, the room reminded Chloe of an alpine cottage, or what an alpine cottage might look like in her fantasies. The high-back chairs near the window were made for drinking hot cocoa and sketching the world outside, and the aroma…spiced pumpkins and pine. Who knew a room could smell perfect?

A fire crackled merrily in the nearby fireplace. Drawn by the warmth, Chloe walked over and held out her hands. Ian joined her, his leather-clad shoulder brushing hers. "This place is amazing," she whispered, unable to keep the enthusiasm from her voice if she wanted to.

"Certainly beats fast food," Ian replied.

"Tell me about it, although part of me feels like I should head out to the barn to milk the cows or something."

"Well, you do kind of look the part." He fingered the edge of her scarf, which she still had tied like a kerchief.

Chloe ducked her head, afraid to look him in the eye for fear she'd get light-headed again. As it was, his touch was having way more effect than it should. Every brush of his hand, every moment of contact brought with it a wash of sensations. Comfort, attraction, closeness, wariness…

so many feelings she was beginning to have trouble naming them.

"I thought I heard the door."

They turned around to find a man standing at the top of the stairwell. "I am Josef Hendrik. Welcome to the Bluebird Inn."

If the lobby was her old-world fantasy, thought Chloe, then Josef was her fantasy grandfather. Portly and gray-haired with a cherry-colored nose, he wore a beige cardigan sweater that barely buttoned across his torso. He leaned on the banister as he worked his way down to the landing, all the while speaking in a faintly accented voice. "I am afraid, thanks to the storm, both of our king-size rooms have been taken, but we still have a couple nice queen rooms available, one with a view of the field...."

"Actually," Ian said, "we're only here to eat. The sign on the corner said you served lunch."

"Only Sunday through Friday." Josef, who was in the process of sliding his round frame behind the front desk, paused. "I am afraid the dining room is not open to the public until five on Saturdays. You have several hours to wait."

"That's a damn shame," Ian replied. "You sure you can't make an exception? We'd really hate to have to go back outside in this weather."

"I am sorry, son," the man replied. Chloe found the idea of anyone calling Ian son rather amusing. "I wish I could, but thanks to this storm, we are understaffed. It is only my wife tonight, and she has her hands full getting dinner ready for our overnight guests."

"Did the overnight guests get lunch?"

"Of course. The kitchen is always open for them."

"Perfect. Then we'll book a room."

Chloe's jaw dropped as Ian pulled out his wallet.

* * *

"I've dated a lot of guys who called themselves spontaneous, but none of them ever booked a room simply so
we could eat lunch," Chloe said, popping a piece of roll
in her mouth. Of course, none of them could have afforded a room, or if they could, they weren't inviting
her to lunch.

"There was nothing spontaneous about it. I was being
decisive."

"Potato, pot*ah*to." Grinning, she popped in another
piece of roll.

She didn't think it possible, but the inn's dining room
made the lobby look modern. Rustic and romantic, the
room relied on windows instead of overhead light. With
the storm killing all sunlight, candles and firelight filled
the void. As the sole occupants—the other "guests" having already eaten—she and Ian were seated by the stone
fireplace, where the heat warmed the wood and flames
cast shadows across their faces.

The shadowy atmosphere suited Ian almost as well as
the coffee shop. Jacket shed, sweater pushed to the elbows, he seemed to occupy the whole room. That's what
happened when you weren't used to dating men of real
substance; they always appeared larger than life. Not that
he and Chloe were on a date. They were two friends taking a respite from traffic delays.

"Use whatever term you want," her non-date was saying. He wiped his mouth with his napkin. "I saw no need
to go looking for a different place when there was a perfectly good dining room right here. You'll notice they
got us lunch."

Yes, they did. As soon as she and Ian "checked in",
Josef and his wife, Dagmar, wasted no time in making
sure they were comfortable, which in this case meant

serving them big bowls of squash soup and a basket of piping hot rolls. The food was delicious, far better than anything they'd grab at a rest stop.

"More coffee, Mr. Black?" Dagmar came out of the kitchen brandishing a coffeepot. Unlike the innkeeper, she was decidedly not Chloe's fantasy grandparent. No grandmother of hers would look like an aging film star. Dagmar brushed a stand of her silvery-blond hair from her face. "I just made a fresh pot."

Ian matched her smile. "Don't mind if I do. Lunch, by the way, was delicious. I appreciate you opening the kitchen for us. I know you've got to get ready for dinner."

"No trouble at all," she said with a flutter of her hand. "The pleasure is mine. If you need anything else, you let me know, yah?"

"Absolutely. I will do just that." He was using the same lazy growl he'd used the day Chloe had met him, the low silk-on-sandpaper voice meant to wrap around a woman's spine. Apparently it was his charm voice.

And Dagmar was definitely charmed.

"Looks like you've won a fan," Chloe said, once the older woman had sashayed back to the kitchen. "And here I thought you were famous for being difficult to work with."

"Doesn't mean I can't be charming when I need to be."

"Obviously."

He raised an eyebrow. "Is there a problem?"

"Of course not." Chloe could hear the sharpness in her voice and it bothered her. What did she care if Ian flirted with some middle-aged innkeeper with perfect hair? It wasn't as if that growl was reserved solely for her. "I was wondering how long you want to stay."

He was busy checking his cell phone. "Not too much

longer. I noticed Josef had a laptop. I'll ask him to check the local weather and traffic before we leave."

"Doesn't look like the storm's let up much," she noted. In fact, conditions appeared worse. They could hear the wind howling from where they sat.

"Hopefully, we're looking at more rain than ice farther west."

"And if we aren't?"

"Then, Curlilocks, we get to see if you turn into a pumpkin."

A shiver ran down Chloe's spine. He was merely making a joke, and a silly one at that, since he mashed together fairy tales. The setting, however, along with his ragged-edged voice made the words sound like a seductive promise.

Ian was checking his phone again, staring at the screen with a frown. "Something wrong?" Beyond current circumstances.

"I left a message for Matt yesterday. I thought he'd have called back by now."

"Did you ask him to call?"

"No, not outright."

"Well, no wonder then." They'd entered her area of expertise now: rationalizing silent phones. "How else would he know he's supposed to call?"

"I would."

"You're different."

Ian settled farther back in his chair. "Exactly how am I different?" he asked, his eyes shining in the firelight.

"You're…" The words coming to mind at the moment—*special, unique, amazing*—weren't ones she wanted to share aloud. Mainly because the fact that she would use such words to describe a man frightened her.

"You were a CEO," she said finally. "You're used to having people at your beck and call. Your son is a college freshman. My experience with guys his age is you have to lead them step by step through everything. And even then they might not get the message."

"When I was eighteen, I was in the army. A higher ranking officer asked and you said yes." Ian's current position had him in the shadows, making his expression difficult to read. Chloe swore she saw a frown. "Come to think of it, I ran my company in a similar fashion."

She was right; she did see a frown. "You go with the world you know."

"I suppose you do."

Silence followed. In the car, the silence had closed everything in. Here, in the empty, half-lit restaurant, quiet felt more like distance. It brought a sadness to the air.

Chloe reached to draw him in again.

"How's Dagmar's coffee? Better than yours?"

His chuckle made Chloe happy. "Don't be ridiculous. We use far higher quality beans."

"That so?"

"You don't notice, since you insist on killing the taste with peppermint and chocolate syrup."

"Hey! You should be nicer to one of your best customers."

"The best," he corrected, leaning into the light. "Not to mention one of my favorites."

What on earth made her think the air had chilled, when Ian was studying her as if she were the only female on earth? A woman could get damn addicted to a look like that. She might even start believing it to be true.

Getting an internal grip, Chloe did what she did best, and acted unaffected. "Just one of? I must be slacking. What's a girl got to do to make top of the list?"

"What makes you think you—"

She was what? Not at the top? Or had a chance? The questions went unanswered as a loud crash suddenly shook the entire building.

CHAPTER SIX

YOU'VE GOT TO be kidding. Ian stared at the giant tree covered in power lines lying in the driveway. Clearly, nature had a sick sense of humor, because the monstrosity managed to block both the road and passage off the property.

As soon as the crash sounded, Ian, Josef and several other guests rushed outside. They stood in a clump halfway down the hill, surveying the damage.

"Tree's been dead for years," Josef said. "I told my neighbor he should call someone to cut it down, but looks like the weather did the job for him."

"Looks like it took power along with it," one of the guests commented.

Sure enough, cables laced the limbs like thin black snakes. Behind them, the farmhouse sat dark, a victim. Ian peered through the trees, searching for light, and saw none. "From the looks of things, the tree took out the whole street when it fell," he said.

Josef's sigh spoke for all of them. "Telephone, too. Hopefully, I can find cellular service so I can call for a road crew."

"Good luck getting a truck out here," a different guest said. "We had a storm like this in Connecticut a couple years ago. Took days before they cleared all the damage."

Peachy.

Above them, pine branches groaned. Instinctively, the entire group looked upward for debris before taking a few steps backward. "Tell the crew I'll double their rate if they get here as soon as possible," Ian told Josef.

"That is very generous of you."

"Generosity has nothing to do with it." He was eager to get on the road, and if money helped bump the inn to the top of the list, he was more than glad to pay.

Top of the list. He'd been about to say the same thing to Chloe when the tree saved him. He was beginning to wonder if she wasn't a test, as well. With her curls and her infectious smile, not to mention those mile long legs, the woman was temptation in high heel boots. He'd been celibate for almost as long as he'd been sober, and for the first time, the lack of companionship ate a hole in him. When he'd wrapped his arm around her waist in the parking lot—hell, before that, when they'd sat in the parked car—images of what he'd gone without had flashed through his head. Beautiful Technicolor images of tawny skin spread out beneath him.

The scariest part of all was his attraction wasn't only physical. She had this way of drawing him out from behind his facade. In one day he'd shown her more of himself than he had anyone, short of the addiction counselors.

Worse, he had this inexplicable desire to know more about her. Like what secrets lay behind that false bravado, for example. A trait so much like his it hurt. But then he thought about all the women whose hearts he'd broken, and he reminded himself he had all he could do to keep his own life together. Complications like Chloe, as intriguing as she was, would only lead to more mistakes.

"You must be psychic."

Ian pulled out of his thoughts to find Josef smiling at him. "How so?" he asked.

"Booking a room. Looks like you will need to stay the night."

Images flashed before his eyes again. Oh yeah, definitely a test. "About that," he said, following Josef and the others to the house. "Do you have a second room available?"

"Really? I assumed…" The innkeeper looked surprised. "The two of you look quite comfortable together."

Sure, if *comfortable* meant being perpetually half-aroused. "Is there a second room?"

"Of course," Josef replied. Ian ignored his disappointment at the man's answer. "I'll do up the paperwork soon as I check to see Dagmar's got the generator running."

"Thank you." That was one test taken care of.

Good thing, too, because Chloe insisted on meeting him at the entrance with a mug of steaming coffee. Wordlessly, she held it in his direction.

"You read my mind," he said.

"In this case, it wasn't so hard to do." She turned on her heels and headed back indoors, but not before shooting him a smile that made his stomach take a strange, hard tumble.

Gripping the mug like a lifeline, Ian watched her walk away. Definitely a complication, he thought to himself. A damn fine complication. He headed off to make sure Josef remembered that second room.

"Extra towels are down the hall. We also keep a supply of toiletries on hand—shampoo, toothbrushes and other essentials. I will check to see if Dagmar has an extra nightgown you can borrow as well."

Somehow Chloe didn't think petite Dagmar and she took the same size, but she appreciated the gesture. "Thank you."

"Do not give it a second thought. Our house is your house."

So long as they were paying customers. Only a couple hours earlier he'd wanted to turn them away. Her fantasy grandfather was quite the capitalist.

Josef filled her in on a few more details, such as where she could find an extra blanket, reminded her that guests could get coffee twenty-four hours a day, and headed off in search of sleepwear, leaving Chloe alone for the first time since their arrival.

First time since this morning, really. She threw herself on the bed. As she lay there staring at the ceiling, her mind automatically went to Ian, who'd stayed downstairs to finish his coffee. His mood had shifted between when he'd left to check out the storm damage and when he'd returned. Lunch's good humor had disappeared. Shouldn't be surprising, seeing how this trip had been nothing but delay after delay. Now they were stuck here for goodness knows how long. The control freak in him must be ready to scream.

Rolling on her side, Chloe took a good look at her surroundings. The room was gorgeous. Small, but filled with all sorts of cozy extras, like fluffy robes and a pillow-laden window seat. Of course it helped that, to save a strain on the generator, Josef had provided her with a battery operated lantern. The light's glow mimicked candlelight in the wake of the setting sun.

An emptiness filled her chest. The Bluebird had been created for couples—real couples, like Del and Simon or Larissa and Tom. She was an outsider amid all the romance, a fact that Ian drove home when he'd reserved a second room. Nothing reminded a woman she was alone like a man sleeping in his own bed.

You'd think she'd be relieved by Ian's gallantry. She

knew plenty of guys who'd assume because they were together, they could share a bed, whether sex was involved or not. Ian respected her privacy—further proof he was different. Sadly, it also made him that much more attractive. It was Chloe's pattern of inverse relationships: The more disinterest, the more attractive. Seriously, though, how could a woman not find Ian Black attractive? Funny, smart, considerate, sexy Ian Black. La-roo was right; Chloe had been fooling herself to think otherwise.

A soft knock sounded on the door. Josef and his never-fitting nightgown, no doubt. "That was fast," she said, opening the door.

"I'm a fast drinker." Ian smiled from across the threshold. His cheeks were still ruddy from being outside, the bright pink adding to his virility quotient and causing her stomach to tumble end over end.

"I thought you were Josef," she said, gripping the molding for support.

"Sorry to disappoint you."

"You didn't." She dug her fingers into the wood. Nothing like blushing in return. "I mean, is there a problem?"

"While I was finishing my coffee, I saw a large branch blow off a tree in the backyard. Got me worried."

"About what?" They'd already lost power and telephone service. What more could the wind do? Topple over the building?

"This," he said, producing a garment bag.

"My dress!" With everything going on, she'd forgotten it lay in the backseat.

"Figured it'd be safer hanging in your room. The way today's going, I didn't want to chance a tree falling on the rental car."

She was touched he remembered. Gathering the bag in her arms, she went and hung it on a hook on the back of the closet door. "Seems like you're forever rescuing pieces of my wardrobe."

"Just don't tell me you owe me. Being stuck here for the night already makes us pretty even."

"Alright, I won't." She unzipped the bag. The dress was still in perfect condition, the azure silk barely wrinkled.

"Pretty gown," Ian said. She could feel him hanging by the door, watching.

"Told you I got a banging dress out of the deal."

"Interesting color."

"Apparently it's Simon—the groom's—favorite shade. I'm only glad the color looks good on me."

"I'm betting most things look good on you."

There he went, making her feel special again. "You've never seen me in bright pink," she murmured, zipping the garment bag shut. Actually, he had, because she was pretty sure her cheeks were that very color. Why did he have to say such nice things?

Josef's voice saved the day. "Turns out Dagmar agreed with you about her nightgown not fitting." The innkeeper appeared in the doorway holding a plaid flannel shirt. "She suggested this. I hope it will suffice."

"It'll be perfect. Thank you." Out of the corner of her eye, Chloe caught Ian trying to fight a smile. "Don't say a word," she warned him once Josef had left.

He did, anyway. "Sexy."

The shirt was faded Black Watch plaid, soft and comfortable looking, but sexy? Not so much. "Whadda you know? There are things I don't look good in."

"Who said you wouldn't look good?"

Chloe had to ball the shirt in her fist to keep her stomach from tumbling again. "Well, you'll never know, will you?"

Hearing herself, she nearly winced. The comment made her sound disappointed, which was the last thing she wanted him to think. Quickly, she stuffed the garment under a pillow and changed the subject. "Thank you for booking a second room." There, that should erase any notion that she expected more. "It was very considerate of you."

"I'm not so sure I'd use the word *considerate*," he replied.

No, he'd probably use *no-brainer* or *common sense*, wouldn't he? *Considerate* implied a deeper relationship. She should stop before she dug herself into a deeper hole.

Fluffing her curls, she moved across the room. "Thank you again for rescuing my dress."

"Wasn't much of a rescue. All I did was carry the thing upstairs. It's not like I saved you from a mugging or something."

"Very funny." He'd brushed off that act with modesty, as well. "For the record, I know a lot of guys who wouldn't have even remembered the dress was in the car, let alone gone out in a storm to retrieve it."

Ian gave her a long look. Such a long look she found herself fidgeting. With nothing close by to play with, she settled for tracing the slope of the footboard with her palm.

"Maybe you should start dating a better class of guy," he said finally.

Yeah, well there was the rub. Better class guys didn't want her. They rented separate rooms. "Or quit dating," she quipped. Just her luck, the light tone she'd hoped for failed to materialize.

"Little young to close the book completely, aren't you?" he asked, sitting on the edge of the bed.

"Am I?" As far as she was concerned, it all depended

on your perspective. A lifetime of guys walking away more than made up for her age.

Ian's eyes had yet to stop looking at her. The scrutiny reminded her too much of the other night when the air grew intimate and unsettled. Taking a seat on the other side of the bed, she grabbed one of the pillows and set it on her lap in an attempt to increase the distance between them. She never should have said anything in the first place.

"I'm sorry your trip's been delayed," she stated, fingering the piping.

"Not as sorry as I am." Gratitude washed over her. As he had in the car, he was letting her change the topic.

Mirroring her actions, Ian grabbed a pillow, too. The Hendriks clearly didn't believe in skimping when it came to bed decorations. "Logically, I know one day's delay won't make a difference."

"But you can't help but feel time is ticking away while you're stuck here."

"Exactly."

He looked surprised. If only he knew. Chloe understood exactly what he meant. Eventually there came a tipping point, when the bitterness became too much to overcome and all the apologies in the world wouldn't make a difference. For a man like Ian, so used to being in control, the idea that such a time might be near would be terrifying. "Your son's still young, though," she assured him. "Plus, didn't you say the two of you have already connected?"

"Yeah…" The sentence was incomplete and she knew he was thinking about Matt's unreturned call.

"Hey," she said, leaning across the bed to get Ian's attention. "It'll be all right. The two of you are already talking. Plus, don't discount the fact you were there for him financially all these years. That matters, too. You could have ignored him or forgot he ever existed."

Too late she realized what she'd said. Stupidly using *forgot* instead of *pretend*. Naturally Ian picked up on the slip. "Is that what happened to you?"

"Sort of."

"What do you mean?"

Chloe ran an index finger across one of the circles decorating the bed's quilt, wishing she might find an answer hidden in the calico. How did a person explain that their father didn't want them without sounding pitiful?

The bed sagged, and a moment later she felt Ian's breath on her forehead. He'd joined her in stretching out across the bed until they lay head to head in the middle. His index finger brushed across her wrist. "Chloe?"

Looking up, she saw his eyes only inches from hers. Up close, the blue wasn't nearly as pale. Tiny pearl-gray lines sprayed from the center, giving the color depth and dimension. He waited for her answer with such sincere interest, she had to look away before her own eyes teared up.

"I told you my father wasn't around much," she began. "What I didn't tell you is that sometimes we'd go years without a word. Soon as we convinced ourselves he was really gone for good, he'd show up again. Somehow, some way he'd convince my mother to take him back, and for a couple of days, maybe a week, they'd be all hot and heavy. Until he took off again."

"Must have been hard for you, not knowing if he was staying or going."

"I guess. Mostly I tried to keep out of the way."

She went back to tracing the comforter, the pattern easier to deal with than the sympathy in Ian's eyes. Might as well tell him the rest of the sad story. "Last time I saw him was on my sixteenth birthday. My mom must have finally had her fill, because she met him on the front walkway and sent him packing. I haven't seen him since."

"Oh, Curlilocks…"

Ian's thumb brushed across her cheekbone. If she'd been crying, he would have been wiping away a tear. Fortunately, she'd stopped crying over her father a long time ago. Still, she closed her eyes, indulging in the warmth the gesture brought to her insides. "You know what I remember most about the visit? Not that my mother kicked him out, but the fact he didn't bring a present. I don't think he remembered it was my birthday. Anyway, that's when I knew."

"Knew what?"

That she wasn't worth the effort. "That my mother had terrible taste in men." Chloe meant for the comment to sound flip, but like so much of her conversation today, the tone missed the mark.

Ian's palm continued cradling her cheek, the warmth of his touch drawing her in. "Your father was an idiot," he whispered.

Oh Lord, if only he knew how badly she wanted to believe those words. To hear him whisper them… The sentiment went straight to her heart. All the pent-up longing, the wishes she so carefully kept locked away behind a breezy facade, threatened to break free.

It was too much. Too comforting. Abruptly, she sat up and brushed at her eyes. To her surprise, they were damp. "What matters is you're not forgetting your son. When he finds out you've been attending—"

"You don't need to pretend…."

"Pretend?" She pushed the curls from her face. "I don't know what you're talking about."

"Yes, you do. You don't have to put on this act as if

what happened with your father is no big deal, when we both know it is."

Busted. She hated how he seemed to see a deeper part of her. Even so, she wasn't about to admit the truth, not when she was so practiced at denying. "What makes you think I'm pretending? My father's been gone for over a decade. Plenty of time for me to process his behavior and the fallout." And if she hadn't…? Who wanted to listen to someone whine about the father who didn't love her. There were plenty of people with more pressing problems. People like Ian, whose amends were the reason she was on this trip.

Outside the wind howled, reminding them they weren't going anywhere that night. Scooting to her feet, she went to the window, only to stare at her own reflection. "Wonder what kind of damage we'll see when we wake up," she mused.

"Hopefully minor. Although I have to say the ice looked pretty thick when I was outside earlier. Going to be a real mess now that the temperatures are dropping again."

"Well, at least my gown is safe."

"Which is what's important." She watched his reflection as he propped himself on one elbow again. "Maybe you should wear it to dinner tonight. Show up the other guests."

"What a great idea, and if I'm really lucky I can spill gravy down the front of me. I think I'll stick with what I'm wearing."

"I guess that means the flannel shirt's out, too." She could see his grin in the glass. He looked so relaxed and at home, sprawled across the bed. As if they should be sharing the space together.

But they weren't. The thought hadn't even crossed his mind.

"I think I'm going to freshen up before we eat," she said, turning around. "Do you want me to knock on your door when I'm ready to go downstairs?"

He sat up, and for a minute she swore he seemed disappointed at being asked to leave. A trick of the low light. The shadows caused everything to look off. "Sounds good. I'll see you then. Hopefully you'll change your mind about the dress…"

"Nice try."

"I'll see you in about ten minutes. And Chloe?" He paused in the doorway. "My father stuck around. Isn't always a good thing."

It was just a glimpse, a sliver to let her know she wasn't the only person whose past had left them scarred. It might have been the best present she ever received.

As soon as the door closed behind him, the room grew cold from his absence. Chloe stole one more look at the rumpled spot on the bed where Ian had lain, before turning back to the glass. Minimal damage, Ian had wished for. He'd been talking about the storm. Why did Chloe have the feeling she should be more worried about the damage being caused inside?

CHAPTER SEVEN

WHY THE HELL did he share that last bit about his father? On the list of topics never to be discussed, the old man owned numbers one through infinity. Yet the comment had slipped right out, easy as pie. *My dad stuck around. Isn't always a good thing.*

God, but it was way too easy talking to Chloe. Listening to her kick herself about her own loser father compounded the problem. It certainly said a lot about the man's quality—or rather his lack of quality—when Ian looked admirable in comparison. Chloe had appeared so lost while telling her story. He'd wanted to wrap her up in his arms right then and there, protect her from all the lousy men in the world. Seeing how he was one of those lousy men, however, he'd held back.

And shared the tidbit about his father instead, giving verbal comfort instead of the embrace he preferred. From the spark in her eyes, his offering was appreciated.

She was waiting in the hallway when he stepped out of his room. Winter coats did nothing for women, that's all he had to say. Day after day, he watched her march to the counter, her long form masked by winter bulk, and the whole time she hid a body made for handling. Thank heaven spring was right around the corner.

"Decided against the dress, did you?" he teased, drinking in her length. Not that he minded the jeans and turtleneck, but he would have enjoyed seeing her wrapped in silk.

"Sorry, you're stuck with me as is."

"As is isn't so bad, either." She rewarded his compliment with a very attractive blush. Better looking than the silk, he decided.

"You shaved."

"Yeah, I decided to look civilized for dinner." Another uncharacteristic move. He preferred uncivilized as often as possible, but for some reason, when he'd stepped out of the shower and saw the shaving gel and razor by the sink tonight, he got the urge to clean up.

"Don't worry." He ran a hand across his chin. "The stubble will return soon enough. I've been blessed with a tenacious five o'clock shadow."

"And here I thought you just liked looking rough-and-tumble."

"Who says I don't?" he asked, winning himself another blush. The woman's cheeks colored on a dime; he liked it.

There were already guests in the dining room when they arrived. During lunch, he'd considered the emphasis on flames and natural lighting over the top, but this evening the lighting looked perfect. If he hadn't spent hours driving in the ice, he'd never know there was a storm outside.

"Glad you could join us," Josef greeted. "Seat yourself. Thankfully, the generator is running without problems, so we will have our regular menu. Unfortunately, we are short on servers so there will be a few delays."

"Thank goodness for generators," Chloe murmured once they'd walked past. "I was wondering if they'd be able to serve hot food."

"Hot food and hot toddies, from the looks of things," Ian replied. Josef hadn't been kidding about being short staffed, either. The innkeeper himself was running around with a heavy pewter pitcher, topping off patrons' mugs. "You know what they say; a little whiskey makes any delay palatable. Would you like one?" He started to raise his hand to signal Josef.

"You wouldn't mind?"

"You having a drink?" He shook his head. "Much as I'd like it to, I can't expect the world to stop on my account. Besides, I've got a replacement vice."

"Dagmar's coffee. How could I forget? I think I'll pass, anyway." She slipped her hand around his wrist.

Ian could let her touch his skin all night. Such long, graceful hands. Before he realized what he was doing, he'd pressed the tip of his index finger to hers. "I see what you mean about wingspan." Her fingers were nearly as long as his.

"You mean my gigantic man hands. Perfect for palming the ball."

"I don't know about that, but those are not manly hands. Trust me, I know a lot of guys."

"Thank you." To his disappointment, she pulled her hand away, back to her side of the table. "For the record, though, I did have mad ball-handling skills."

"I believe you, Curlilocks." He was sure she could handle a lot of things well. Grabbing his water glass, he took a long drink, wishing the unwanted sentiment out of his head.

Silence settled over the table while they studied the menu. Or rather, Chloe studied the menu. Ian couldn't take his eyes off her. It wasn't that she looked any different. Sure, she'd touched up her makeup a little and combed her hair, but she was essentially the same woman who'd slipped into his car this morning. And every bit as alluring. "Know what you're getting?" he asked, breaking the silence before his assessment grew out of hand.

"You mean from the menu option of one?" she replied.

Looking down at the paper before him, he saw it described a set four-course meal. Fortunately, Chloe mistook his question for sarcasm. "Guess asking for a burger is out of the question."

"You've got to love a good hunk of meat."

And a woman with simple tastes.

Suddenly, he noticed her frown. "Is this the same table we sat at for lunch?" she asked, looking around.

He'd been caught. "What can I say? I'm a creature of habit." More like a creature who enjoyed the way the flames colored her skin from this angle, and wanted to watch the transformation again. "Blame my rigidity on the army."

"How long did you serve?"

"Eight very long years."

"I take it you didn't enjoy military life."

"Enjoy?" He shook his head. "The army is all about team building. One big unit working toward a common goal. I'm not exactly a team player."

"Let me guess. You didn't take orders well, either."

Coming from anyone else, the comment would have made him bristle. "Guilty as charged."

"Then why did you…"

"Enlist?" Did he dare share more? Tell her how it was either enlist or let his father suck what little life he had left out of him? The mood was too pleasant to spoil with the dirty truth. "I didn't have a lot of options. School wasn't a choice, and neither was sticking around."

He cast a quick glance over the top of his water glass

and was nearly done in by the understanding in her eyes. No explanation was necessary. "I stayed to prove a point."

She cocked her head. "A point?"

"That I could stick it out." *You won't last two weeks in the army. You'll be right back here like the nothing you are.* He didn't want to talk about those days anymore. "What matters is I lasted long enough to know I'm better at giving orders than taking them."

"Not to mention figuring a way to make the world a better place," she replied.

It was the first time anyone had suggested he made anything better. "You're going to have to explain."

"Your blood coagulator. If you hadn't gone into the army, Ian Black Technologies would never exist."

"Oh, that." Guilt, his old friend, tapped him on the shoulder. Here's where he started letting her down.

"What do you mean, oh, that? Your product has saved countless lives."

No doubt, and there were days when he was damn proud of the product. The product, not himself. "You know I'm not the one who actually created the coagulator patch, right? All I did was pull together the people who did the work for me." To make money. To prove another point.

"In my business, we call that person the idea man. Every successful business needs one."

Until it didn't need him anymore. Or until the idea man became drunk and volatile and his own worst enemy. Ian grabbed his water, quickly washing the sour taste out of his mouth.

Once more, Chloe mistook his action. Grasping her own glass, she saluted him. "And now you're saving the world again," she said.

"How's that?"

"You said yourself that without coffee, man would kill himself. You're saving lives with high quality beans."

The gloom he felt creeping over him receded in a flash. "I like the way you think, Curlilocks. You're good for my ego."

"Good. When you become a big-time coffee magnate and need an agency, make sure you hire CMT and give me credit. That way I can score points with Simon."

"Simon, as in Simon Cartwright?"

"You know him?"

Yeah, he knew him. Or rather *of* him. Apparently, they possessed similar tastes in women. "We had a few...mutual acquaintances."

"Is that society-speak for dated some of the same women?"

He could feel the color creeping up his neck. "I wouldn't call me the society type." Certainly not like Cartwright, who, if Ian recalled, had been born to the roll. "But yes."

"In other words you're a serial dater."

"Interesting term." Sounded fatal. Considering the stack of apologies he'd written, the word was spot on.

He sat back in his chair. "I suppose I have dated my fair share. Hard to be monogamous when your soul's focused elsewhere."

"You mean drinking."

Sure. Let alcohol take the blame. Even if the liquor was only a by-product of a bigger demon.

"Not that I'm judging," Chloe continued. "By Delilah and Larissa's standards, I'm every bit as bad. But then they're overly romantic right now."

"Aren't all new brides?"

"I don't know about all, but those two certainly have taken the lovesick pills." She reached for her water. "I keep trying to tell them not everyone in the world has a soul mate. Statistically, it simply isn't possible."

"Because there isn't an equal number of men versus women."

"Exactly!" She saluted him with her glass again, her eyes glittering as though she'd proved some great scientific theory. So flushed and gorgeous, he had to squeeze his goblet to keep the blood from rushing below his belt. "You do realize there are more men than women in the world, right? Meaning men are the ones on the short end of the soul mate stick."

Chloe's smile faded. "Thanks for killing my theory."

Great, he'd gone and dimmed the sparkle. Why the hell did he have to say anything? Because the idea of her spending her life alone wasn't cause for celebration, that's why. Any notion that involved a woman like her being alone wasn't.

"You will, you know," he said. "Find your soul mate, that is." Wouldn't be someone like Aiden, either.

"You assume I'm looking for one."

"You aren't?"

"Let's just say I'm going to leave the veils and flowers to people like Delilah and Larissa."

That so? "Even though statistics are back in your favor?"

"Statistics aren't the only reason." Her smile was as indecipherable as her answer. Didn't matter. She could toss out all the nonchalant, enigmatic comments she wanted; he didn't buy a single one.

After eating, most of the guests either went back to their rooms or headed into the living room for an after dinner drink. Ian, however, leaned close and whispered, "Feel like exploring?"

Seeing how his question wrapped around her spine like a naughty suggestion, Chloe should have said no. The reckless side of her took charge, however, and she leaped at the offer.

Josef had told her the Bluebird's history when he was showing her to the room. The original structure dated back to the Civil War, while additions were added over the years based on the owners' needs. As a result, the first floor was a crazy pattern of rooms and hallways.

"Should we tie a string to one of the doorknobs in case we get lost?" she asked Ian.

"Where's your sense of adventure, Curlilocks?" he teased. "Besides, the place only looks confusing because the lights are out."

Precisely her problem. She wasn't sure if Josef and Dagmar were trying to reduce strain on the generator or discourage guests from roaming, but the rear of the inn was dark except for some isolated night-lights and lanterns. "Aren't these people worried about law suits?" she asked, tripping over a raised floorboard.

"Don't worry, I'll catch you if you fall."

Would he? She'd made him make the same promise in the parking lot this afternoon, only she wasn't sure she meant literally anymore. Ever since their conversation in her room, her insides felt like one of the wind-tossed trees outside.

It hardly helped matters that their conversation over dinner had further strengthened the connection she felt toward him. Nor did it help that he stood so close to her she could smell the wool of his sweater.

They rounded a corner and came to a small reading room.

"This must be the library Josef mentioned," Ian said.
As was the case in the other rooms, the lights were

off, leaving a small fireplace as the sole source of illumination.

"How many fireplaces are there in this place?" Chloe asked. "Must take forever to light them all."

"Maybe, but you won't hear me complain."

"Me, neither," she hastened to assure him. "A night like this one screams for a warm fire." And the flames were far too inviting. She held up her hands. The heat burned her palms, causing the rest of her body to shiver from the temperature difference.

"Cold?" Ian appeared near her shoulder.

Chloe shook her head. "I like firelight, is all. You know, that's how I started going to your coffee shop."

"We don't have a fireplace."

"No, but your walls are fire-colored. All the red and orange—very warm and appealing."

"I had no idea. And here I thought you came in because of Aiden."

Aiden. Those days seemed so long ago. "He's why I started going so often, but I first walked in because of the decor."

Spying the fireplace set, she picked up the poker and began moving the logs around so the flame would burn brighter. "Blame the visual artist in me—I'm attracted to bright colors. There's something about them that's very....welcoming. Like fireplaces."

"Remind me not repaint, then. I wouldn't want you to feel cold."

He was joking, but the comment still made her tingle from the inside out. She gave the logs another poke. Sparks popped and floated upward. "You really want me to stay warm in your café, turn the heat up a couple notches."

"Let's not get carried away. I said I wanted you warm,

not the whole damn customer base. How about I loan you another sweatshirt instead?"

"One's enough, thank you. A second would require another mugging, and I think I've had my fill."

The fire burned brightly now. Content, Chloe gave the log one last poke, then set the implement aside, as Ian squatted down next to the hearth.

"You're right," he said. "The fire does feel nice."

"Doesn't it? Too bad we don't have marshmallows we could toast."

"We could always raid the pantry. See what kind of secret stash they keep in there."

Chloe plopped down next to him. "Not much of a raid when you've got the hostess wrapped around your little finger."

"What makes you say something like that?"

"Oh, I don't know…how about 'Do you want more coffee, Mr. Black? How do you like the crème brûlée, Mr. Black? I hope the meal met with your standards, Mr. Black.'" With each "Mr. Black" she imitated the woman's lilting Scandinavian accent. The innkeeper had been very solicitous.

"She was simply being a good hostess."

"Toward you, maybe. I had to wait twenty minutes for my iced coffee. In fact, the only reason I got served at all was because she wanted to bring you a refill."

"Now you're just exaggerating."

"Am I, *Mr. Black*?"

A small smile threatened the corners of Ian's mouth. If Chloe didn't know better, she'd say he was purposely trying to goad her. "I suppose it's possible the woman recognized my name and was a little impressed."

"If you say so, although…" It was Chloe's turn to do a little goading of her own. "…I don't think it was your name she was staring at when you walked to the men's room. Unless that's what you're calling your behind these days."

Ian laughed. The carefree sound made Chloe's heart give a tiny bounce. "How would you know she was staring at my rear end? Unless you were watching, too?" He gave her shoulder a nudge.

"I was simply following her line of sight."

"Uh-huh."

"Seriously. I was not staring at your rear end." Actually, she was, but she certainly wouldn't admit it to him.

"Too bad," he replied. "Because then I could feel less guilty about staring at yours."

Chloe did a double take. "You were not." When did he have the opportunity? When she'd gotten up to use the ladies' room? "No way."

"You'll never know, will you?"

He was mimicking her comment from upstairs, although in his case, the words sounded far sexier. Then again, she was pretty sure he could read the fine print on a contract and make it sound sexy. Her skin grew hot. She couldn't help herself. Every compliment, implied or otherwise, took up residence in her chest, leaving the space between her heart and lungs so full it was hard to breathe.

Suddenly, the atmosphere shifted, and what had started as lighthearted grew still and expectant. The mirth disappeared from Ian's gaze, replaced by a new light, hot like the center of a flame. Outside, branches slapped at the house as trees bent and swayed to nature's will. Looking into Ian's eyes, Chloe swore she was bending and swaying, too.

"Dear God, but you're beautiful," she heard him whisper. His knuckles brushed across her cheek, the featherlight touch making her shiver. "Thank—"

His kiss swallowed the rest.

A whimper caught in Chloe's throat. It was a slow, sensual kiss, full of passionate promise.

Her eyes fluttered closed. He tasted like coffee, and the small part of her brain still working realized she would never think the same way about the beverage again.

"Oh! I did not realize anyone was in here."

Josef's voice broke the spell. Ian's arms dropped away, leaving Chloe swaying for purchase. As she struggled to regain her composure, she swore her ragged breathing was the only sound in the room. Frankly, she wouldn't be surprised if they could hear it on the upper floors— along with the sound of her racing heartbeat.

"I was coming in to check on the fire before heading upstairs," the innkeeper said. From the way he hovered in the door frame, he didn't know whether to complete his task or not.

Ian was the first to recover. Shooting Chloe an indecipherable look, he turned and smiled at the innkeeper. "Go on upstairs. We'll take care of the fire."

"Well, if you are sure…" He, too, gave Chloe a look, which she returned with a weak smile. Hopefully the embarrassment creeping up her spine didn't show too much. Being caught necking in a darkened room. Talk about awkward.

Especially since the kiss felt like way more than mere necking. Making out had never left her aching with such need before. It was as though her soul had woken up from a long nap she hadn't realize she'd been taking.

"All you need to do is close the glass door. The fire will burn out on its own."

"Will do," Ian told him.

Unable to voice anything more than a whisper, Chloe gave a small wave goodbye. Her heart had yet to slow down. If anything, her pulse kicked up another notch as soon as Josef disappeared around the corner. She turned back to Ian, expecting to find a desire to match.

His face was shuttered. "I…it's been a long day."

No need to say more. She wasn't good enough for a serial dater. Why make the moment worse with a whole lot of false apologies and excuses?

At least now she knew how to take all his implied compliments. "You're right," she said. "I should be heading upstairs. See you in the morning?" The hopeful note that sneaked in at the end of her question made her want to kick herself.

Ian nodded. "I'm not going anywhere."

True. They were stuck together until this trip ended. And she'd thought Josef walking in on them was awkward.

Straightening to her full height, she turned and walked away. It took effort, but she managed to reach upstairs without running. She'd be damned if she'd let Ian see how much his rejection hurt. Her blood pressure might shoot through the roof, but she would spend the rest of this road trip with a smile on her face. What she didn't understand, she thought while brushing her teeth, was why he'd kissed her in the first place. Some kind of game? A challenge? Or was she remembering the moment incorrectly, and she'd been the one who'd made the first move?

Whatever happened, it was her fault for letting her guard down. Something about being with Ian had her opening up about parts of her life she never shared with anyone else. For crying out loud, she'd told him about her father!

As if she wasn't disgusted by herself enough, she took a good look at her reflection upon donning the flannel shirt. She looked like a plaid circus tent with legs.

And swollen, thoroughly kissed lips.

Dammit, Ian. Stepping back into the bedroom, she found her attention going straight to the rumpled spot on the comforter where he'd lain earlier. He'd looked so comfortable stretched out there. So weirdly…right.

It was an image too good to be true. For her, anyway.

For the first time in eighteen months, Ian rolled out of bed cotton mouthed, and lucky him, he hadn't had to drink to get it. No, he'd earned the bleary-eyed state by spending most of the night thinking about the woman next door. The woman he had no business kissing, but had kissed anyway. Might as well have been alcohol, because once he started, he didn't want to stop. Thank heaven for Josef. God knows what might have happened if he hadn't shown up.

Ian pictured the disappointment that had flashed across her face when he'd stepped away. If only she knew how hard it was.

Once his body cooled down and common sense returned, he'd realized just how smart it was for him to stop. Maybe if she'd been some mercenary socialite… but she wasn't. She was sweet and funny. His past was already littered with good women who'd offered their hearts, only to discover he was incapable of returning their feelings. He didn't want Chloe to become one of them.

Man, though, could she kiss…. He could still taste her, still feel how her long lean body had ground against him.

He groaned aloud. Thinking about last night did not help. If he was back in New York, he could distract himself with the paper while watching the staff brew the first pots of the day. Lying here, he had too much access to his thoughts.

It was the quiet that had woken him. All night he'd listened to the pelting of freezing rain against the glass. There was no rain now. No wind, either. The only sounds Ian could hear were those of birds chirping.

A tug on the window shade revealed a mottled sky of blue and gray. The storm had left damage, though. The entire world was coated in ice. Branches, cars, even the sides of a work shed glistened as part of a frozen wonderland. Fortunately, he saw some of the branches already beginning to drip. This time of year, ice never stuck around long. The downed tree in the road was a far bigger problem. It couldn't be moved until the power company cleared the lines. Who knew how long that would take? Chloe and he could be stranded here another night.

He ignored the thrill that arose at the thought.

Yanking on his jeans and sweater, he headed downstairs in search of coffee. If this place kept its promises, then a pot would already be brewing. Otherwise, Josef and Dagmar would have to deal with him making his own.

Chloe's room was silent as he walked by. Nice to know one of them could sleep following last night. As he passed, he ran a hand across the door's painted surface, a poor substitute for Chloe's burnished gold skin, but probably the closest he'd come to a caress again.

"Good morning!" Josef stepped through the front door as Ian reached the landing. "You are up early. Did you sleep well?"

Ian gave the man credit; he acted as though last night's awkward encounter had never happened. "Very well, thank you," he said, playing along.

"Glad to hear it." The man propped a hiking pole against the wall, then hung his jacket on a wooden hook. "I was spreading salt on the front steps. If you and your friend go for a walk this morning, you will need to be careful. Until the sun warms everything up, the ground is an ice skating rink."

"Any word from the power company?" Ian asked.

The innkeeper joined him at the buffet and poured himself a cup of coffee. "I called this morning and got a recording that said they had crews on the job. Unfortunately, I also heard on the radio that there are power outages all over the state. Forty thousand people without power, I think they said. Even with your generous offer, I have a feeling repairs will be a while. I hope you were not in too much of a hurry to leave."

"Would it matter if I was?" Ian asked.

"Not really." Josef offered him the creamer, which Ian declined. "I noticed your car has New York plates. Were you coming or going?"

"Going. My son is a student at the state university. We were heading out to see him."

"What a shame you were unable to make the trip. But I am sure your son will understand."

"Hope so." The man had no idea how much. As Ian stared at the black contents of his mug, he wasn't so sure.

Behind him, the stairs creaked softly. "Good morning," Josef greeted. "I wondered if you would be joining us at this hour or not."

Ian's body tensed in awareness. Without turning around, he could tell who it was Josef spoke to. His insides sensed her approach.

Sure enough, when he turned, Chloe stood on the bottom stair.

He'd been wrong to tease her about the flannel shirt. The oversized garment looked sexy as hell on her—even with the jeans she'd tugged on to cover her legs. Soft and flowing, with a wide neckline that revealed the honey-colored skin around her neck. His body tightened as he remembered just how that skin tasted.

She'd pulled her curls into a topknot, but a handful of corkscrew tendrils had managed to work their way loose. It was those she brushed at with her hand before offering a small wave. "Good morning," she replied.

She smiled as she joined them, but Ian could tell it was for Josef's benefit only. The corners of her mouth were pulled too tightly, and while her eyes avoided looking directly at him, he still caught the embarrassment shining in their depths.

"Hope there's enough coffee left for me," she said, turning to their host.

"Why, of course. Allow me to pour you a cup."

"I thought you preferred to drink iced coffee," Ian remarked. He hoped the innkeeper took the hint and went to get some ice so the two of them could have a moment alone. Chloe, however, must have known what he was doing.

"I've been known to drink both. Besides, if you add enough milk, the coffee cools down fast and it's almost like iced."

"Almost but not quite."

"Close enough." She took the cup Josef offered and began adding what amounted to a second mug of cream. All to avoid standing alone with Ian. So much for friendship. He wanted to kick himself.

"Ian and I were just talking about the two of you spending an extra night."

The knuckles on the hand gripping her mug handle tightened. "Is that so?"

"All our guests will, unless we can get the tree moved by the end of the day. At the moment, it does not seem likely."

"Josef, can I get your help in the kitchen?" Dagmar's voice called out.

The innkeeper drained the rest of his coffee. "The boss beckons. I had best see what she wants."

"Will you be coming back?" Chloe sounded so nervous, Ian's stomach dropped.

"Afraid not. When Dagmar signals she needs help, it is usually the end of my spare time for the day. I will let you know when breakfast is ready to be served. Hope you two like eggs because we have a lot of them to cook up."

"Farm fresh eggs," Ian remarked. "Don't see those every day."

"No, I suppose you don't."

Chloe's smile had vanished along with Josef. "Another day, huh?" she said, staring at her mug. "You must be disappointed."

"A little." At the moment, he was more disappointed that she continued to avoid his gaze. Unable to stand her evasion any longer, he caught her chin with his forefinger, forcing her to look in his direction. The apology in her eyes tore his guts out. "We need to talk."

CHAPTER EIGHT

BUT NOT IN the main salon. There were too many opportunities for interruption. Before Chloe could say a word, Ian grabbed her hand and led her down the hall to the first empty room and shut the door.

She blinked in disbelief at the unlit fireplace. Startled as she was by Ian's abrupt maneuver, it took her a minute or two to realize they'd returned to the library. "I didn't think you'd feel comfortable going upstairs," he explained. "And this way we can speak in private."

"Do we have to?" If he wanted to talk about last night, Chloe would rather not talk at all. She'd spent enough time rehashing the evening while not sleeping.

"I think we do."

That's what she was afraid he'd say. She took a seat on the edge of the leather sofa, while Ian stayed by the door, arms folded, leaving miles of distance between them. As she waited for the inevitable "it's not me, it's you" litany, she struggled to keep from tugging at her neckline.

Wearing the flannel had been a mistake. That they both knew she'd slept in the shirt left her feeling more exposed than the wide-open collar. Exposed, foolish and a thousand other adjectives. Didn't matter that Ian had yet to look her in the eye, choosing instead to focus on a spot on the floor; she still felt naked.

"I owe you an apology," he said.

"No, you don't." *Please don't,* she added silently. Apologizing meant he regretted kissing her, and she didn't want to hear the rejection out loud. No matter how confused her thoughts, she needed to believe he'd wanted her, even if only for a moment. "You kissed me and I kissed you back. End of story."

Well, the end except for the fact that her skin still burned where his lips had touched her, and that staring at him this morning, she ached for him to kiss her again.

He lifted his eyes. Chloe immediately wished he'd go back to staring at the floor. "I had no right—"

She couldn't do this. Couldn't sit and listen to his excuses. "Look, we're both adults." This time, she held up her hand. "Last night was…We got caught up in the atmosphere after a stressful day. It happens. There's no need to make a federal case out of it." Considering how her insides were trembling while she spoke, she applauded herself for sounding so mature.

"Are you sure? I don't want things to be awkward between us."

"They'll only be awkward if you keep apologizing for something you don't need to apologize for." Or that she wanted to hear him apologize for. Hearing the note of relief in his voice was hard enough.

Besides, she realized there was some truth to her statement. Between their conversations and the storm, yesterday had been an emotionally draining day. They probably did overreact to the romantic atmosphere. Things between them would be much different now that the sun was out.

If he would stop studying her, that is. With her hand clutching at her open neckline to cover herself, she rose and walked to the window. On the other side of the glass, a sparrow hopped from shrub to icy shrub. Chloe watched, grateful for a distraction. "Believe me," she told Ian, "if you needed to apologize, you'd know. You'd be wearing a cup of coffee."

There was no missing the relief in his chuckle. "Lucky me, then, since I don't have a spare shirt."

Before she could blink, he'd joined her at the window. Leaning on the sill, he stretched his long legs in front of him. "Far as I know, only the cars in the parking lot are stuck here. The rest of the street should be fine."

Chloe frowned. "What does that mean? You planning to buy someone's car?"

"Nothing that drastic, but I was thinking there's got to be a train station within a town or two. I could walk up to one of the neighbors. See if they'd be willing to drive you there."

So he could ship her back to New York. "You want me to leave?" She was surprised by how much the suggestion hurt. She'd rather have the apology.

"This was supposed to be a one-day trip. I've already derailed your weekend. There's no need for you to miss work, too."

"I appreciate you thinking of my career."

"And your friend's wedding. We're assuming they'll have the tree cleared in twenty-four hours. Could take longer. Don't you have maid of honor duties to do?"

Yes, she did, and his arguments made sense. There was absolutely no reason to stay if she could find a way back to the city. Better yet, he was offering her a way to escape the romantic fishbowl they'd found themselves in. Seeing how the sun was shining and his nearness still ignited a longing sensation in her chest, heading home might be a good idea.

Except…in laying out his argument, he'd left out a

very important reason, perhaps the most compelling of all. "Is this what you want?" she asked. "Do you *want* me to go back to the city?"

"You've long since paid me back for the purse snatching."

She'd forgotten that's how the trip began. At some point between New York and this morning—the moment she'd slid into the passenger seat of his car, most likely— obligation had stopped playing a role. "Maybe I want to see this trip to a successful conclusion."

"What about your friend the bride?"

"Delilah? She'll be fine. So, if you'd like me to stay, I will."

If Chloe hadn't been holding her breath, waiting for his response, Ian's slow smile would have taken it away. "I'd like that," he said in his sandpaper whisper.

Her heart did a little victory dance. "Good."

Turned out Delilah wasn't fine with the decision. "What do you mean you're stuck in Pennsylvania?"

"Long story." Chloe took a few steps away from the building. With the storm over, she'd discovered she could get a faint cell signal by standing on the back patio, and so she'd called to update her friend. "I'm here to give Ian moral support."

"The guy from the coffee shop? Are you nuts? You barely know him."

And yet Chloe felt as if she'd known him forever. "I know him better than you think," she said aloud.

"Seriously? Three days ago you thought he was an unemployed slacker."

Only three days? Wow, it seemed so much longer. "Since then I've learned a great deal more about him."

On the other end of the line, Delilah sighed. "You've

done some crazy things, Chloe, but this…? Going away for the weekend with the man?"

"We planned on it being a day trip. Just long enough to drive to the state university and back."

"Awful long way to go for a day trip."

"He wanted to visit his son. They've been estranged for years, and this was the first time they would meet in person. I thought he could use the support."

She chewed her lower lip and waited. Delilah knew enough about her past that she didn't have to say much more. "Does he appreciate the gesture?" her friend asked after a moment.

Chloe thought about the smile she and Ian had shared in the library. "I believe he does.

"Look, I know what I said the other day, but he's not at all the guy I thought he was. In fact, he's very…" Sexy. Funny. Incredible. "He's nice."

"You like him then."

"Of course I like him. I just told you he's a nice guy. Why else would I agree to take an eight-hour car ride with the man?"

"That's not what I meant."

"Nothing romantic is going on. Ian's not—that is, neither of us are interested in romance."

"Never stopped you from falling before," Delilah replied. "In fact, isn't 'disinterested' a job requirement?"

"Very funny." Just once she wished her friends didn't pay such close attention to her behavior. "You're as bad as La-roo, you know that?"

"We try."

"In this you can stop trying. I can guarantee nothing's going to happen." Ian had made it quite clear. "You can pass the message along to Larissa, too. I don't need her calling and gushing about some potential romance that isn't."

"I will, if I can reach her. She hasn't answered her phone all weekend, either. Maybe she and Tom got stuck in the storm, too."

"Either that or the two of them are spending the weekend reading the hotel brochure for the thousandth time. Or making little doohickeys to give away to the wedding guests. Did I mention I'm grateful you don't worry about those kinds of details?"

"Right now the only detail I'm worried about is whether I'll have a maid of honor. Promise me you won't run off to Hawaii with your new boyfriend until after the ceremony, please?"

"I promise," Chloe replied, refusing to comment on Del's using the word *boyfriend*. "Besides, I spent way too much money on that dress not to walk down the aisle."

A few minutes later, she clicked off the phone with a sigh. Something Del had said disturbed her. Not when she called Ian her boyfriend—that was typical teasing— but earlier. *That's never stopped you before.*

"Ow!" An object smacked her head. Looking up, she saw that pieces of ice were falling from the tree. All around her tiny chunks were melting on the patio. Funny how quickly things could thaw. By evening, much of the ice would be gone. Already, the same frozen crust that she'd had to jam her heel into yesterday to cross had turned to slush.

Voices sounded from the driveway. Picking her way across the parking lot, she found a circle of male guests staring at the tree in the road, pointing out other large branches that littered the area. It was easy to find Ian in the group. He was the most masterful figure there. How on earth did she ever think him a slacker?

One of the men said something, causing him to laugh. The throaty sound reached her insides despite the distance, lodging in the center of her chest like a warm fuzzy ball.

Delilah, annoying as her comment was, had a point. When it came to men, the more disinterested, the more attractive Chloe found them. Ian, with his sexy smile and his insistence that he wasn't made for a relationship, fit her bill perfectly. He was exactly the kind of guy she chased.

So why did being with him feel so different than the others?

The question nagged her most of the day. Actually, a bunch of questions nagged her. How was it that being with Ian could feel as natural as breathing, while at the same time scare the heck out of her? Made zero sense. No wonder she'd told La-roo she needed a break from the dating world. Clearly, the whole Aiden catastrophe had left her brain fried.

"So this is where you've been hiding."

Chloe jumped, her pencil skidding across the paper on her lap. Ian stood propped against the door frame, arms folded across his chest. As usual, her insides took a dive roll the moment she saw him.

"Who said I was hiding?" she said, brushing some stray curls off her face. Stupid topknot wouldn't hold them all. "Since you and all the other male guests were busy surveying storm damage, I figured I'd come upstairs to take a nap, is all."

"You always nap with a pencil and paper?"

"Obviously, I'm not napping at the moment." She'd tried, but her thoughts wouldn't let her relax. "I found some scrap paper in the desk and decided to do some sketching."

"Really? Can I see?" he asked, stepping into the room.

"Um…" She looked at the papers in her lap.

What started as a sketch of the pines had turned into a series of doodled logos for Ian's coffee shop. "Sure. Why not?"

She handed him the designs. "For me?" he asked, surprise in his voice.

"I was goofing around with some ideas. Nothing serious."

"I like them. The middle one especially. The lettering isn't hitting me, but the concept is right."

"What if I…" She grabbed the paper back and quickly rounded off the letters, giving them a more fluid look. "That work better?"

"Like you read my mind."

She tried not to take the comment seriously, but her heart beat a little faster, anyway. "Then your mind must be easy to read," she told him, pushing the feeling of connection aside.

"Funny, but my old employees never said so. Then again, I was half in the bag most of the time, so mind-reading would have been difficult." He went back to studying the sketches.

Chloe pulled her knees closer to her chest. It dawned on her that his honesty regarding his drinking bordered on self-abusive. "Why do you do that?" she asked him.

"Do what?"

"Mock the fact you had a drinking problem." Listening to him put himself down the way he did hurt. "Shouldn't you cut yourself a little slack?"

"Should I?" he countered. "Have you forgotten why we're on this road trip?"

"Doesn't mean you should beat yourself up."

He let out a long breath. "You're a sweet kid, you know

that?" Before she could protest the kid label, he sat down on the arm of her chair. "I have to mock," he said. "It's the only way I can get past what a bastard I used to be."

"Used to be," she reminded him. "You're not a bastard now."

"That's because you're seeing me on my good days."

If he meant to warn her off, the attempt didn't work. "I still think you're being too hard on yourself."

He smiled and brushed her cheek with the back of his hand. "You'd think differently if you saw the damage I caused. My list of amends is pretty damn long."

At least he was making amends. To her, that's what mattered. Although she doubted he'd believe her.

She settled for changing the subject. "You never did explain why you picked coffee for your next business adventure."

"I didn't?"

Chloe shook her head. "Care to share now?"

"Do you want the public relations version or the truth?"

He stretched his arm across the back of her chair. What started as his being perched on the arm suddenly turned into a crook with her nestled close to his chest. "Truth, please," she replied.

"I like coffee."

Chloe waited for the rest of the answer. When one didn't come she started to giggle. "Seriously?"

"Deadly. This way I can control my vice."

"You want control? I'm shocked."

He poked her shoulder. "Speaking of control, the power company arrived. They're busy clearing the downed wires as we speak."

"That's great. You must be happy."

"I am." Strangely, his voice lacked enthusiasm. Chloe chalked it up to nerves.

"Of course," he continued, "clearing the wires is only the first step. We still need to cut the tree into sections and move it from the road."

"We?"

"I convinced a couple of the other guests that if we did the work, the job would go faster than if we relied on Josef and the neighbor across the street—who, by the way, is older and about half Josef's size."

Chloe laughed at the description. "Sounds like a wise decision."

"We thought so. If all goes right, the road will be clear by early evening. We'll be able to head out west first thing in the morning."

Bringing an end to their stay at the Bluebird Inn. She was surprised at how disappointed the thought made her feel. You'd think she'd be relieved, given that, contrary to what she'd told Ian, she'd spent the day hiding from him.

"Sounds terrific," she told him. "Thanks for finding me and letting me know."

"Actually, giving you a road update is only part of the reason I was looking for you."

"Oh?" Drawing her knees close, she swiveled in her seat so she could look up at him. "What's the other part?"

"To tell you I have a surprise planned for after dinner."

"A surprise? For me?" Images of last night's kisses flooded her senses, making her pulse race. "Why?" *Please don't say to make up for last night.*

"Because…" She wasn't sure if he paused to think of the right words or if he changed his mind about answering altogether. "A guy can't do something nice for a friend?"

Friend. The word didn't fit as right as it once had. Friends didn't make her insides ache with longing.

"Truth is," Ian continued, "I wanted to thank you for coming along with me this weekend."

"We've already been through this. You don't have to thank me."

"Stop spoiling the fun."

"Sorry. The gesture just caught me off guard." After all, surprises were reserved for couples, not *friends.*

"You're supposed to be caught off guard," Ian replied. "That's why it's called a surprise."

He grasped her chin, tilting it up until their faces were so close Chloe thought for a moment he might kiss her again. "Six-thirty in the dining room. Don't be late."

Don't be late? How could she possibly? She would be counting the minutes.

Much to her chagrin.

"No peeking, now."

Chloe felt Ian's lips against her ear. "Your eyes are closed, right?"

"Sealed tight. Is this really necessary? I feel a little silly." Not to mention anxious. Ever since Ian had mentioned an after dinner surprise, she'd been a bundle of anticipatory nerves, and now, with her eyes closed, the expectancy had her other senses hyperaware of the man propelling her forward. Ian's hands rested on her shoulders, the pressure of each finger finding a way through her turtleneck to excite the nerves beneath. She felt his broad chest hovering behind her. She could even sense the soft knit of his sweater brushing up and down her back as he breathed.

It was probably time for her to accept that she'd gone and done exactly as Delilah predicted: fallen for Ian.

Never one to take your own advice, were you, Chloe? Much as she hated to admit it, she was hopelessly and deeply into the man.

"Relax," he said, mistaking her tension for self-consciousness. "No one's here to see you."

True enough. As soon as the road opened, most of the guests had piled into their cars and headed home, leaving Chloe and Ian the only couple left. As a result, the two of them ate dinner with Josef and Dagmar. The arrangement only added to Chloe's nerves, since she had to spend the entire evening pretending not to notice the knowing glances being shared around the table.

Ian turned her body to the right. "Ten more steps," he told her.

"You counted?"

"Of course. We wouldn't want you tripping and falling on your face, would we?"

"Ah, that means we're heading someplace with obstacles."

"Maybe." His voice appeared in her ear again, low and rough. "Then again, for all you know, I could be messing with you."

In more ways than one. She swore that, with every step, his body moved closer to hers.

One of Ian's hands left her shoulder, and a moment later she heard the click of a doorknob. A soft gust struck her face; a door being pushed open.

Two steps forward and the air temperature suddenly changed, becoming warmer. Chloe heard the sound of crackling wood. "Is that a fireplace?"

They were in the library. Last night's kiss flashed before her, stirring a heat she was afraid to let take hold.

"Okay, open your eyes."

She blinked, adjusting to the darkness. Someone had

moved the furniture. Pushed the sofa and chairs toward the wall. In their place lay a large tablecloth, the bright red square spread in front of the fireplace like a picnic blanket. At the far corner, she saw a silver tray bearing a tea set and several covered serving bowls.

She arched a brow. "A picnic?" This *was* a surprise. She didn't see Ian as the picnic type, let alone a picnic by firelight.

"Not any old picnic," Ian replied, taking her hand. He motioned for her to sit, then reached for the tray. "I'll have you know, by the way, I worked extremely hard on this." Based on his grin, Chloe couldn't tell if he was serious or making a joke.

He lifted the first cover. Chloe slapped her hand over her mouth to keep from laughing. "Oh my God, you raided Dagmar's pantry!"

"More like charmed her into setting this whole thing up," he replied. "Told you I worked hard."

She bet. More likely Dagmar had caved at the first smile.

One by one Ian uncovered the dishes, revealing marshmallows, graham crackers and chocolate squares. "You said you never cooked s'mores over an open fire before, so I figured…"

He'd give her the opportunity. Chloe stared at the tray in disbelief. It'd been a casual comment, babble really, nothing more, and yet he'd listened. The men she knew didn't care about any of her life's details. They certainly wouldn't go to this much trouble to help her live out a childhood fantasy.

Attraction shifted into an emotion she couldn't name. The strange feeling filled her chest, squeezing her lungs. Her vision blurred.

"Hey, hey, hey." Ian moved to her side. "There's no need to cry. They're only marshmallows."

"I'm not crying. I'm…" She blinked the tray back into focus. "I can't believe you did all this."

"Dagmar did the work. All I did was smile and say please."

They both knew he'd done more than that. It was wonderful. *Sweet, wonderful*… Words couldn't describe the fullness in her chest, so she settled for wrapping her fingers around his, hoping the connection would speak for her. "Thank you," she whispered.

"My pleasure, Curlilocks."

With his free hand, he brushed her cheek, and Chloe wondered if he felt the inadequacy, too.

"Ian…"

He broke away. "Enough with the thank-yous," he said, reaching for a skewer. "We have marshmallows to toast."

For the next few minutes, they sat cross-legged in front of the fire, watching as the flames licked their marshmallows brown. When the surface of hers began to bubble and expand, she let out a giggle. "This is already better than using the microwave," she told him.

"You are way too easy to please."

"I wouldn't be so sure. If this tastes as good as I anticipate, then you will definitely have to install a fireplace in the coffee shop."

She pulled the crispy, gooey confection off the end of her skewer and popped it into her mouth.

"What happened to the rest of the steps? Aren't you suppose to stack them all together?"

Mouth full of marshmallow, Chloe shook her head. "Didn't want to spoil the toasted flavor."

"Terrific. I made Dagmar unwrap all those candy bars for nothing."

Laughing, Chloe sipped her hot cocoa. "A woman never lets chocolate go to waste." To prove her point, she picked up a piece. The square had turned soft in the heat and she had to lick the remains from her fingers.

She was running her index finger over her lower lip when she heard a soft hiss. Looking up, she found Ian's stare glued to her mouth, his gaze hot and needy.

It was the *needy* that did her in.

They moved as one, their bodies coming together in a tangle of mouths and limbs. Last night's kiss promised passion, tonight's delivered. The moment Ian's lips slanted across hers, instinct took control. They moved in sync, until even the sound of their breathing shared a rhythm.

And then, suddenly, Ian broke away. Swearing, he buried his face in the crook of her neck. As she listened to his breathing, Chloe continued to hold him tight. Her head was spinning. What had happened?

Swearing a second time, Ian lifted his head. "Do you have any idea how many times I promised myself I'd quit drinking before I actually went to rehab?" he asked.

Rehab? Why on earth was he talking about drinking now when he could be kissing her? Chloe was about to ask that very question when she caught the anguish in his expression. The question clearly mattered.

She shook her head. "How many?"

"Too many to count. I'd promise, and fifteen minutes later I would toss my resolve out the window. And do you know why?"

Again, Chloe shook her head.

"Because I'm a stubborn bastard who always has to have his way. Makes resisting temptation very difficult," he added, brushing the curls from her eyes. Chloe felt his fingers tremble as they moved across her skin.

He wasn't talking about drinking. He was talking about kissing her. "It's not temptation if we both want something," she told him.

His laugh was hollow at best. "If only it were that simple."

"Maybe it is," she replied. "Maybe we're simply over-thinking."

"Or not thinking at all." Sighing, he rolled away, his departure causing Chloe to shiver. "You're a sweet kid, Curli, you know that?"

Kid. He'd said the same thing this morning. It was, she realized, his default answer whenever things turned inti-mate. As if using the term helped him keep his distance.

"I'm not a kid," she reminded him. "I'm a grown woman."

"I know." He shot her a look that would melt steel. "Believe me, I know."

"So, I don't understand. What's the problem?" Any other man would be leading her to his bedroom by now. "Is it me?" Of course it was. Stupid question.

His horrified expression was little comfort. "Oh sweet-heart, no."

She wanted to believe him. She did. "Then…?"

"Because I like you."

Her heart stuttered. Ian rose and walked toward the rear window. "I've got a list of amends a mile long," he told her, looking out into the darkness. "Do you have any idea how many people I've let down over the years?" What he was really saying was *how many women.* "I don't want to see you dragged down, too."

"In other words, you're being noble." Funny, for a rejection—and a clichéd rejection to boot—the words went straight to her heart. Call it wishful thinking, but his expression reflected in the glass looked so regretful it made her feel special rather than cast aside.

Pulling herself from her paralysis, she joined him by the sill, her heart cringing when he looked away. Up close, she saw traces of self-reproach mixed with his regret. Further proof of his sincerity. This time it was she who brushed his cheek. Her silent way of telling him nobility wasn't necessary.

"You deserve—"

"Shhh." She didn't want to hear the protest. Not when, right here, right now, she knew there wasn't anyone in this world better than the man next to her. They'd been dancing around this moment all weekend; both of them afraid of what would happen if they let their guard down. She was tired of being afraid. She wanted him. Wanted him in a way that went far beyond sex.

"I've got all I need right here."

In case he didn't believe her, she forced his gaze to meet hers. Every muscle in his body was tense, shaking from restraint. In the shadowed blue light, she saw the desire struggling to break free. "Right here," she repeated, and brushed a kiss against his lips.

A groan tore out of his throat and he wrapped an arm around her waist. Chloe found herself yanked tight against his body. "Do you have any idea how difficult you are to resist?" he growled.

The roughness in his voice turned her insides raw. "Show me," she challenged, her rasp matching his.

He did.

CHAPTER NINE

CHLOE LAY ON her side watching Ian breathe. Sleep managed to do what consciousness couldn't, and that was to erase the stress from his face. He looked younger, less burdened. She traced the planes of his face in the air above him, down over the curve of his shoulder and along the scar on his arm. The raised cord was the only imperfection on his flawless body. She followed along to his wrist, ending at the hand splayed next to his pillow. One hand from a pair that had so masterfully played her body. While she wasn't as experienced as she often pretended to be, she recognized a skilled lover.

Why then, if Ian was so amazing, was she wound tighter than a drum?

You know why. Ian was different than other men. Waking up and seeing him lying next to her felt way too natural. He inspired words like *complete*, *real* and *forever*. Scary, troublesome, dangerous words—at least for her. She felt as if she stood on the edge of a steep cliff, one with the lip pulling away from beneath her feet. Every instinct told her to take a few steps back.

But then she'd remember last night, not the lovemaking, but the fullness that had gripped her heart when Ian revealed his surprise, and the words took hold again.

"You look a million miles away."

She started at the sound of Ian's whisper. Pulling away from her thoughts, she looked over and caught the gleam of his eyes as he watched her in the dark. "What time is it?" he asked.

"Four o'clock."

"What are you doing awake? Everything okay?"

The darkness made the concern in his voice sound urgent. So much so that for a second, she worried he'd heard her thoughts. "Fine," she lied. "Couldn't get comfortable is all. I didn't mean to wake you."

"You didn't. I wasn't sleeping all that well to begin with." He scrubbed his hand over his face, his strangled sigh loud in the darkness. "Too much on my mind, I guess."

Regrets? Her insides steeled, ready for rejection. "Anything I can do?"

"You've already done more than enough," he replied, rolling to his side. "In fact, you've been pretty darn incredible."

Chloe fought the urge to burrow under his arm. Afterglow compliments were no doubt standard operating procedure for a man with Ian's experience, and he still managed to say the words with such tenderness, her insides melted. "Are you trying to make me blush?" she asked, grateful for the darkness.

"I do like the color your skin turns." He nuzzled her curls. "I knew," he murmured against her temple. "From the minute you walked in wearing those high heeled boots, all curls and attitude. I knew you'd be a force of nature." He pulled back. "Why do you wear those high heels?"

"So the world will see me coming." And be forced to acknowledge her existence.

"You're very hard to ignore." She felt him smile. "Even

before you tossed your iced coffee. Now—" he gave her a quick kiss "—how about we see what we can do to make you more comfortable."

Rolling on his back, he wrapped an arm around her shoulder and pulled her close. She nestled into the crook of his arm, burying her face against his neck.

"Better?" he asked.

"Definitely."

It was her second lie of the night. Being in Ian's strong embrace wasn't better; it was *the best*. Once more, the words she feared danced before her eyes. *Complete. Real. Forever.*

Something was off, Ian thought as he pried open his eyes, and it wasn't the empty expanse on the other side of the bed or the sound of the shower.

In point of fact, it was *exactly* those two things, along with the tightness in his gut when he noticed them. Usually, on mornings after, he was the one up early, looking for a drink and a way out.

Perhaps that was why he felt so unsettled. Not only had he given in to temptation—enjoying every blessed second, he might add—but here he was, lounging in bed without any inclination to move.

The shower stopped, and a few minutes later, Chloe stepped into the room wrapped in a towel. As soon as she spied him, she flashed a smile. "You're awake. I was afraid I'd have to throw cold water on you."

Still might, he thought, adjusting the blanket. There was way too much honey-colored skin on display. Pushing into a sitting position, he pretended to lounge against the headboard until he could get this body under control. It was a lost cause. As Chloe bent over to scoop her clothes from the floor, all hope vanished. Man, he really did suck when it came to resisting temptation.

"Actually, I'm surprised I slept as late as I did. Guess all that tossing and turning at 4:00 a.m. caught up with me."

"I hope it wasn't because I used you as a pillow."

"Curli, you using me as a pillow was the second best part of the night."

There it was, that gorgeous pink blush. The same color her skin turned when she was aroused. "Last night was pretty…um…" She bent to retrieve a stray sock. "What time would you like to leave?"

"Leave?" The hem of her towel had risen, affecting his concentration.

"I'm assuming you must be eager to hit the road so you can see Matt."

"I am." Unsure where this conversation was going, he drew out his answer. The way her eyes were glued to her clothes rather than on him gave him pause. "Why do you ask?"

"No reason. While I was in the shower, I got to thinking that maybe…" She crumpled the sock in her fist. "Maybe I should have you drop me off at the train station, after all."

"What?" He sat up straighter. "I don't understand. When I asked you yesterday, you didn't want anything to do with the idea."

Why the one-eighty?

"Yesterday you were talking about hiking through the ice and asking a total stranger to drive me. Now that you're back to driving, the situation is different.

"Besides," she added, "you're going to want privacy when you talk with Matt. I'll only be in the way."

Mostly I tried to stay out the way.... Why did that comment pop into his head?

"You would have been in the way Saturday, too. That didn't stop you from tagging along."

"Saturday was before…"

They slept together. Of course. Typical Chloe with her bravado. She was trying to act casual, something she was clearly not accustomed to doing. Guilt stabbed him in the gut. *You selfish bastard.*

"Don't be ridiculous. I want you there," he told her. Finally, she showed her face. With her clothes clutched to her chest, she eyed him warily. "You sure?" she asked.

"Positive," he replied. So much so, it shocked him. "But first, there's someplace else I want you." Drawing back her side of the covers, he patted the mattress.

Chloe's eyes widened. "I thought you were in a hurry to see Matt?"

"We've got plenty of time, Curli. Plenty of time."

He'd forgotten how big the state university was. Driving onto campus felt more like entering a small city. It didn't matter if it was raining; students still roamed everywhere.

Just as Ian turned a corner, a flash of red rushed by his driver's side window. He sucked in his breath, only to realize it was a false alarm.

Chloe shifted in her seat, reminding him he wasn't alone. "We played in a tournament here once. I remember the girls from their team were Amazons."

Picturing her long, muscular legs, he smiled. "Like you should talk."

"I was downright petite in comparison, thank you very much. Did Matt text you?"

"Not yet." Ian had sent a message before leaving the Bluebird. "He's probably in class." He ignored the lump in his stomach determined to remind him it'd been three days since the first call, with no word.

"What are we going to do then? The campus is a little big to simply wander around asking if anyone knows Matt Black."

"Only place we're going to wander to is the president's office. I'm sure with a little persuasion we can get ahold of Matt's schedule."

She stared at him. "In other words, you plan to buy your way around the privacy rules."

"Hey, perks of being rich." If only his insides matched his outward confidence. The closer they got, the more he wondered if this plan, which had made such sense in New York, was going to work.

A familiar silhouette near the center of the parking lot caught his eye. Driving closer, he discovered the boy had brown hair. Another mistake.

He parked and let his forehead drop to the steering wheel.

"How are you holding up?" Chloe asked.

Holding up? His stomach was stuck in his throat. "I keep seeing kids I think are him," he told her. Of course, the odds of Matt simply walking by were slim to none.

"You'll see him soon enough," she said.

"I know." The thought made his pulse race. Thirteen years was so very long. "What if it's a mistake?"

"What are you talking about? Of course it's not a mistake."

"No, I mean being in his life at all. What if…" Ian struggled against the fear rising up inside him. "What if he's better off without me?"

"He's not," Chloe said. "He's going to want his father in his life."

She believed that because of her own father. "Not all dads are worth having. Mine was a miserable drunk."

"You are worth having."

Damn, did she have to speak with such assurance? "You don't know that," he said, shaking his head.

He turned his wrist so their palms faced each other, and entwined their fingers. The connection calmed him. He thought of how many times and ways she'd comforted him this weekend. Now he was about to lean on her once more. She should hear the whole story, though. "I didn't build Ian Black Technologies to save lives. I built it to make a fortune. So I could rub my success in my father's face. Nothing else mattered. *Nothing.*"

Years of working nonstop. Drinking and working. Leaving the people who cared because he was too drunk and too driven to give them what they needed.

"I wanted so badly to prove him wrong," he said, staring at the rain-covered windshield. "Instead, all I did was prove I was as miserable a bastard as he was. What if being around me does the same thing to Matt?"

Slowly Ian turned to face her, expecting reproach. Instead, he saw a sheen in her eyes brighter than ever before. "It won't," she whispered.

"How do you know?" For crying out loud, he'd hurt so many people on his way to the top. How could she possibly be so certain still? Especially after what he'd said.

"Because." She cupped his cheek. "You're different. You're better."

Ian let the silence settle around them while he sat holding her hand. What did he do to deserve her crossing his path? She'd been a gift, his Curlilocks. The kind of woman a man could not only draw strength from, but who he could go toe-to-toe with, as well. A challenge and a comfort. If only he'd met her earlier. Before he'd crashed and burned.

"Ian?" Brown eyes shimmered with concern.

"I'm sorry," he told her.

"Sorry for what?"

For leaning on her so much, for pretending he didn't notice her casual air this morning was a little forced, for being selfish. Any of those answers worked.

What he said was "For suggesting we find a way to send you home Saturday. I…" He squeezed her hand. "I'm glad you're here, Curlilocks."

Pink colored the edge of her smile. "There's nowhere I'd rather be than with you," she said.

The emotion shining in her eyes was more than he deserved. Unable to speak, he kissed her. Hard and greedily. "For luck," he whispered when they broke apart.

"O-okay." Her eyes were dazed, her lips swollen and glistening like the rain. A picture, he suspected, that would be in his head for a long while.

Slowly, his insides untwisted. They were here. No way would he turn back now. Planting one more kiss on her hand—for extra luck—he grabbed the door handle. "Come on, Curlilocks, let's go track down my son."

It took a lot of persuasion, as well as a donation to the new building fund, but Ian eventually walked out of the office armed with the information he needed.

"I don't think I want to know the amount on the check you wrote," Chloe said as they crossed the quad toward the building that housed Matt's last class.

"Money talks, Curli." A small price to pay as far as Ian was concerned. He'd paid far steeper sums for far less important things.

At least they were in between rainstorms. The morning's steady downpour had faded to a drizzle, meaning more students would be out and about.

Checking his watch, he saw it was five after the hour. "Class ended a few minutes ago. Why's he hanging around after?"

"Talking to friends, I bet. If he's done for the day, he's not in any rush."

"You're right." Ian couldn't let his impatience get the better of him. "I'm sure he…"

The doors to the building opened and a trio of students stepped outside. One look at the shock of auburn hair sticking out from beneath a baseball cap and Ian caught his breath.

He'd recognize the cocky strut anywhere. The determined shoulders. He was looking at a younger version of himself.

"Matt!" His voice rang out across the quad. The trio stopped, and so did he, a few feet shy of closing the gap. "Matt!" he called again, softer this time. The boy turned. It took a minute, but eventually his eyes widened in recognition. Ian raised a shaky hand. "Hey."

Silence filled the quad, stronger than before. "What are you doing here?" Matt finally asked.

"I came to see you," Ian replied. His heart permanently jammed itself in his throat. After all this time, they were finally speaking face-to-face. So many things he wanted to say. Where did he start?

"Did you get my messages?"

"I got them."

"Good. I didn't know if the storm—"

"If I wanted to talk, I would have called back."

What? Ian froze. "I don't understand. I thought we…" Words failed him. "We've been talking."

"I answered a couple letters. That doesn't mean I'm ready to get all buddy-buddy."

If he wanted you to know his phone number, wouldn't he have given it to you? Jack had said. Ian had screwed up. Again. He shoved the self-pity aside. This wasn't about him, it was about making things right with Matt. "I'm not looking to be your best friend. I understand I don't have that right."

"And yet you're here."

God, but the kid sounded so much like him it hurt. "If you'd give me five minutes—"

"No."

A slap would have hurt less.

"You need to hear your father out." It was Chloe. While he and Matt were talking, she'd stepped up to stand at his shoulder. Her fingers brushed the back of his hand, a featherlight gesture of support. It was all he could do not to grab hold.

Less appreciative of her presence, Matt stared her down. "Lady, I don't know who you are, but I don't need to do anything." He washed a hand over his features. "Look, I can't do this right now. I—I've got study group."

The worst thing about his son's rejection was Ian deserved every single bit. Mentally, he backed away, giving the kid the space he needed. "I'm sorry, Matt. I never meant to hurt you."

"If that's the case, then leave me alone. Find some other poor schmuck and call him. Just…ust…" He made the same face Ian made when searching for the right words. "Just back off."

"You want us to call security or something?" one of Matt's friends asked.

"Won't be necessary. Right?"

Ian nodded.

"You don't understand. Your father—"

"Let him go, Chloe." No need making things worse than he already had.

Incredulity filled her expression. "Are you nuts? You can't let him leave without explaining."

"Chloe—" Ian reached out to grab her arm, only to have her break free and jog after the trio.

"He's trying to make things right!" she called out to the kids. "Don't you understand what that's worth? How lucky you are?"

"I'm lucky?" Matt whirled around, his eyes hard as stone. "I don't know who you are, but that man did nothing for thirteen years. I'm not dropping everything because he decided to play father today. Now, leave me alone."

"But he—"

"Chloe, stop!"

Ian had had enough. Matt didn't want to listen. The only thing Chloe's pushing would do was drive the boy further away.

She refused to give up the fight, however. Her eyes had a desperate, manic shine to them as she gripped his arms. "Go after him," she demanded. "Tell him about all the events you attended. About graduation. He needs to know you were there."

"He doesn't want to hear it."

"Then make him! Follow him and make him listen."

"And how do you suggest I do that? Tackle him and hold him to the ground?" Didn't she realize he would if he thought forcing him would make a difference? Ian had messed up, pure and simple. What he needed to do was go home and regroup. Figure out how to fix what he'd destroyed.

He watched as Matt and his friends moved toward

another building. For one brief second, while standing in the doorway, it looked as though Matt glanced back in their direction, but he was merely holding the door open for someone else before vanishing behind the glass.

"Jack warned me. He said I should be more cautious."

But Ian hadn't listened, and as a result, he and his son might have had their one and only meeting. To think he might never hear Matt's voice again cut him in two. What had he done?

He never got the chance to apologize.

Chloe still wouldn't give up. She paced back and forth, her boots hitting the ground with hard steps. "You've got to go after him," she repeated. "We cannot come all this way, go through everything we went through, only to turn around. Tell me we aren't. That we aren't quitting."

"For crying out loud, Chloe, will you be quiet? We aren't doing anything." The words burst out of him like bullets, loud and fast. "This is about my son. You want to work out your father issues, do it on your own time."

She looked as if she'd been struck. "I can't believe you said that."

He could. He'd known it was only a matter of time before the monster inside him hurt her. This, he thought, as angry tears brightened her eyes, this was why he should have kept his distance.

The rain had returned. Chloe could feel the drops spitting in her face as she watched Ian walk away. With each step he took, the hope she dared to let hide in her chest grew fainter.

"You were supposed to be different," she whispered. Not like the others. He was supposed to stay and fight for the people he cared for. In her mind, the little girl she used to be gave up believing things could ever be different.

She found Ian in his car, staring at the steering wheel. "I told you I was a miserable bastard," he said.

"You had a rough day. It happens." The lame answer came from someplace she didn't recognize. Guess the hope hadn't completely died, as she was willing to forgive the outburst, even after he greeted her explanation with a humorless laugh.

"I should have listened to Jack."

"You said yourself some things can't be communicated in a letter."

"Because I know so much about parenting and relationships?"

"You weren't the only one who thought coming here was a good idea."

"Oh, I know."

He drawled the response, coating the words with bitterness. Chloe's hackles stood on edge. "What are you saying? You're not blaming me for this trip, are you?"

"Don't give yourself so much credit. You only confirmed what I wanted to hear."

Slowly, she pulled her scarf from around her neck. The wool was damp from the rain, but she spread the cloth over her legs, anyway. Kept her hands busy. "Nice to know I had such influence," she said, smoothing the plaid.

Ian replied with a long exhalation. "I'm sorry."

For what? Insulting her or bringing her along in the first place? There were so many ways she could take the comment. "I'm sure you are," she replied.

He jerked the shift stick out of position. "Might as well get going. We've got a long drive ahead of us."

An interminable drive at that. This time, however, it wasn't the weather, but the distance between driver and passenger making the trip uncomfortable. Ian didn't say a word and Chloe was too hurt, too frustrated, to try and draw him out. She spent the miles watching the rain streak her window.

The few times she looked in Ian's direction, her stomach churned into knots. His profile had turned so hard and reproachful, it hurt to look. Then there were her own insecurities. As much as she tried to tell herself it was the failed meeting with Matt causing his turmoil, she couldn't help worrying. If Ian could quit on the one person he claimed mattered more than anything in the world... With every mile that passed without contact or conversation, his angry words rang louder, and her insecurities grew stronger.

By the time they pulled up to the curb at her place, she was so tense she wanted to bolt straight from the car. "Home sweet home," she said softly, as much to the window as herself.

"Sorry I wasn't much company."

Said in the same terse voice he'd been using since leaving the university, the apology didn't hold much weight. He might as well have said "thanks for the good time" or "get out" for all the emotion behind his words.

Well, she'd be damned if she let her hurt feelings show. "Guess I'll see you at the coffee shop tomorrow."

"Sure." At last some emotion broke through. Unfortunately, that emotion was regret. Compounded by his finally reaching out to touch her. His hand gently cradled her cheek. "Good night, Curlilocks."

He meant goodbye. She saw the truth in his eyes. It took every effort, but she managed to step onto the sidewalk without showing her pain.

And to think this morning she'd actually almost thought about forever.

* * *

At least she could finally change her clothes and use her own hair dryer. Riding up in the elevator, she tried to list as many positives as possible. Anything to take her mind off the man who'd just driven away. She wouldn't have to sleep in Josef's nightshirt again, for example. One night was more than enough, thank you very much.

She much preferred sleeping in Ian's arms....

Stop being a crybaby. Ian had endured a devastating rejection. He had every right to be distant and preoccupied. Only a self-absorbed ninny would make this moment about her.

Except his kiss *did* feel like goodbye....

And what if it was? The elevator doors opened and she stepped onto her floor. Not the relationship type, remember? You both said so. Relationships were for people like Del and—

"Larissa?"

On the floor next to the door sat her best friend, knees pulled tight to her chest. As soon as Chloe said her name, she looked up with red-rimmed eyes. "I'm sorry I didn't call," she said. "I don't have my phone."

Her voice trembled as though she was barely holding it together. Chloe was frightened. "What happened? Are you okay?" A terrible thought occurred to her. "Is it Del—?"

Larissa shook her head. Fresh tears filled her eyes. "T-T-Tom left me."

What? "Oh, sweetie, no." She gathered the woman in her arms and hugged her tight.

Once Larissa calmed down a little, Chloe led her into her apartment and sat her on the love seat. La-roo immediately curled into the corner like a miserable blonde ball.

"I'm going to call Delilah," Chloe told her. This was

the kind of problem the three of them dealt with best together.

"No, don't," Larissa said. "This is her big week. I don't want to ruin it for her with my bad news."

"What happened? What do you mean, Tom left?" All Chloe could think was that Larissa misunderstood. Or she misunderstood Larissa.

"He said he met this woman at work, another broker, and they 'clicked'." She framed the word with her fingers. "Said she 'got him' better than I do. At least I think that's what he said. Honestly, I wasn't listening. I was too interested in getting out of the apartment."

"If that's the case, maybe you didn't hear the whole story," Chloe told her. That had to be it. "Maybe he had impure thoughts about this woman or something, and simply felt guilty. I bet if you call him—"

"He said 'I don't want to get married.' Not much there to misunderstand."

Dammit. Speechless, Chloe sank onto the sofa. Larissa was one of the good ones, too. Sweet, kind. Lovable. How could Tom walk out on her? What did that say about people like Chloe? "I don't understand," she murmured.

"I know. Everything was going so perfectly, too. We had the wedding all planned out…. "Oh my God, the wedding. What am I going to do about the wedding?" She burst into a fresh round of tears. "Why did this happen?"

Because men leave, Chloe thought as she rubbed her friend's back. No matter how wonderful they make you feel, they eventually walk away. The best thing you could do was to walk away first before they could cause too much damage.

CHAPTER TEN

"I KNEW YOU'D go off on your own the minute you hung up the telephone. Do you ever listen to advice?"

"You can skip the lecture, Jack. I already know I made a mistake." In more ways than one.

Squeezing his eyes shut, Ian massaged his temples, hoping the pressure would chase away the headache pounding in them. "I got impatient. You know as well as I do I suck at self-discipline."

He heard Jack let out a breath. "Self-discipline isn't your problem. It's stubbornness."

"You forgot selfishness," Ian added, raising his mug.

"Where are you now?"

"Where do you think? I needed solace, and I didn't want to go home." Another mistake, as things turned out. Opening his eyes, he looked around the vacant coffee shop. For the first time since buying the place, he found the atmosphere didn't bring comfort. Instead, the bright walls mocked him. Reminded him of firelight and spiral curls.

Amazing that it was Chloe he found himself thinking about. Matt was everything to him. His flesh and blood. The one real accomplishment in his life. Yet here he was, filled with as much self-loathing over hurting a girl—make that a woman—he'd known for less than a week as he was over hurting his son. How the hell did she get under his skin like that?

"See what I mean about self-discipline?" Jack was saying. "You could be in a bar."

"Doesn't mean I don't want to be. Only reason I'm not blitzed is I figured I'd screwed up enough this weekend."

Unfortunately, Jack could help him with only one of his mistakes. "I knew he was angry, but… I'd been so focused on apologizing." He'd never stopped to think about Matt's role in the equation. Ian had been selfish and stubborn as always.

Chloe's reaction had woken him up. He could still see her on the quad, desperate to make him to change his mind. And what did he do? Lose his temper. That's when it hit him. Time pulled back and he was once again hurting someone he cared about. Only this time he didn't have alcoholism to blame. Only himself.

"So what are you going to do?" Jack asked.

"Let her go."

"Don't you mean he?"

Right, they were talking about Matt. "What can I do? I can't walk away. I need to apologize."

"You did apologize, Ian. In your first letter, remember?"

Ian remembered. "I didn't tell him the whole truth, though. About the alcoholism, about watching him grow up." *He needs to know you didn't forget him.* Wasn't that what Chloe would say?

On the other end, Jack let out a long breath, a sign he was about to deliver a lecture. "Do you remember step nine?"

"You know I do." Make direct amends wherever possible. "I've been living the step for the past eighteen months."

"I know. Obsessively."

"What's that mean?"

Another long breath. "It means you don't have to be obsessive, Ian. 'Wherever possible.' Sometimes the best we can do is try."

"And if the attempt fails?"

"You live as good a life as you can and hope someday you get another chance."

"In other words, I can't make things happen on my timetable."

"I take it back, you did learn something."

Too little too late. Matt was furious with him, and Chloe...how the hell was he supposed to make amends to her? He wasn't sure he could be in the same room without wanting to pull her into his arms. Even tonight, frustrated and angry as he was, he longed to drive back to her apartment. So he could hold her again.

He must have sighed, because Jack asked, "What?"

"Nothing," he replied, then laughed. "Would you believe woman problems?"

"This the 'her' you're thinking of letting go?"

His sponsor was damn perceptive. "She's unlike any woman I've ever met, Jack. Sweet, innocent..." Vulnerable, kind.

"She sounds special."

"She is." Too special for the likes of him. A man whose entire legacy was causing pain to people he cared about.

"So what's the problem?"

"Nothing you can help with, unfortunately. This is one problem I have to solve myself." His eyes fell on the black garment bag lying on the counter.

He had one more amend to make. This one would be for her.

Having been up till five in the morning, Chloe did not appreciate hearing her apartment buzzer at nine-thirty. She rolled from bed, stole a glance at Larissa and headed into the living room. It was probably Delilah, worried over her two best friends calling in sick for work. "You could have phoned," she snapped into the speaker.

"I don't know your home number."

Ian? She was so surprised to hear his voice that for a second she forgot last night's resolve. "What are you doing here?"

"Can you let me in? We need to talk."

Actually, they didn't. Chloe was pretty certain their time for talking had ended when he'd kissed her goodbye last night. Anything Ian had to say now would only hurt. *But what if you're wrong?*

The oath came out soft but sharp. *You're a glutton for punishment, Chloe Abrams.* "Fine." She unlatched the front door, then rushed to the bathroom to brush her teeth, purposely avoiding the mirror. She already knew she looked like a disaster; checking would only lead to panic. Instead, she grabbed a ponytail holder from the vanity drawer and shoved her curls atop her head. No sooner did she finish than Ian knocked.

It wasn't fair, an inner voice whined. Did he have to look so good? He wore his usual leather jacket and sweatshirt, with the familiar ginger shadow again covering his cheeks. Yesterday's sad, withdrawn expression remained as well, she noticed, only today a new emotion joined the mixture. Resignation. Defeat.

Disappointment settled in the pit of Chloe's stomach. She'd so hoped he might be different. She hated how he made her think that way.

At least now she knew the truth. His expression said everything she needed to know.

With a glance at the bedroom, she stepped out into the hall, closing the front door halfway. No need for Larissa to be dragged into the conversation. "What are you doing here?" she asked.

"When you didn't show up for your morning coffee I called your office, and they told me you phoned in sick. Are you all right?"

Wait a second. "You noticed I didn't come in for coffee?" He'd been looking for her.

Ian's response was to gaze at her as if she had two heads. "You've been coming in for thirty-two straight weeks. Of course I noticed you.

"You're a little hard to ignore," he added with a half smile.

Damn, but she hated how her heart fluttered when he gave his answer. Her heart had never fluttered until Ian. Further proof she'd made the right decision last night. Larissa's devastation was a harsh reminder of how important it was to protect your heart. For so long Chloe had told herself people got what they deserved. Until this weekend, when she'd let herself hope she might find forever. She'd been kidding herself. Ian was no different than any other man she'd let into her life.

With one exception: Ian had the power to break her heart if she let him get close.

"You didn't answer my question," he said. "Are you all right?"

"Fine." Man, but her face felt tight. She swore she wouldn't show emotion one way or another, but the action killed her check muscles. "Larissa got some bad news, and we spent the most of the night talking. I called in sick so we could get some sleep."

"I hope the news wasn't anything serious."

"Her fiancé broke up with her. He found someone else."

"I'm sorry."

There was sympathy in his eyes she didn't want to see, so she turned her attention to the weather-stripping on the side of her door. "Yeah, me, too. She deserved better."

"She wouldn't be the only one."

Chloe didn't want to discuss who deserved what; she simply wanted to get this conversation over with. The sooner she ripped the bandage off, the sooner the sting would start to heal. "Why are you here, Ian?" she asked. "Surely you didn't come by simply because I forgot my coffee."

"You left your dress in the backseat of the car."

For the first time she noticed the garment bag draped over his shoulder. "Figured you'd be looking for it come the end of the week," he said.

"Thanks." Gathering the bag in her arms, she held it tight, not caring if the dress wrinkled or not. Clutching helped her cope with the latest wave of disappointment. You'd think at some point she'd stop holding her breath for his response. "If that's everything…"

"I also wanted to talk."

And there it was; the true reason. He was going to stand in her hallway and tell her this weekend had been a mistake, or a one-time deal or, or, or…she knew a zillion excuses a man could give, and even if Ian did have the decency to deliver one of them to her face, she didn't want to hear it. Not from him. Not right now.

She started backing into her living room. "This isn't really a good time. What with La-roo being upset and everything."

"You said Larissa is asleep."

"Yeah, but…"

Ian reached around to pull her door shut. "This won't take long."

"Then why bother at all?"

He blinked. The question came out far sharper than Chloe meant it to. Usually she could fake indifference with the best of them. Thing was, she didn't feel indifferent this morning. Disappointed, agitated, but definitely not indifferent.

Taking a deep breath, she started again. "Look, what I'm saying is we both know the deal, so why go through the pretense? Why don't we save ourselves the hassle, agree that this weekend was fun while it lasted, and move on?"

"Do you really mean that?" Ian moved so that he shared the door frame with her, his broad chest consuming what little space her own body didn't. When he folded his arms across his torso, the action brought him right up against her. With a narrowed gaze, he looked her in the eye. The intensity made Chloe want to squirm. She missed her high heels and the height advantage they gave her. They were eye to eye right now, and she'd never felt more pinned down in her life.

"Sure," she said, finding her voice. "Don't you? I mean, isn't that why you're here? To end things on a nice clean note?"

It was his turn to squirm. She'd made up her mind last night that this time she would walk away first. "Some people aren't cut out for relationships, right? Wasn't that what you said?"

"I wasn't talking about you. You're—"

"No." He did not get to play the martyr and feel better about himself. "I'm the same as you, Ian."

"That's where you're wrong." Before she knew what happened, his fingers were playing with the loose curls by her face. "You, Curlilocks—"

"Stop calling me that!" Her frustration boiled over and she slapped his hand away. Forget indifferent. "You do not tell me what I am and what I'm not. I'm the one standing in my hallway in a pair of ratty yoga pants being tossed aside, so I get to be the one to walk away. Me, not you. And if that leaves you feeling bad or guilty or un-lovable, then tough. Deal with it."

Her vision started to blur. Dammit, she would not lose control more than she already had. She reached for the door handle, only for Ian to catch her by the wrist.

"You are not unlovable," he whispered.

Of everything she'd said, why on earth did he pick that word to zero in on? Keeping her jaw clenched, she stared straight ahead. "Hey, we all get what we deserve, right?"

His stuttered breath gave her a small measure of sat-isfaction. "I never meant..."

"Cross my name off your list, Ian. You've made all the amends here you're going to make."

Breaking free, she finally managed to open her door and get herself inside. Ian didn't stop her.

Did you expect he would? Chloe let her head fall back against the door. Walking away wasn't any better than being brushed off.

"Did I hear the door?" Larissa asked, stepping out of the bedroom. Her face still bore mascara traces from last night's cryfest.

Chloe quickly mustered a smile. "I left my dress in the backseat of Ian's car. He stopped by to return it."

"I thought it might be Tom."

"Sorry." Based on everything she'd heard last night, Tom wouldn't be stopping by in the near future.

Larissa shrugged and shuffled toward the kitchen. "This is Ian from the coffee shop, right? The rich slacker?"

"One and the same," Chloe replied.

"I thought you said you weren't interested. How'd you end up going away with him for the weekend?"

"Long story." A long, depressing story, and La-roo had enough on her plate to deal with. Opening the fridge, Chloe searched for the orange juice. "You don't want to know."

"Come on; tell me. I need to talk about something other than my problems. What happened?"

Chloe told her the bare-bones story.

"Wow. Stranded at a mountain inn. That sounds so romantic."

"Only because you're addicted to romance," she replied, handing her a glass of juice. Even as she protested, however, scenes from the weekend laid themselves out in her head.

"Maybe, but you're not nearly as unaffected by it as you pretend to be," Larissa retorted. "You cannot tell me you spent the entire weekend under those conditions and didn't feel even a little spark."

Chloe's heated skin betrayed her. She tried to hide behind her orange juice, and failed.

"Oh my God, you did!" Chloe's skin burned hotter. "That's wonderful! Makes me glad to know both my friends have decent love lives."

That was Chloe's line. "Better change the number to one."

"I thought you said you and Ian…?"

"We did, but it was only a weekend fling."

"Why?"

"Because." Because she wasn't worth more. "You know I'm not interested in a relationship. That's yours and Del's thing."

"I'm doing real well in that department, aren't I?"

Seeing the dejection on Larissa's face made Chloe's

already beat-up emotions feel worse. "I'm sorry, La-roo. I didn't mean to be insensitive."

"You weren't. My new single status is something we both need to get used to. But I also don't believe you. You may say you don't want a relationship, but I don't buy it for a minute."

"Don't be ridiculous." The conversation was getting uncomfortable. "Do you want me to make breakfast or do you want to head to the diner corner?"

"I'm not hungry. Do you want to know why I don't believe you?"

"Because analyzing me will cheer you up?"

The blonde shook her head. "Because you make the same speech every time you end a relationship. You make a very big point of stating how you weren't emotionally invested."

"Because I usually wasn't," Chloe reminded her.

"Methinks the lady protests too much."

Seriously? She was going to psychoanalyze, and quote Shakespeare? "I need coffee if you're going to do this," Chloe muttered.

She reached for the coffee pods, grabbed one and dropped it into the brewing chamber. "And for the record, I do not protest too much. Some people simply aren't meant to find love. I'm one of them."

For a moment, the only sound in the kitchen was that of the coffee streaming into her mug.

"Why on earth would you think you aren't meant to find love?" Larissa asked after a moment. Did Chloe really say that out loud? Damn.

"I meant be loved. Be in love."

"Use whatever phrase you want, it's still not true. You're as worthy as anyone."

"Have you checked my dating record?" She tried to sound flippant, but the attempt sounded flat.

"No offense, Chloe, but that's because you tend to date losers."

Maybe you need to date a better class of guy. Ian's words repeated in her ear.

"I thought this time I was."

"What?"

Seeing the confused look on Larissa's face, she realized she'd spoken out loud. "I thought this time was different."

"You mean Ian."

Chloe nodded. "But he walked away, too. Or he was about to."

"What do you mean, 'about to'?"

"I beat him to the punch."

Larissa's jaw dropped. "You broke up with him? Chloe, what were you thinking? You don't know if he was planning to walk away."

"Yes," she said, "I do."

"How?"

"Because I've been dumped enough times to know the signs, that's how!"

She shouldn't have shouted, but arguing the point made the wound raw again. Larissa didn't taste the good-bye in his kiss or see the regret in his expression.

"He told me I deserved better," she said in a softer voice. "All I did was preempt the inevitable."

Tears threatened to burn her eyes. Refusing to give them a chance, she slid to the floor. Drawing her legs tight against her, she let her forehead fall to her knees. The same pose she'd found Larissa in last night.

"Oh, Chloe." A warm presence materialized on the

floor next to her, followed by an arm around her shoulders. "He's a jerk. Tom's a jerk. All men are jerks."

"I'll give you Tom, but Ian?" She shook her head. Much as it hurt, she couldn't call him a bad name. "He was nothing but honest from the start." If anything, she was the one who wasn't special enough to change his mind.

"You really like him, don't you?"

"Yeah," she whispered into her knees. At last she admitted the truth she'd been fighting since Friday night. "I like him a lot." More than liked, actually. Somehow he'd gotten past all her defenses and captured the very thing she swore she'd never risk. Her heart.

No wonder breathing hurt.

"At least Delilah found Simon, and those two are definitely soul mates," Larissa was saying. Good old La-roo, looking for the silver lining. "So they do exist. We'll have to wait a little longer to find ours, is all."

Chloe bit back her discouraged reply. No doubt Larissa would bounce back and find true love, but her?

She couldn't help but believe her soul mate had kissed her goodbye last night.

Given how she felt, only an idiot would go to the coffee shop the next morning.

"We could go to the place across the street," said Larissa, who met her on the corner.

Chloe didn't want to go to the place across the street. "Absolutely not. Do you plan to stop eating dinner at the pub?" she asked, referring to the little restaurant where Larissa and Tom used to grab dinner.

"No, but that's different. The pub is in my neighborhood. I was meeting you guys there before Tom and I met."

"This is the same thing. I've been visiting this coffee

shop for months. I didn't stop coming after Aiden, and I refuse to stop coming now." It was a matter of pride.

Plus, possibly, she wanted to make a point of showing Ian what he'd given up. She'd taken extra care with her appearance, going for a leather jacket and dangerously high heels, the kind that turned heads on the subway. The cut on her chin was almost healed and she'd done her makeup to perfection. The only way anyone would know she wasn't 100 percent together was if she removed her sunglasses and revealed the circles underneath her eyes. Vestiges of another lousy night's sleep. She didn't plan on removing the glasses. Not in front of Ian.

Forcing her head high, she strutted down the sidewalk with such long strides Larissa had to double-time to keep up. "What are you going to do if he wants to talk?" the blonde asked when they were four doors down.

"I'm not. We said everything yesterday." And she wasn't ready for friendly small talk.

No more banter, she realized. The back-and-forth might have lasted only a week, but she couldn't picture being in the shop without Ian's sandpapery voice teasing her about something. She'd miss talking most of all. The sense of connection that had them finishing each other's sentences, as though they were two halves of the same brain.

Great. Two doors away and she was already getting emotional. Maybe she should have gone to the other place, after all. Blinking away the moisture, she adjusted her sunglasses and pulled open the front door.

Ian's absence was the first thing either of them noticed. "I thought you said he hung out at the front table?" Larissa remarked.

"He usually does." The table sat empty today. "Must be out back."

Her sixth sense said otherwise, though. There was a noticeable chill in the air that wasn't normally present, while the red and orange walls—which she'd told him inspired warmth—looked garish. Even the furniture possessed a worn indifference. They were missing the ingredient that brought them to life.

As if fate wanted to truly hammer home a message, Aiden waited on them. "Ian's not here," he said. "He said something about having to take off for a few days."

"See?" Chloe said when the barista turned around. "Told you he wouldn't want to talk with me."

She couldn't have felt worse if she tried.

CHAPTER ELEVEN

FOR THE AMOUNT of money he'd donated the past two days, you'd think he could get a decent cup of coffee. Obviously, the university president didn't appreciate flavor as much as he appreciated signed checks. Then again, beggars couldn't be choosers. The man was already treading a thin ethical line by doing him this favor. Ian set his half-empty cup on the desk and resumed his pacing. Every so often his eyes would stray to the clock on the wall. Checking the time. Wouldn't be long now.

He'd made the drive in record time. Motor across a state three or four times in as many days and you got used to the route. He'd done this trip in one straight shot, no stops.

Although he did slow down when he passed the exit for the Bluebird.

Ian rubbed the center of his chest. Damn heartburn had bothered him since leavng the city. Simultaneously sharp and throbbing, the pain felt as if something had smashed a giant hole in his sternum.

Make that someone. The hole had formed the second Chloe closed the door in his face.

If only she knew how badly he'd wanted to bang on that door, drag her back into the hallway and kiss her senseless. Thankfully, he'd kept his impulse reined in.

He'd done the right thing, walking away. Sure, she hurt now. That so-called casual attitude didn't fool him for a bit—even before the meltdown. In time, however—in the long run—she would be better off. She'd find a great guy, fall in love, and make his mornings better by being there when he opened his eyes.

Ian rubbed his sternum again.

We get what we deserve. Her parting words, and his wish for her. If that meant he had to deal with heartburn for the rest of his life, then so be it.

The door opened, stopping him in his tracks. "I got a message to come see you— Crap, you don't give up, do you?"

"Not when it matters," Ian replied. Crossing the room in two strides, he reached over the teenager's head to shut the door. "I'm not letting you walk away this time."

"Seriously? You're not letting me walk away."

Ian winced. The kid wasn't making things easy, but Ian held his ground. Today's visit wasn't about him. He was here to set Matt free, and for Chloe. So she'd know he cared enough to fight. "Five minutes. And when I'm done, you never have to speak with me again."

Matt stared at the oak door. The kid was wavering. Otherwise, he would have walked out by now. "How much did it cost you to get Dean Zobreist to do your dirty work?" he asked.

"You don't want to know."

"I hope you get your money's worth."

"I already have. You're still here."

"Okay." He turned around and folded his arms across his chest. "Five minutes," he repeated, chin jutting forward. "Four minutes and thirty seconds actually."

Talk about a chip off the old block. Ian took a deep breath. "I was wrong to surprise you the other day. I—I wanted us to reconnect so badly, I didn't stop to think about how you might feel."

"So you decided to surprise me again to apologize."

There was a certain irony to the arrangement, wasn't there? "Not to apologize. To give you this." Reaching into his breast pocket, he pulled out a letter. His final letter of amends. "This explains everything that happened over the last thirteen years. When you're ready, I hope you'll read it. After, if you want to talk, you call me. I'll meet you whenever and wherever. You call the shots."

Matt stared at the envelope. "That's it?"

"Unless you want to talk now."

"I'm not—"

"Ready. I know." Ian stepped away from the door. Matt immediately reached for the handle. "I love you very much, Matt. I always have."

"You have a funny way of showing it," his son replied.

"Love isn't always visible. Someday I hope you'll realize that my being around would have only made things worse for you."

The teenager started through the door, only to stop and turn around. "I believe you, you know," he said, the words going straight to Ian's heart. "But it would have been nice if I'd had a choice."

He was getting one now. For the third time in three days, Ian let someone he cared about walk away, and it ripped his insides in two.

He waited until he was back in his car before calling Jack.

"How'd it go?" the lawyer asked.

"About as well as could be expected. At least he didn't throw the envelope in my face."

"Good news there. Who knows? Maybe the kid'll come around someday."

"Maybe," Ian replied. Although he didn't think he'd hold his breath, waiting for the moment. There were many layers of resentment and disappointment to be worked through even if Matt did read his apology. Could scars like that ever truly be healed?

Ian thought of Chloe, who was still hoping for an explanation from her own father, and wondered. Wondered if the man ever sat in his car kicking himself for ignoring such a beautiful, unique, amazing woman. If so, Ian hoped the guy felt as guilt-ridden as he did.

He let his head fall back against the headrest. "Do you think I was right to keep my distance all those years?"

"Between the alcohol and the Jeanine factor, you can certainly put forth a good argument. Why?"

"Just wondering. Matt said something on the way out the door. Made me wonder how bad the damage would have been had I stayed in touch."

"I'm going to guess there would be damage caused either way. You were a bastard until you got sober, or did you forget?"

"How could I when I've got you to remind me?"

"True." There was a brief silence on the other end. Ian could picture the lawyer grinning. "What exactly did he say, anyway?"

"He accused me of not giving him a choice."

"Of course you didn't. He was five years old and you were…"

"A drunk, I know." Chances were, if he'd stayed, he would have inflicted the same damage on Matt that his father had inflicted on him.

"Either way," Jack continued, "there's little you can do about your decision now. What's done is done. Best you can do, if you did make a mistake, is try to fix things, and hope you don't make the same mistake again."

The thing was, had he learned? All the way back to the city, Ian couldn't shake the notion that he'd forgotten a piece of the lesson.

Matt's comment kept ringing in his head: *I didn't have a choice.* Jack was right, of course. The kid had been five years old at the time. Ian walked away to protect an innocent boy. He couldn't offer Matt a choice. Maybe, if he'd been an adult…

You mean like Chloe?

Crap. Ian practically slammed on the brakes, the thought reared up on him so abruptly. What did Chloe have to do with all this?

A stupid question. She and Matt had been twisted together for days now. Think of Matt's abandonment and Chloe's story wasn't far behind. Picture Matt's angry face and Chloe's disappointed expression followed. Hell, think of anything and thoughts of Chloe tagged along. In a few short days, she'd managed to permanently attach herself to his brain. More than his brain, he amended, rubbing at the hole in his chest.

The more he thought about it, given their shared childhood experiences, the commonalities between Matt and Chloe didn't surprise him. Ian wondered if his son faced the world with the same edge and bravado. The first day she'd strutted her way into his coffee shop…man, but she'd looked so sassy. He realized now she wore her attitude like a shield. All her talk about not being the relationship type? Her way of getting out in front of any hurt the world might deal her.

It's what she'd been doing yesterday morning, too. He could tell because her eyes had the desperate sheen to them that came from trying too hard.

But when she dropped her defenses… Then those eyes grew so soft and vulnerable, a man could drown in them.

Ian could see her now. Eyes brimming with emotion in the firelight. She'd given him a gift, he realized. A window into a part of her she didn't share with too many people. That glimpse stole his heart.

Who was he kidding? She'd stolen his heart the moment she gave Aiden a peppermint latte shower. All Saturday night did was cement her hold on Ian.

But he'd pushed her way. Just like with Matt, he'd pulled back because he'd decided distance was for the best. He took away her choice.

"Idiot." Ian added a few other choice adjectives as well while pounding the steering wheel. All his talk about no longer being selfish, and here he was, being as selfish as ever.

How many losses would he have to endure before the lesson kicked in? His son, his company, years of sobriety—all lost because of his stubbornness. His insistence on doing things his way. And now here he was, insisting he knew best again. He'd already lost Matthew. Did Ian want to be sitting in his car twenty years from now, mourning Chloe, too? Because Lord knows, he wouldn't find another woman like her again. She was one of a kind.

The car behind blared its horn, then passed him on the right, the driver offering up an obscene gesture on the way by. Ian started to glare in return until he glanced at the speedometer and saw he'd slowed down to thirty miles an hour. He needed to get his mind off Chloe before he caused an accident.

Would if it were that easy, he said to himself as he pulled over a lane. The upcoming exit sign caught his eye and he gasped. Looked like the universe was full of messages today, wasn't it? Flipping on his direction signal, he eased right again and prepared to turn off the highway. Same exit he and Chloe had taken leaving the Bluebird. With luck Josef and Dagmar would have a room he could use for a few days. He had a lot of thinking to do.

"They look great together, don't they?" Larissa asked with a sigh. "So much in love."

So much in love it hurt, thought Chloe. She licked the cinnamon from the rim of her appletini and watched Delilah get twirled around the dance floor by her new husband. Their friend had two left feet. Every so often she would trip over her partner, the stumble sending both of them into giggles and kisses. They were perfect for one another.

They danced in the center of a lantern-lit floor. The Landmark Hotel ballroom had been bathed in white satin for the evening, the only color being the blue of the centerpiece flowers, which coordinated with the attendants' dresses. Beautiful and perfectly matched. Like the couple on the dance floor.

One of the groomsmen approached the table. "Would one of you ladies like to dance?" he asked. Chloe sipped her drink and pretended not to hear him, leaving Larissa to smile and take his hand. Not, however, before shooting a quick glare in her direction.

She should probably feel bad about throwing La-roo under the bus, but honestly, she didn't think her friend truly minded, and even if she did, she would still make a far better dance partner. While she might be heartbroken, Larissa still loved weddings, and was pouring her all into enjoying this one. Chloe, on the other hand, had all she could do to keep a smile on her face. It wasn't that she didn't wish her friends every happiness in the world. She did. It was that every time she looked at Simon and Delilah, she saw a happiness she'd never have. Seeing them was like sticking a knife in her heart.

Nearly five days had passed since she'd closed the door on Ian. Four days since she'd seen his face, heard his raspy voice. The sucker in her insisted on visiting the coffee shop every morning, looking for his ginger-scruffed face sitting at the front table, only to be disappointed. According to Aiden, Ian hadn't returned from his "getaway." She wondered if he wasn't simply avoiding her.

Shouldn't the pain hurt less by now? She licked more cinnamon and wondered. Granted, this level of heartache was new, but she hoped she'd be feeling better. That the emotions ripping her apart every time she thought of his name would begin to fade. No such luck. It appeared that when Ian went, he'd left behind a giant hole too big for filling.

"Why aren't you dancing? You should be dancing." A giddy Delilah, her eyes glittering manically, plopped down at the table. "That dress looks way too stunning to be stuck behind a table."

"Larissa's showing the dress off for us both," Chloe replied. "I need to stay on alert in case important maid of honor business comes up." It was the same excuse she'd been using for two days to avoid socializing.

Apparently Delilah had figured out her plan, because she waved off the excuse. "Your duties are officially over. I'm Simon's problem now. Wait, that didn't come out right."

"How much champagne have you had to drink?"

"Not as much as you'd think. I'm simply really, really, really happy." As if Chloe couldn't tell. Delilah's face glowed so brightly she could power Manhattan and half of Brooklyn, too.

"I'm glad," she replied, meaning it sincerely. "You deserve happiness."

"Thanks. I can't help feeling a little guilty, though, what with you and Larissa having such rotten weeks."

"Don't you dare! No guilt allowed on your wedding day, Mrs. Cartwright. Larissa and I will be fine." Chloe looked over at her fellow bridesmaid, who was chatting away with her dance partner. "In fact, I think La-roo will bounce back quite nicely."

"What about you?"

She managed a smile for Delilah's sake. "I'll bounce back, too." Eventually. She was nothing if not resilient.

"I hope so," Delilah replied. Before Chloe could say another word, she gathered her in a tight hug. Wrapped tight, Chloe allowed the emotion to bubble to the surface. She squeezed her eyes and her friend.

"For the record," Delilah whispered in her ear. "Ian Black's an ass."

Chloe sniffed back her tears. "Yes," she said, "he is."

The moment was interrupted by the band leader speaking into the microphone. "May I have your attention, please. It's time for the bride to toss the bouquet."

"Oh man," Chloe groaned. "I thought you decided not to."

"Larissa insisted."

Of course she did. With luck her friend would catch the foolish thing, too. Chloe sat back to sip her drink.

"What do you think you're doing?" Delilah took the glass from her hand. "As maid of honor you're required to be on the dance floor."

"You said my duties were over!"

"I lied."

Standing on a dance floor fighting over who caught a bunch of flowers was the last thing she felt like doing, but since Delilah and Larissa had their hearts set on it, she would go join the crowd. Someone else could do the catching, though, she decided, grabbing her drink. She made her way to the back of the area while a beaming Simon led his bride to the stage. Delilah grinned at the crowd, turned her back and tossed the flowers high. Too high, it turned out. The bouquet struck the chandelier and ricocheted straight down, landing at Chloe's feet.

A tuxedo-clad arm reached down to retrieve the fallen blossoms. "What's the matter, Curlilocks? Rebounding a little rusty?"

Silk over sandpaper ran down her spine, stilling her heart. Slowly she turned. This couldn't be real. Ian was not standing there clutching a bunch of limp flowers.

He offered the bouquet with a cautious smile. "Thought maybe you could use a dance partner."

She tossed the appletini in his face.

"Are you nuts?" Larissa and Delilah had cornered her in the ladies' lounge.

"Three days!" she snapped at them. "Tells me I deserve better and then takes off for three solid days. Do you have any idea how miserable I was? Now he shows up acting like nothing ever happened. What did he think I would do—throw myself in his arms? Who does he think he is?"

She pressed her hands to the marble vanity, hoping the coolness beneath her palms would help sort the feelings swirling inside her. "What is he doing here?"

"My guess would be he's here to see you," Delilah replied.

"In a tuxedo," Larissa added.

"Don't go there." Chloe should have known the blonde would find Ian's appearance romantic. "Every man in the room is wearing one."

"Every man in the room didn't crash the wedding,"

she shot back. "He came to see you. Maybe he wants to try again."

For how long? Until she got her hopes high enough for him to dash again? "And what if I don't want to?"

"What are you talking about?" Larissa's reflection stared at her in disbelief. "You're crazy about him. You told me so yourself."

Maybe so, but she wasn't crazy enough to have her heart stomped on a second time. She wouldn't survive. "He should have acted while he had the chance. I don't think I'm interested anymore."

"That's a crock and you know it. You've been going to that damn coffee shop twice a day, hoping to see him. Now he shows up and you say you're not interested? Pul-leeze. I'm blonde, not stupid."

"All right, fine!" Chloe should have known her in-difference act wouldn't work. "So I'm crazy about him. How do I know he's going to stick around this time? That he isn't going to make a whole bunch of promises and take off? Face it," she said, staring down at the marble. "Men suck."

"Not every guy leaves," Larissa said.

"Tom did."

"Simon didn't." Delilah appeared next to her. "Do you remember before Simon and I got engaged? When we were having problems, and the two of you helped him track me down to talk?"

"Of course I remember. But you and Simon were a completely different situation. The two of you were mis-erable without each other."

"And you've been miserable all week."

"Look," Larissa said, "no one is saying you have to give Ian any kind of chance. He broke your heart, and if you want to kick him to the curb, then we'll help. Before you do, though, aren't you the least bit curious to know why he tracked you down?"

Chloe had to admit she was. Her friends had a point. She should hear him out. If for no other reason than to keep her hopes at bay. Then she'd kick him to the curb.

"He's right outside, waiting," Delilah told her. "He wanted to come in and corner you himself, but we convinced him it would be safer if we did."

With her heart stuck somewhere between her chest and her throat, Chloe opened the lounge door. Ian stood across the corridor, wiping the front of his shirt with a napkin. "I forgot how lethal you were with a glass of liquid," he remarked when he saw her.

"You caught me by surprise."

"Clearly."

No wonder Larissa had pointed out the tuxedo. Ian might be dressed like the other guests, but none of them wore the suit nearly as well.

"They told me at the coffee shop you were out of town?" Not the question she'd planned to ask, but the first one to pop out of her mouth nonetheless.

"I went back to Pennsylvania."

"To see Matt again?" Did that mean Ian hadn't given up on his son, after all?

That still didn't mean anything had changed between the two of *them,* she reminded herself when hope threatened to blossom. Matt was his flesh and blood.

"I decided to change tactics. One of the things we learn in rehab is amends aren't about you. They are about making things right for the other person. I was so focused on completing my plan, I forgot."

"How'd it go?"

"Verdict's still out."

Chloe nodded. No matter what happened between her and Ian, she hoped he made peace with his son.

She stared at the man who'd upended her world. Too shocked by his arrival to notice before, she realized now how tired he looked. Tense, too. Reminded her very much of Saturday afternoon, when he'd been so stressed over meeting his son. "Why are you here?" she finally asked.

"Isn't it obvious?"

"Frankly, no. I thought we said everything Tuesday morning."

Ian crumpled in his fist the napkin he'd been holding. "I made a huge mistake that morning," he said.

"Look, if this is another amends mission, I already told you you're off the hook."

"Not this time."

Chloe sighed. She hurt too much to assuage his guilt. "Well, then I guess you'll have to deal."

"Chloe, please wait." She'd turned to leave, only to have him catch her hand. A week didn't diminish the effect of his touch. Every inch of her skin tingled with memory. "I need to say this," he told her. "Give me five minutes. Then, if you want me to go, I will."

CHAPTER TWELVE

FIVE MINUTES. SAME request he'd asked of his son. Pulling her hand away, she tried to still the tingling by squeezing her shoulder. "Five minutes," she repeated. Then she was out of there.

"My whole life I did things on my terms. The way I built my company, the way I dealt with my demons. The way I raised my son."

"You're eating up your time," Chloe said. "I know all this."

"Point is, because I was rich and successful, I figured I had all the answers. That I knew best. That included measuring my mistakes. Because I thought Matt was better off without me, there could be no other solution. The kid never had a choice. I did the same thing with you. I decided I wasn't good enough for you, so I decided to pull away.

"Only you beat me to the punch," he added.

Chloe, however, was stuck on something he'd said earlier. Not good enough for her? Seriously? "So, what, you're back because you've decided you are good enough for me?"

Ian stopped pacing. "No." Chloe's heart sank.

"Do you have any idea how amazing and special you

are?" he went on. "I don't think I'll ever be good enough. Not in a million years."

Perfect words, but could she believe him? "Words are cheap."

"You're right, they are. I wish I knew an answer to make you believe what I'm saying, but I can't. I'm learning love doesn't come with guarantees."

If only it— *"Love?"* The word hung between them, waiting to be claimed.

He looked down at his hands, a frustrating move because it meant she couldn't see his face. After using the word, she needed to read his eyes.

"After I left Matt the other day, my mind wouldn't stop spinning. I needed a place to think."

It wasn't the direction Chloe expected their conversation to travel. With her nails digging into the palms of her hand to keep her body from trembling, she waited for him to make his point.

"I went back to the Bluebird," he told her. That was a surprise.

"You wouldn't leave my head. One minute I'm driving, thinking about you, the next I'm staring at the exit. I took it as a sign that that's where I needed to go.

"I spent the past couple days in the room we shared, trying to pinpoint what made our time together so incredibly right. When I wasn't in the room, I was talking to Josef and Dagmar. They gave me some pretty sound advice. Did you know they've been married thirty-five years?"

"That's very sweet, but at the moment I don't care." Chloe's nails were carving permanent lines in her skin. This journey of self-discovery was all well and good, but he'd mentioned love. She needed to know what he meant.

"Ah, my sweet little Curlilocks, I love how impatient you are."

There he went again, throwing the word *love* around. Each time, her breath would catch, as she waited for the reality check. "Ian, please, what are you trying to tell me?"

"I'm saying I've got a lot of baggage."

Reality struck. The damn baggage again. She should have known.

She turned to leave.

"But…" His voice stopped her. "But," he continued, sounding a step closer than before, "sitting in that room surrounded by thoughts of you, it dawned on me that so does everyone else in this world. It's what we do with that baggage that counts. Look past, move forward."

"I don't understand." Actually, she was afraid to try. His words sounded too good, made her heart too hopeful. It was getting harder and harder to keep her feelings reined in. If she let herself believe and she was wrong…

The hands that suddenly caressed her shoulders didn't help. "All this time I've been focused on earning people's forgiveness," he said. "Turns out there was one very important person who never made the list."

"Who's that?"

"Me. I ignored one of the most important lessons of all—to forgive myself for my mistakes. Matt, the drinking, the pigheadedness. Of course, when you stop to think, it makes sense. I was being pigheaded about forgiveness."

Despite her churning nerves, she had to smile at the irony. "Sounds like a great epiphany."

"And it's all because of you."

Her? She turned to see his face. The sincerity in his expression shocked her. "What did I do?"

"Walked into my life," Ian replied as he swiped a thumb across her cheek. Almost as if brushing away a tear. Blinking, she realized that's exactly what had happened. She'd been so busy reining in her heart, she didn't register the emotion wetting her eyes.

"One of the reasons I was so intent on fixing the past was because it was all I had. Other than the coffee shop, I didn't have a future. At least I didn't until a gorgeous, curly-haired drink-tosser walked into my store. I couldn't resist you."

He'd said the same words in Pennsylvania, only with far less devotion. "You called it your weakness on Saturday night," she reminded him.

"You're right, I did say that. Because I was too blind and stubborn to see I was weak for a reason. That I'm completely and utterly nuts about you."

He cradled his face in his palms and stared into her eyes, the posture so much like their first kiss she nearly fell into his arms then and there. Not yet, though. All his sweet talk was wonderful, but the fact remained, he'd cast her aside once. He could do so again. Her fear must have crossed her face, because there was his thumb brushing her cheek again. "I know I hurt you, Chloe. In my mind, I thought I was doing the right thing by walking away, but in reality, I was only dooming us both to being miserable. Truth is, I love you, Chloe Abrams."

Her heart stopped. "You—you love me?"

"With all my heart, and I want nothing more than to spend my days and nights showing you how much."

"I don't know…." Breaking away, she stumbled toward a nearby credenza. *You idiot*, her insides screamed. *Ian Black just said he loved you.* Her heart had recovered and was pumping with joy, the beats so loud everyone in the hotel could hear.

Fear, however, refused to let up its grip. Say she gave in, admitted she was as much in love with him. What would happen a week from now? Two? What if he decided his baggage was too much to handle, after all, and left? "I'm not sure I could handle another rejection," she murmured.

"I know. Which is why I'm not going to pressure you. It's an amazing rarity, in that I actually learned a second lesson this weekend. Forgiveness doesn't come on my schedule. That's why, as crazy as I am about you, I won't force you to decide anything today."

The hands returned to her shoulders, this time gently turning her around. His eyes were as dark and passionate as Chloe had ever seen. "I'm not walking away," he told her. "I'm waiting for you. And I'll wait as long as it takes"

His kiss was tender. Sweet without pressing, and so full of love, Chloe ached. Needing purchase, lest she fall, she grabbed his forearms. When the kiss finally ended, she kept her grip. Ian was her stability.

"See you soon, I hope, Curlilocks," he whispered. Pressing one last kiss to her forehead, he started to walk away.

Chloe clutched at her middle. *Run after him*, her heart screamed. Not only did he claim to love her, he'd said he would wait until she made up her mind. No man had ever done that. Forget being rejected. Ian was right, love didn't come with guarantees.

Her feet still wouldn't move. She was still too scared.

A flash of white distracted her. From the corner of her eye she saw Simon grabbing Delilah's arm to prevent her from coming over. He whispered something in his bride's ear, and kissed her cheek. The softness in his expression took Chloe's breath away. She'd seen the exact same expression on Ian's face when he'd kissed her.

What kind of idiot walked away from such a gift? Ian was offering her the opportunity to be loved, as well as the choice to walk away. Knowing his need to be in charge, she sensed the call to hold back had to be murder.

She might love him more for that sacrifice alone.

"Ian, wait!" The bouquet lay on the credenza where he'd left it. She grabbed the flowers and heaved them across the hall. Ian caught them the second he turned around.

"You know what it means when you catch the bridal bouquet right?" she said, rushing up to him.

The adoring expression returned to his face, filling her heart and making her realize she'd made the right choice. Her. Chloe Abrams, who was never destined for love, had finally picked the right guy. "It means the maid of honor falls in love with you."

She gasped as Ian pulled her close. "If that means getting you, I'll catch a thousand bouquets."

"You only need one." Hoping her eyes reflected the love he'd unlocked, she shoved her fear aside and kissed him.

Five weeks later, spring finally and permanently arrived in New York. With the arm of the man she loved draped around her shoulders, Chloe let the sun warm her skin. "Today is the perfect day," she said to Ian. "I can't believe Larissa would rather be in Mexico."

"Personally, I'm having a harder time believing she went on her destination wedding alone."

They were walking back to the coffee shop after seeing Larissa off at her apartment. The blonde had surprised everyone last week by announcing she planned to keep her hotel reservations, and go on her honeymoon. "I spent a year of my life planning this trip, practically down to the shells on the beach," she told them. "I am going regardless."

"I've got to give her credit. She seems to be handling the breakup with Tom a lot better than I thought. In fact, I think she was more emotional about having to give up the wedding."

Ian pressed a kiss to Chloe's temple. "I've been thinking, when we get married, we should have a destination wedding, too."

"Yeah?" A thrill passed through her when he said the word. Ian spent a lot of time mentioning weddings and their future. Most of the references she believed were to ease her fears, thinking that the more he talked about forever, the more she would believe he planned to stay. Thus far, the tactic was working. Every day that she woke up and saw his face on the pillow next to her, or heard his voice on the telephone, she grew more and more convinced she'd found a love to last a lifetime. "Where were you thinking we should go? Mexico?"

"Pennsylvania. We could go back to the Bluebird Inn and celebrate where we began."

Chloe couldn't think of anything she'd love more. "Why wait for a wedding?" she said, snuggling closer. "I bet the inn is beautiful this time of year."

"I like how you think." He stopped to give her a lingering kiss.

"Um, hi."

She felt Ian stiffen as soon as he heard the greeting. He reached for her hand as Matt pushed away from the coffee shop door to walk toward them. The youth stopped a couple feet away. Hands shoved in his back pockets, he scuffed his running shoe back and forth across the sidewalk. "Did you really attend my graduation?" he asked finally.

He'd read Ian's letter. Thank heavens. As good as things were between her and Ian, she knew the loss of his son ate away at him. Keeping his promise to give Matt space hadn't been easy, but he'd kept his word.

"I went to a lot of things," Ian told him. Both spoke softly, as if worried that a raised voice would make the other bolt. "Just because I kept my distance didn't mean I forgot about you. You were always part of my world, Matt."

The teenager nodded. Scuffed his toe again. "I, um, the sign says you're hiring."

"We lost one of our baristas the other day. He gave his phone number to some guy's girlfriend and caused a fight."

"Bummer."

"Not really," Chloe chimed in. "Are you looking for a job?"

Matt glanced at her and back to his father with a blush. "I'm going to be spending the summer with friends here in the city, and I thought maybe, I might…"

He was offering an olive branch. Ian, wise man that he was becoming, snatched it. "Let's go inside and I'll tell you about the position."

Chloe lingered on the sidewalk, watching as the man she loved held the door for his son. In a way, she and Ian both had come full circle. After all, if he had never tried to reconnect with his son, the two of them wouldn't have found each other. Without Matt's rejection, Ian never would have learned to forgive himself. Nor would she have learned to take a chance on love. Now, with their lessons learned, Ian might finally have a chance to know his son, as well.

Sometimes you did get what you deserved.

"Hey, Curlilocks," Ian called from the doorway. "Are you coming? I can't do this without you."

And sometime, you got even more.

Her heart fuller than she could imagine, Chloe took Ian's hand and walked inside.

* * * * *

MILLS & BOON®
By Request

RELIVE THE ROMANCE WITH THE BEST OF THE BEST

A sneak peek at next month's titles...

In stores from 9th February 2017:

- **One Night With the Prince** – Caitlin Crews, Chantelle Shaw & Fiona McArthur

- **Come Fly with Me...** – Scarlet Wilson, Pamela Hearon & Fiona Brand

In stores from 23rd February 2017:

- **His Little Secret** – Maureen Child, Andrea Laurence & Janice Maynard

- **I Do...** – Michelle Major, Dani Wade & Barbara Wallace

Just can't wait?
Buy our books online before they hit the shops!
www.millsandboon.co.uk

Also available as eBooks.

0217/05

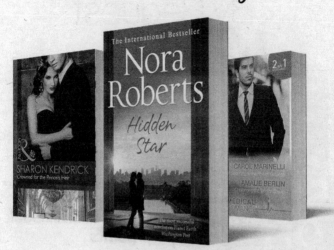